LADY OF THE SOUTH WIND

Javier García Sánchez

Translated by
Michael Bradburn Ruster
and Myrna R. Villa

P R E S S   S A N   F R A N C I S C O   1 9 9 0

La dama del viento sur was published in Spain in 1985
by Montesinos.
Copyright © 1985 by Javier García Sánchez
English translation copyright © 1990 by
Michael Bradburn Ruster and Myrna R. Villa
Printed in the United States of America

LIBRARY OF CONGRESS
CATALOGING-IN-PUBLICATION DATA
García Sánchez, Javier.
 [Dama del viento sur. English]
 Lady of the south wind / by Javier García Sánchez ;
 translated by Michael Bradburn Ruster and Myrna R.
 Villa.
  p. cm.
 Translation of: La dama del viento sur.
 I. Title.
PQ6657.A723D313 1990
863'.64—dc20   89-36925

To Arantza Garaizar

TAURUS
(21 April–20 May)

Confusing day, one you won't forget. Nor
has your absence resolved the personal
conflicts you provoked; but you will soon
achieve the permanent disappearance you
so yearned for. You have become the invisible which endures.

Die Stimme (The Voice)

LADY OF THE
SOUTH WIND

MY NAME IS Andreas Dörpfeld, although that fact is not important, and if I have decided to tell this story it is simply because I believe I was the only firsthand witness to what happened to my friend and colleague Hans Kruger as a result of having met Olga Dittersdorf, a young woman who worked with us: a relationship that had a profound impact on him, but which despite everything I became aware of only gradually, when the actual unfolding of events—simple in appearance but with a murky undercurrent I still haven't been able to fathom—completely overwhelmed me.

For Hans, I'd say, the story began almost as a joke. But little by little his obsession with Fräulein Dittersdorf grew to such a degree that he ended up being virtually out of control.

The fact is that little by little Hans himself related to me, somewhat involuntarily, I think, the details of his relationship with Olga. And of course, now that some time has passed, I realize that he concealed certain things from me at first, from particular aspects of the relationship to feelings he already had at that time, so that one might say I was his confidant, but only up to a point, not realizing until some months later the true magnitude of what now, without the slightest doubt and with the critical objectivity accorded by distance, I venture to consider a passion worthy of being transcribed, or at least recalled. Which is precisely what I intend to do, as faithfully as possible, bearing in mind that Hans Kruger told me in a fragmentary fashion what he felt for Olga. There was one evening, however, when Hans decided to talk. I recall his having pressed the button to turn off the windshield wipers of his car. It was nearly two in the morning, and a torrential rain seemed set on preventing us from seeing through the car's windows. Unable to move, he thought about what for some time had been happening to him. It was then that he decided to tell me everything, or at least a first version that was fairly close to the reality of the situation. With his head leaning against the car window and his gaze fixed on the huge drops of water slipping down the invisible grooves of the glass, he scrutinized for the umpteenth time the origins of the fever raging in him.

Olga Dittersdorf had joined the company shortly after Hans. She was perhaps more attractive than our other co-workers, but that was not, he would remark, what made him notice her. In general terms, one might say that Olga Dittersdorf was the prototypical woman who immediately sparks men's interest. She was tall, svelte, with straight hair parted to one side always playing across her forehead, which compelled her to toss it back in a gesture that was automatic yet fraught with sensuality. She was generally inclined to indulge everyone with her cheerful laughter. Indeed, that affability made her more accessible, according to Hans. Thus she was not, in his view, the typical marble statue who seems to count out her smiles with an eyedropper, depending on where she stands in relation to the light, knowing all along that her beauty, because of a long and to some degree logical process, has deteriorated to haughtiness.

Nevertheless, it could indeed be said—and this opinion I shared completely—that her beauty was classical. The lines of her face would have been the delight of any Renaissance sculptor, of anyone enamored of antiquity. Well-proportioned lips, barely more than a pair of carmine segments that contracted gracefully, but also compulsively and rather voluptuously, when she spoke. With regard to her enormous blue eyes, Hans told me they were like the sky on a spring day, and that on rainy days, like the one we had just had, they would assume the olive tone of those family photographs which, owing to an ancestral and inexplicable awareness of finitude, plunge us into a profound melancholy when we gaze upon them, as though we recognized in them something of our past that will never again return. Her skin was fair and smooth, of a hue like the sand on a desolate beach that neither seagulls

4

nor castaways would ever dare approach. That's how I remember his describing Olga to me that night.

All our office mates, moreover, had approached her at one time or another with more or less clear intentions, which Kruger said he had noticed during the period he had been observing her as if his very ability to go on depended on her, on Olga Dittersdorf's nonchalant gait through the company hallways and offices. They would use any excuse to attempt such an approach. Sometimes an absurd interest in having Olga itemize for them particular data from the last inventory, of which almost all of them, it so happened— at least those directly concerned with the matter—possessed a brand-new photocopy. Hans and I worked in the Publicity Department, so that our dealings with the people in Administration were more infrequent.

And one by one they would fall, Hans remarked, once they found themselves in her presence. That pair of eyes like coral reefs would instantly cast them down and make them relinquish any obscure strategy to obtain what Olga Dittersdorf, aware of her own powers of attraction, knew in advance they were after. A date, only one. To invite her for a drink, only one. To be near her and consequently, perhaps, to feel different from the others, among whom each and every one felt himself to be in competition: Werfel, Jürgen, Helmunt, the head of Publicity Franz Stoppel, everybody. To have dinner once, just once. That long chain of things and circumstances that occur among people when one of them exerts a great power of attraction.

Hans Kruger, in contrast, assured me that he had looked at her with stubborn skepticism ever since she had arrived. For several months, he told me, he hadn't a single reason to become interested in Olga Dittersdorf, nor had the occasion arisen to speak with her. Nothing but routine phrases, and always in order to finalize particulars relating to work. On such occasions he had the opportunity to notice two details, which initially disturbed him somewhat. In the first place, he realized with some surprise that while they were talking Olga would glance away in an instinctive, automatic manner every five or six seconds. That, he assured me, deeply disturbed him, as he had no idea what might give rise to this gesture, which was in all likelihood not without cause.

But it was some while later, he said, that he had discovered something that

5

would entirely change his attitude toward Olga Dittersdorf, something at first glance insignificant, yet that acquired for him an immediate and tremendous importance: she bit her nails. The truth is, he had never found her engaged in that physical punishment, which is undoubtedly the result, among people who have the habit, of a high-strung temperament. Olga would move her hands quickly, as she did her neck and waist, but musically and with a discreet exuberance. She never let them lie still in one place, where they might fall under someone's gaze. From that instant Hans was aware that there were moments when Fräulein Dittersdorf could quite furiously assail those fingers, which remained long and agile in spite of it all.

Those fretted fingertips were nonetheless a disfigurement when compared with Olga's perfect and seductive appearance. A disfigurement she alone fostered, which began to bother Kruger to a degree surprising even to himself. That was the beginning of the joke, Hans said. Soon thereafter, without knowing how, when, or why, he would cross over the threshold of a nightmare. Until that moment it had been a placid and incomprehensible nightmare that had provoked in him feelings he'd already forgotten. Not in vain did Hans frequently call to mind that at age thirty-six, despite everything, loneliness proved to be the most bearable torment of all the emotions he could imagine.

From then on everything was to happen fairly quickly. He admitted to having been surprised when, one typical morning on arriving at Leipzigerstrasse beyond the avenue that borders the river, he caught himself looking eagerly for the yellow Volkswagen that Olga drove to work every day. She would park it on the street, actually positioning half the car on the sidewalk, a visual point of reference that soon became a lure for him: something that, depending on whether the car was there or not, would comfort him or fill him with great anxiety. It was then, he said, that he began trying to avoid running into Olga in the company hallways or at the corner bar, an attempt frequently unsuccessful, since he realized at once that his will, fragile as the branch that yields time and again to the impulses of nature, would propel him toward her like a spring. After not having seen her for several days, however, Hans believed he had rid himself of such feelings. He even went so far as to think he would soon forget about her.

Perhaps he might have succeeded had it not happened that, coinciding with his increasing preoccupation with Olga Dittersdorf's tortured fingers, he chanced to overhear an offhand remark about her that Hans at once realized or believed was directly related to her fretted nails, bitten down to the quick. The remark had been a double one—made, in other words, by two colleagues who came across her unexpectedly and without being seen, in different parts of the city and on different days as well, two remarks that in essence coincided: they had seen her in the company of a man, the same one, judging by their description of the fellow, and on both occasions she seemed to be "sad and pensive." These were more or less the exact words of the two people who had made the remark. It didn't take much for Hans to conclude that in all probability the man was none other than her husband, Peter Sömmering, an athlete quite well known in the city's sports circles, and who, it was rumored, might even represent the country in an important competition to be held shortly.

There was nonetheless something, Hans told me, that didn't quite fit the picture. If Olga Dittersdorf usually appeared cheerful and open in the office, why should she be seized by depression once she'd left work? What was the cause of the essential sadness that seemed to take hold of her, to change her into someone reserved and taciturn? That aspect of her character, combined with the detail of her nails, led Hans to believe that this broad-shouldered woman with the feline gait was dragging along a secret that tormented her, a deep sorrow of which perhaps not even she was aware. Something was torturing her, so Kruger thought. So he wanted, so he needed, to think. But, he told me, even he was not aware that behind that need lay the abyss, that precisely there was where the joke ended and reality began.

Thenceforth Hans, by his own account, was bent on finding a formula that might allow him to delve into a reality that was beginning to deprive him of hours of sleep, that would make him take a wrong turn when going to places he knew perfectly well, that from day to day could so absorb him that it prevented him from concentrating on his work.

He had always been suspicious of people who were excessively cheery, he said, and perhaps that was due simply to his own inability to relate fully to others. This was possible, but that night in the car Hans hastened to explain that in Olga Dittersdorf's case, even apart from her beauty—that of a goddess drowsy after the bacchanal—he was impressed by the fact that she had been able to awaken in him a feeling infinitely superior to desire, inasmuch as desire is generally, Hans added, as fleeting as those stars that cleave the sky scarcely giving us time to perceive their passing: the single, furtive suspicion that behind that smile was concealed something painful and perhaps even irreparable. Rare were the occasions in the weeks that followed when he managed to slough off that feeling of doubt, the mortifying hypothesis that was gradually nullifying him as a person.

Until that very night, he said as we were getting out of the car, he'd been unable to catch even a glimpse of anything that might lead him to reject the idea that the entire thing was a monumental piece of stupidity hatched inside his head. He said this in a tone at once solemn and distracted. I couldn't claim that I knew him well, of course, but I had never seen him behave that way. At the instant the cold, damp wind lashed across our faces, I realized that the alcohol he'd consumed prevented him from reflecting coherently. He was attempting to gauge every gesture, every step, as though in doing so he sought to dispel the suspicion that it was a miracle that such a thing should happen specifically to him, and at that stage of his life.

Strolling down the wet streets that night, I recall, Hans told me he was convinced that she herself was the genuine miracle: the look in her eyes, the impossible dream scented with nail polish, her laughter that of an empress drunk with power, perhaps the miracle of her beauty or even of her secret, the single dark spot in the electrifying aura of that daughter of light. And Hans, dazed like an animal surprised by a crack of thunder, said that deep in his heart he sensed the conviction evolving that those nails of hers, devoured with unflagging indulgence down to the lunulae, were but a reflection, a mere glimpse of her soul.

A couple of weeks went by before Hans spoke to me again about Olga. Earlier I had come upon him on Magath Avenue, but I was with some friends and, although I suggested he join us, he said he was in a rush. Around that time I remember having seen him talking quite a lot to Rolf, a colleague from Publicity who had just started working there. Hans' only complaint in those days was about a problem related to payroll, one which Wehmeyer, the one in charge of Administration, seemed not to be resolving satisfactorily. After those two weeks had passed, I chanced upon him at breakfast, and the

8

subject of Olga came up by itself. They had gone out one evening, and Hans proceeded to tell me what had happened.

"Tiny circles were beginning to appear," he said, "in what until then had been the bright stillness of the puddles, when Olga craned her neck, trying to pierce the tavern windows with her gaze.

" 'Listen to me, Hans, one needn't complicate life with foolish things,' she had said, 'we all do things we'd rather not do. In the end hardly anyone can avoid that. Not even the managers.' "

One after another the cigarettes smoldered away in her mouth, the pronounced arch of her eyebrows slackening with each puff. She would let her cigarette dangle, slightly tilted, and would speak very quickly, giving it a slight quiver that ceased only when she paused or tossed back the lock of hair falling over her brow. He strove to not even blink. He just looked at her, feigning an interest in what Olga was telling him that he didn't really feel. "I didn't blink," he said, "for fear that after one swift, instinctive movement of my eyelashes she might suddenly be gone."

He admitted to having been weak, since not even he had succeeded in resisting the temptation of putting his vanity to the test, and on a couple of occasions had suggested to Olga a glass of the delicious port to be had at a certain bar near the Kommenplatz arcade. The place was located a considerable distance from work, almost at the opposite end of the city, lending his proposition an air of tacit complicity which, though Olga basically seemed not to take the whole thing seriously, didn't seem to bother her either. Now at last the moment of their date had arrived, although in fact they had chanced to meet shortly before the designated hour, quite near the Kommenplatz bar. It was then, being near her for the first time, that he became aware of the undeniable loveliness embodied in that face. "It was as if I'd just been born," he said, "as if I'd been born anew." They went on chatting for nearly two hours, and the profuse combination of port and martinis didn't confuse Hans remotely as much as looking at Olga Dittersdorf's lips did. From time to time, for a brief instant, she would catch him carefully examining them. Then once again she would toss back that lock of hair and ask, "Why do you look at me that way?"

According to Hans, Olga seemed disinclined to discuss subjects unrelated to work. As soon as he made a reference to leisure time, to their respective pasts, to particular likes or preferences, she would give a swift turn to the conversation and soon the familiar allusions to managers, work schedules, and trivial quotidian problems would crop up. "If my schedule weren't limited to mornings and I couldn't have the afternoons free, you can be sure I wouldn't work there for anything in the world. Come two-thirty, I'm gone. I forget about everything. That's when I start to live," she had told him at some point. Suddenly, Hans told me, she made a gesture as if about to bite her nails. That, coupled with a word uttered a few seconds before, made him think he had felt the impact of a lightning bolt in the depths of her pupils. Olga had shrugged her shoulders as she said it: "Well, I'm happy, I can't complain." It was at that instant, when she uttered the word "happy," that she had craned her neck to look at the puddles of rain in the street.

It had been at just that moment and no other when he heard, for the first time, her voice floating above what she was actually saying. It was, Hans said, as though another Olga Dittersdorf were speaking simultaneously through that mouth with its honeyed lips. "My life is like those cigarettes slowly smoldering away, no fanfare, no fireworks," her eyes had said, or so he thought. "Like any one of those cigarettes piling up there, leaving me not even a vague memory, not even a sensation."

"Believe me, I don't have enough time for everything. You know, I've even stopped attending classes at the academy of design. Things just pile up. I wind up having to choose among several alternatives," was what she had actually said.

Hans was gazing at her without making any comment whatsoever, bewitched by the sporadic, fleeting apparition of her tongue, whose tip would appear now and then amid reckless laughter, with the ingenuous perversity of a snake raising its tiny head from beneath a rock and provoking a shudder in every creature who sees it, rational or not, obtaining by its mere emergence their acknowledgment of its irrefutable supremacy. At a particular moment, Hans went on telling me, the snake recoiled as if it had been abruptly cudgeled. Without realizing it, Olga had admitted to having scarcely any friends, although in saying so she was assisted no doubt by the alcohol, yet she also declared she was aware that many men desired her. It had always been that way. It was normal. She bore it with a certain disdain and an assumed apathy.

"What am I to do? How can I avoid it? I look, make a mental note of it, without any ill will, you know. Then I decide, I choose very carefully what suits me and what doesn't. You understand, don't you?" she asked, widening her eyes exaggeratedly.

Hans told me he had to cover his mouth with his hand to keep from repeating what he was truly hearing from those eyes, imbued with a confidence so fragile that a gust, a puff of warm breath would have made them vanish, disappear like an emerald that melts from the effects of heat. "I need to be loved with a much greater intensity than any other woman I know. That both pains and pleases me. That's how it is, something else I can't avoid. I'm tortured by the idea that I don't do what I want. And I deceive myself by repeating aloud time and again that it's not really so. I can't convince myself that what I want is something else, that I'm in the habit of doing things I would rather not do, and I find I'm powerless to resolve it. I end up believing that whatever doesn't cause me problems from the start will ultimately bring me happiness. Yes, I wind up doubting everything. What I really want is for someone or something to come and change my life, at least to help me change it. To give me the final push. I wish my life would change entirely. Just like that, suddenly. I want to lead a different life. To travel, travel a lot, all over the world. I'd like to fall in love with Peter again, with anybody, to do so again every day, to feel the enchantment of the first kisses, the impatience of not knowing how a man would treat me as a lover. To vibrate with an embrace, a simple embrace. To keep embracing someone, with no need to say anything. To go dizzy when I notice someone's lips. To believe that nothing in the world exists but those lips. Nothing else. Returning to childhood or living another life would be all the same to me. Exactly the same, but I want to be loved in a different way, if that's possible. I'd like that kind of love to be invented for me. I'd like to forget it every night, before going to sleep, and see it born all over again when I awake. I want to be awakened at every moment by the slap of love."

That is what Hans believed he had read in her gaze.

"Quite a little row we had over the last inventory," Olga had said while placing, in perfect alignment between herself and Hans, the ashtray, a pack of cigarettes, and the matchbox. "Ah, but it won't occur to anyone to ask just what's going on with the overtime they owe us. And that hardnose Schroeder always ignoring the issue, as though it weren't his problem. I've already told Ingrid and Hansen, 'either Schroeder says something soon or one of these days I'll stand up to him.' It won't be for lack of trying," she added while, as a direct result of Hans' silence, his gaze intense and fraught with questions, she placed the two glasses in the manner of a wall between her own hands and his. And that was the moment when Hans interposed:

"Have you realized that this looks like a minefield?"

The question disconcerted her, causing her hand to withdraw into her lap. She made as if to tilt her face, but then knitted her brow before looking pointedly at the surface of the table.

"What do you mean?"

"This. You've created a genuine barricade between us. If there were anything else left, you'd put it there as well. In a while I'll have to peer over them in order to see you."

Hans smiled on remembering that astonishment and coquetry mingled in a fresh, rather nervous peal of laughter and in the demolition of the tower which the vertically placed matchbox resembled at that instant. A tiny wrinkle appeared between the lower part of her nose and the left corner of her lips. She was trying to be serious but wasn't succeeding.

"That's too much psychology for me. I know, I know—" she protested, her hands gesturing conspicuously "—every movement arises from something, they each have some concrete meaning. I think it's wonderful, but to reckon this is a minefield, a wall, is to seek out vain interpretations for something simple, as simple as breathing."

"As breathing," Hans repeated, his gaze shifting back and forth between Olga's eyes and lips.

"Yes, breathing," Olga said, glancing discreetly at her watch.

Hans gingerly moved the empty glasses to either side, then did likewise with the ashtray and Olga's pack of cigarettes. He placed his hands where the agglomeration of objects had been a few seconds before.

"See? And it doesn't explode," he said.

"Don't be such a tease," she replied, smiling, not without first removing her elbows from the edge of the table. "It's my belief that thinking to excess is harmful. Thinking too much tends to lead to inactivity. And often the act of thinking too much is the greatest lie against ourselves. Just look how serious we're getting!" she exclaimed in a lighthearted tone, drawing back a little. She then proceeded to stare at the empty space Hans had opened up by clearing the objects from the table's surface.

"I am like a child who starts to cry without really knowing why," he went on reading, he told me, in her gaze. "I need to be loved just as a child cries, showing his displeasure with something he doesn't understand but which hurts him. I suppose what I'd really like is to be eighteen, to return to that age when every gesture ended in a display of rebelliousness and strength, if not in scandalous fun. Why, these days there's no genuine fun to be had anywhere. I suppose my real desire is not to be eighteen but thirteen, when I discovered that men looked at me in a special way as I walked, so that even I would watch myself doing it. When one could be happy making stupid faces in front of the mirror. To be eight again, to be five, when you loved your dolls and were loved by them unconditionally, purely . . ."

"Take my advice and don't complicate your life too much, it's tangled enough already. It's a matter," Olga had said with conviction, "of appreciating what we have, great or small, whatever it might be. Don't you think I'm right?"

He, Hans said, had not replied. He was incapable of doing so. He merely heard the incessant hammering of that other voice of hers, emerging from her closed lips: "It was during that period, around fourteen or sixteen, when I could somehow channel laughter, the most abject passions, or the tenderest feelings at will. The power, the magic of love, resides in its discovery. It makes no difference whether it's the first time or every time. And I'm aware of being overwhelmed when I realize it might never recur—that plenitude of wonder implicit in having once felt myself to be the center of the universe, the first time Peter separated the glasses and took my hand to caress it while he continued talking about I don't remember what, almost, I thought, the way you were about to do at any moment. He was decisive. Besides, I loved him. I would never have withdrawn my hands. And had you done that . . . You? Who are you really?"

"Well, it's getting a bit late," Olga said, calling to the waiter. Hans said he had made for the bar to pay for their drinks. On the street, heading toward their respective cars, they spoke again about work, scarcely exchanging a glance. They were no longer face to face.

Through Olga's half-open handbag, Hans could see the pack of cigarettes and the matchbox. They bade each other farewell, and on getting into his car the first thing he did, so he told me, was to stare at his hands. They were burning, as if some potent device had exploded near them.

I must confess I was quite impressed by all that, not so much on account of the content of his detailed explanation—though he had, after all, recounted to me almost verbatim parts of a conversation held some days before—but rather because of the peculiar manner in which he did so, especially with respect to his knowing or believing he knew what Olga had been thinking while they were conversing. And Hans' face, his expression when uttering her supposed thoughts, was what suggested to me that in some way or another that young woman had made a profound impression on him.

I also realized it because of the effusiveness with which he described certain gestures of hers, gestures he believed were invested with special and important, perhaps even occult, significance. I recall, for example, that he referred in that vein to her way of allowing the tip of her tongue to surface just seconds before she would laugh, or indeed her way of opening her eyes uncommonly wide, leaving them like that for several seconds when something was bothering her or she couldn't quite understand a particular aspect of a conversation that directly concerned her.

I also recall that at that time I couldn't help being surprised by the fact that Hans should use the metaphor of a minefield when referring to the unconscious obstacles he said Olga had placed on top of the table in a tavern, thereby averting closer physical contact. Perhaps it was precisely because we worked for a large explosives firm, a national enterprise also geared to exports, although we were completely removed from the manufacturing process of these materials, our offices being responsible for handling purely technical and bureaucratic tasks. It had become a frequent joke among our colleagues. According to Hans, Olga herself when referring to Herr Schroeder would say: "Even if they pay us in TNT, as long as we get the back pay they owe us."

I don't know what her reaction must have been in light of a remark (the one about the minefield) fraught with sarcasm and allusions to work. But the way Hans told it, Olga didn't seem to have caught the presumed double meaning of his words. It was all she could do to master a situation she hadn't anticipated, one that, judging from his description, caused her some discomfort.

Over a period of approximately a month and a half, Hans spoke intermittently to me about Olga no fewer than seven or eight times. At first they were trivial remarks which I realized he almost wished to avoid. But I finally got him to elaborate a bit, something he really needed to do, and to disclose the present state of their relationship. They had seen each other on a couple of other occasions, and Olga's attitude toward those rendezvous appeared to be totally indecisive. On the one hand she offered no objection to them, yet on the other she seemed tense, even though she attempted to conceal it. This created a great insecurity in Hans. According to him, it gave rise to a habitual pattern: Olga always appeared to be in a hurry, for example. If they made a date for nine in the evening, no sooner did they meet than she would allude to how soon she had to be home that evening, or to how early she had to get up the following morning. She might even spend much of the time glancing swiftly at her watch, which clearly, understandably, put him ill at ease. Oddly enough, Hans explained to me, once that first spell of nervousness and furtive glances at her watch had passed, the clock might well strike three or four in the morning while they ambled zigzagging down the streets, naturally after several drinks too many, with Olga apparently having completely forgotten the hour, or that time even existed.

Nonetheless, that torment of suspicions would arise again at their next meeting. Uncertain, then, not so much regarding her feelings, but as to just what her motives might be in these encounters, which for him had become something fundamental that he anticipated with genuine impatience, he chose to repress entirely his desire to see her.

I believe that somehow or other, in spite of everything, Hans must have been aware that not only his emotions but even more his general attitude toward Olga was not what is usually expected of someone his age. I say this because at some point he asked me, with genuine interest in my reply, whether I thought what was happening to him was normal. Obviously I told him I was probably the person least qualified to answer that, for various reasons: in the first place, I had never fallen in love, and I no longer hesitate to use that term, because that and nothing else was what had happened to Hans. I had never gone so far as to fall in love with someone like Olga. I told him that perhaps this was the result of some ancestral and unconscious prejudice against excessively beautiful women. I saw other qualities in them, I explained, aside from the fact that until then I'd not even had the opportunity to determine whether or not Olga Dittersdorf indeed possessed those qualities that might, in theory, attract me in a woman. But I also confessed to Hans that I found it all somewhat out of phase, out of tune perhaps. Everything he would tell me from day to day reconfirmed my initial supposition that Hans was a born romantic, though his character was also quite immature. The fact is, I endeavored to temper my words so as not to hurt him in the least, but nonetheless I didn't let slip the opportunity he had allowed me to remind him that things were done differently between a man and a woman nowadays, in perhaps a much more straightforward manner. As for myself, I must admit, I couldn't quite understand whether there was a clear physical attraction there or not. In any case, based on the way Hans himself recounted their meetings to me, I thought he was sublimating the fundamental aspect of Olga's powerful physical attraction to a secondary plane. Furthermore, I remember being certain that he was completely deceiving himself in that regard, excessively idealizing her, conferring upon her phrases, gestures, and deeds an almost mystical halo, which I, of course, could not possibly perceive.

But Hans didn't appear to be bothered by any of this. On the contrary, he listened attentively to my opinions, and once I had finished he admitted to being very surprised by everything I'd said. "So you think that's how it is, you really believe that's what's going on with me?" he would ask incessantly. For my part, I advised him to take things calmly. "Even if you haven't got both feet on the ground," I recall telling him in hopes it might help him somehow, "you can be sure she does. And if you are not a realist, at least with Olga you should attempt to be one, as long as you intend to get anywhere with her, of course." Hans made no reply to this remark, and I fear he didn't because he'd no idea what to say.

He promised me, in any case, that he would consider what I'd told him and reflect upon it as objectively as possible. So I was left temporarily at ease,

16

and it was much to my surprise that I learned a few days later that he'd taken a turn for the worse. He told me once again, over breakfast, how he was faring. On only a couple of occasions during the entire time did he remove his gaze from the blackish, shimmering surface of the coffee. He spoke of feeling that the city was deserted and that Olga's shadow seemed to be following him everywhere. He would walk about crestfallen, comprehending nothing at all of what was happening to him. He would either dodge the puddles or wade right through them with utter disregard, soaking his shoes and socks. I recall his saying that he would even switch on the television, which, given the circumstances and the context in which he mentioned it, seemed as extremely symptomatic. Everything struck him as odd. It was as if he were discovering the world with every step. He breathed with difficulty, and the thought of her produced a suffocating sensation in his chest. While telling me this, his voice was keen but remotely pleasant. He would place his hand on his chest only to withdraw it a few seconds later. Presently, he would repeat the motion, which left him confused and rather shaken.

Things gradually acquired a constant rhythm, which Hans admitted to having realized right from the start he couldn't change. Everything was simple and unrelenting, as though it were written that he should behave in that way and in no other. That was his explanation.

The first nearly sleepless nights—in which time and again he imagined Olga's face, her hands, her body, in a thousand and one positions and attitudes—were followed by abrupt awakenings. Rare were the nights when his sleep was not shattered during the wee hours of the morning. It would occur suddenly, and when he awoke he would realize he was drenched in sweat, sometimes trembling as though he were ill, feverish. He would heave for a few minutes, his neck resting now against the pillow, until he was able to calm down. Then he would fall asleep again, thinking he saw Olga's silhouette among the curtains, her face in the shadows and chiaroscuro of the ceiling. After considerable efforts to regain sleep, he would fall into the quagmire of dreaming with her movements etched in his mind. And the discreet perfume Olga wore, he said, penetrated his skin like a poisoned dart whose effects were more hallucinatory than harmful. He would call to her silently then, as though afraid the sheets would hear the name that created a knot in his throat each time he uttered it. He said he had begun to pronounce her name anywhere at all, at all hours of the day. Very quietly at first, in a barely audible fashion, later on spelling it out with a certain delight.

But he told me still more. He was capable of staring through one of the windowpanes facing the garden of his house for hours, and little by little his need to know things about her would become so pressing that it drove him to do something he was not conscious of until it was too late, when he couldn't escape the trap he himself had created: in his conversations with other colleagues he would endeavor to bring up the subject of the women at work. He would spur on their desire, provoke them, do anything at all just so long as he could hear her name mentioned. It was all the same to him whether they uttered vulgarities or obscenities, which I imagine must have been fairly common, especially if such comments came from the likes of Jakob Grober, Rolf Vuttke, or Martin Hartwig. He had heard her name on the lips of others, and that seemed to satisfy him. She did exist. Olga was a reality. Perhaps this rather masochistic habit compensated for the fact that he couldn't discuss her with anyone, or at least not with the frequency Hans must have needed. I think it quite likely that, where I was concerned, his timidity prevailed and raising the subject of Olga ended up becoming an enormous predicament. When he succeeded in having others refer to her, he would relax, but that sensation was transitory, since carrying Olga about in his mind every hour of the day had convinced him that in some way she was his. And the almost immediate discovery of his mistake, he said, usually led to many drinks at some city bar. More than his system could bear.

During the period following that first meeting in the tavern by the Kommenplatz and their subsequent encounters, his conduct at work became, by his own account, absurd, not only with regard to Olga Dittersdorf but even to himself. He would just as soon go to great lengths to avoid encountering her as he would seek out infantile excuses to send her coded messages in the form of notes attached to invoices, overdue statements, and other documents of which she had no need whatsoever. He even went so far as to send her photographic material whose use was restricted to the Publicity Department, with notes in the margins.

Apparently the top drawer of Olga's desk was always unlocked. Most of the staff locked theirs, but not she. It seemed to be open precisely so that

Hans might leave those papers along with a simple note. "Here is the info re: department payments for the last quarter. There is some data missing that I'll forward to you as soon as I get it. Are you still as happy as ever? I hope so. Hans." Or even more laconic: "Olga, these are the statements that were missing. I try not to think, but can't help it."

Taking care not to be seen, he would leave them in the drawer, which Hans—obsessed by the idea that this was the only way he could communicate with Olga—came to believe signified, as long as it remained open, that she was impatiently awaiting his message: her small and ingenuous signal; he was certain that if one day he were to find it locked, it would mean that Olga was saying "enough" to a game that, at least as far as he was concerned, was not one at all, and to which she didn't seem to attach the slightest importance, because chances were that the day after receiving one of those notes that Hans would deposit at a time during the evening when no one remained in Olga's department, she would pass by him without even looking at him, without making a single remark to let him know that she had somehow received his message. At that point Hans' spirits would fall, rather like a candle attempting to keep its flame steady in a draft.

But there was something, he explained to me, that hindered any resolution he might make concerning Olga Dittersdorf: the fear of boring her, the dread of the scant interest she might feel toward a fellow like himself, tormented him until he became a passive individual consumed by his own cowardice and impatience. The situation struck him as totally incongruent when analyzed objectively, but at that moment it seemed to Hans like a dead end: What attitude must he assume with her, even supposing he might get her to agree to another meeting alone with him in a secluded place, under conditions conducive to unburdening himself? Olga led an orderly life, had a stable relationship. Her time and her opportunities to go out would thus be quite limited. What could she see in him, he asked himself over and over again, if they had talked for but a few hours, and so hastily besides? What could he say to prolong their encounters indefinitely, when he was certain to meet with her more or less discreet rejection? What might he talk about when he craved only to gaze at her, to lose himself in her eyes and her mouth?

He recognized himself that he had changed. He told me that, contrary to his former reaction, if I mentioned Olga at work it disturbed him to the point where he had to restrain himself to avoid immediately walking away. Actually, apart from what he told me in that regard, I myself could observe that he was undergoing a profound change. He would walk about looking at the floor, and I noticed he was totally absentminded. In spite of all this, I also realized that the care devoted to his outward appearance increased considerably. Hans recognized that himself. When he fancied he might run into her at work, or even when he was ready to force such an encounter by any means, he would select his clothing only after much deliberation. He lingered a long time before deciding what best suited him. He said he had gone so far as to buy a shirt before daring to enter the office. Then, hours before those hypothetical encounters, he would look at himself continually in the mirror. His showers were longer than usual. And he was using at least twice as much shampoo on his hair. Perhaps that way, he admitted with a smile on his lips, his hair would be softer and more blond.

The fact is that on some occasions, while he was relating these things, I came to believe that Hans might be mocking not only me but himself, especially himself, and I abandoned the idea only after realizing that he spoke with total conviction, his face taking on a scowl of contagious seriousness. He spoke of walking tall, straighter, when he would step into her office or pass before her, as though he were walking on air. In an instinctive gesture, he would thrust his chest forward a few centimeters, his jaw set, his gaze fixed on some indefinite point ahead. Usually, if she was accompanied, he didn't have the courage to stop and see if she would look at him, thereby initiating a dialogue. If on the other hand there was no one there, he would confine himself to giving her a fleeting smile. Later, alone again at his desk, came the feeling of failure, the conviction that the woman hadn't a single reason to be attracted to someone like himself, the sense of having been ridiculous in devoting such care to his attire for nothing.

His own timidity about approaching her was undermining his self-confidence with respect to her. Indeed, Olga herself, largely ignorant of what was happening to Hans, must have observed a certain coldness and aloofness toward her, which must have left her quite baffled. As for Hans, it tortured him to prolong that situation, and the evidence of his lack of courage even to look at her, let alone address her, marked the beginning of what he himself deemed an "acute depression."

During this period, he told me, he avoided places Olga might wander by. He averted a chance encounter on the office stairs or in the elevator at the expense of completely upsetting his schedule, devising the most complicated pretexts. Nevertheless, every so often at nightfall, when scarcely anyone was left in the offices and nobody at all in Administration, he would enter stealthily, prepared to explain, should anyone surprise him at that moment, that he was about to make some photocopies, to pick up letterhead stationery, to get carbon paper for typing. Anything at all.

That was one way of sensing Olga's presence, the distant echo of her voice, of staring at the chair where she had been sitting the entire morning, of gently touching the pen she had used only hours before on a multitude of occasions. He would gaze at her vacant desk without blinking, peering into the semidarkness until his eyes smarted. Sometimes he would approach it to caress the surface with his fingertips. Everything there had been touched by her hands, those soft, long, rather bony hands, their nails bitten for some reason, which, he confessed in a tone of grave resignation, possibly had nothing to do with the one he had imagined, with the one he had needed to imagine so as to avoid feeling he had lost the battle beforehand. Because Hans' battle, as he dubbed it that morning while we breakfasted, truly began at the moment when, between jests, he asked Olga what her secret was and where it resided, to which she, abruptly serious, replied: "In the wind." It would be a long time yet before I was to perceive the import of this assertion, on which Hans seemed to bestow an extraordinary significance, although he hadn't the faintest idea what Olga could be referring to, if indeed her words went beyond sheer poetic license owing, perhaps, to the alcohol.

He admitted that at home he was beginning to behave like a caged animal. He would put on a record, scarcely letting it play before taking it off. He would light a cigarette and then forget it in some ashtray until he found the butt consumed and fuming. He would carry objects from one place to another without there being any need to do so. Thus, he would suddenly find himself conveying an empty glass into some room or other, changing the position of a chair, cleaning something he had cleaned only minutes before, or standing bewildered before some decoration which, having occupied the same space for several years, suddenly bothered him.

The fact is he became worried about the frequency of these incoherent gestures, which kept increasing in an alarming manner. The apex of that inexplicable spiral into which he had been drawn came at the moment when he caught himself with a fork in his hand on the verge of placing it in the freezer. It was all he could do, he would confess to me with somewhat disturbing candor, to repress a sob on realizing that, next to the ice cubes and some frozen foods, there already lay another fork. He had absolutely no recollection of having put it there, but of course he was the only one who could have done so.

It was shortly thereafter that Hans took a few days' sick leave. Upon his return he seemed quite changed, as though his absence from work, and consequently from his almost daily contact with Olga, had lent him a certain equilibrium. On the other hand, however, I also noticed that he seemed to have deteriorated physically. Nevertheless, I was glad when Hans stated after a few weeks that he had again been out with Olga several times, though he didn't specify how many, and that everything was progressing. "I don't understand her, Andreas. She acts on impulse, and I don't know what to do," he told me, "but at the moment things are much better than before." Those were exactly his words. Nor did I inquire any further, and thus the end of the summer and part of the autumn passed. On the few occasions when I spoke to Hans during that fairly wide span of time, our conversation was limited to work-related matters. Then, abruptly, everything was to change. I think something must have happened between them, something that continued over a period of several weeks until well into the winter, which made his personality at work tense and completely overwhelmed his spirits, rendering him taciturn and irascible.

At that point there occurred a bit of a scandal at work involving a colleague, a somewhat older man named Handke, with whom nobody got along and whose manner was frankly unpleasant. Hans had already quarreled with someone over the telephone that morning, and it was only a few minutes later that the altercation with Handke took place. Even now no one has figured out just what really happened, although it's more than likely that by this time everyone has forgotten. The fact of the matter is that we were stunned by a tremendous uproar coming from Handke's office, shouts and exclamations of pain. I was one of the first to arrive there, and I'll never forget the spectacle: Handke was sprawled on the floor trying to cover his bloodied face, and Hans was delivering blows all over his body with real savagery. I remember, too, that what horrified me was to realize that in Hans' right hand I could see a heavy desktop ashtray, which he seemed disposed to go on wielding right up to the ultimate consequences. The disproportionate strengths of the two men made the struggle quite pathetic. Margrit Hauff, a colleague from Administration, another person, and myself all flung ourselves on him to prevent him from smashing open Handke's head. Hans looked like a maddened demon. He was panting and his teeth were clenched. Twice he broke free from the lot of us, attempting to finish what he had started, but we managed to restrain him in time.

Once having separated him from Handke, who was taken to a nearby clinic by a few of the company managers, I was able to calm Hans down somewhat and took him into the bar. There we had him drink something and try to collect himself so he might tell us what had occurred. But he scarcely said a word. He wanted only to go home and rest. Since he appeared to have regained his composure, we let him go, though not without some concern, at least on my part, on account of his condition. Before taking the taxi, he asked that after a few days I convey his apologies to Handke. I still remember him with the scratch across his face as he spoke, and at that precise moment I, too, was sufficiently excited not to realize that "after a few days" implied that he didn't intend to come to work for a few days.

So I awaited him in vain for some while, at least a week, and in Personnel they told me only that Kruger was under medical supervision, and that as soon as they knew something definite they would let me know. I was thinking about going to his house to visit him and ask after his health when I received a call from his sister. She informed me, to put it briefly, that Hans had raised no objection at all to spending a while in a specialized clinic, about which (being herself a psychologist of some renown in the city) she had heard excellent reports. I admit it made quite an impression on me to hear from her lips that Hans had been confined to some sort of former spa with thermal springs that was currently functioning as a psychiatric center. The place was located near Chemnitz, in the Hohenstein-Ernstthal area, and his sister said she didn't know how long he might have to remain there. Fearful, I insisted on knowing whether or not it was an insane asylum, but she replied that it wasn't. It was, in her words, simply a recovery center for specific types

of mental disturbances and was staffed by a very competent team of profes-
sionals. She also said that during her visit to Hans over the weekend, he had
requested that I alone be told where he was, that he was sure he would wish
to see me before long, and that she should therefore let me know once a few
weeks had gone by. That period had not yet elapsed, but his sister preferred
to let me choose the moment to visit Hans, advising me in passing that he
would remain there for at least three months, if not longer.

I therefore allowed a prudent interval to pass before deciding to travel
as far as Chemnitz to see for myself how Hans was faring in that spa-
sanatorium of which his sister had spoken so favorably. I immediately recognized what must be the sanatorium as soon as I distinguished, at the top
of a hill, the old-fashioned architecture of a white mansion with handsome
arches in the central portico. The wrought-iron gate was open, and I left the
car next to some others parked at one end of the garden, which disappeared
beyond a grassy slope. I could hear the sound of a stream that must have been
flowing nearby. In the background, to the right of a pronounced knoll that
rose above a grove of beech trees, the landscape became more mountainous
and abrupt.

It was shortly past mealtime, which I assumed to be the reason there were
no people about. The fact is I recall everything about that day in a confused
and tangled manner, as though it were a dream which even now is difficult
to interpret. I shall attempt to recount it just as it happened, striving not to
omit important details. I asked a young man loaded down with some tubing
and a bundle of wires the whereabouts of Hans Kruger. He asked me to wait
a moment. Within a few minutes another young man came out, wearing a
white smock, extending his hand and asking if I was the one who had come
to see Hans. I replied affirmatively, and he said simply: "Well, here he is
now." I turned, and indeed there was Hans, who was at that moment de-
scending the garden stairs in my direction. When I turned back to the man
I had assumed was a doctor, he had withdrawn a few meters, summoned by
the youth with the tubing.

It's difficult for me to think about that situation, about what I felt just
then. It felt quite odd to find myself in a place like that, for although it might
seem stupid, I kept trying in vain to get the term "insane asylum" out of my

24

head. I didn't know what to do or even say when I found myself facing Hans, which had concerned me since the incident with Handke and, more specifically, since his sister had informed me that although I might find it strange, he felt like speaking to me. That's why, when I saw him approaching, I did nothing more than return the smile with which he welcomed me. He was bundled up in a thick woolen sweat suit with a gray plaid muffler coiled around his neck. He wore sports shoes and had his hands in his pockets, and although at first I wondered whether he would offer me his hand, I soon realized he was not going to remove it. In spite of the slight, pleasant glare of sunlight hovering over the garden, it was cold. I noticed that because of the vapor issuing from his mouth as he breathed.

For me, it all continued to be a bit unreal, something I felt was about to end at any moment. As though without warning he might say: "Well, it's been a joke, the comedy's over." It was hard to believe that the fellow before me was the Hans Kruger I knew, and it proved difficult to imagine that someone I knew should need to be in such a place. I believe I had the feeling that the whole thing was a film in which I was at once a spectator and an actor, and that at any moment the film was going to end. But not so.

I recall perfectly the gesture he made once we were facing each other. Without losing his smile, he shrugged his shoulders and released another mouthful of vapor, which would have blown right in my face had it not been for the breeze circulating about the place. Then he stood there staring at me, saying nothing. I must have asked him how he was, to which he responded with an evasive, "As you see." Whereupon he asked me, "How's it going?" and I, somewhat uncomfortable with all that, briefly related my journey from Emden. He looked at the ground and, interrupting me, suggested we go for a stroll. My reply was unnecessary, for Hans had already begun to walk heavily, almost dragging his feet and as though his thoughts lay in the earth we trod. I recall having asked him what he normally did there, to which he replied: "Marble." I was about to ask him to explain what he meant by that when, raising his gaze to the grove of beech trees, the place where we seemed to be headed, he began to inquire how things were going in the city. It was clear that he intended to deal in ambiguities. I admit I became quite nervous, and I therefore preferred to keep quiet and wait for him to initiate the conversation. I had no inkling of what only moments later would come pouring down on me, as indeed there had been nothing that might lead me to predict such a thing.

But I was in fact able to foresee it an instant before Hans began to speak in a deliberate tone. In the split second when our eyes met, almost without warning, I observed a strange flash in his gaze. "This is very tranquil, very. It's rather nice here," he said. We walked on in silence for a stretch and, since he had again withdrawn into utter muteness, I decided to ask him point-blank. That's why I had come so far. "But just what is going on with you, Hans?" Again he exhaled vapor, and I heard him say without looking at me: "Do you really want to know?" His question was completely ingenuous, as though he were surprised. I insisted, noting that he slowed the pace of his steps. It was then that he began to speak:

"I don't know, I just don't know. I really understand very little of what is happening to me. I mean, I don't understand it at all. Everything is confusing here, yes, and repetitive. Things are repeated. Like repetition being re-peated, as if it were trying to perfect itself. The days go piling up one after another, and I still don't quite know what I'm doing in this place. I suppose you wonder the same thing," Hans said. "I usually go for walks, I walk a lot, beyond the grove of larch and beech trees, past the stream. Nobody goes near there, no one from the hospital, I mean. Because I'm perfectly aware that this is a mental hospital. Yes, perfectly aware of it. That's what it's called, isn't it? Yes, mental hospital. These days they give everything a name, even though it might not mean a thing. Hospital. What nonsense. And in saying 'mental' one seems to be assuming the nonexistence of the hospital. But it does exist, as do its humidity and cold and contorted faces. Some even cry in the middle of the night. I hear them. In the upstairs floors, which are always closed, with their wardens in green coats reading magazines in the door-ways. They—the ones who cry—must think I don't hear them, but I do. I hear them as if they were moaning here in my ears. As though they were nerve fibers in my eardrum. If I concentrate I can even guess the reason for their crying, yes," Hans said, "in the sanatorium there is no distance. And if there is, it's a *tactile* distance, that can be touched, but at the same time you're not able to think about it the same way you would elsewhere. To figure out the distance, yes. We all know what everyone is doing at every moment.

Every gesture. Some have gone on telling the same stories for almost a quarter of a century. The oldest ones, I mean," he said. "Unbearable. They're the ones who call this a 'spa.' A spa, yes. I don't suppose that falls short of the truth. Everything that is not tactile is, I suppose, indemonstrable. Consequently it may be false, but may also contain a portion of truth. This, in addition to being a building is also, I think, a concept, an intention. Everything is a lie, I suppose, and the proof is that there is a truth for each person, for each collectivity, for each ethnic group, yes and above all for each ideological bloc. We are, I suppose, a herd of antelopes in great tumult. A chaotic flight, I think, in search of an ideology, any one at all, that might justify existence. We are motivated by the lie of the conflagration we intuit. We can't see it but, just as animals in the jungle do, we know it's there, that history is blazing beneath our feet, behind our backs. Yes, the flames almost reach us," Hans said, "and that's why we run and run without knowing, I suppose, toward what. Yes, since I've been here in the 'spa,' I suppose a great deal. I never stop supposing. I suppose that I suppose that I could suppose this or that. And so forth. I know or believe I know which is the most passable shortcut toward the infinity of suppositions. The only shortcut possible, I believe," he said. "I say 'spa,' and I suppose that I've said spa and not something else. I could have said 'sanatorium' or 'madhouse,' but I didn't. I have only supposed that, because I've heard myself say 'spa' and not the other things. The others are suppositions. Everything here is supposition. I am a supposition, but an absolute supposition, because the rest of the suppositions proceed from me. Yes, a thinking supposition. You, on the other hand, are an *accident*. Usually you're not present, I mean not present in the spectrum of suppositions, in the chain of daily suppositions. Today you are right alongside the primordial supposition, myself, and therefore you're being supposed from the center. In that sense you too, I believe, are an absolute supposition. I don't know if you follow me. I don't want to confuse you. I am already quite confused, I suppose. I told you that everything here is very confusing, didn't I? Yes, I believe I did," he said, "but that's really how it is, just as I'm telling you. Everyone supposes. They—the rest of them—suppose that I suppose, but they don't know what I suppose and vice versa, no. Although if I think about what their suppositions might be, I have a better chance than they do of knowing what it is they suppose, what they think, and what they suppose I think," Hans said, scarcely pausing in his monologue at all. By that point I was stupefied, almost frightened to see the diabolical swiftness with which he was spinning out phrases and the mechanical tone with which he expressed them. I recognized neither his manner of speaking nor even his voice. He seemed to slacken the fluent rhythm of his words only when he uttered a term he wished to emphasize, to accentuate. Then, for but a fraction of a second, he took a deep breath, only to go on presently: "They also know that I am in the habit of going for walks *alone*, that I don't accept their company. But it's not necessary to tell them. They know it. They suppose what I'm thinking. Always the same stories. Very boring, I can assure you. I acquiesce to sharing certain activities with some of them: baths, meals. If they ask my advice about choosing a book from the library, I give it to them. Yes. I usually mislead them," Hans said in total seriousness. "I recommend difficult things, things I know they won't understand, whose sense they'll only manage to suppose. Nothing else. That way they're trained for daily life. Yes, acting without understanding anything, letting others act upon us and supposing that we understand but knowing it's not so. It fascinates me to know they won't understand what I recommend, that their reading is going to prove arduous, irritating. In fact, it fascinates me as much as it does to see a person writing in a public place. You suppose, you try to suppose what he's writing, but your efforts are always dashed against his busy silence. To suppose and suppose, despite everything, may sometimes come to be a relief. Yes," Hans said, "in cutting marble, for example, that peculiar, shrill noise becomes unbearable. When you polish the edges and get sprinkled with dust, when the electric saw strikes a vein, the stinging sensation runs through your blood, and you feel at times as though it's going to smother you. Then you make the effort of supposing that noise, you detach it from your identity. It's there, you're supposing it, and you're thinking beyond its range. It comes to be a part of you, yet it doesn't bother you. It's simply there, produced by your own fingers vigorously plying the machine. It's a matter of *will*. I mean not hearing it is a matter of will, just as thinking it, thinking that noise, would be a matter of *necessity*. Many have become disturbed in the marble workshop," he said. "Yes, I suppose they had to leave because it was very difficult for them to go on hearing that buzzing inside their heads hour after hour. You hear it even when it's not there, especially when it's not there. As a matter of fact, I suppose it's just the same as with Olga," he said. He had uttered Olga's name for the first time, making me freeze. He had done so without warning, without changing his tone a whit. "I remember that when she was there, I mean when she was beside me, even when I knew she was in a particular place and doing a particular thing in particular clothes, in a particular mood," he said, "when she was with me I would obviously sense her presence at every instant. It was a sensation of anguish and indefinable plenitude. Yes, I think that was a sensation rather than a supposition. What I mean is that Olga was always there, but if we weren't together her *presence* was even greater, it was a contact without fissures, like one of those marble blocks I begin carving in silence at dawn, when everybody is still sleeping. That's why I requested they transfer me to the room right across from the workshop. I mean, the contact with marble came to be a kind of transmutation of the contact with Olga. Yes, Olga was always there, goes on always being there, though I suppose my being here and not in the city (where I'd have more possibilities of being with her, I mean in a purely physical sense) has turned thinking about her into yet another supposition. That supposition is by turns sweet or bitter, and although I can't determine the course or consequences of such emotions, I can claim to exert some authority over my own will with respect to Olga as a *supposition*. I know, I realize that I control something," Hans said, "but I don't quite know what. In fact I only suppose that I control it, I merely suppose so. I also control a portion of your thoughts right now, at this very instant. Mentioning Olga's name, Olga as a supposition, or at best mentioning her as a supposed reality—since ultimately she's obviously not a reality now—Olga's name, I was saying, its sudden appearance during this walk, must have confused you quite a bit. You were expecting it, I'm sure, but I'm also sure that you wouldn't have dared mention her to me so easily. Yes, that I suppose with a fair degree of certainty. Olga was floating between us, I can tell, she's in the atmosphere, floating there at this moment, but you probably wouldn't have found the opportunity to mention her specifically; I know you're thinking: 'He is here because of Olga,' I mean, I suppose you must be thinking that. Yet I also suppose that you would never have mentioned her regardless. With every minute that passed, seeing that I didn't bring her up, you would have thought it more and more inappropriate to talk about her. I suppose that beyond the supposition of this *sanatorium*, it's impossible to suppose

that I am here because of Olga. I simply ask that you suppose so. Only that.
Let's say it was a possibility, I mean, that I understand it's a possibility that I
am here because of Olga. But the point is that Olga herself, her very existence, has often seemed to me to be a remote possibility made flesh. And curiously, that possibility made flesh came to justify my own existence, since
hers—as I've said—was inexplicable to me. Given that I never really had access to her private life, I was obliged to suppose, on and on. To suppose her as
a possible reality was frustrating, perhaps because we didn't desire the same
thing from each other, I mean, I suppose I did desire something from her,
perhaps I still do, though what it is I can't tell for certain, while the reverse
probably wasn't true for her. That's why, as I was saying, I was obliged to suppose her as a possibility, never as a possible reality. I believe there is a great
difference. Oh, yes. Much more qualitative than quantitative. Yes," Hans
said, "I suppose she was born to be desired. In any case, I suppose Olga was
always evanescent. She was there *without being there*, yes, in some sense
when she *was* there, it was I who could find myself on another plane completely opposite hers. In the end I think I no longer knew whether she was
there or not. When she wasn't, when there was really no one beside me, I
couldn't fathom the reason for her not being there; in fact I could honestly
feel her presence there beside me. On the other hand, when she was with me,
I suppose I behaved as though she weren't, because the moments when she
hadn't been were so firmly rooted in my mind. I doubt that Olga realized
that," he said, "but as I was saying, she was there, she always is, and what I
feel is neither her presence nor the sensation of her, but rather the *sensation
of her presence*. I don't know if you follow me. Well, that's what I suppose, as
I said. So, at those moments I would think I should tell her this or that, but I
had done it so many times in silence, at a distance, from that tactile distance
I spoke of before, that when the time came to do it, I kept quiet. Perhaps she
would suppose what I desired to tell her, but if not I think that sometimes she
must have felt very confused. In other words, I suppose I kept quiet because
I never knew for certain what I ended up saying to Olga. Nor why I said it. I
do know, however," Hans said, "that she's always there. That's all I know, but
I know it with absolute certainty. I know it because I suppose it, think it,
sense it, feel it. It's the tangible part of the supposition, yes, the absurd supposition my life itself is. I know, too, that certain inclinations I felt with rel-

ative intensity even before coming here, to the sanatorium—and about
which I recall having spoken to you at some point, though perhaps indirectly—have considerably intensified as a result of thinking about her only
as a supposition, without any possibility of seeing her. And I know, I suppose, that I should sort out my ideas about Olga, indeed that I must sort them
out here, because given the possibility of her physical presence, it would be
completely out of the question. The only alternative to that is the perpetual
supposition, I don't know if you follow me, I mean entering the sanatorium
as a concept. Granted, I suppose it's hard to admit. Something tells me that I
compelled my coming here so as to think better, calmly, to think of her as
supposition rather than as possibility. Here," Hans said, "I've now managed
to see more clearly those *inclinations* I alluded to before. I don't know, I suppose that was not a supposition. I'm referring to the act of seeking Olga
everywhere. I did that before, I mean, I sought her in a morbid way, I would
seek her even where I knew I couldn't find her, especially where there should
theoretically be no trace of her. Perhaps that territory was exclusively my
own, one of things and places that might have been with Olga. Whereas
now, here, I think about the way I sought her, I try to analyze simultaneously
not really the causes of my having done it—causes I realize I'll never come
to understand fully—but rather the specific effects provoked by that search
in the general supposition which she herself is. I don't know, I fear I'm not
explaining it very clearly. I mean to say, my actual experiencing of the places
where we happened to be didn't occur when we were there, physically and
temporally present, but rather when I returned to them to assure myself that
we had in fact been there and some possibility thus existed that the general
supposition Olga represented could at any moment become a reality. The
truth is, in referring to myself, I can't help feeling that I'm talking about
someone else. An inner voice tells me that I went there, to those places we
both visited just recently, as an attempt not so much to understand the magical aura that surrounded her and those moments when she had been present
(an aura she had conjured up and which I've never truly understood), but
rather to kill her image," he said, "the image of the general supposition
within me. In killing the supposition, I suppose, I would have killed the possibility. And of course in killing the possibility, I think one kills the reality.
Don't you think so?" Hans asked, not even glancing at me as he walked,

seemingly engrossed, toward the grove whose first trees were now fully discernible. "Yes, I suppose I wanted to kill the reality, my reality. A reality without her was not real." After having remained silent a few seconds for the first time since we commenced our walk, he suddenly said, "I've never been a gambler. Moreover, it seems to me that chance, games of chance are a supreme folly, the greatest waste of time imaginable, precisely because one engages in them to kill time, but I dare say that in some sense I was always aware that my round with Olga was lost, and I can also state that at those moments when, just hours after having visited them, I went back again to the places where I had been with Olga shortly before, I would make an attempt to wipe her out entirely, to convince myself that what I felt wasn't real, or at best a supposition of the possibility, never a real possibility, as I said. And as a matter of fact I realize that I came here, that I compelled my coming here to consummate that attempt to wipe her out from a distance. 'To forget her,' you'll think, but no, that's not the point. It's not so much a function of memory as it is a function of consciousness," Hans said. "I can't forget the very thing that gives character and essence to the general supposition of my life. And if I say *wipe her out*, it's in a literal sense. To erase her from my existence, in other words from memory, by means of consciousness. But while memory is founded in an uninterrupted series of images from the past," he said, "she goes on being there with an undeniable protagonism. I should have to cease to exist in order not to think about her. Do you understand what I mean?" he asked, giving me a fleeting glance. "To cease to exist. Though I think that's a possibility, too. Nobody can assure me that if that were so, if I should really cease to exist, I would stop thinking about her. Nobody can convince me that nothingness, in other words the direct result of nonexistence, will be an absolute nothingness, without the possibility of that state being transmuted into something. What I'm saying is that I've never had doubts in that regard, I mean doubts about immortality. And I haven't had them because for me that was never a question of faith, but a theoretical, ethical one. Olga herself, however, has been the manifest proof that nonexistence can be reality, or at least the remote possibility that the real might cease to be possibility and become reality. Indeed, I suppose that for me there always existed *two* Olgas, or perhaps it was simply a matter of one double Olga: the real one and the possible one. Yes, and I could never do without either of them. They formed a strange symbiosis that seemed to have coagulated in my veins. She had a real way of smoking," Hans said, "she was constantly offering me cigarettes. I would ask her why she was so insistent about it, about offering me cigarettes, as indeed she would do each and every time she smoked herself, but her reply always tended to be the same: 'To break down your health for when the time comes to run together.' But I believe it was a gesture not so much of politeness (which Olga undoubtedly possessed), but rather of nervousness in view of the possibility that I might *observe* her while she lit the cigarette and smoked. On the other hand, of course," Hans said, "she played a lot of sports, I mean, I suppose she did, for I never saw her running or playing other sports, but she said she did so whenever she could. Yes, I suppose that must be normal when one's around an athlete. She would do it 'to fight fatigue,' in her words. We talked at some point of running together. Yes, but our meetings on that score kept being postponed on account of major obstacles. Obstacles on her part, naturally. I always waited for those obstacles to disappear. But they didn't, they continued being there. Now, after much thinking and supposing that the possibility of running was something more than a real possibility, I've come to the conclusion that when she told me we should 'run together' one day, not even she knew exactly what she meant. Yes," he said, "I don't know if she was talking about running physically or if she was referring to some other kind of *running*. 'Running is a risk,' she used to say, 'you may feel stifled in the attempt, but afterwards you're always satisfied.' Yes, that's what she'd say. I'm completely certain she would say that," he added pensively and as if he had attempted to corroborate the fact in his memory. "When the day we were to run together finally arrived, she didn't show up. She couldn't come, she said. But she said it later, I mean some time later. I no longer remember just how much time passed from when she suggested the idea of running until the moment, the day to run, arrived—though now that I think of it, it was to be at night. And still less can I recall how much time elapsed from that day, that night rather, until she apologized with a vague excuse that hurt me, I suppose, quite a bit. To find out that something that for me was vital was in her eyes optional, secondary, would understandably wound me quite a bit. My self-confidence kept dwindling from day to day. Yes. *Major* obstacles. Because Olga's obstacles were always major. But even that night, running alone, I think I was able to struggle somewhat against the memory of her, yes, that too must have been a means of wiping her out. I remember sweating and sweating. I had gas and felt I couldn't breathe, but I kept on running until I nearly collapsed. I ran furiously, so as to forget everything. Yes, perhaps momentous things can only be done furiously. I could feel the pain in my thighs, in my legs. Sharp pangs in my kidneys and shoulder blades. Everything was spinning around," he said, "but I kept on running. I always thought that running with her would have been auspicious. I don't know, perhaps because it would have been a way of becoming integrated into her world, into a *zone* of her world explored by very few people, I suppose—the athlete, yes, and perhaps some other sports friend. Because I am certain that Olga carefully selected those people with whom she was going to run, just as a good drinker selects those with whom he knows he's going to get drunk. We always ritualize everything, it seems to me. I don't know, perhaps she intuited that for some reason it was counterproductive for me to know that zone of her world, perhaps she intuited that our running together was also a way of wiping her out. Yes, because one can only kill what one knows. The unknown may excite or alarm, but it can't be wiped out," Hans said. "And the same thing happened with those places that we both frequented, I mean, I had to wipe out those places as well, it was necessary. There they were, many of them I'd see daily, they were Olga. Yes, she in the shape of a *place*. She in the abstract. Her echo, her movements, everything was there, a perfect emblem of Olga. In fact," he said, "there was one place above all, a certain bar not too far from her neighborhood, right on the corner of Birminghamstrasse and Joachim Sörolt Avenue, which I used to feel was particularly mine, or rather hers, because it was Olga. The nook at the back, every flagstone, every chair. I've had countless drinks nestled in that corner next to the smoked glass windows," he said, "yes, the ones through which you can see clearly what's going on outside, but from the street you can scarcely distinguish anything inside the bar. I don't know, perhaps my memory of Olga is rather like that. I, seeing her in a bluish tone, from the inside, but seeing her fully, and she barely making out a silhouette leaning forward on the other side of the windowpanes, yes. We went there several times. I would speak and she would listen. Yes, she always listened. The bar was called the Sörolt. The light there was special and even the infernal noise of the game machines seemed to be translated into a tolerable, muted tone.

And her eyes: in that corner Olga's eyes would shine enigmatically, yes, in those instants she was on the verge of becoming a real possibility. Because when we went there together I would yield *my* corner to Olga without her being aware of it. I obliged her to sit there, knowing that in a few hours I would occupy that seat in search of the warmth she had left. Yes, at the Sörolt I would feel a genuine euphoria. One evening," Hans said, "I became so nervous that I nearly cracked my head when I went up to the little restroom on the upper floor. It was a filthy place, with a very low ceiling. On returning downstairs I told her to avoid ever going up to that restroom. It was no place for her. Filthy, I said. An elegant swan like you should never see *that*, I said, yes, and I remember she liked that, I think she really liked the allusion," said Hans, having apparently forgotten that I knew her too and, unlike him, was still seeing her daily, "and for an instant, striking my head against that dirty ceiling covered in dampness, I feared that if she went up the same thing would happen to her. I think a blow to Olga's head would have hurt me more than her, I don't know how to explain it to you, I suppose you can make an effort to understand me, yes, in fact I think you're the ideal person to do so, I mean to come relatively close to understanding me. But earlier, I think, I shouldn't have said 'euphoria' but rather 'enthusiasm.' Being there with her I came to feel waves of enthusiasm," he said. "It was an indefinable sensation that would make me talk incessantly, yes, always talking constantly. As I spoke I would take slight pauses, in which I would swallow one whiskey after another, giving my palate a brief respite. Then she would look at me as if expecting more, but also making it very clear by her silence that she didn't actually know what to say, or at any rate if she did know, was making a great effort not to say it. In retrospect, Olga never told me a thing, or rather, *almost* nothing. I think that used to frustrate her. I believe she needed to talk too, and something about me—something in me—hindered her. Yes, but I couldn't prevent that, I didn't know how, nor of course whether I ought to— I mean, I insisted that she give free rein to what she thought, to what she thought she wanted to say. I'm not sure, on one occasion I received a brief message from her at work. I found it in the drawer one morning shortly after one of our dates," Hans said, "yes, it was like a tremendous blow right in the face when you're not expecting it. I sat there like an idiot, not knowing what to do for a quarter of an hour or more. In fact I suppose, but I only suppose, that I didn't want to break the spell of that situation, didn't want to tear open the envelope and read what she had written. It was the first time she had sent a message to me. It came sealed in a white envelope, with no inscription whatsoever, but I knew immediately it was hers. It couldn't have been from anyone else," he said, "it *must not* have been. In that message, referring to my way of talking incessantly, she said it overwhelmed her, that I overwhelmed her with my words. 'You leave me speechless,' she wrote on that sheet. I don't know, I was actually unable to control the internal impulse that drove me to talk. On those occasions, I suppose, speaking in torrents must have been a kind of medicine, the only possible therapy for containing a dike threatening to burst. Just like now, in fact," Hans said, raising his gaze toward me, which totally disconcerted me, for it shattered the comfortable role of listener he had obliged me to maintain until that moment—"You've been listening to me for a while now and I notice you've fallen into doing just what Olga does, letting me talk on and on, and when I stop doing so you both avert your glance as if to avoid confronting my silence. Yes," he said, "she was *disconcerted* by my silence. She would automatically light a cigarette every time I stopped talking, yes—I mean, I suppose she would. I'm certain she would. Her way of lighting a cigarette was inimitable, I remember it well. I told you before, a real way of smoking. To see her expel the smoke was to perceive an immediate delight right here, between the lungs. Yes, a sort of asthma of satisfaction, I mean, satisfactory. Olga would move exactly as I had desired, just as I had imagined she would for so many nights prior to our meeting. Yes. My life and my feelings were internally linked to her, I can't even explain that precisely. I don't know, in some sense I always knew and was aware of what was going to happen, of what was happening. Until the very instant when I'd fall silent I was able to control the situation, though never her feelings. That's why I think I would have wanted us to run together that evening. We were one and the same thing, I mean, *within me* we were one and the same thing. A single thing, yet nevertheless detached in specific areas such as playing sports, I mean worshipping the body, in a sense. My life without her—which is why a while back I told you I wasn't partial to games, you remember? . . ." At that moment Hans became quiet, apparently engrossed in something he seemed to have seen or heard over in the forest, or perhaps on the peaks in the background. "Yes, well, I suppose I go from one thing to another without making much sense, every so often I get lost and then I have to take great pains to get back to the starting point . . . yes, my life, as I was saying, my life without Olga was like a true gambler's, just like a professional gambler obliged to play a round of poker on something other than green felt, the typical little green surface for poker games. Yes, I suppose that's how my life must have been at those moments. Something that was her very own, something that belonged entirely to her. I controlled everything up to a certain point, as I said. Her disquiet when faced with my silence, for example, a silence that forced her to assume various physical attitudes, and her relative ease with regard to my incessant talking. If I wanted to break that passivity, if I really desired to break it, then I would tell her things that were meant to be pleasant. In saying them I always thought she would like them. I know for a fact that they didn't displease her, but I don't know to what degree she liked them. I never knew. Indeed, *almost everything* concerning her was unknown to me, and only at the end did I have the vague awareness that she was, in some sense, quite a stranger even to herself. You're the air I breathe, I would tell her. And Olga protested, saying no, all that was nonsense. And she attempted to change the subject as soon as possible. Even now, on many mornings here at the sanatorium or while I inhale the vapor of the thermal springs, I inwardly repeat that phrase. You're my air, I say," Hans said. "And I hear her voice protesting from afar. It's true, I still hear her. Well, I suppose it's a supposition, because Olga isn't here, but I do hear her. She protests and with her habitual nervous gestures dismisses the comparison and everything provoked in me by those gestures. Yes, I understand her feeling relatively *at ease* in the chaos of words and ideas with which I would accost her. My chaos was preferable to my silence, which, had I forced it, might perhaps have entailed immediate chaos for her. I mean a chaos not only of her ideas but above all of her feelings. But as I was saying, I knew at all times exactly what my situation was. Certainly, I always had a notion of what I was doing, although not of what I wanted from her. I only became disconcerted the first time, I mean, when I got that envelope, the *message*. Yes, when she sent me her message, no more than half a page on one side, I was immensely surprised. I suppose that was the first time Olga disconcerted me altogether. Yes. Quite exceptional. I thought she would never repeat it. Usually Olga never repeated anything, but at that moment, yes, at that moment I suppose I already knew,

I was aware that every day, for as long as I worked for the firm, I would open the drawer every morning, not so much expecting to find another envelope with a fresh message from her—because I supposed that wasn't going to happen, that she would never allow that to happen—but rather to gaze at the empty space in my drawer which that first and only envelope had occupied for a few minutes before I arrived at work. But it was the first time," Hans said, "and I supposed it would be the only one, she never said so, but I supposed as much. It pained me to suppose that, I wanted to suppose something else, but my instinct told me the contrary. She herself, while I would speak to her about feelings—trying to make her believe I was referring to a man's overall feelings toward a woman, to *affective generalities*, to give it some sort of name, when in reality we both knew I was recounting my particular feelings toward her—she herself, as I was saying, asked me on some occasion if *that*, if that kind of passionate feeling (because that's what she called it, never losing a certain coolness in her composure) was something I'd experienced *frequently*. Other women, I know she was thinking. But she didn't mention them directly. She didn't share her throne with anybody. She was too proud for that sort of thing. She pretended not to know the meaning of the word 'throne,' but at the same time she assumed the countenance of a queen when I uttered it. Olga was above all that. To evince the contrary would have meant falling into a contradiction, and a woman as straight as she was couldn't allow that. Yes," he said, "I must talk about Olga's *propriety* so that you understand in a general sense what all that was about. Yes, she asked me about the frequency of those feelings. I'm not sure, I suppose I responded with the truth, which I think she expected to hear, I mean, which I suppose she expected to hear: that no, it had happened to me only a very few times in my life and—what was most remarkable and exciting for me—that I had almost completely forgotten such feelings. Those were only words, she said. Yes, words. Desire, anxiety, uncertainty, I think I may have said, yes. Disturbance, upheaval. Yes, she went on listening without batting an eye. But I think I lied. In fact, I had never felt anything similar, nothing. To see her was to sense my feelings translated into bliss in a matter of seconds. I sensed it in my skin. And I would tell her: 'I see you and I begin to feel a surge of happiness flowing through me, do you realize that?' Then her protests would intensify considerably. What I did know at those moments, just as I know now, and in fact always knew, is that although at one time I had thought of something more or less similar in resolving not to involve myself again in what is deemed a *passion* for someone—in this case Olga—on this occasion, with Olga, I knew it was to be the last time, I mean, I suppose I was fully convinced then that this was, this must be, the last time such a thing should happen to me. Now, on the other hand, I no longer suppose, I know it. I simply know it," Hans said. "But I don't know how or why I know it. Nor does it prove easy to face up to it, to that thought. So let's say that I know I suppose it's the last time. Often a person tells himself repeatedly that it's the last time this or that will occur. Later on it happens again, but the truth is, he already knew that's how it would be. This is not the case," he said, "I'm strictly supposing a certainty. Being here, at Chemnitz, has allowed me to suppose many things. Things that before coming here I knew or thought I knew, yet which I've subsequently considered in a different light. I've already told you, I believe, that here one is constantly supposing, one is driven to suppose. In almost every case they tend to defer to other *patients*—that's what they're called by the doctors and the relatives who come to visit them during the week or on Sundays. With me they don't do that. I can even suppose the arguments they'll put forth in response to a request of mine concerning anything. That's what happened when, having just arrived at the sanatorium, I asked them to transfer me to the marble polishing workshop. At first they refused, yes, but I made them understand that I wanted to think about nothing but marble, only marble. About nothing other than marble. Marble at all times except during meals, walks, and sleep. I suppose I threatened them as well, I mean I threatened the doctors with thinking and behaving *accordingly* if they didn't grant my desire for admission to the shop. I spoke to them, I think, of my inveterate passion for marble. I made them understand that, besides neutralizing me and keeping me away from the other *patients*, they could avail themselves a little of my unrestrained, voracious passion. Marble or nothing, I suppose I must have proposed to them. Marble or all-out war, I said, because all-out war would have meant futility, and they didn't like that, no sir, I've been able to observe that with other patients. It makes them nervous, makes nervous those who have always dealt with nerve problems, with nervous individuals. Nobody wants war in a place that should be tranquil. Yes, I suppose I felt the same certainty with

Olga from the beginning of our relationship, although now that I think about it, I don't know whether to call what happened between the two of us a relationship because, as I told you before, I don't even know if anything happened. I suppose it did, although I don't know what, probably something that was left *half-finished* happened, yes, the real possibility, I think, that something might really have happened. But it so happens that there are moments when that supposition collapses all by itself. Then I find myself surrounded by darkness. Completely surrounded. Darkness on all sides, yes. Nothing but darkness. Here, there, within me. Mist everywhere. Wherever I looked during those moments, I would see myself dressed in black, saber in hand, attempting to dispel the fog with strokes that sliced the air with a characteristic whoosh. Slicing the fog with a saber, yes, and I wearing a black cape that swept the ground, the ground I couldn't quite see in any case, since the fog prevented me. That was a strange vision. I never entirely understood it," Hans said, "it was simply there, within me, and would appear every so often. The man in the black cape battling against the mist. A poetic image, I thought then, The Man in the Black Cape and the Desperate Saber Slashes to the Heart of the Fog. Maybe so, I don't know. But every image is poetic. I mean every image—or rather, any representation of the will—has an unsurpassable poetic essence insofar as it takes the form of a sheer evasion of reality. Reality, I think, is the eminently *antipoetic*. Although now that I consider it, if someone were to ask me what facts I'm relying on to determine that the man with the cape and saber was myself, I wouldn't know how to reply. I should have to speak of probable suppositions. I know it was I because I saw myself in him, in the man with the cape, and my own fist delivered every stroke of the saber, yes. I've often asked myself, where is the heart of the fog? It's an odd thing. Those suppositions, as I was telling you, were the visible part of the immense disintegration that would take place within me whenever something mangled the certainty that Olga might eventually become—not so much some day, but in or by means of some idea—a real possibility, thus immediately leaving her almost bereft of the poetic, in the sense that she would cease to be an evasion of reality only to become a *manifestation* of the results of that reality. I don't know if I'm making myself clear, I want to make myself clear, since this is important, very important. To make her real," Hans said, "to turn her into a feasible possibility was and always had been a challenge, but to maintain her in supposition ended up being a torture. The pain was unbearable. I was telling you that I do know—though I don't know how I know—everything concerning Olga. Although not as much, at those very moments when she was *present*, as I should have and could have known. I know things I couldn't have imagined, about myself, about this place, the sanatorium, about Olga herself—although with regard to her, taking the leap from supposing to knowing was very problematic. I know these things with a certitude that frightens me, I suppose it frightens me tremendously, though I also suppose that the dreadful pitch of that fear isn't directly related to the desire that it be so, but to the part of my will that escapes the very awareness I still possess of that will. It's as though I were aware of everything surrounding me, as though I knew it because I myself provoked it," Hans said. "I know you're uncomfortable right now, yes, I can tell how uncomfortable you are, and at the same time I'm absolutely certain that it would be entirely impossible for you to stop listening. Earlier I thought that you, just like Olga, were frightened by chaos as an alternative to silence. You both believe silence is equivalent to lucidity, I think, but I also think you're mistaken. Silence, in certain circumstances, I mean under certain circumstances and in certain people, the acceptance of silence, the actual assumption of it, implies an *ethical* acceptance of the defeat that each and every one of us embodies. I say defeat, yes, because finitude is defeat, and what characterizes us is our condition of finitude in the face of the encompassing infinite. But that's not really important," he said, "that's how it's always been, yet nevertheless people have not ceased to feel dread before the imminence of that finitude, by which I mean death, in spite of the fact that life is usually an arduous apprenticeship in the school of courage for when *the moment* arrives. It makes no difference, I was saying, and our discussing this now is not going to change anything. I don't even think you'll remember it clearly a few hours from now, once you're no longer here. As far as that's concerned," Hans said, "you might perhaps think I'm raving, but I'll tell you, Olga has helped me a lot in thinking about that. Yes, she's the only person with whom I've managed to spend a few minutes in silence, with whom I've even remained silent at will. Something was there, between the two of us, I think, that *replaced* silence, I mean, what is normally filled by silence. Well, I don't know, I suppose before I was attempting to talk to you about certainty

in general and certainty in particular. The former would have to do with me
and the world, in other words, myself as a person and an integral part of the
cosmos, and the latter—the specific certainty applied to something or someone—would be the certainty I felt regarding Olga, things pertaining to Olga
and even Olga's feelings. Because Olga, aside from the determination she always showed to be faithful to her *idea* of propriety, was an inexhaustible
fountain of feelings, I know that. In truth," Hans said, "I can state that she
never demonstrated it to me, yet I know it. I know it had to be that way and
no other. Here, as I've told you, by dint of so much supposing—that uninterrupted supposing that flows incessantly through every nook and cranny
of the sanatorium—one ends up knowing everything, I mean almost everything. I never had actual proof of her feelings, but I sensed them there, hidden, seething within her being. Yes, I know for sure that she made me breach
the limits, my limits, in many respects. I always knew that with absolute certainty. Olga was like a toothache, something that's there inside you, vexing
you little by little, unhurriedly. From time to time the pain is alleviated by
incidental remedies, which are in fact worthless, because that pain returns
promptly and with renewed vigor. Yes, that's it," said Hans, completely al-
tering the expression on his face (which I had seen all the while in profile), a
change one might assume was due to having discovered something midway
between his mind and some thickets we were passing at that instant, at the
verge of the stony path we trod, "—a toothache. When I had toothaches I
would take a swig of cognac in my mouth, holding the liquid in the affected
area for a little while. But that didn't do much good. On the contrary, having
gone through several bottles, you become immune to the effects of alcohol,
and it seems that the nerves become considerably sensitized, so that what
would normally hurt you a little hurts even more. I doubt I'm the only one
for whom this holds true. I suppose the problem of toothaches is a general
problem. Olga was like that, a general problem quite closely related to toothaches, as I'll explain to you. Naturally at the time I also began taking shots of
French cognac to alleviate that pain. I managed to recover somewhat, but the
hook gnawing at the roots of my molars, of my thought, of the carious molars of my thought—to take it further—didn't quit. I thought and thought
about her. Sprawled on the floor of my house, between bouts of vomiting
and fantasies whose contents on several occasions wound up surprising even

me. Yes," Hans said, "while driving, talking to someone on the telephone, eating, drowsing on the sofa, while looking into a shop window. She was everywhere, in the changing of traffic lights, in the noise of a bottle being opened, in the creaking of a door, in the movement of curtains, in the hands of the clock, in the sudden braking of a car, in a lighted sign, in the distant sirens, in shoelaces, in the waft of morning coffee, between the lines of a book, in the weakness of my knees after a nocturnal binge. Yes, because Olga crowned my nights and my days. On those occasions she would appear by surprise. She would ask nothing. She would appear like a flash and vanish. For me Olga was a constant surprise, though a surprise not because of what she did or didn't do—for in fact she was in the habit of doing practically nothing but observing me and smiling as she nodded agreement—but rather in terms of what her mere presence inspired in me; something, I mean a feeling, that from the first few times we saw each other had burst the dam of reason. Indeed, seeing her I always or almost always had the sensation we have upon viewing filmed images of a building being dynamited, an immense, perfect, mute building, which suddenly comes tumbling down under the impact of some charges strategically placed in the foundations. Because you know perfectly well," Hans said, "that even blowing up an old building has to be done with grace, with art. Yes, even destruction can and should be an art. It's an indefinable sensation, yes, indefinable is the word. Even the commentator's voice seems to contract. An instant of silence, an instant which is also indefinable, and then everything comes down. Ashes, smoke. Thus with Olga," he said. "I would see her and have an identical sensation, yet without images, the sensation alone, an *unadulterated* sensation. I think perhaps I should have to speak of a perception. Yes. I don't know. I really don't know, no matter how much I reason it out, I can't know that. In any event, I think, sensation must be that within us that possesses certain physical characteristics. Take that hook, for example. I mean the *hook* of her absence, occasioned by her absence. Perception, on the other hand, may be a sensation more or less foreign to us, generated and incubated internally, but *actualized* outside of us. I mean: fully actualized. I used to tell her, for example, that I thought about her constantly. A mistake, I suppose, but now that's neither here nor there. I was telling you that not at any moment did I conceal from her that my thoughts gravitated toward her nearly every hour

of the day. But Olga would never have acknowledged that the same thing
happened to her with respect to me even if it were so, which it wasn't. On the
other hand—and this I've figured out here—she was in the habit of saying
that she had thought about me for the most inconceivable reasons. 'Yesterday
a couple of friends came to the house for dinner,' she would say, speaking
very quickly, 'and brought a bottle of whiskey with them. When I tasted it I
thought of you.' That's what she'd say. Bewildered as I was by the general atmosphere Olga always managed to create around her, that went in one ear
and out the other. I mean it didn't affect me, I almost didn't hear her. And yet
she had said it. She had told me something similar to what I had confided to
her, but in her own *language*. Because Olga would speak in code. Following
the breakdown of one or another of her household appliances, or having
heard some nonsense on television, she would come to me and say: 'I thought
of you.' She was incapable of giving more, of feeling more, but I repeat: at
the time I wasn't even aware of that. Yes, I suppose that what she would
transmit as *sensation* I'd understand as *perception*, a fact I realized in all its
magnitude only some months later and after much reflection. Her voice, as
well," Hans said, "the effect of her voice would help to explain this point. I
think of her voice when she had a cold. It was a child's voice, something that
filled me with tenderness, something that impelled me to jump for joy on
hearing it. Your voice is like that of a schoolgirl, I'd say. Naturally, she'd deny
it. She usually denied everything," Hans said. "It was a sort of defense mechanism that, I suppose, must have produced good results in her relations with
people—well, at least in some relationships with some people. 'Oh sure,' she
would respond. That was her reply, yes, a denial. For the sake of denying,
Olga would deny even her supposed propriety. When I alluded to it, partly
to provoke her, she almost got annoyed. She never realized I was talking
about an idea of propriety, and also about a willingness to assume that idea
of propriety. But I'll talk to you about that another time," he said, "first I want
to explain fully, I mean as best I can, my own experience of those perceptions.
Although now that I think about it," Hans said, "another of those perceptions arose precisely whenever I mentioned her propriety explicitly. Yes. For
an instant she seemed to soften, and I'd feel her *draw near* me at such moments. She would deny it emphatically, deny it over and over, but before
long, once she was aware of my provocation, she'd emphasize with infinite

calm that as a matter of fact I wasn't provoking her at all. 'You're not going to upset me, relax,' she reiterated. Then she would assume a hieratic disdain, which I guess I supposed was real, yes, I think she had fared quite well and wasn't upset by my mordant allusions to her propriety. 'I'm sorry,' she would say later, when I was again reduced to ashes and smoke. The building, you know," Hans said, "that instant of silence. Nevertheless at such moments she displayed a Parisian elegance. Her attitude was one of rejection, yes, but eclectic, somewhat superficial and forced, yet certainly Parisian. I suppose you understand what I want to say, it would be tragic if you didn't understand what I want to say," Hans averred, noticeably worried. "Despite everything," he went on, "I want to make it very clear that Olga was, I mean is, a wonderful person, yes, a great person, someone with a great deal of humanity. She takes pleasure in thinking she's cold, though she sometimes feigns a kind of indignation when she's accused of it, yet at heart she knows she's not. I know, I mean I suppose, that she is capable of becoming *fiery* about anything. I never really found out what her firing mechanisms were. On many occasions I intuited that they were there, within reach, within my grasp. But no. They vanished as if by magic. Yes, to get Olga to catch fire was a task for heroes. What did not vanish were the perceptions—on the contrary, they kept intensifying and sharpening as time went on. Since I've been here, at Chemnitz, I've clearly beheld the feeling I frequently experienced when I was with her, a feeling caused, I would say, by a perception, and thus in some sense foreign to me, yet proceeding from me. Every perception, I think, needs the foreign element, from without, while a sensation is sufficient unto itself. I don't know, I'm referring to what Olga, I suppose, must have felt when faced with the sort of *accident* I must have been in her life, which I insist was ruled by a strong will to establish herself within propriety, to fashion a whole, I think, with her source of happiness lying not so much in the practice of propriety as in the absence of problems. I don't know, I think in the final analysis we all aspire to that, to the absence of problems, but I also believe there are people who feel drawn to risk as to a magnet, to what will unquestionably end up causing them problems. Olga, on the other hand, was very circumspect in this regard. The absence of complications in her life, more perhaps than being a source of happiness, was the measure by means of which she sought her emotional stability. But I maintain that I've become aware of all this only with time. Only now have I seen myself making a genuine effort to *track down* what affected Olga. I mean, I'm now tracking it down mentally, but back then I was doing so *physically*. I've already told you how I used to go to the bars the two of us had visited at some point. Just like a little dog who sniffs everything in an attempt to find something his instinct craves. That's how I was," Hans said, "like a little dog. I gave no more thought to that possibility, I suppose, until much later. Suddenly I understood, I knew—I don't know, maybe I only supposed it—that her behavior toward me was that of people who lose their temper with their little dog and strike it in a moment of irritation only to caress it immediately afterwards. She would initiate an attempt at a partial break with me and then would appear *solicitous*. Solicitous only partially, too. I don't know if Olga went so far as to caress me at some point, I suppose she did. Olga simply allowed herself to be caressed so as to demonstrate that she bore it—my caressing her hand in a total daze, for example—with a certain stoicism. That Parisian elegance I mentioned before. Yes," Hans said, "she must have understood that had she brusquely withdrawn or rejected me, it would have been very hard for me, as a sensation, and also for her in terms of perception: that's why she let it happen, I would even say she let it happen with a certain morbid complacency, but never really pleasure. Never any emotion. I don't know how, but I guess I killed the spring that generated emotion—the real possibility of real emotion in her—as soon as we met each other. That's what Olga was always incapable of showing: emotion. Which doesn't mean that she didn't feel it, but that if she did feel it, she experienced it in a very particular way. Perhaps she was restrained by my chaotic way of speaking and expressing myself, which on the other hand meant her comfort and also her confidence with respect to me, the general attitude she should adopt with me. I could kiss the knuckles of her fingers, nibble at them for quite a while, yet her changed expression revealed almost nothing but initial surprise at an act— my boldness—that she really wasn't anticipating. 'You can keep going until you get tired,' she would say with a wry smile on her lips. Parisian elegance, you see, yes, but from the *center* of Paris, not from the suburbs. Because Olga, in spite of believing the opposite—I mean, in spite of being bent on believing the opposite—was never suburban, at least in my experience. She was always at the center," Hans said, "always. And I think she goes on being there, I mean, I suppose so. I always searched avidly for that center, which translated to the level of sensations ended up being, for example, the places or things that reminded me of her. Once, in jest, I put the raincoat I was wearing on her. Well, I never wore it again, I would have found that impossible. If by mistake I ended up with half a pack of Olga's cigarettes, I couldn't bring myself to smoke them either. One day she told me she would like to live in one of the houses by the river, you know the ones. 'They get a lot of sun,' she said. Until then, oddly enough, I too had thought about looking for a house in that area. Afterwards, the mere act of going by those houses on either side of the Leer made me feel queasy just looking at them. Anything she mentioned was instantly branded forever. It was forbidden ground. Something similar happened with the bars, I believe, especially the Sörolt. Yes," Hans said, "the Sörolt, oddly enough, will never be just a bar, but rather a mutual bar, it belongs to both of us in the sense or at the point in which sensation and perception cross in space and time. Yes, I was searching for that center which I knew even then was my center of gravity, although that might be a perception manifested in sensations, in everything that was directly or indirectly related to Olga. I suppose I should explain this to you with a practical example. Indeed, there are so many," Hans said, "that my entire life seems to have been reduced to practical examples of my way of being and the influence she had over that way of being, because unlike what may have happened to her with regard to me, in my case Olga meant constant *practice*. At first, I think, the practice of inertia, since I was totally incapable of doing anything except thinking about her. Later, after several weeks, it was the practice of and in sensations, but also of particular perceptions that I recycled in what was perhaps a desperate search for the nourishment that would sustain me in the actual practice of life. In the end, when I entered the phase of what may be akin to hysteria, at least to what I call hysteria, in other words, being permanently *on the brink*, the fact of her existence outside of me, in the end, as I said, after overcoming that incapacitated state, I remained entrenched in what I call *passive hysteria*, yes. Well, in all likelihood that's not an adequate term to define what was happening to me, probably not. If that's how it is, I'm sorry, because you're not going to understand me and, having arrived at this stage, I believe it would be dangerous if you didn't understand me, if you misinterpreted my words, and above all I would feel sorry because

I truly desire to make myself understood, to have someone understand me. I just don't know," he said, "I'll confess that perhaps the worst part of the whole business with Olga, that disagreeable and sad business—but about which in spite of everything (and this may seem to you an enormous contradiction) I have absolutely no regrets—the worst thing, as I said, may be that I've *never* spoken to anyone about Olga. With you, and I still don't understand why, I did unburden myself somewhat, but only a little, I mean, I suppose only a little. I don't recall exactly," said Hans. "That was the period of cognac for my tooth—which in fact at that time was really causing me a lot of pain—and I got into the habit of having a few too many. That Parisian elegance, I think, could only be borne in a relatively Parisian manner with French cognac. Yes. I also spoke to my sister on one occasion about Olga, but only a little. I really did speak to her only *a little*," Hans said, "and my sister, who is an excellent psychologist—I mean, whom I believe to be an excellent psychologist, since she has many clients in her practice and tends to appear in magazines and such—more than anything else intuited my general condition, saw it clearly right from the start, yes. And precisely because she is an excellent psychologist, I suppose, she tried to play down the subject. Because my sister classifies everything into subjects and areas," he said, "yes, she classifies everything. Olga as a rule denies everything and Angelica classifies it. It would seem that mentally denying and classifying everything were part of the same activity. Yes, that must somehow or other be the most typical mode of extroversion for those who are strong. You see, I think it's rather odd: each of them with such delimited activities. To deny and to classify. Neither *gives*. Perhaps that's why they're doing well in life. At any rate, I suppose they're doing all right, at least that's what they say, or at least what Olga used to say. Angelica grasped my condition perfectly. That's why she refused to speak about the problem directly. She, too, I suppose, kept on listening to me, attempting to make something out of it. I think she hoped I would give her a new element that might end up invalidating the construct or the outline of a construct she had envisioned regarding my *quote-unquote problem*, as she called it. It's typical that intelligent creatures like Angelica—like Olga in her own way—should have the ability to trivialize what lies close to the bone. Capacity for abstraction," Hans said, "but I suppose, I only suppose, that every fact I gave her ended up completely invalidating her former view of

48

my *quote-unquote problem*. At the time, at first, she offered no opinion whatsoever. Angelica never gives her opinion about anything lightly. She just listens, combines facts. She works with the details as she hears them," he said, "in that respect her conclusions are always *a posteriori*. And often, of course, one doesn't even learn what they are. She must discuss them with her husband. I don't know. Probably. If not, with whom does one discuss that sort of thing? Yes, possibly with her husband," Hans said, "I believe so, I'm certain, almost certain. Yes. At the beginning, when I told her superficially what had been happening with Olga of late, I mean, because of my feelings toward her, Angelica said bluntly: 'You're still like that at this stage?' An adolescent, she must have thought. Yes, I bet that's what she thought, although she never got around to telling me so. She must have mentioned that to her husband, as well. Yes. It's natural for these things to be said to a husband, at night before going to sleep, or while eating," he said, "those moments when, I suppose, one doesn't hear a thing but responds correctly and automatically to everything. Yes, I think even she never understood what was really happening to me. At bottom, I think, *something* in me or about me inspired fear in her. Normally Angelica was much more brutal in her speech. Yes, it's part of her therapy, free of charge when dealing with friends or family. Some while later she had to come to the office to give me an urgent letter and entrust me with some errands. She was going away on a trip. Olga happened to be at the switchboard of the reception booth, you know how she sometimes covers that post for a few minutes. So," he said, "on that day Angelica marched up to my desk, flinging at me point-blank a phrase that would later give me a lot to think about. Yes, my sister is very intelligent, I've already told you that, her packed office proves that, or at least indicates it, and I repeat, she always measures her words carefully. That day, on the other hand, after seeing Olga through the glass in that incubatorlike reception booth, she planted herself before my desk, and what she said even carried, I think, a strong dose of contained rage. 'She's a bonbon! Don't you even realize it? A bonbon!' Yes, that's what she said. I recall Dietrich, two desks away, looking baffled at such a sudden display of irritation from someone who, although not with the firm, had approached me in such a familiar manner. Later on I spoke to Angelica again about my *quote-unquote problem*. Just once. Yes, I never did so again. It was fruitless. Like talking to a wall. Deep down I was hurt, I mean, I suppose I felt hurt by her remark about Olga. Once she was calmer, my sister attempted to explain how she believed she understood me perfectly, yes, that's exactly what she said: perfectly. And she added further: 'in its proper perspective.' I don't know, the content of that conversation strikes me as odd. I do know, however," Hans said, "that Angelica insisted that in life—and note that at no moment did she refer to mine, to *my* life, but to *life*—one does come across bonbons. There are lots of bonbons, she said. And I recognize, if you like, that one doesn't find bonbons where one expects them to be, they're not invented, Angelica said, but in spite of that there are other bonbons. It's a question of looking for them. She pronounced judgment. I don't know, the point is that later, carefully considering my sister's remarks—her theory of looking for a bonbon to sweeten the unpleasant sensation of having lost another bonbon and so on—I wound up feeling indignant. Yes, you heard me. Once I had thought about all that, I was very indignant, I mean, quite indignant. I had never become so indignant with anyone, and particularly with her, with Angelica," he said. "But to become indignant with a psychologist—I mean with an intelligent psychologist who furthermore is your sister, and who had always adopted a severe but maternal attitude toward me, despite my being older than she—is completely fruitless, you know. A discussion, I suppose, would have been fruitful, but I felt I had neither the strength nor the capacity for it, I mean the *mental* capacity to undertake a confrontation of that sort. I couldn't remain calm and impassive before someone who asked me, 'But what is it you see in her?' No. That was beyond me. I could have told her Olga's story, could have spoken to her about the wind, I mean about Olga's *provenance*, about her relation to the wind, but I know that Angelica would not have understood anything. I'll explain that point to you later," Hans said, giving a light kick to a stone that lay in his path. "Yes, I'll tell you because, after all, that really is Olga. Without that, without knowing that story it would be difficult for you to understand everything else, to understand me. But going back to my *quote-unquote problem*, as my sister disparagingly called it on that occasion, I suppose she had already covered that ground, I mean discussed it with her husband, who is also a psychologist. Both of them, Angelica and her husband, came over to visit last Sunday or the one before, I'm not sure. My *quote-unquote problem* didn't come up at all," Hans said, "I talked to them about marble, yes, lately all that appeals to me is talking to people about marble. Here, of course, 'people' means those in white smocks or green ones, and *patients* like me," he said. "Marble at every hour of the day, yes, and she too—my sister—attempted to steer the conversation toward the blow I dealt that poor old Handke. Old Handke, so unsociable and stupid," Hans said. "Oh, yes, but I didn't fall into the trap. I said what I always do: that my striking old Handke was a result of having momentarily lost my patience with him. The same story as ever. The ones wearing the white smocks had to hear the entire thing countless times: 'Why do you think you hit him?' they would ask with uncommon interest. And I'd say: 'What reason could there be not to hit a chronic moron who's spent years making your life impossible? Give me a reason, just one.' Oh yes, they would speak about the unseemly nature of any aggression, and I would ask them about the *other* acts of aggression, the ones we suffer everywhere daily, on the street, at work, in our own homes. Yes, very curious, like a conversation between deaf-mutes over the telephone. I don't know," he said, "I'm not going to deny that there were in fact many other things behind that blow—well, that uninterrupted series of blows I gave old Handke. If I say 'blow' it's because I really meant to deal him just *one* blow. The other blows were dealt by my hand, I mean, by my lost patience or my overwrought nerves, but not by me. I don't know, I understand an explanation like that must be difficult to grasp, especially seeing how poor old Handke ended up. I told Angelica that I was truly sorry about what had happened and that I supposed (although I actually knew) that if I was now confined to the spa—and I did say 'spa,' but I also said 'confined'—it was because of that, because of the blow I dealt old Handke. Period. We spoke no more," he said. "In spite of everything, I see quite clearly the reason my sister put my *problem* in quotes from the beginning. Yes, I think there's a certain kind of person, or rather a certain kind of woman—more specifically *intelligent* women, and my sister Angelica is one—who comes unhinged at the mere sight of certain women, I mean certain *beautiful* women. Yes," Hans said, "I think Olga's beauty not only disconcerted her to a great extent but also deeply hurt her. Undoubtedly she must have seen something in the perfection of Olga's features that struck her as repulsive, I imagine so, yes, because one thing I'm completely sure of is that my sister could see only her face through the glass in the switchboard incubator. Yes, she didn't like the beautiful, wild features of that face. Had she said anything else I would have understood. Feline features, catlike, none of that would have bothered me. But to call her a 'bonbon' seemed vile to me, the result of a thoughtless and unbridled resentment that comes from who knows where, or why. Yes, I always thought that those features of Olga's face had something animal about them, I don't know, something indefinable as well, like her behavior itself. I understand how they might bother a lot of people, especially progressive people, and above all progressive women like Angelica. Beauty tends to wound the senses, I think. I also believe," Hans said, "that beauty somehow tends to wound especially those who think to excess. Indeed, the beautiful doesn't let itself be thought about unless it's to corroborate that beauty, that's why it bothers a lot of people. Yes, to meet Olga was to confront an entire world of subjective evaluations as contrasted with general knowledge, which often clash with each other. It's impossible to know if we behave in a certain way because of what we know or because of what we feel. Don't you think so?" Hans asked quickly, keeping his gaze fixed ahead, "yes, the beautiful spoils us, I mean it becomes a habit. And we cannot do without it, although other alternatives may be offered us, even appealing alternatives. I don't know, everything is confusing, but I suppose it has to do with my own theory as opposed to Angelica's bonbon theory. Yes, bonbon. That's what my sister said. And my sister, as I've told you, is not only a progressive and intelligent person but also one who possesses an innate degree of brilliance that quickly becomes evident. Oh yes, a brilliant woman, with character, according to everyone who knows her. I believe so, too, but I know her gesture of discomfort when someone says she's very *attractive*. Really, ever since she was a child, they've been telling her that everywhere she went. Attractive. And despite all that, she couldn't stand Olga's beauty, she despised her right then and there, without knowing her or discovering what lay behind that lovely face. Sometimes I think that had she simply found her pretty, what someone like Angelica would actually have felt might have been indifference. But she must have seen something beyond her beauty. Don't get me wrong," Hans said, "even I don't know, I mean I don't know for certain, because I've sometimes gone so far as to think that Olga, Olga's attitude, Olga's beauty, everything about Olga, was a question of *certainty* and of nothing else. Olga's way of proceeding was never very philosophical. Nonetheless, I believe she herself was not very inclined to excessively beautiful things. For example, it disturbed her tremendously when people alluded to her beauty, she became really upset. I don't think she was pretending, I mean, I suppose she didn't pretend. She didn't need to. So, when she was reminded of her beauty, she'd talk about her unkempt hair and her excessively large body, yes, that's what she'd say, her hips were too wide and her feet enormous. Indeed, Olga wasn't one of those people who go about looking at themselves in all the mirrors and shopwindows they happen to pass. I would tease her, saying, oh yes, she was a genuine freak of nature, and she seemed to accept that. She tried to conceal her hands whenever possible. It's as if she hadn't any hands," he said. "If at any point I grasped them, I mean if I'd consumed enough al-cohol to make me uninhibited enough to take hold of them for a few seconds, she, Olga—always with that Parisian elegance I told you about—would abruptly withdraw them and hide them, as though they were frightened snakes. Perhaps deep inside she didn't believe one bit all that about her beauty. She had two other sisters who, she maintained, were much prettier than she was. She would even speak of 'the pretty one' whenever she referred to the older one. But to think of her sister in terms of 'the pretty one,' with Olga in front of me, struck me as an insult, a joke in bad taste. Olga was— and I quote her very words—the one in the middle, with everything that im-plies. In fact, almost the *ugly duckling* of the family. As I told you, a genuine freak, as far as she was concerned. No, Olga didn't enjoy things that were too beautiful. That's why she didn't like roses. I mean she did like them, but in a very peculiar way, since on one occasion she confided to me that she would always have her home filled with roses. Yet something about roses repelled her nonetheless, something about their nearly absolute beauty. She never got around to explaining why. Yes, I think that wasn't really necessary, I mean, I think so now. At the time, naturally, I was left half in the dark. Had she ex-plained it *totally*, she wouldn't have been Olga. There would have been something wrong. She preferred daisies, yes, they were her favorite flower. 'I like what grows freely, spontaneously,' she'd often say for no particular rea-son. Yes, 'spontaneously' was a word that sounded delectable on her lips. It sounded actual, as though the spontaneity she referred to were translated into something substantial at the moment it was uttered there, in the moist depths of her palate. Yes, I remember her saying, 'Roses are *too* beautiful.'

That's what she said. Yes. 'Like you,' I thought of responding, but I didn't dare say it. In that respect, in speaking about her beauty, I was constantly afraid of hurting her. You see, I didn't dare tell her that I found her *too* beautiful. Yet perhaps, had I done so, she would have liked it. I don't know, I won't ever know that. I suppose I restrained myself then and many other times not out of shyness or cowardice so much as out of weakness. Yes, weakness, that's what I think," Hans said. "The weak always lose," he said, "just watch a sparrow attempting to peck at some bread crumbs while surrounded by pigeons, enormous pigeons. He can't do it. He loses. The sparrow always loses. It's his destiny to lose. And it's not because of cowardice, but rather weakness. He uses every means to attempt it, but ends up losing. Oddly enough, I think, pigeons frightened Olga, yes, and dogs as well. Whenever a dog approached while we were walking down the street, she would seize my arm, thoroughly convinced it was going to bite her. As for pigeons, she admitted that she had never been able to feed them from her hand. In that respect, I believe it was also weakness that veiled my attempts to *draw near* to Olga, to everything pertaining to Olga, to anything Olga had done. You already know about the bars, yes, that whole pilgrimage—fetishistic, I suppose—to the places that reminded me of her, that sort of voluntary calvary. Well, the business about the bars, though, is merely the tip of the iceberg. Yes, there's much more," said Hans, "things no one knows about. It's true: things even my sister failed not only to realize but even to intuit. I mean to intuit from a distance. Nor her husband. No, not him, either. Things even Olga never supposed, though I myself told her about them in lavish detail, and I understand now that was a grave mistake, since at the time, at those very moments, she was *unable* to understand them, and therefore she would dismiss them or merely laugh, saying that if I kept teasing her, I'd have her tearing out her hair—her 'ugly, unkempt hair,' she'd say. Because sometimes she supposed to excess, as well, even when—as was the case with those things I mistakenly confided to her—she was faced with a total reality, which doesn't mean that I believe there are realities that aren't total. No, that's not it. What I mean to say is, I was even beginning to doubt those realities subject to my control. Or perhaps I should correct that, yes: realities conceived in a totally uncontrolled way, yet about whose certainty I had no doubt. Yes, I'm referring to something worse than the business about the bars, quite a bit worse than the thing about the

54

bars: the places that really *were* Olga's, those places that, because of family, in some way or another belonged to her. Her uncle's house, where she tended to visit frequently, comes to mind. One evening," Hans said, "I discovered by chance that it was located quite near my own, in my neighborhood, in the upper part of Grossen. I remember her pausing in front of 48 Paul-Klee-Strasse. She pointed to the entrance and said: "This is where my aunt and uncle live." Yes, that's what she said. Just that. Then I believe she went on walking as if nothing had happened. What Olga never knew is that from that night on I would periodically go for walks down that stretch of Paul-Klee-Strasse where her uncle's house stood. That gilded *48* encompassed by a circle became an obsession, a further obsession, like that of the wind, which I'll explain to you later," Hans said. "It was one more image that prolonged the chain of thoughts with which I had to fill my sleepless nights. That door-way haunted me relentlessly. I suppose it was just an ordinary entrance," he said, "with nothing special to distinguish it from the others on that street. And I, standing like a statue at the corner on some sort of pretext, glancing toward it every so often. Although the truth is that in order to do so—to stand there quietly a few meters from the uncle's doorway or to stroll up and down the very sidewalk Olga traversed several times a month when she vis-ited her relatives—I needed no pretext of any sort. No," Hans said, "I did it just because. As if it were really a *mission*. It's odd, I've always believed in doing things just because, but I've never put the idea into practice. That was something I did just because. Prowling about, that is, on that street. If I hadn't done that, I wouldn't have known what to do, I mean, what to do with my time, with my life. That was Olga's sidewalk because she had set foot there. And I felt genuinely sad whenever I had to leave the place, it's true. But don't think I was hoping for an encounter. Not at all, the worst thing that could have happened to me, I can assure you, would have been precisely to run into Olga there. That certainly would have required an explanation, a convincing explanation. 'What are you doing around here at this hour?' she would undoubtedly have asked. 'Right in front of my uncle's doorway.' And I wouldn't have known what to reply, she would have read it in my eyes. Though as a matter of fact I don't suppose any reply would have been pos-sible. Yes, now that I think about all that—I mean, about those strolls down the sidewalk of the street where Olga's relatives lived, and of my thoughts back then with regard to the possibility of a fortuitous encounter with her, which in reality wouldn't have been so fortuitous, since I was always aware that Olga frequently passed by there—I think about it, as I said, and it all seems like a trifle compared to the business with Olga's car," Hans said. "That damned yellow car. At some point I told her what was happening to me with her car, but I know she didn't understand me, well, I suppose she had no desire to understand me. 'I find it amusing,' she said, 'and if it's true you'll get over it before long.' Yes, that's what Olga said. And she quickly changed the subject. As easy as that. As a matter of fact, Olga, unlike me, never considered that one had to do things just because, yet that's the way she did them. I don't think she believed it, I mean I don't think she believed the story about me and her car. No, she understood that she oughtn't to believe it. Yet nevertheless that phrase indicated something: 'If it's true you'll get over it before long.' I suppose she was lucid enough to grant that minimal margin of veracity to what I was telling her, to think it might be true and not merely my imagination. I don't know, but it was always obvious to me that the two of us experienced that sort of thing in distinct, diametrically opposed ways. I'm referring to the business with the car, for example. I think I even raised some doubt in her mind as to whether I was making fun of her, or attempting to flatter her with arguments of that sort. Yes, I always thought that those situations—situations I provoked—must have reminded Olga of the smell of stagnant water, evoked for her the sensation of stagnant water, or rather the sensation of the smell of stagnant water. Something neither good nor bad, but distinctive," Hans said, "something unmistakable and indestructible if only we didn't think it smelled like that, like stagnant water. I don't know if you follow me. *Stagnant water*," he repeated mechanically, "a sensation that perhaps took her back to her youth, to her adolescence, to when she was thirteen or fourteen and for the first time felt an inclination toward someone or someone felt an inclination toward her. Because I have sometimes thought that for someone to feel an inclination toward Olga must, all through her life, have created an immediate turmoil for her. Yes, I suppose she needs to know that she provokes that sort of inclination in certain people, but I'm also sure that she's never known how to gauge the proportion between her need to be desired and her willingness to give. Yes. She didn't know herself very well, and when you often have to display strength, that winds up being dangerous. Perhaps she did think about these things too much, I mean, mulled over in her head the advantages or disadvantages of having someone break through the wall that preserved her privacy, or what she believed to be her privacy, since Olga was in fact too sincere and spontaneous to keep anything really important inside. Well, at least that's what I believe. For example, I think that from the time we met, she began to evaluate our relationship before it even took shape. I don't know, I suppose she must have experienced all that with a certain *anticipatory disenchantment*, a disenchantment imposed by circumstances, because Olga was always very adult, I mean, very adult in her behavior. Yes, not one slip. Not one false step. As for her thoughts, I don't know. Actually, I was always afraid to know more in that regard. On the other hand, my general feeling toward her had nothing to do with anticipatory disenchantment imposed by circumstances, but rather with something much more tangible, something very similar to what we feel on waking up amid total darkness in a strange bed. Yes, groping desperately about, knocking things over, even falling out of the bed, trembling before a wall that isn't there at all. Yes," said Hans, "I had that feeling of helplessness when Olga was not beside me, which tended to be most of the time, I mean, *nearly always*. That's why, I think, it was very difficult for her to really understand the thing I had about her car, her damned yellow car. The fact is, the affair with that car ended up being sheer hell. I wound up hating all the yellow cars in the city, the country, the world, above all yellow Volkswagens, of which this city, it seems, is particularly full. You turn over a stone and out comes a yellow Volkswagen. Sometimes I think I see them going through the air in perfectly aligned squadrons, yes, as if they were flying brigades. Well, when I arrived at work in my red car, I'd immediately park it near hers. At first I started edging it a little closer to hers, then a bit closer. Yes, inch by inch I was bringing it nearer to hers, to her damned yellow Volkswagen, in such a way that for a time even I thought it was a purely circumstantial detail. At first I would tell myself: nudge in right alongside hers so other people can park with ease. It was simply a matter of politeness. Although in fact, I remember that there were always a lot of spaces yet to be filled along the street. Yes. There came a time in which, whenever I didn't ride the bus to work, I would literally press my car up against hers. I brought it so close to hers that the two bodies came into *contact*. Yes, they would be touching: metal against metal. She had to have noticed it more than once. When she started her damned yellow car, she must necessarily have felt the vibration of that other car touching her own. But she never said a thing, no, not a word, despite the fact that, as I said earlier, I had already talked to her about it at some point. There, too, her Parisian elegance in such matters never betrayed her. Yes, I think she found it amusing, though it's also likely that she eventually got bored with it. Yes, I'm afraid Olga was one of those people who tend to get bored very quickly with everything. I suppose that made me seem especially sensitive about any behavior of mine that I thought might bore her: gestures or repetitious phrases. I recall that one of the first times we talked, she assured me she was firmly convinced that life consisted of nothing other than deriving the greatest possible benefit from routine. But she said it with the expression of someone already living a routine existence, which, as you might suppose, left me feeling totally glum. Yes, right from the start that made me feel I was bothering Olga: yes, bothersome like a cough in the middle of a concert. I, the cough, the unstoppable fit of coughing," Hans said, "she, the concert, the symphony. To my misfortune, I always thought that Olga was a sensible woman from head to foot. Because she *did* have a head on her. Once she even defined her own head as 'more than just a lump that separates my ears.' Yes, it was a precise definition, I'd even say devastatingly precise. She would repeat, I mean, every so often, just so I'd never forget it, she'd repeat to me that she was the type of person who has 'only four ideas in her head, but very clear-cut ones.' Paradoxically," Hans said, "in time I came to realize that she also referred somewhat sarcastically to certain people as 'one of those people who have only four ideas in their heads, but very clear-cut ones, you know.' Yes, Olga's capacity for self-criticism was ferocious. She had never been a militant member of a group or any such thing, I mean, she hadn't learned the *techniques* of self-criticism in any organization with ideological aims, but she treated herself ruthlessly on that score. Yes, hers was a clear head. So clear, I think, that her allusion to the clarity of her ideas was a neat, an overwhelmingly neat and of course exquisitely Parisian way of telling me that she really couldn't care less whether I was afraid of boring her with my behavior, be it gestures, repetitious phrases, or whatever. Just as it didn't matter to her that I pressed my car up against hers, her damned yellow Volkswagen, which really constituted a repetitious gesture,

I recognize that, but also a *desperate* one. Yes, that was a gesture of sheer desperation, my only means of contact with her, at least at that time, of course. Because whenever I did that, pressed my car against hers, it meant we wouldn't see each other after work. Sometimes I would park my car not behind or in front of hers, but alongside, so close to one of the doors that she was obliged to make countless maneuvers to avoid damaging both cars. And of course she had to get in through the passenger door, not from the driver's side. Yes, I suppose it really was a signal, a violent signal. But not a word out of her, not a single word. With Olga, as far as that sort of behavior—or response to certain behavior—was concerned, reticence and indifference came to be one and the same. And in the end, I mean the last few times I recall having done that with the car, I literally tried to make it touch the driver's door of the yellow Volkswagen. Then she was forced to get in through the other door, which she did without batting an eye, even when she was accompanied by other co-workers whom she was driving downtown. Even then she didn't lose her poise. She pretended not to notice it. One evening she alluded in passing to my *tactlessness* in putting her in such a situation in front of her colleagues. Yes, that poured cold water on things, and I stopped parking my car next to hers. That was always the way Olga proceeded: in passing. But she didn't say anything offensive, she never really said anything offensive. Perhaps some stray allusion, in jest, but really nothing. No, that wasn't her style. I suppose that witnessing day after day my fruitless gesture of despair with the cars, mine seeking a symbolic contact with hers, was not the only thing that made me desperate, but also seeing her passivity in response to what at some point I believed might stimulate her, I mean Olga with that same passivity always and at every turn when it came to anything stemming from me. Olga never *did* anything," Hans said. "Having gotten to know her, I think, I learned that letting things happen wasn't so much a comfortable attitude as it was an art, a most difficult art. It was as if the other—extracting a forceful, direct reaction from her—was impossible, like resurrecting the dead or arresting the Earth's motion. Yes, and Olga wasn't dead, oh no, far from it. Her vitality was frightening, I assure you. I know she was lively, I frequently heard her laughing at work, in her office, cheerful and pleasant with everyone, not with men in particular but with everybody. With me, though, if I managed to beguile her into drinking one whiskey too many, in other words, if she consented to letting herself be beguiled, making me believe I was beguiling her by making her drink more than her share of whiskeys, she also appeared cheerful, but only that. Cheerful. When the one really beguiled in this whiskey business was not Olga but I. Yes," Hans said, "the first time we went out she drank martinis and port without saying a word about it. Later, when on subsequent dates we moved on to whiskey, I thought it would go straight to her head, since she wasn't accustomed to it. Much later I realized—to my astonishment and almost with indignation—that she was an unrepentant whiskey drinker, yes, that was the initial mistake on my part, something that only served to caricature a more general, more important situation. She was able to distinguish not only one whiskey but one *bourbon* from another by the smell, with her eyes closed, and only very rarely was she wrong. Olga drank and drank," Hans said, "and I was shocked to find out it hadn't the slightest effect on her, you know, I suppose at heart I had the quaint idea that a woman whose body is full of alcohol is more vulnerable, more *uninhibited* about everything. And in the end—as long as I didn't recognize Olga's capacity for drink, I mean—it was always the same spectacle: I was the one whose speech became slurred, I felt almost incapable of thinking, my legs went all wobbly, and there was Olga right before me with the same cheerful expression. Yes," he said, "I never thought cheerfulness could wear a smile of ice. It was quite a surprise. And I became fascinated, naturally, when I discovered that in spite of all my tricks and stratagems, whatever I might try, Olga never *did* anything in my presence. But I repeat, she wasn't dead, no, not a bit. Each time she seemed more alive. Her penchant for life increased from day to day. Everything in her was life, even her icy gaze or letting herself be beguiled into drinking that extra whiskey, or even her allowing a *fleeting* caress. At least I suppose that's what they must have been, I mean, for her those caresses must have been fleeting, insignificant. That's what they must have been, I think," Hans said, "even though I spent entire days wondering how and when to venture them. Yes. Each time more alive. And to the same degree that she was more alive, I on the contrary felt more dead. Yes, I think my mental deadness in that sense, I mean my proclivity toward inertia—maybe owing to contamination or perhaps simply to my inability to shake off the condition that had taken hold of me—began to wax in direct proportion to her *regeneration* with respect to life, and at my

expense. Because the one thing I'm sure of," he said, "is that the regenerative
process by which Olga sought greater activity never suffered severe relapses,
though on occasion it must have stagnated. I don't think the period immediately before I entered her life—I mean before I burst, before I flung myself
into her life—I don't believe it was anything new, really new for her. Later,
I suppose, she automatically became more and more alive. And I more and
more lifeless. It was as though I were giving her my life in the abstract sense
also, which affects one's moods. That I do see clearly, at least now, because it's
here, at Chemnitz, that I've reached this conclusion: that my total inertia, in
the sense of a progressive atrophy of my ability to react, resulted from my
extremely intense mental activity during that period. Little by little my brain
was becoming atrophied too, I'm not sure, something strange happened to
me. Sometimes I have the feeling that, even though I said it was I who *flung
myself* into her life, I underwent a kind of process of vampirization through
her. I don't know if you follow me," Hans said, "I declined and she ascended.
Because Olga's ascent was always a constant. Yes, as she grew older—and
this I know not only because at some point she told me so but also because I
realized that's how it was—the more she gained, I mean, in years and experience, the more alive she became. I suppose, but I'm merely supposing,
that she had unconsciously set herself some sort of goal to live intensely up
to that point, and afterward to pour all that willpower into the pursuit of her
emotional stability, the need to become serene. Yes, I think I ended up with
the worst part. I arrived at the most unsuitable moment, I mean I flung myself into her life when she least needed an intrusion of that sort. Yes," Hans
said, "I think that desperate gesture of pressing my car against hers was
nothing when compared to other things I did because of Olga—and I say
did inasmuch as those things were carried out, things of which I was perfectly well aware, for the fact is I saw them taking place before my eyes—but
which she, I think, just as with what happened with the car, never really
quite believed, though I even tried to inform her about them, at least superficially, without insisting too much, since I realized that was counterproductive to my intentions, if indeed I really knew at any time what my intentions
were. But as a matter of fact," he said, "since I've been here, in the sanatorium, or spa, or whatever exactly this place may be, I believe I've finally come
to understand that my intentions with respect to Olga were precisely to elicit

a *response* from her. Whatever it might be, but a response, to get her to do something for once. I suppose she did give me the response I was actually expecting, a negative response, of course. Let's say she responded by not responding. Her reticence or indifference, I suspect, was her response. Her way of responding. Her only way. But it so happens that there were *other things* as well, other elements that left me baffled and induced me, perhaps wrongly, out of desperation, to invalidate those previous signs of rejection, responses after all. I don't know, in my life I, too, have had a few ideas that were clear-cut. For example, I always thought it was a trait of sensible men to be drawn to nooks. When Olga and I went someplace, she always yielded the nook furthest from the heart of the bustle to me. It was a gesture on her part, yes. But Olga herself, what she represented for me," said Hans, "was another one of those clear-cut things: sharp, I'd say, yes, of an incredible transparency, like her smile when she would look at me without a word, saturated with whiskey, and my vision would cloud over. The point is that I wanted Olga to do something because of me, with me. Yes, sometimes I still feel like laughing when I think about what I did because of her. And she, Olga, found out from me that on one occasion I even went so far as to do something outrageous just to be near something of *hers*: I'm talking about her dentist, about going to see her dentist," Hans said, "one of the most perfect and aseptic forms of *torture*. But even that, I think, she believed partially, only half-believed it. Yes, I say outrageous because, as is the case with many people, nothing strikes me with such horror as a dentist. As a child I used to think hell was full of dentists," Hans said. "Yes, statesmen, war heroes, artistic geniuses, inventors, executioners, all crumble before the dentist. Not so much at the pain the dentist causes us, which at times is not so great, but rather as a result of a man inserting tools into your mouth, instruments of a frightful aspect that produce a diabolical sound. It's like marble, I mean, like polishing marble, but hellishly, on yourself, inside you. I myself," Hans said, "have let months, entire years go by, immersed in a pain that ebbed and flowed before taking the step of going to the dentist, before allowing those instruments to be inserted into my mouth. And as a matter of fact, during that period, I mean, in the period immediately after meeting Olga and going out with her one night, I was suffering from a severe toothache. Yes, I believe I mentioned it to you at some point. Cognac," Hans said, "that's when I became fond of cognac, which eventually was useless in alleviating my pain. Well then, with the aim of getting close to something that was connected to Olga, or rather, that referred to her, I was bold enough to go to her dentist, who was in fact located on 'the other side,' as she termed it, meaning just across the Dutch border. It's curious," he said, "'the other side' seemed to be a place of magical reminiscences for Olga, despite its being less than a hundred kilometers from the city. Yes," Hans said, "for her, 'the other side' was something like another world, what may be seen from up on the trapeze, I suppose, a place that attracted her for reasons still opaque to me, like nearly everything about her, and where she had found a very good dentist, so she said. But we also have dozens of good ones, acceptable dentists, those butchers in white smocks who insert instruments of torture into your mouth and assume a bored, smug look when you shudder at the sight of the drill, I mean when the drill's *not yet* running, because once it's shrilling away it's far worse. Yes, and you know I've sometimes even thought," he said, "that my own experience with Olga was something like that, but not necessarily in a bad way, of course. That feeling of knowing that you're going into *open-heart* surgery, that you're the one who'll enter the operating room in order to submit to something doctors probably talk about without ever looking into their patients' eyes, as if to lessen the importance of the event; I often had that feeling, I was saying, when I was with her, when I was going to be with her and I was unable to get to sleep for several nights before that. Sometimes it was painful, others sweet. But I was telling you about the dentist," Hans said, removing his hands from his pockets and slipping them inside the elastic waistband of his sweatsuit, "Yes, it was just across the border, near Winschoten, on the road to Groningen. A butcher who looked like a magazine model, and who would automatically repeat 'Relax! Relax!' every time he saw me looking with horror at his diabolical gadgets. But he was none other than *her* dentist," Hans said. "Oh yes, I thought about that constantly, over and over. It was a means, I suppose, of overcoming the fear inspired in me by that individual and everyone of his kind. I know a good dentist in Emden. Yes, a very good one. And my sister Angelica usually goes to him. But as you see, I chose Olga's. Crossing over to the other side isn't something I'm in the habit of doing," Hans said, "no, in fact it had been over six or seven years since I'd set foot there. For Olga, on the other hand, crossing the border every so often was *inevitable*, going over to the other side in search of who knows what, because the truth is, she wasn't always accompanied. Furthermore, I imagine that, given the circumstances surrounding these trips, she must have been in the habit of going alone. For example, when she had an appointment with her dentist, I know (because she once told me so herself) that she would go alone. But Olga did that sort of thing. She was very strict about some things, totally inflexible in her habits. If for whatever reason she didn't like some bar, I could grovel and beg to no avail: a flat and final no. That was Olga. At some point I invited her to go down to Gronau someday. She loved Gronau. So, then," said Hans, "she got very solemn and replied, 'I only go to Gronau when it snows.' Naturally I thought that was her way of declining my invitation, of avoiding a trip with me. But no, as the months went by I found out that she simply didn't want to go to Gronau if there was no snow in Gronau. I don't know, she finally got around to telling me that maybe she might compromise and go to Gronau without snow, but the fact is we never did, I mean, we never *really* went there. Mentally I did take the trip to Gronau with Olga. That was quite a pleasant fantasy. Just like our going to the Swiss Alps. 'Sometime soon I'll invite you to spend a few days in the Alps—how does that sound?' I once asked her. And she, to my surprise, replied, 'Fine, but what will we do there?' I don't quite recall what I answered, although I more or less told her, 'I'll read *The Magic Mountain* and look at you.' And do you know what Olga replied, do you want to know? Well, what she said was, 'I'll walk with my feet sunk in the snow and look at you while you read *The Magic Mountain*.' That's what she said, yes, and I think it was one of the most wonderful moments I've ever experienced. Deep inside I knew we'd never go to Gronau or the Alps, but it didn't matter, really, I also knew that when she said it, to some degree she truly wanted it. Yes," Hans said, "I think one of Olga's greatest battles was for independence, for her own independence. She isolated herself as much as possible. And in that respect I never figured out how she endured living with that fellow, with Sömmering. Olga's nature was methodical but at the same time unpredictable. Yes," Hans said, "for example, before going to work on Saturday mornings she'd drive around a considerable part of the city in her car. If necessary she'd get up an hour before usual so as to drive about in her car, in her damned yellow car, down the still-deserted streets. Well, that's what she'd say, although I never saw her

driving down the streets on a Saturday morning, because *I did* drive along
those streets where she might be," Hans stressed, suddenly raising his voice.
"I must have done that on three or four Saturdays. Around eight or a quarter
past. Yes," he said, "after nights when I hadn't gone to bed or when, having
awakened early, I found it impossible to get back to sleep. So I'd get dressed
and drive around the area where I had a hunch she might turn up. I never
saw her, I mean, perhaps she drove by me at some point but I didn't see her.
From time to time the sound of an engine similar to her car's would startle
me, yes, make me feel like a cornered animal. But it wasn't she. And I have
no doubt she did drive about in that same quarter of the city on many Saturdays. Olga never lied. Absolutely not. I think lying didn't fit into her system of values, it was completely foreign to her. She did, I think, practice a
certain *concealment* with respect to her feelings or opinions. But she didn't
lie. She never lied to me, I'm certain of that. Utterly certain. In that sense I
think dealing with Olga was rather difficult, because on occasion her sincer-
ity could wound. Yes, it was like trying to avoid making a sound while eating
soup that's nearly boiling. If Olga said she drove about in her car at around
eight, I know that's what she did, even though I didn't see her. I suppose that
to see her, after all, would have been nothing but to behold an image that had
in fact haunted me during the preceding hours, filling my dawn. I know she
drove around there, yes, I know it. I don't know how, because in fact I should
have seen her one of those times, but I know so," Hans said, "I believe so. It's
quite possible, I think, that we passed each other in our cars and I didn't see
her. I tended to drink a lot those nights. Cognac for my teeth. Yes, and whiskey, a lot of whiskey. Sometimes it was hard getting home, I'd take the wrong
street. The truth is that for months on end I saw Olga's car pass dozens and
dozens of times. It's true, I had a knack for coming across it anywhere at all,
and always after working hours, of course. But I insist that lying and Olga
were incompatible. Yes," Hans said, "she was noble—frank and a bit intro-
verted with certain people, but noble, not a liar in the least. At times, I think,
she might even display a certain asperity in her behavior, in her hasty manner
of speaking, interrupting whatever I might be saying when she did speak,
which in fact almost never happened. That, however, was mingled with her
Parisian elegance, with her innate tact in avoiding or sailing through those
situations where *sparks* might fly. Although I think I must have been the one

seeing those sparks. I was always aware that Olga knew perfectly well which things were most likely to bother me, but she never brought them up, not even in passing. I can say as much for myself, I too knew the places where she was most vulnerable. But no matter how much we might verbally assault each other, no matter how high the tension between us might rise, those areas were unmentionable, yes," Hans said, "we had established, I think, a kind of tacit pact forbidding any real aggression. Neither of us ever lacked the necessary tact to avoid offending the other. I recall that sometimes, while she was driving with me sitting beside her in the damned yellow car, which I had to take great pains to get into—because by then we (I mean, the car and I) were in the midst of a cold war—while she was driving, as I was saying, I would observe her without speaking at all. I'd simply look at her. Yes, it seemed to me that a couple of times Olga got nervous, quite *nervous*. She even fumbled when changing gears, and her hands moved incoherently and pointlessly over the steering wheel. But in spite of everything, I still think I was the only one who perceived those sparks. Yes, I'm entirely certain of that, I could swear to it. Because I'm not sure if I've told you that every time Olga's eyes and mine met I felt a spark, I saw it flash and then fade before me. I've always been under the impression that people with light eyes gaze with more intensity," he said, "and Olga herself even said something once to that effect. It seems that a gaze so limpid captures your attention better. Naturally I was a prisoner of her blue eyes. Yes, her oblique glance while she was driving, and of course when we were face to face, was like a permanent succession of little electrical discharges that completely sealed my mouth, rendered me incapable of uttering a word or, on the contrary, drove me to talk on and on almost torrentially, which happened quite often. Yes," Hans said, "they were sparks. I know, I knew it all along. And what was curious about all that, I think, is that for a long time I lived immersed in a *perpetual spark*. I know, I mean, owing to experiences I had years ago I know that in these matters one eventually reaches a zenith, after which passion declines. A kind of natural law," Hans said, "something inevitable, like my enthusiasm as soon as I'd see her. That did happen to me on one occasion when I was younger. With Olga, on the other hand, it was a *linear* zenith, there was never any decline in the voracious anxiety of wanting to be with her, or with anyone who had some relationship to her, like her dentist or her co-workers, or even with some-

66

thing that referred to her, such as all yellow Volkswagens, at first, and eventually all yellow cars, until I wound up being obsessed with all Volkswagens, regardless of their color, and with any car whose lines or color remotely resembled Volkswagens and yellow. Something I don't recall ever having mentioned to her was that for me yellow has always been the color of eternity—in other words, if eternity had a color, it would be yellow. Yes," Hans said, "and it was hard for me to realize, in contrast to all these things, that for her I was something that just *can't be* avoided, yes, like those things one can't avoid despite repeated attempts to do so. Like a headache," Hans said, "like that gesture people tend to make when boarding a bus, taking the only seat that's totally vacant, even though it's a double, there are other empty places, and they have to go down the length of the vehicle in order to isolate themselves. Yes, I'm talking about the kind of solitude syndrome that comes over almost everybody when boarding public transportation. We shun each other as though we smelled bad or suffered from a contagious disease. That's how she must have seen me, even if that seems an odious comparison, and perhaps a bit exaggerated. She wanted to avoid me," Hans said, "that was clear, to avoid at any cost my entering into the course of her life. But instead of throwing me off the bus that so perfectly depicted her life, the orderly program of her hours and her days, she simply placed herself at a distance, yet where she knew I could see her. Yes," Hans said, "deep inside I think it was immensely cruel on her part to permit the slow, progressive annihilation first of my pride, and later of my wishes. Yes," he said, "I don't understand how she allowed herself to ride the bus of her life, even if for only a brief stage of it, with a shapeless heap of ruins. It must be unpleasant to hear someone confessing such a thing about himself without too much self-pity, but that's how it is. Deep inside I can't feel any, because I knew perfectly well what a woman like Olga might give under normal circumstances. Yet I know I have *something* of hers, I know what she gave me, I'm the only one who knows that. Yes," Hans said, "I suppose I was a sheer ruin, a total and absolute ruin, smoking rubble. And to this day I can't quite understand her reason for not throwing me off the perfectly synchronized bus of her life earlier. At times, I think, I've gone so far as to believe it was coyness, pure and simple. The abject, vile coyness of women, of some women. An irrepressible proclivity to feel and know they are first of all desired, then unconditionally loved, and

67

finally idolized. But I suppose that coyness," Hans said, "is nothing but a mode of self-defense. That's what I think, anyway. I don't know, there might actually have been something like that, but I suppose it would in any case have been to a slight and of course unconscious degree. At other times I think it must simply have been sorrow over having caused someone—in other words me—greater harm than I think she ever intended to inflict on me. And indeed, that rejection would have been tremendously harmful to me, would have had an obviously destructive effect no matter when she'd done it, I mean her throwing me off her bus. Yes," Hans said, "at any rate, the feeling defining *what* it is that lies between coyness and mercy, where it's a matter of letting oneself be loved on the one hand, and on the other not wanting to cause any pain, probably isn't to be found in any dictionary. It's a question of inventing a name for it, if only to explain what must have happened to her in relation to me. Obviously by that I don't mean it was a blend of mercy or sorrow with coyness. No, not in the least, I think that feeling, her feeling toward me, lay halfway between the two emotions. But never a blend. The truth is, as clear as Olga seemed to be about her concerns—and there's no doubt that for a certain while I was one of her *concerns*—she was always very *contradictory* with me, she always made me feel insecure. About our dates, above all. Yes, that was a torment. I could be excited about a date, looking forward to it impatiently for two or three weeks, but I knew that five minutes before leaving to go there, to the place where we were to meet, the phone might ring and it would be she, offering some excuse or other for cancelling or postponing our meeting. Olga was never really able to appreciate the importance of those meetings, I mean, the importance they had for me. But I insist, I don't believe it was a blend of coyness and something else. I think one has to be very careful with blends. Yes, sometimes they can prove to be *explosive*. Just look how often people who know very little about them tend to talk about explosives. We ourselves work for a firm dedicated to making and exporting explosives, and we know about only a slight fraction of them. Of course," Hans said, "we're in the technical and administrative section, not in the lab or the warehouse. But that doesn't matter. Yes," he said, "I've always been afraid of blends. And during my military service I myself learned to use a good number of the explosives that the firm now manufactures and exports. Yes, I know you're aware of that because we talked about it at some point. I remember a couple of years ago Herr Wahlen insisted on having me join the research lab in Oldenburg. I explained to him then several times that if the warehouse were not there, I might perhaps be tempted to transfer to that unit, but besides having no desire at present to move to another city, I'm scared of explosives, I can't help it. Nobody can help it. Not even some technicians with whom I've had a chance to talk. For example Martin, the warehouse security guard, when he comes to collect every month. He spends many nights glued to the door, unable to sleep a wink without knowing why. Yes, a cigarette butt, a safety device that malfunctions, a short circuit, or even a burglary. In any case, for me Olga was the most powerful, most dangerous explosive imaginable, the most frightening of all the ones I'd ever had the opportunity to see explode, or even whose effects I'd studied in specialized books. In spite of that, I repeat, what she felt toward me was not a blend of feelings. It was rather that indefinable intermediate point which makes an explosive—when combined with a degree of harmony, not mixed in a disorderly, loose way—destructive to a greater or lesser extent. Yes, it's a very specialized realm. If, for example, you use two kilos of flematized pentrite and explode it by remote control, the material being buried one meter below ground, the effect won't be the same as if you had two kilos of nagolite. It's very curious. Yes, the blast varies a lot from one instance to the next. The same holds true for the action of nitric acid on cellulose or of picric acid on glycerin," Hans said, leaving me completely baffled by the abrupt turn he'd given his discourse. He was no doubt extemporizing in the course of the walk, but despite my having gone a very long while without uttering a single word, attempting to breathe and walk almost cautiously so as not to interrupt his monologue, I wasn't able to comprehend it no matter how much I thought about it. "Yes, one has to be rigorous, although it requires nerve and a great deal of tenacious study to ascertain, for example, up to what point melinite and the combination of nitroglycerin and ammonium nitrate produce distinct or even opposite *effects* on the surfaces selected as testing sites. This is the aspect, I suppose, where people get everything confused, but not Herr Wahlen. He knew very well that I had handled such materials for over two years, or rather, that I'd been required to deal with them despite the fear they provoked in me. That's why for a time he insisted that I go to work at the lab. 'After a brief training period,' Herr Wahlen said, 'you'd be a good technician.' Yes, I think that's what he said. But who knows, I don't assume one really needs all that much knowledge to see the difference between a charge of dynamite in a quarry, a mine, or a building about to be demolished, and a mass comparable in weight but consisting of hollow charge plastic explosive. No," Hans said, "all that's required is to be rigorous and to know what elements you're dealing with and what immediate effects the action of those elements will have. Yes, it's quite simple," Hans said, "if nagolite explodes at a specific degree of compression, it produces a highly dangerous undulating wave. In addition, plastic explosive is quite treacherous, yes, its expansive wave can acquire an angle whose degrees are directly proportional to the diameter of the conical cavity in which the material has been set to explode. The wave concentrates right in the apex of that hypothetical cone and when it exits, if it's carrying solid particles, for example, it fragments, and can go so far as to penetrate even very hard surfaces. Yes, it's very *curious*, this world of explosives," Hans said. "Each one of them possesses its own peculiarity, some unique detail not reflected in any other. One of the most visually spectacular is trinitroglycerin—when it explodes, I mean. Yes, and I believe that ammonal is one of the most destructive. Its effects are *instantaneous*. Those materials fill me with terror, and at times I've thought about what it must be like to have an accident with them. Something rather like *being hurled into the instantaneous*. Yes," he said, "to be and not to be. But with no transition. Being and nonbeing fused, simultaneous. To be and to cease being all at once. A curious evolution that must last much less than a fraction of a second: to pass from the summit of pain to the portal, the threshold of nothingness in a silent apotheosis. The instantaneous, yes, it's a concept that fascinates me, and perhaps it does so because Olga was something instantaneous in me. I don't know if you follow me. But I keep thinking, I mean, even now I think it's a matter of being sure about the blends. Anyone can learn just as I learned. I suppose so. It's not beyond anyone's reach to research and work with certain types of materials, which can be acquired separately and in small quantities. Yes," said Hans, "without stepping out of the house, one can make some very dangerous things. One has only to go into some store and ask for two low frequency remote control filters with a tone modulator, a twenty-seven megahertz receiver, a three-volt transmitter, also at twenty-seven megahertz, and a remote control mechanism that can be bought, as I said, in any electronics store. Naturally, the dangerous things can rarely be acquired all at once, but only *separately*. Yes, that's the way it's always been. Anything worthwhile, difficult, requires effort. Yes," he said, "you just have to put on an innocent face and go about buying things little by little. And, you know, it's because the state sometimes doesn't anticipate intelligence, that's beyond the parameters of its actual power to control. Little by little everything tends to function smoothly, like a clockwork mechanism, I mean, like well-made clockwork, devised with intelligence and patience, like meticulously crafted clockwork. Yes, because all clockwork worthy of its name should always *function*. Yes, of that I'm certain. And also that Olga was very much like precise clockwork, not designed to ever explode but rather, I think, to have her expansive wave affect other people who might cross her path at some particular moment. Thus it was with me. That's really how I see myself, yes," Hans said, "I as the one affected, dazzled by a phantasm of raging light that blinds him in an instant. But it was the way she said one day—or assented to a particular suggestion I made one day—that she, too, liked things done little by little, done well and *calmly*, through calmness and out of calmness (like a piece of clockwork, I thought): that, I meant to tell you, is what made Olga disturbing. You can't imagine the face she made when she said it. Yes, maybe that was the Olga who was susceptible to coyness, who perhaps needed affection and flattery, even though she never actually acknowledged it. Because in a way, I think, there was in her a sharp contradiction in this respect. Yes, as you know, on one hand she was methodical and organized, her convictions absolutely unshakable. I suppose it was a kind of armor—impenetrable armor, I can tell you—whose plate no shrapnel was capable of piercing. Yes, very hard," Hans said. "After I'd spend several hours—and I say several hours because they were not minutes but hours—talking about feelings in general and about my feelings toward her in particular, which though confusing were feelings nonetheless, she— Olga—would look at me intently and say: 'Things are as they are. Period. You brood over things far too much.' Yes, she'd say that, fully convinced she was right. And all the while, not a muscle in her face would move. Just as she'd show no affectation whatsoever when, at my insistence that we see each other for a while in the evening after work—just for a brief while, because I had something *very important* to tell her—she would reply: 'Things are as they are, and today it's no. Period.' But if today it was no, that didn't mean, coming from her lips, that it would be the same tomorrow or the next day. Yes, that's just what I meant when I told you Olga must have experienced a sharp contradiction with respect to me. On the one hand wanting to be rid of me, and on the other, not wanting to lose me altogether, I mean, not wanting to lose what I offered her, above all the special treatment, affection, attentions, *many* attentions, ranging from gifts to passionate letters (which I suppose were more suitable to an adolescent than to a thirty-six-year-old man) and even to the most unimaginable things. Yes, I think for a certain period I must have been, in Olga's eyes, like a toy, like one of those little dogs one takes for a walk with an extensible leash that can be adjusted at will by pressing or releasing the mechanism you hold in your hand. Yes, inside, deep inside, I'm convinced she was always a contradictory person, hurt by her own contradictions, which at the same time she never had any intention of resolving, or at least, I believe, never felt any real interest in resolving. That would have meant a sympathetic detonation with *unforeseeable* results. Yes, like a poorly monitored explosion, like a detonation initiated from a distance in the process of which some unexpected element has interfered. Who knows, it could be any number of things. The condition of the material, the condition of the ground, dampness. The problem, I mean her problem, is that she very often must have thought she had been born for *something else*, for something other than what she was actually doing. You know, at times it seemed to me that she was going to say something important, something that had been internally gnawing at her for a long time, especially when we were talking over the phone, and she would only mutter something like onomatopoeias. Sounds that were almost guttural. She wanted to tell me something, but she would stifle it. Yes, I've always wondered where all those things she was about to tell me, but never did, must have ended up. There's a whole history of those things she was on the verge of telling me," Hans said, "still fresh in my imagination. I don't know, perhaps on that score she demonstrated a lack of intelligence, since by not telling me, I could amplify or diminish them as I saw fit, always distorting them in any case. Well, Olga never chose to consider even remotely the possibility of causing a *perfect explosion*; I suppose, nevertheless, that it couldn't help but hold a certain fascination for her, though, mind you, I only suppose so, because it's an impression due to that other Olga, of whose infinitesimal gestures I became somewhat aware only at the end, when it was *too late*. Yes, as a matter of fact, at those moments I didn't know what she was trying to convey to me, or indeed if she was trying to convey something to me or not. But to dynamite the foundations of one's life and change it entirely, I mean the possibility of blowing it all up, that's something that can hardly fail to tempt a troubled person. And Olga was that. Very much so, yes. Even though she never explored that possibility. Troubled people perhaps consider that possibility continuously or periodically, even in a somewhat orderly way, but always within the limits imposed by a morbid specter, I suppose I'm referring to the morbid specter imposed by their own proclivity to routine, outside or beyond which they find it impossible to ponder that, the great explosion, the *real* change in their lives. The same thing happens to a lot of people with the alternative of suicide. Yes," Hans said, "at some point everyone considers that possibility to some degree or other, and yet no one can explain what might make a person who until a given moment had only thought about it, *do it* at that instant. But regardless, certainly Olga's explosion would never take that course. Yes, she'd prefer to sell herself to any person or concept before doing that, and in this respect I don't believe that my perceptions about what Olga may have thought during that period differ much from what she actually thought. Because Olga was very strict and orderly, yes, but she also went around bumping into every corner. It's true," Hans said, "she herself once admitted it. 'I go around smacking into everything. It's chronic with me,' she used to say. Yes, and in fact I noted that even though she would say it lightheartedly, she didn't like being that way one bit. At other times—and this I was able to observe—she would *forget* to park the car, completely forgot about it. Yes, we'd be going down a street and she would leave it there, almost in the middle of the road. Only when I reminded her did she come back down to earth. Or who knows, perhaps it was simply that she felt uncomfortable with me in her car, sitting next to her inside her car. In any event, I think, I've reached all these conclusions—if they can be called conclusions without committing a fundamental, perhaps etymological, error of judgment—later on, in other words, only fairly recently. As a matter of fact," he said, "I think I've reached that stage of understanding while here, at Chemnitz. The daily contact with marble, the sharp, penetrating sound of the machine when it's polishing the contours of those blocks, cold as a tomb, cleared my mind, it classified certain thoughts that had until then been subject to a tremendous pressure that prevented their surfacing, I mean surfacing in my memory, isolated from all the other images and sequences that make up the whole of thought. Yes," Hans said, "marble has helped me to concentrate and to understand some of the keys to the curious puzzle that lay at the heart of Olga's character. Her propriety, which it so annoyed her to hear about, her orderliness, I think—and I have thought a lot about it since I've been working in the shop for so many hours—was an externally imposed order, perhaps even from outside her consciousness. It was not a natural, spontaneous order by any means," Hans said. "No, Olga had her own release valves, her own therapeutic methods to withstand the slow pace of life which, I'm sure, was spurned by her restless, I'd almost dare to say adventurous, nature. Her whole existence revolved around bad moments—especially the ones at work, against which she would employ the weapon of her smile and a hollow cheerfulness—and the others were moments of escape, which compensated for everything else, yes. For what she called her 'special moments,' she would play Ravel's *Boléro*. Time and again, methodically, automatically. I never really knew just what she was referring to or what she meant to refer to when she spoke of those 'special moments.' That there should be a 'special moment,' even one, in the orderly schedule that comprised her days, was enough to elicit my surprise. It signified that she, too, was vulnerable, that she needed an occasional refuge. Yes," Hans said, "furthermore, those moments would apparently occur rather frequently, so that my initial surprise turned to bafflement, yes, sheer stupefaction. I don't know, everything was inexplicable. I'm referring to everything, encompassing first of all the fact of meeting Olga, then becoming interested in her, later on devoting all my time to her, and finally the circumstances surrounding our last encounters. I remember that in the period after I met her—and in fact this went on almost until the end—I began spending the afternoons shut away in my house, listening to the music they played on the radio. Whatever it was. Yes," he said, "quite incredible, I mean incredible *for me*. As soon as I would get off work, almost without worrying about eating, I'd dash to the radio and avidly tune into the station that, from noon until well into the evening, played the current top fifty hits. As I said, it was a *mad dash*. And now I understand that was a plainly self-destructive attitude. Incredible, yes, but I have come to the conclusion that it was incredible, as I've tended to conclude about everything else since being here, at Chemnitz, rather than at home. My house was a prison then, a comfortable prison where each and every object seemed to emit a chorale of reminiscences that in one way or another had some connection with Olga. She *might* or might not have touched every object if at some time she had come to my house, she *might* or might not have liked each object. Those were days of enormous confusion, and back then I knew or supposed that it was simply odd, but never incredible. Yes, I used to spend the evenings immersed in commercial rubbish, quite unusual. I suppose it must have been a kind of sedative. None of the more than four thousand records on my shelves were of any use to me. No, Olga was something new in my life, she had come into it like lightning, and those records, in contrast, were part of my past. I tried to find Olga in those tunes that, evening after evening, week after week, month after month, formed a strident conglomerate in my mind, with a refrain here and there that wasn't too offensive to the ear. Yes," said Hans, "it was something of a strange phenomenon, unrepeatable I think, because my true sedative, dating back nearly fifteen years, had in fact been music, music not so much as passion or escape but as passion that was prudently escapist. Yes, and also as the opposite," he said, "as an escape that was entirely passionate, but over which I always exercised the control necessary to curb certain emotional impulses that might turn me into an unmitigated *addict*. Neither more nor less. I've always held that the spheres of art and emotion should be kept as far apart as possible. Yes," Hans said, "and perhaps unconsciously I thought likewise with regard to love and emotion. Until I met Olga, of course. Olga herself was music, her whole being *sang out* as she moved, as she spoke, but I think that until I met Olga, as I was saying, mine was a rational addiction, perhaps manipulated at will, that's possible. But her coming into my life, or rather, into my thoughts—because I think that after Olga made her physical appearance I ceased being alive and operated solely on the basis of thought—when she stormed in, saturating, demolishing everything, you know, everything else vanished immediately. Habits, history, preferences, fears, future. Everything," Hans said. "I think even the ample gamut ranging from Mozart to Webern stopped making sense, it instantly lost its aesthetic and even its sentimental value, it stopped being escapist passion or passionate escape, which obviously could have occurred, I mean, to a certain degree it accorded with logic, my logic, my own code of logical values, that among those thousands of albums," Hans said, "among those dozens of thousands of hours of music, it accorded with logic, I was saying, that I could and should have found the music that would somehow help me to bear or to face the Olga problem, the *quote-unquote problem*, as my sister Angelica would say. Yes, but something strange happened, as I said: I'd look for her among the top fifty hits. It's also true that during that whole period of wandering through all the corners of the house I had a terrible toothache and, therefore, my relationship with cognac was more intimate than I should have allowed. Yes," Hans said, once again putting his hands in his pockets, "cognac when she wasn't there, especially in the afternoon, and whiskey at night. What happened is that there came a time when we also saw each other in the afternoons, right after work. Yes, but with her it was never cognac. Olga herself was all whiskey, she smelled of whiskey, you know, that taste between stale and vanilla. Yes, she was music and whiskey all at once, like a phrase of alcohol. So much so that I even thought of her as 'my sweet whiskey score.' The tunes, then, were a kind of accident in my life. And once here," he said, "bent over the marble surfaces until my head throbs and my kidneys ache, my eyes permanently squinting so as to avoid as much as possible the fine dust that scatters when I polish, I came to the conclusion that, if not all those tunes, at least some of them were exactly the ones that were playing in most of the bars or pubs we went into while our relationship lasted, I mean the most visible phase of our relationship. Although I suppose it wasn't so much a normal relationship as a series of dates to have a few drinks, the two of us, and for me to do all the talking, at least most of the time, a relationship or whatever you might call that intermittent series of small explosions, which is how I perceived them, and which for her, I think, must have been merely conflicts in her schedule, I mean in her planning of daily tasks, because for Olga almost everything was reduced to a permanent task, she was freed from that only in her 'special moments.' The point is that in those tunes that were always playing everywhere," Hans said, "through those tunes that had pierced me as thorns pierce the skin, without my being aware of it, through those tunes, I was saying, I was looking for fragments of Olga's phrases, fragments of Olga's gestures that my memory had failed to retain in their entirety—a memory that on the other hand was not served one bit by my nervousness, nor by the sapping effects of alcohol—fragments of fragments of Olga's gestures, fragments of fragments of fragments of Olga's words that had perhaps been sketched in imperceptible gestures. Fragments I suppose I must have found scattered, adrift among those tunes on the radio, because otherwise there's no justification for my remaining for weeks and months in that perpetual calvary, which is in fact how I view enduring the music broadcast on those airwaves. Yes, suddenly Mozart and Webern ceased to exist," Hans said. "It was as if all the musicians and the music that fall between the two composers had also vanished into thin air. The redemptive *gamut* I mentioned earlier. Yes, curious, quite curious, I suppose. All of a sudden that's what happened: no Mozart and no Webern. Yet Olga, in contrast to what I was going through, remained faithful to Ravel's *Boléro*, which after all was for her the synthesis, I suppose, of all that music concentrated in the gamut from Mozart to Webern, I mean, the emotional synthesis of that gamut. She—Olga—never entered into the dynamic of that calvary of radio tunes," Hans said, "she didn't fall into that mire, because the fact is, she wasn't searching for me in those jingles. This isn't something I've learned on account of the marble, I knew it then. Marble has simply helped me to *solidify* that thought. But in contrast, she did listen to Ravel, with the headphones on, until 'her eardrums nearly burst.' Yes, that's what she used to say; until her eardrums nearly burst. But that bursting, I think, was also *controlled*, I mean controlled in the sense that it was always Ravel, or at least Ravel in particular moments, or Ravel at particular special moments in, of, or throughout particular special moments of his *Boléro*. The special moments," Hans said. "*Her* special moments. Yes, I don't know if you follow me," he said, "I suppose it might be rather difficult to understand what I'm trying to say, to grasp it in its actual context. Well, at any rate, being only partially understood by people has always worried me. I *hate* rhetoric, I mean, patently rhetorical attitudes. I'm certain, or rather I'm almost certain, that people who engage in them conceal serious psychological problems behind those patently rhetorical attitudes. As if behind the curtain there were a vast quagmire. Yes. That's why knowing I was extremely rhetorical with Olga, why being rhetorical to the point of boredom was, as it were, a doubly harmful contradiction, though the truth is I never found out if she had been bored

77

with my stories. Because as a matter of fact," Hans said, "I don't have the slightest idea what stories I may have told her, for I've never had a story, I mean I lack a definite history. Yes, at times I've thought I've lived in a profound state of coma, a state of coma disturbed only by slight agitations, until the sudden advent of that *atomic mushroom cloud* that was Olga. But even in this," Hans said, "she was following a certain thread of coherence. Yes," he said, "I suppose, though I merely suppose, that it must have been a way of behaving or of facing the situation created between us, the one I created for her every single time we'd see each other. Because even today I reflect with surprise upon the fact that Olga and I actually met quite a few, many times. Usually she would always say *yes* to my proposal that we go out. She only said *no* when I really needed her to say yes at all costs, when I was going through what no doubt must have been one of my 'special moments' and not seeing her would mean utter delirium. Yes," Hans said, "our typical situation was always the same: she, never talking, almost attaining a sophisticated level of continual and attentive muteness, as I once pointed out to her, and I producing stories in industrial quantities. But every once in a while she'd go off, starting to talk on and on as though someone had wound her up. Then I would end up feeling dazed. My interest in grasping all she said was such that I thought I had to focus my full attention on everything she was saying. Unconsciously, then, I'd watch her lips, yes, and at that point I was *lost*. Her lips were total darkness, the abyss," Hans said, "yes, Olga could be truly frightening when she would suddenly start to talk. Perfect clockwork, as I think I said before. That's how Olga was. Yes. Then, I recall, she would speak in such a rush that all I could do was try to take shelter from the cyclone of words that descended upon me, a cyclone that, while I scarcely realized it, was already exhausting me. Olga would talk about anything at all, in the same way she would do anything at any moment and without taking into account the circumstances surrounding her. It was, I believe, during one of those fits that she explained to me her ritual with the headphones and Ravel, yes, but she also often listened to louder, more rhythmic, current music. 'Until my eardrums burst,' she said with a cryptic smile. Yes, that's exactly what she said. That other music didn't fit in with the 'special moments.' Only Ravel. It was during those verbal fits that she would confess to things one would never for a moment have thought her capable of. For instance, that she always bit her nails *at night* and always when *no one* could see her. Yes," Hans said, "always at night, never in broad daylight. I suppose all that might seem Draculean. You already know how preoccupied I was with Olga's nails. And the truth is I never stopped being somewhat obsessed with them. Yes, I remember perfectly one particular evening when she looked especially beautiful. The light in the pub illuminated her face from one side and there was something Transylvanian about her expression. I remember saying to her: 'If I kiss you, my lips will be smeared with blood.' And she answered simply: 'Try it if you dare,' but I didn't. Not at that moment, and for several reasons. One," Hans said, "because she had just raised her glass to her lips to finish her whiskey. Two, because she looked too beautiful, I didn't want to deprive myself of that beauty even for an instant, and three, because I was fully convinced that my mouth really would be smeared with blood if I kissed her. But I was telling you about the times when Olga would break out talking as if she were mad. Who knows," Hans said, "even in those frantic diatribes she might ask me if I could imagine, if I had ever been able to imagine what it must be like to work in a funeral home, or she'd tell me she couldn't stand the smell of powdered milk, that she abhorred that smell even from several meters away. She couldn't bear the smells of pharmacies and of certain warehouses either. They were, she said, smells *beyond* her strength. Yes, Olga talked and talked, and at those moments I was seized by a sensation similar to what we feel after visiting a foreign country, usually an exotic one, in the shortest time possible. Yes," Hans said, "that sensation one has on returning from a place about which one really doubts everything, despite having just seen it, is the very one I had when Olga made up her mind and plunged into doing or saying things. Because I suppose the composition of the two written messages she herself had conveyed to me at work also belonged to such a phase. Yes," Hans said, "messages she gave to me in person, which passed directly from *her* hand to *my* hand, an operation that to some extent involved the risk of being observed by someone who might start making silly and malicious remarks, which on the other hand, in one way or another, wouldn't entirely have lacked substance. That was a risk, a possibility that struck her, I knew, as awful. Olga could have sent them, I mean the two messages, in a letter, by mail, using the appropriate stamps, and of course without identifying the sender. I would have received them a day later and everything would have been *neater*. I always sent my letters to her without a return address, always at work, always without hope. But it wasn't so much for the sake of anonymity, the need for which was obvious at work, but rather because when I wrote to her I actually *forgot* my own address. I swear I didn't write to her from a specific place. At best I wrote to her from the void, from the sensation of anticipated void I felt on knowing she would never answer any of those letters, some of them funny, others begging for help almost as if for alms. No," Hans said, "I knew I would only get muteness from her, but that drove me to write compulsively, as it were, on and on. Even if I had seen her just minutes before and I was to meet her that same evening, I'd hurl myself into writing to her, often not really knowing what I was writing or what I wanted to tell her, with the sole, obsessive idea of writing *for her*. But in fact," Hans said, "I think I never wrote for the silent Olga, the one who requited my displays of affection with silence, but for another Olga whom I also knew and who surfaced only very rarely. Yes," he said, "I'm referring to the Olga who was able to laugh at the expression, between jolly and witless, of a doll we'd seen in some shopwindow in town, in the wee hours of the morning when the streets are deserted, and I could hear only her voice saying: 'Do you hear the silence? There's no one, absolutely no one.' Or the Olga I saw on another evening uttering words of wisdom to the waters of the fountains. Because I'm not sure whether I've told you that Olga spoke to fountains in a completely *natural* way. Listening to her, my heart would beat faster, would merge with the swift, enigmatic flow of the water, I would feel intoxicated gazing at that Olga who conversed so ingenuously with the fountains. But don't think it was on account of the whiskey," Hans said, "as much as something instinctive in her. To send me a letter at work would have contradicted those attitudes. But even so, at times I was convinced that sooner or later she'd do it. Yes, I mean what I said, completely convinced. I expected it, I anxiously awaited that moment," Hans said. "But no, that would have meant that she, too, accepted the game, or the furtive sort of relationship I had in some sense tried to impose on her. Because, as I said, I *did* send her several letters at work like that: without a return address. I don't know, I suppose receiving a letter without a return address, especially if one doesn't recognize the handwriting on the envelope, must be one of the greatest *sensations* there are. At least for solitary people. Yes," Hans said, "one feels tempted never to open them, to preserve them like that forever. The fact is, I think, that Olga was on the verge of doing that, of sending me a letter at work, when in fact we were sometimes *obliged* to talk more than once in a single morning. But she changed her mind at some instant, I suppose at the *last instant*. She may have even gone so far as to tear up the envelope once it was sealed and stamped, only to slip the note into another, fresh one, discreetly folded, without a single phrase or word written on it, which she would deliver into my hands herself while talking about something else, almost always inconsequential. Yes, I suppose even though handing me those notes could be ostensibly much more intimate or even more emotive, Olga knew that to send them through the mail would mean something entirely different, and I think perhaps she couldn't quite figure out where that difference lay; maybe she had only an inkling, but the fact that I did it—I mean, used the ordinary mail to communicate with her despite our working less than ten meters apart and seeing each other sometimes once or twice a week after work—that fact, I was about to say, must have convinced her not to participate in an act she may have deemed punishable and tinged with the clandestine, and in which I suppose she did enjoy being the recipient, at least for a while. Yes, and her reticence concerning my letters," Hans said, "made it impossible for me to determine the reason for her curiosity or excitement about receiving my letters. What it was I don't know even now. Because Olga was very indecisive about everything, both in speaking and *doing*. Yes, terribly indecisive. And both of us were very clear about her having been born to be desired and loved, not to love. Yes, that was very clear. She herself always recognized it even though she remarked, quite candidly, that such a circumstance disproportionately fostered her selfishness, which, she would say, 'has reaped very good results for me.' Yes, Olga gauged everything, everything was measured. In that sense, her brain had a mathematical bent. And I still think," Hans went on, "that the evidence of her having been *on the verge* of writing to me in the same peculiar manner in which I often communicated with her indicates that she unconsciously weighed the pros and cons, in the end opting to do something that was much more congruent with herself, with her spontaneous, open, forthright manner. To hand me those two notes. Yes, 'Things are as they are. Period,' which she repeated over and over, as you know. Well, the truth is that the ordinary Olga, I mean the everyday Olga, wasn't like that. For me, the Olga who every so often would *open up* always meant a long, exciting trip abroad. And I understood perfectly the language of that foreign land she became once she opened up," he said. "Somehow I could almost claim that I would *see* that language, I mean, that I was aware of what she said to me, yet on the other hand, I perceived the *landscapes* of that region in a rather eclectic fashion. The whole thing was like a kind of vision in the desert, resulting from the relentless effect of heat and sand. Yes," Hans said, "something of that sort. As I mentioned earlier, in spite of everything our relationship at work was quite intense, although conflictive because it wasn't fulfilling for either of us, particularly for me, I'm afraid. Quite frankly, I was at pains to figure out a way of approaching her when she was in her office. Yes, I suppose I regarded the territory that was Olga as adverse, perhaps even dangerous, like an explosive with a high amount of moisture, but that other territory delimited by her work schedule, by her office, was totally hostile to me. My salvation or my definitive sinking into the mire of frustration (I still don't know which it was, even though I've ruminated on it a lot since I've been in the marble workshop) came when Olga, because of a management request and as a gesture of fellowship toward a co-worker—for indeed she could have flatly refused to comply with it—started to fill in for the operator at the central switchboard while the woman went to lunch at a nearby restaurant. Yes," Hans said, "even in this Olga proved to be extremely methodical. It was she who specified from the start that although she agreed to fill the vacant post, she wanted to make it clear she'd do so only between one thirty-five and five past two. Give or take a few minutes, of course, but in fact that was never the case, except for some special reason. Even in this there was a sense of clockwork," he said. "Even in arriving at work. At some point she confided to me that, while in theory one punches in at nine o'clock on the dot, she never did it just then but rather at *one minute* after nine. 'With watch in hand,' she said, yes. She used that stray minute to finish her cigarette before going in, or even to have a friendly chat with one of the managers who usually hover about the main entrance at that time. Yes," Hans said, "she was very strict in that respect, I mean, *also* in that respect. 'I don't feel like punching in at nine o'clock. I've no intention of ever doing it, even if they kick me out,' she'd say. And I imagine she never did. I, on the other hand, arrived many mornings ahead of time, yes: I liked to work in isolation, without the din of machines and all that. Always, as if programmed, I'd look at my watch at a minute after nine. Never before or after. At one minute past nine. Deep down," Hans said, "I always thought that Olga was a troublemaker, but I wouldn't say she's one of those people whose aim is to sow discord through continual strife wherever she is, but rather something of a small-scale revolutionary, a great troublemaker who developed her global strategy *through order*, through strictness. Who knows, perhaps it had to do with an infiltration of the enemy's ranks, I mean, those absolutely normal people, those people whom I suppose she hated as much as or more than I did. Yes, and I think that if I had somehow realized the true extent of her follies, of the follies that at least if you took her at her word, she was always ready to act upon, perhaps I could now devise some sort of reliable chart of her potential to be a real troublemaker. Everything about her was mysterious, most of all—as I've mentioned before—her halting manner of talking, giving the impression of being about to say something extremely important and then saying nothing. Yes. I suppose she implied at some point that she'd committed *several* of those follies during one of the stages of her life she generally refused to discuss: I mean the three years she spent in Düsseldorf. Yes, she lived in a flat with several friends, and I never managed to coax anything substantial out of her concerning that period. Yes, it's curious," said Hans, "I've been here for several months, almost four, and I'm still exactly where I was when I arrived. I constantly ask myself questions about her, I attempt to resolve them mentally because they were always left up in the air. Yes, conversations, acts, follies, everything always *half-finished*," he said, "everything up in the air. And she herself, Olga, once remarked that she was 'fascinated' by things left half-finished. That's what she said—tremendous. Yes, I say tremendous because she made that statement at a very special moment. I recall having surreptitiously taken her hand seconds before—while she, that is, talked about something I was incapable of hearing—yes, as I was saying, I had taken the part of her hand that was unable to *slip away* from the mild pressure of my own—her fingers, I mean—and I was softly kissing them while she gave little instinctive jerks in order to prevent it. As tremendous as when she talked about liking things done little by little. I never found her as sensual as on those occasions. Yes, that was amazing, I can assure you. Olga's skin on my lips, on the *inside* of my lips, is something I'll never be able to forget. Yes, it was then that she said that. Anyway, I imagine I won't be able to forget Olga's lips in an overall sense, either: I mean the imprint of her lips, the imprint of that part of her body on *any* part of my own. But that's another story," Hans said, "or rather I know it's part and parcel of the same story, yet something relegates it to the margins, only to the orbit of the general problem that was Olga. Yes," he said, "as a matter of fact, perhaps I was too insistent with her. At first I just wanted to be friendly, that's all, really, but circumstances compelled me to be insistent, which is something I never intended. I hate people who force you into think-ing that they're *insistent*. At any rate," Hans said, "in this sense I understand that I might have been very insistent with Olga. Quite. Too much so. I wanted to avoid it, but her mere presence hindered any effort or intention on my part to do so. And my only excuse for not desisting was always the same: I wasn't about to give up unless she herself told me, 'Go away!' consistently enough to make me believe she meant it. And in fact, I think as early as one of the first times we went out together I made her say it, I literally forced her to tell me that. And in the end, of course, she did; after a lengthy enumera-tion on my part of the troubles that being with me might create for her, she shrugged her shoulders and said: 'Fine—go away, then.' Yes, I remember that Olga perfectly well, but I also remember *another*: I remember her al-most as I would a still from an old movie. It was the Olga who, while at the cinema, most likely watching an old movie, took hold of my left hand and kissed the knuckles of my fingers. Oh yes, but that was later on," Hans said, "when I didn't understand anything whatsoever, when as I told you before, her mere presence had the power to *disorient* me entirely. Perhaps that's the neuralgic part of the problem, a problem that I believe was much bigger than me. Yes, like the desire to work with marble. Something inevitable, I sup-pose. For example, I reached the height of insistence in the scant half hour when Olga filled in for the receptionist at the central switchboard. Yes, that damned incubator, after her damned yellow car, was another one of those obsessions I couldn't get rid of, no matter how much I tried. But while I might run across her damned yellow car a few times during the day, I mean in the afternoon or evening and anywhere in the city, I ran into the damned incubator without fail at least ten or fifteen times a day. Yes," Hans said, "but as long as she was there, she was mine, *entirely mine*. All I had to do was dial

a number from the phone at my desk, simply dialing a number would result
in her picking up the phone in the incubator. The fact is, I requested that
Olga place so many calls during the brief interval of that half hour when she
filled in for the receptionist, I mean I requested her to make such a high number of calls that more than once I must inevitably have *blocked* the switchboard. Yes, completely blocked it," Hans said, "rendered it useless. All of it
for me. I wanted them just for me: the switchboard and Olga. I don't know
how to explain it. It was hard to bear the thought that others were *also* re-
questing that she place calls. I don't understand how the company wasn't
economically undermined by the blockage I inflicted on the switchboard.
But mind you, it was almost like a military blockade, something well
thought out and with a clearly defined strategy of calls behind it. I suppose
that backfired on me, completely backfired, like so many, many things I did
because of her and for her, but I imagine that around that time I developed,
instinctively and to the utmost, a whole logistics of siege, of *emotional siege*,
I mean. Yes," Hans said, "in theory, all my calls were justifiable; none of them
were of a nature unrelated to work. Every one of them arose from genuine
business reasons, oh yes. What was curious, I mean, what I knew to be curious, was that all those calls should be placed between one thirty-five and
five past two in the afternoon. At times I even thought to myself, 'Hans,
you'll ruin the company, totally ruin it with so many calls.' But my fingers
had a will of their own. They went on dialing the magic little number, after
which Olga's voice would emerge. Yes, had Olga been in a distant place, the
phone bill would have bankrupted the company. Surely. I actually leafed
through my phone book several times from one end to the other, making
calls and talking to people I hadn't been in touch with for years. I would approach them with one excuse or another, but the idea was to *request* those
calls—to request that she place them—in a businesslike manner and as
though my life or the economic future of the company were truly at stake as
a result of those calls. Yes," Hans said, "I made dozens of calls, and nearly all
of them just to hear words such as 'Yes?' or 'All right.' But those words had
issued from *her* lips, directly from her lips. They were the nourishment
thanks to which I could subsist during those afternoons and evenings, that is
to say, the afternoons and evenings after having heard those words or similar
ones, because at work there was little else I could hear. Later during those

afternoons and evenings I might waste several hours walking in the rain, something I'd never done before, driven on by a strange inertia. Yes, an inertia whose source, reason, or purpose I couldn't fathom," he said, "but I do know that I'd walk down the street totally lost, lost to myself. Although I keep thinking the mistake was mine—I mean the mistake of not having figured out how to really win Olga over. In that sense, she never made *mistakes*. It's only logical that behind her more or less passive attitude there should be less likelihood of making a mistake. It was almost a bet of a mathematical nature. You know, even at those moments when I thought I was affecting her most deeply, Olga maintained the distance and *common sense* typical of her. Yes, in connection with all this about realizing or not realizing one's mistakes, I remember finding out that at some point she had gone out with her best friend, and I also learned that she had talked with that friend about me. I don't know," Hans said, "if I hadn't been quite certain that what she had discussed with her friend was favorable to me, I naturally wouldn't have wanted to know about it. But I insisted over and over. I wanted to coax her into confiding it to me, but Olga cut me short by saying: 'I can't tell you what I said to her, it would be a *mistake*.' Most important, her reserve, her rare capacity for introversion—when in truth she was really very open—also carried over into the realm of feelings. That was a lot harder to bear. Sometimes you need to hear what the person who spends hour after hour in your company is feeling. And at those instants Olga was quite capable of alluding to what a mistake it would be to tell me how she felt. Or what's worse," said Hans, "another evening she suddenly flung at me something that left me stunned for several days. 'Don't bother asking me what I feel,' she said, 'because I feel nothing. I'm here and that's enough. You understand? I don't feel anything.' Who knows, I think if she'd said that under other circumstances, I would have understood it differently, but the fact is, she said it when I had been kissing her neck for quite some time, my arms encircling it from behind, and I could see the *effect* of those caresses. Yes, I'm convinced I behaved insistently, I admit that, but it's just that Olga, too, was very peculiar about certain things. Take the way she'd wink at me, for example, yes, *wink*, you heard me," Hans said, repeating himself no doubt on account of the surprised expression I must have made when I heard what he was saying, "a gesture she excused or attempted to excuse by claiming that giving a wink was actually something she did with nearly everyone, which I knew wasn't true. She loved it, or at least she said she loved it; from which, as you see, I can only suppose that she loved to wink at me slyly on a particular day of the week, when some colleagues and I went to her office to deliver certain receipts. Yes, Olga was very peculiar about that sort of thing. She used to tell me she winked at *everyone*, but she didn't, she winked only at me, and furthermore she was very deft about doing it in such a way that no one else around her would notice. I think perhaps that's how she showed her flirtatious side, I mean the part of her that was inclined to flirt, a fact she denied, trying to put forth convincing arguments one might understand and even believe right up until the moment she winked. Then everything else would vanish into thin air and one would be left with only the desire to be God, in order to arrest time at that instant," Hans said, "at *that* instant and at no other. Yes, as a matter of fact I suppose I felt like God in some sense, every time I saw her, when she stood before me. Do you realize how tragic that was?" Hans asked of no one in particular, with a hint of anguish in his voice, "Olga inspired *that* in me, while for her I remained an odd, even interesting sort of fellow on account of the things I would say—affectionate at best. Someone who, I became increasingly aware, no matter how much I might do, would never manage to cross the frontier into being an *integral* part of her life. On the other hand, she was not at all flirtatious about other things, when she really could have been—I'm referring now to her appearance. Having been singled out for her beauty since she was a child might have left a decisive mark on her, but it didn't, it was almost the opposite. Olga developed a rare defense mechanism that kept her from truly believing that her undeniable beauty was a genuine attribute with which to avail herself in life. Yes, and her propriety," Hans said, "the propriety I used to allude to in order to upset her, was along the same lines. Even while being a serious woman, she could have taken better advantage of certain qualities she undoubtedly possessed. Yes," he said, "she could and should have, I think, treated some things more frivolously, and she didn't, at least not with me. But I think that deep inside, although with others she might have made a slight change, she must have behaved the same way with everyone. Just to give you an example, she was extremely serious when referring to Sömmering. Yes, almost two months were to go by, during which we saw each other an average of three or four times a week—I mean, saw each other that often *after* work—before I learned that she was living, and had been for several years, with this Sömmering, that they were not 'husband and wife' in the literal sense of the word, as I had thought at first, but that they shared their lives nevertheless, the life of an established *couple*. That had a great impact on me," Hans said, "it changed everything. I suppose that on the one hand it explained a multitude of little doubts concerning Olga's *propriety*, and on the other it made me become aware of the motives behind her many and varied attitudes toward me. For example, the fact that there *was* someone waiting for her at home, beyond midnight on those days we'd get together, was not the same as having no one expecting her. At first that was distressing, as indeed for me everything was reduced to a question of weighing, I mean wondering whether she would prefer to be with me or to go home because someone was expecting her there. That was another whopping mistake, I know that, but my selfishness won out, my *need for her*. Yes, and the truth is I never knew what she would have done had she not had someone waiting for her at home. I didn't even really imagine it, I didn't want to imagine it. In spite of everything," said Hans, "when we got together she would stay out quite late, I mean very late, even *too* late for a person who had somebody expecting her home. Yes, I would weigh all that mechanically and even unconsciously, but in fact I wouldn't fully grasp that situation until many hours after our meeting, when I could consider more calmly and from every possible angle the moments spent in her company, as though attempting to introduce, like serum into my veins, the sequence of those images experienced with Olga. Despite everything, I think my tendency to be gallant toward her was very detrimental to my interests—if, I repeat, I actually had at any point *specific* interests regarding her, or if at any time I knew what those interests were. Yes, it had to do with another type of insistence, *objectual* insistence. I'm talking about the gifts. I knew how much they bothered her, yet still I endeavored to shower her with gifts every chance I got, which was often, although I knew nothing of her tastes, knew virtually nothing about her. Or *almost* nothing, yes. It's true," Hans said, "even though she'd talk on and on, in reference to things in her life, even her private life, I never quite understood the true meaning of everything I heard. Painful though it may be to admit it, I believe Olga never truly intended to communicate with me, which is why I'd crash against the

88

wall that her reserved nature so often became. Yes, the sensation I had each time a new date drew near was that of going to an examination—a sensation that, as time went by and in view of Olga's increasing reluctance to go out with me, as more and more difficulties surfaced in seeing each other—that sensation, I was about to say, took a turn for the worse. Yes, then it wasn't simply going to an examination but rather being *condemned*. Having been condemned and awaiting your own execution. All of that fostered my insecurity about her, as well as about myself, beyond words. Yes," Hans said. "My terror about her not showing up for our next date never faded. Actually, I suppose I was always somewhat convinced that Olga might not show up, that as people commonly say, she might stand me up. And therefore each time she showed up for a date—which, by the way, she always did—I'd be filled with joy. She couldn't understand why, and I noticed that. In that sense, Olga was always a *discovery* for me each time I was with her. What I can say, however, is that the way she communicated with me evolved as time went by, yes, it was all like a phenomenal drinking binge, like a hemorrhage of words and images, something similar to the way time is passing for us right now, you know what I'm trying to say?" Hans asked suddenly, leaving me absolutely perplexed because, until that moment, I hadn't actually stopped to think about the time we'd been walking while I let him speak. Perhaps it had been several hours, maybe a couple, but the truth is that, paradoxically, I hadn't had time to reflect upon or consider the period that had elapsed since we began our walk from the steps of the sanatorium. Hans was silent now, as though expecting a response on my part, but I was incapable of uttering a single word. I nodded in agreement, as it was already quite a strain for me to grasp the bombardment of phrases to which I was being submitted. But I soon heard his voice rising again in the cold crepuscular air of that wood, enveloped during those moments in a dense mist. "Well, I'd like you to understand it in any event. As I was saying," he continued, though now in a lowered voice, "Olga had a special way of communicating, not only with me but with people in general. Yes, I think Olga's capacity in that sense was prodigious. Every gesture of her hands, of her fingers, the way she moved her neck. Everything in her was unique and *replaced* words. Merely the way she smiled was unnerving. Yes," Hans said, "I remember a certain occasion when we were in the midst of a wooded spot. It was rather like this one, but more rugged. We had stopped the car, her damned yellow car, at the verge of the road and we walked about a hundred meters into the woods. Yes, she looked very beautiful," he said. "She exhaled vapor slowly, calmly, and yet I could have sworn she was restless. Yes, very *restless*. I don't know, perhaps it was the fact of being there with me, in that place, surrounded by that absolute, overwhelming solitude. I looked at the high treetops and uttered, I think, a meaningless phrase. Then she, with her eyes fixed on the pine trees in the background, said she didn't like pine trees. 'I don't like pine trees,' she said flatly. I heard those words but didn't *understand* them, and then, almost mechanically, instinctively, to clarify what she had intended to say, she added, 'They're rather like . . . ,' and she stopped altogether, without finishing the phrase. Yes," said Hans, "but her hands had already sketched a quick picture in the air. The vapor from her mouth had dispersed because her hands, when she used them to express herself, I mean, to *finish* or to begin to express herself, were like daggers. Yes, like swords wielded by a samurai, something very special, which I'd be at a loss to define. Much like a snake's cunning and fatal strike, attacking without knowing why, yet certain not to miss. Yes, I've already spoken to you at some point about Olga's hands resembling snakes. But in any event, on that occasion she said, 'I don't like pine trees'; she gestured like that, and I *understood*. It was sufficient, I think. Yes, and I also think the same thing happened in quite a few other respects throughout our relationship, I mean while we saw each other every now and then. I think I even managed to understand everything, or nearly everything, I'm not sure. At least I understood certain things. We were an integral part of the same scene. She the general and I the particular. Yes, I think Olga was like a cage. Meeting her and already being *caged* were instantaneous, much like being hurled into the instantaneous, which we were just discussing—well, which I discussed," Hans said, once again surprising me with his lucidity in realizing that he had just chosen the wrong word, the subject that would designate both of us as speakers. In a fraction of a second, and of course without interrupting his speech, he had corrected himself, demonstrating in passing that he exercised some degree of control over everything he was saying, which, I must admit, had not been the impression he'd given me at every moment. "Yes, I used to feel like a little bird going from one perch to the other and thence to the wires in his tiny trajectory within the cage that was Olga. Her cordiality was a cage, much the same as her discretion in some instances or her bluntness in expressing certain things—never *feelings*, mind you, but *opinions* concerning something. Her partial disdain was also a cage, surfacing only at particular moments, often mingled with the uneasiness of not knowing how to resolve a problem which I, even without intending to, had raised," Hans said. "Her apparent affection for me, at other times, was a cage as well, the worst sort of cage in that the pain of absence—her absence, that is—was even greater after she had been *affectionate* with me, albeit affectionate in a controlled way. And I was always, I think, tugged at by that control or attempt at control, originating with her rather than with me. Yes," he said, "I believe that went on for many months. I did delay my necessary pending calls, and also the totally unnecessary pending calls, until those moments when she was handling the phones in the incubator. Yes, and I can say the same about her briefly stepping out of her office in Administration to use the photocopy machine that sits a few meters from my desk. Just a few meters away. Six or eight at the most. In that instance I also managed to have perfect control over my impulse to dart over to the photocopy machine so as to coincide with her—doing the impossible to make it happen, often even standing there with nothing to photocopy, empty-handed and awaiting my turn after her, in order to photocopy *nothing*. Olga realized that. And she would smile," said Hans. "She just smiled. I think it should have been possible, merely possible, to be able to photocopy her smile at those moments. It was at once terrifying and soothing. Yes," he said, "with a diaphanous touch that, nevertheless, made her impenetrable. Exactly the opposite, I think, of the gesture she made with her hands to explain why she didn't like pine trees. Yes, people understood Olga's smile, while I, in contrast, never managed to do more than approach *comprehension* of any of her gestures. It's curious, now that I think about it: she, on her part, also controlled when she came to make photocopies, never glancing in my direction, although she had, must have had, some inkling of what my reaction on seeing her would be. Yes, I'm sure, absolutely sure, that Olga knew I would rush to the photocopy machine, often with nothing in my hands, or on the contrary, remain seated facing sideways and without glancing in her direction, completely ignoring her, ignoring her sullenly and theatrically. Rather pathetically, I think. Or perhaps, I guess, it's possible that at some point that held a certain charm for her.

What I mean to say by all this is that she controlled those two disparate re-actions, and she controlled her poise in the face of such reactions, for she knew I would do nothing else: either approach her with an almost Olympic sprint or pretend I was ignoring her, that I didn't see her. But I was being con-sumed inside," Hans said, "especially when I adopted the latter stance, I mean remaining seated in my chair looking as though I were working. My whole being was a *fire*. Yes," he said, "an internal fire with towering flames. An outrageous fire of extraordinary proportions, a fire consuming acres upon acres of life in each of those situations that she, with her back to me, controlled *in her own way*, often even forgetting, I suppose, that I was there, a short distance away. That's how Olga was. And in fact, I still believe that had I done just the opposite in both cases—in other words, what's normal with a co-worker: greeted her, cracked a joke, or actually continued work-ing, that is, gone on working without *secreting adrenalin* at a frenetic rate— if I had done that (behaved naturally, that is), she might perhaps have been puzzled. Maybe at that moment all my turmoil and confusion might have been transferred to her, lightening my heavy load a bit. But no: she, Olga, controlled those reactions perfectly, she anticipated them, and thus they were never strange to her. They never disconcerted her. Yes, she was relatively easy to overwhelm, with words for example, but she was not easily disconcerted. Moreover, I would even venture to say that Olga was never really discon-certed by anything or anyone. She was too worried about feeling so over-whelmed to think about the possibility of being disconcerted. Curiously enough, however, I believe she could indeed be disconcerted by other kinds of *attentions*. Some of them she actually found droll. Yes," Hans said, "she found my nervousness, for example, charming. Yes, that's what she said at some point. *Charming*. At least I know she regarded it as charming for a while, at the beginning, when she barely knew me and still thought the whole thing must be a show, a pose. Yes, and to realize gradually that it wasn't, that I was truly *nervous* in her company, was something which I sup-pose in one way flattered her, in another put her ill at ease, and in yet a third, amused her. And the blame," said Hans, "lay squarely upon her eyes. Upon her immense blue, almond-shaped eyes. Which is exactly what I would tell her, but Olga would simply laugh it off. She always laughed when I brought up her eyes, and she would laugh even more, I mean more intensely, when I specifically referred to the physical effects her eyes had on me. Those physical effects, I think, were translated into an ever-increasing nervousness. Because Olga's eyes were something very special. Their color changed according to the weather, yes, they were never the same shade of blue by morning as by night. They would shine more or less depending on the season of the year. And the way they would shine in autumn was absolutely *unbearable*—I'll tell you about that some other time. Yes," Hans said, "I've actually seen her eyes looking chestnut, green, yellow, every imaginable shade of color. Yes, my nervousness was directly proportionate to the effect those eyes produced in me. On a certain occasion I was talking to her in the reception booth, or rather she was sitting on the other side of that sort of showcase or counter, and I was standing outside. Olga had slid open the glass separating us and I was about to drink a coffee I had just fetched from one of those coin machines, you remember the one? Yes," Hans said, "they removed it shortly afterwards. Well, I had the plastic cup with my coffee leaning on the ledge of that damned counter. I was looking at her and trying to understand what she was saying to me. Yes, the eternal struggle, to comprehend what she was saying to me, and all the while having to *endure* her face being there, a few inches away. Suddenly I stared into her eyes and the coffee spilled *right into* the reception booth. Yes, it was frightful to realize that it had splashed everywhere, that everything in that hellish incubator was spattered with coffee. Yes," Hans said, "it was as though the coffee in the plastic cup—the small, only half-filled plastic cup—had multiplied infinitely. Almost a miraculous event, defying all known laws regarding fluids. I remember there being coffee everywhere, all over her clothes, the telephone, the papers she'd been consulting just before turning to me, all over the desk, the pile carpet, the drawers, the chair, along the metal strip of the window. Everything drenched. Yes, all of it drenched with coffee, with the aroma of coffee. And I, growing ever more nervous, was asking her where the devil all that coffee could have come from if what I'd spilled on her was only a small cup and not a thermos or an urn. And she, Olga, was laughing away while pronouncing the word 'spilled' again and again, apparently finding in it some highly comical meaning. Yes," Hans said, "but what followed was almost worse, my bewilderment turned to spurious efficiency, I mean an attempt at efficiency, when I insisted on cleaning all that up myself with some filthy sponges I found in the restrooms. Yes," he said, "into that task I poured a zest and zeal worthy of a housewife in a television commercial. But I was spattering it about even more because I forgot to wring out what I had just wiped up with the sponge. The whole booth was swimming in coffee. Yes, and Olga laughing away incessantly. Eventually she had to calm me down and force me to stand still and watch while she took over the task of cleaning up. I insisted that the *blame* lay with her eyes, but I think that time she didn't understand what I really wanted to tell her. Nonetheless it was true, entirely true. Her eyes, I think, held the same devastating power over me as would certain hard drugs. I suppose she made a supreme effort *not* to understand me. Yes, with the affair of the coffee she'd had enough," Hans said. "That reaction, I think, indicated unmistakably what I might have done in her presence if that flood of coffee hadn't come between us. But it was clear that in her overall assessment of the situation, of the unplanned and always unexpected circumstances I could create every time I approached her, she couldn't take into account that coffee machine that had just been installed in the building, a machine that was usually out of order, in fact, and was therefore removed. I suppose that, had she taken into account the presence of that machine and my desire to speak to her while handling the coffee cup, she would no doubt have fled in dismay. The truth is," Hans said, "that machine, too, even though it lasted such a short time at work, became one more obsession. Yet another. Yes, I've already mentioned that Olga always took her coffee without sugar. Ah, but with that machine she usually took it with milk. Don't ask me why, but the fact is, she did. Another day I had the bright idea of offering her a black coffee, without sugar. Yes, horrible. Never before had I seen her put on that look typical of revulsion. Yes, several little wrinkles formed on either side of her nose, and she assumed a very amusing expression. I was the only one able to elicit it, by making her drink that concoction. As on so many, many occasions, I tried to be *attentive* toward her, but something went wrong. The point is, as I was saying, that the machine, too, became another one of those damned objects. Yes, my life was soon surrounded by damned yellow cars, damned photocopy machines, damned coffee machines. And I'd rather not talk or think about the invisible presence of Sömmering's damned face, that fellow who lived with her. It's counterproductive, I know that. I looked for him in the face of each and every one of the fellows I would come across, though I never knew him personally. Only once, I think, while on the bus, I chanced to see Olga's damned yellow car: beside her sat a man whose knees and shoulders were all I could glimpse. Yes, although my first reaction was to turn away, the truth is that I came very close—driven by my curiosity to know what the fellow looked like, to know once and for all what his face was like—very close, I was saying, to *tumbling* out the window. But I couldn't see him," Hans said, "well, all the better. Later on it would have been worse, especially bearing in mind that he, Sömmering, played a fundamental role, I think—though unwittingly—in Olga's conscience in regard to what one might call the denouement of my story with her, but I did say I'd rather not dwell on that damned topic. Although I do think he was decisive in our relationship, at the time I always thought he was marginal. Olga was Olga and I was I. I mean she was herself and I was *also* hers, but the one doesn't alter the other. I was telling you about my nervousness at knowing I was so absolutely hers," Hans said, "yes, Olga controlled my nervousness, but not the nervousness when, being near her at certain moments, I held some solid object in my hands or there was stuff between us. Yes. It was normal that if we were chatting while having a drink and there was an ashtray full of cigarette butts on the table, at some moment, without warning, I'd *blow* in such a way that Olga ended up all covered with ashes. Yes, mind you I never blew on purpose. Most likely I'd say a word in a loud tone with my mouth very near the ashtray, or cough, or laugh about something. The truth is," said Hans, "as she once remarked, quite amused, being with me was like venturing into the desert with the simoom whipping violently about. But if attentions like the one with the coffee, or rather my attempts at being attentive with coffee as an excuse (for indeed I remember that I spilled it on her because I wanted to offer her a little bit, too insistently, I suppose), if that sort of attention, I was saying could strike her as droll, it wasn't so with others. And I poured all my enthusiam into those other attentions so that she would be pleased by them, or at least, not be bothered by them. It's curious, I think, how important the word *enthusiasm* became for me after I met Olga. Yes, first I regained it, if in fact I'd ever had it. I was all enthusiasm. And later I lost it entirely. Just so. Yes," Hans said, "I'm afraid that among all those attentions there was one in particular she never really liked at all; rather the contrary, I suppose it made her feel besieged even beyond our peculiar relationship at work, peculiar outside of work as well. Because the relationship between Olga and me was, I think, really *peculiar*, no matter where. Yes, she never understood the ultimate layer of that attention, that joke which in fact I indulged only six or seven times with her. I don't exactly remember the number. I'm talking about the horoscopes. Yes, a joke, just a joke I thought she'd find amusing, that would capture her attention, be a sort of lure for her, but it wasn't. The fact is that one day, naturally quite a few months ago, I was talking to a journalist friend of mine, yes," Hans said, "he's in charge of the horoscope in the local paper. I mean not only the horoscope but the entertainment pages, games and all that, you know. Suddenly he asked me how I'd like to do the horoscope for him once in a while. He was fed up with always printing the same things, of talking about his co-workers and making references to them. Yes, I recall that I'd just recently started going out with Olga and around then we had actually talked about the signs of the zodiac and so forth. Well, that was a subject I'd read a bit about. The fact is, I agreed to send him an occasional horoscope, never really committing myself to anything, and in them I set out to depict and above all advise old friends and co-workers. You yourself, I think, showed up in it a couple of times. Yes, I imagine you're surprised," he said, "I grant you it was nonsense, but I had fun with it for a time. No one except Olga knew about that pastime. Of course she always appeared in the sign of Taurus when I did the horoscopes for the paper. She was born precisely on the first day of that sign, and I would tell her— teasingly, you know—that she was Queen of Taurus. Yes," he said, "it seemed a pretty name for her . . . But in light of certain things I wrote in some of those horoscopes, she suddenly felt uncomfortable, very uncomfortable. Yes, I set about writing them at important moments for me, at moments when our relationship, our peculiar relationship, had suffered some internal collapse in one sense or another. At first Olga attached no importance whatsoever to the horoscopes I devoted to her, which weren't that many at any rate, as I said, but I suppose that in one of them I must have told her *something* she didn't like. Yes," Hans said, "and she and I were the only ones who knew that it was always a message, a coded message no other colleague could understand in the least, although most of them, naturally, read the paper every day. In this regard, I recall her telling me one evening that it was like 'feeling she was being watched from outside,' yes, those were her words exactly. She added no more, in keeping with her habit of avoiding use-less disquisitions on topics that, for one reason or another, she considered entirely *settled*. Olga couldn't bear, above all else, feeling she was being watched, which was tantamount to saying *controlled*, even though she, I think, exerted considerable control over everything around her, especially in the realm of feelings, and even more, she hated having to give explanations about her private life. Then she was even liable to lose her head. I don't know," Hans said, "I suppose I was clumsy enough to write another two or three horoscopes, and crowned my mistake by making sure she'd know the specific day the horoscope would be printed. Yes, I recall that in a round-about way I even saw to it that she got them before she might have a chance to come across them in the pages of the paper. Although I knew she usually read them every day, especially after learning that a message directly ad-dressing her might appear at any moment. Yes," he said, "yet I couldn't help fearing that, on just those days, Olga wouldn't glance at the paper, or wouldn't take notice of the horoscope, and for that reason I took the *step* of conveying them to her promptly. I understand now that I shouldn't have done it, neither that nor many *other* things. I think I didn't even give her the opportunity to reflect calmly upon whether she wanted so much attention, yes, I suppose I barely let her breathe with such a torrent of attentions. That, I think, was evidently the moment when I decided not to devote any more horoscopes to her, even though my friend the journalist kept insisting for quite some time. Yes," he said, "and even now, at Chemnitz, I find myself mentally reciting one of those horoscopes, always a new one that I think about while I'm working, even though thinking clearly while polishing and carving marble proves to be quite difficult, I can assure you. It's a task that requires *enormous* isolation, though it's more cerebral than physical, yes, al-though a certain degree of bodily concentration—of certain parts of the body in relation to thought—is also necessary. That noise," Hans said, "fil-ters into the brain, fills it, gradually annihilates it, you hear the voice of the drill in dreams and in the deepest silence of the most remote stretch of forest. It goes wherever I go. Yes, it's *the other face* of my thoughts. Because, as I've already told you, I think a lot here, I think incessantly, I think I should avoid being always and constantly thinking about something, but were I to do so, I mean if I were to stop thinking for even a moment, it would be still worse.

I don't know, I wonder whether this sanatorium might perhaps be the ideal place to think, or at least the ideal place to think about *certain* things. You already know that Angelica was the one who decided on this place, I suppose because someone had spoken highly of the medical team and the thermal waters. She had initially talked about taking me to another one in Schlangenbad, or to one near Wiesbaden. I remember there was also some talk about the possibility of going to Bad Schwalbach, where an aunt of ours spent some time convalescing from some sort of illness when we were children, but she finally decided on Chemnitz. The truth is," Hans said, "I'm glad to be here. I've done what I truly wished to do, the *only* thing I wished, to go on thinking incessantly, to think without placing any bonds on the tumultuous course of my thoughts. Yes, in just that way I've arrived at curious conclusions; for example, concerning the noise marble makes while it's being worked. I've already mentioned that upon my arrival I could have chosen to engage in some other task at the sanatorium. There are several workshops. You haven't seen them because they're in the rear pavilions. Yes, but as soon as I heard from afar the noise coming from the marble shop, I told myself, 'That's what I want to do, I want to be *in the midst* of that all the time.' Precisely that and nothing else was what I wanted to do, it was exactly what I needed. And mind you, I heard that noise by chance, because no one was working in the shop during the weeks immediately prior to my arrival. I heard it as soon as I stepped into the garden to take my first walk. 'That, that is it,' I said to myself. And later, after some days, some months, with the continual memorization of that oppressive noise, I've realized that it's very similar (although higher-pitched and considerably more unpleasant) to the one emitted by the upper part of the gear shift in Olga's damned yellow car. Yes, that little black ball screwed onto the gear shift must have been rather loose and that's why it vibrated as the car began to pick up speed. That little black ball was always a bit loose, it had always bothered Olga when she was driving, for months or perhaps even for years, and she was forever talking about fixing it. 'Maybe it's just a matter of tightening down *some piece inside,*' she replied once when I remarked that if the noise bothered her so much she could have had it fixed by now. Yes," Hans said, "I think perhaps that belonged to the pile of things that Olga left *up in the air* for some strange reason. And at times she even became entangled in out-and-out battles with

that little black ball while driving. She'd take one hand off the wheel and vigorously seize the little ball so as to muffle the noise, which became a very an-
noying whine once the car passed a given speed. Occasionally, stifling my
horror," Hans said, "I even saw her letting go of the wheel with *both hands*
in her eagerness to choke the little ball. She'd do it only for a few seconds, of
course, but I ended up feeling that our physical well-being was endangered.
I suppose that fact—finding a certain similarity between the noise of working on marble and the noise emitted by the gear shift in her car—wouldn't
have been reason enough to grant such importance to my gradual discovery
(since, I repeat, I became conscious of it little by little), it wouldn't have been
sufficient, I was saying, had it not been for another circumstance, I mean, a
circumstance essential in enabling me to understand the workings of my
memory when faced with the sudden phenomenon of a noise that was familiar to me. Olga's *hand*," said Hans, with an abstracted air that was to last
several moments, "yes, her hand and mine. I think that's what is important,
that her hand and mine would occasionally meet over that little ball on the
gear shift of the car. When she tried to grab it to stop the noise, she was partially disabled, I mean, she couldn't stop looking ahead, paying attention to
the road, nor could she let go of the wheel with her other hand except, of
course, in those fits of hysteria I've already mentioned. Yes," he said, "when
Olga placed her right hand on the black ball, she was as trapped as when she
was in the incubator of the reception booth at work, and just then, availing
myself perhaps of the fact that she could only look at me for a few seconds,
I would place my hand over hers and we'd go on like that for a spell, yes, until
for whatever reason she needed to let go of the shift handle. That, too, has
become part of the palpable noises that have for some time now given shape
to my existence. Yes, I think it's as though some noises solidified, as if they
acquired a certain corporeality without leaving their unsolid state. I don't
know if I'm making myself clear. Rather strange, I suppose. It has to do, I
think, with a sensation I notice between my lungs in just that area of my
body. I don't know, I know only that I feel this sensation right here when I
think of the noise of marble. And, on the other hand, you may well imagine
that almost the entire time I hear the noise of marble, I *also* hear, I mean, I'm
quite likely to hear the noise of the little black ball on the gear shift in Olga's
car, and at the same time I have the optimum tactile and acoustic mental con-

ditions to think. Yes," Hans said, "cold as marble. Her hand, nearly always cold. I don't know why Olga didn't take her hand away when I'd place mine on it, I mean, I don't know why she *sometimes* left it there, especially at first, when that gesture wasn't as frequent as during a somewhat later time. I suspect that contact didn't entirely displease her, or that at least she wasn't as displeased with it as with some of the other attentions of which I made her the object. But I think that what Olga used to call 'my offerings'—I mean my little attentions, things I would give to her quite frequently, things I bought for her *against* my will; it was against my will to purchase them and particularly against my will that they should be conveyed into her hands directly from mine—all those gifts, I was saying, ended up making her extremely uncomfortable. I know that if on the one hand they inspired in her the delight natural in one who is the object of such a gesture, on the other I think they made her feel obligated to be grateful, or even worse, attentive to me, and at times, even *especially* attentive. Yes," said Hans, "attentive to the point where she showed absolutely no hesitation in telling me that she, too, felt the need to give me something, to give me anything for whatever reason, which I think wasn't at all true. No," Hans said, "I don't believe Olga ever felt the need to give me anything. In the first place because the very idea of gifts made her uncomfortable, and secondly because she must not have known what to give me, which might ultimately demonstrate, particularly given the disparity in the gifts we exchanged, that she never knew me well enough to know what might delight me. I don't know, I think that in that respect our relationship must have been like cross fire. Yes, for example, I recall one very special weekend. I suppose it was no more nor less special than other weekends during that period, but it was special nonetheless, because a few days before I had told her that on that weekend—that very weekend—I intended to shut myself away at home, to shut myself off completely, not even going out into the garden, without venturing into the street at all; not turning on the radio, or playing music of any sort. 'No rubbish,' I told her, 'not even that pop rubbish.' That's what I told her. No Mozart, no Webern, I must have thought of saying, though I don't remember if I told her the last bit. Nothing: I'd devote myself to thinking, thinking intensely about a way to wipe her out, about how to wipe her out mentally, of course, once and for all. Well," Hans said, "I recall that just minutes before work ended on Friday, on the eve of that weekend, of course, I ran into her in one of the halls at work, or rather I suppose that for once *she* ran into *me* and told me there was 'something for me' in the trunk of her car. I went down to see what awaited me in the trunk of her damned yellow car. Yes, it was droll: I opening the trunk of her damned yellow car, of that odious yellow car with its odious trunk. I withdrew a plastic bag from it. Inside was a bottle. Yes, there was a bottle of my favorite whiskey, not a terribly expensive brand, but one I re-served solely for my 'special moments,' a fact I had conveyed to her. Once we'd gone upstairs again I indicated the bottle, asking her something that Olga herself always had on the tip of her tongue, a devastating word she used always at the most critical instants: 'Why?' Yes, I remember her looking so beautiful, particularly beautiful—I'd even say radiant—and she said sim-ply: 'For your toothache.' I know that at that moment I *fell apart* inside. That weekend, all vain threats aside, I really did want to shut myself away at home without going anywhere, not even into the garden, so as to be done with Olga, to *destroy* her within me. I realized that the gift, coming just a few hours before I was to initiate that process of destruction long deferred by cir-cumstances, was due to something more than mere chance. Yes, I immedi-ately recognized it wasn't a coincidence, a fortuitous gift. But I couldn't really betray my doubts to her in such a crude way. I don't know, the whole affair was rather confusing, yes. Several times," Hans said, "I made the same resolution: to put an end to her, to cancel her out, to erase her from my life. But the whole thing proved fruitless. If she was the best—I mean, if Olga was the best thing that had ever arisen within me—how could I make her vanish so easily? At any rate, at least on that weekend, I was firmly resolved to do it. There had taken place in recent days a series of rather sad and dis-appointing events, so that was the ideal weekend to attempt it, I mean, to put an end to her. Although the truth is, I was oblivious to everything, I was going about like a sleepwalker, yes," he said, "I expect I felt a similar sensation to what we feel when, being on a train that has stopped at a station, another train suddenly comes to a stop right alongside. If we look out the window, staring at the car beside us, and one of the trains, ours or the other one, slowly begins to pull away, for a few instants we're unable to distinguish which of the two trains has started moving. You know what I'm talking about," Hans said, "yes, that was the feeling of disorientation I experienced then. I also think that about that time I was seeing ghosts everywhere, ghosts which made me suspect that she, Olga, could actually think what I was thinking at the *very same instant* I was thinking it, ghosts which made me realize that indeed I myself quite often knew what she was thinking, although hardly ever at the moment when she was theoretically doing so, but rather *a posteriori*, when the blaze from her eyes could only partially harm me, when I could only be hurt by the *heat* emitted by that blaze, not by the fire itself. I expect you understand me. I'm referring to the expansive wave of the immense explosion Olga was when she moved, when she spoke, when she would appear down the street. I suppose that more than once, in an acute state of intoxication, of course, I intended to appear before her dressed as a fireman, yes, a *fireman*," Hans repeated to himself while smiling sarcastically, "with the fireproof uniform, the helmet and everything. Yes, that would have been a splendid way to show her how her gaze could burn, and to what degree. She would have had quite a laugh, I'm sure. As a matter of fact, on one occasion when I was absolutely drunk, as I was saying, I even considered asking Hoffmann, from the Oldenburg lab, for one of those uniforms used by the blasting technicians for some of their special jobs, you know, when serious complications arise in a mine or quarry and they have to deactivate some explosive. Yes, just thinking about it amused me. So that afternoon, the afternoon when she gave me her gift, I again asked her: 'Why?' And it was just then that I understood Olga also took a certain interest—what sort of interest I don't exactly know, but indeed some interest—in that process of destruction, or rather that attempt at destruction I was bent on subjecting her to in order, I suppose, to free myself from a *total*, an absolute destruction, which I also began to glimpse at that time. Olga herself lived immersed in a process of destruction that she was unable to conceal, however much she might try. Her personal and family circumstances—and also, I think, some kind of affective lack I was never able to pinpoint—either were or constituted the *outline* of such a process. And I recall that her reply to my question about the *intent* of that bottle containing what she knew was poison to me was nothing but 'It's so that you can wipe me out better.' Yes, she didn't add another word. Not one. I had to imagine everything else myself, I mean in solitude, in the frightful solitude of my house that weekend of seclusion, shutters closed, scarcely any light, listening only to the dripping of a kitchen faucet that I was unable to stop or didn't want to stop because somehow or other I realized in time that the dripping was absolutely *essential*. My sole point of reference to the world, I don't know if you follow me. Yes," Hans said, "I was completely drunk on *her* whiskey, thinking what she herself, I guess, must have been thinking at that moment. But I believe, or rather I'm absolutely convinced, that Olga was aware that I was thoroughly incapable of thinking about or feeling anything but a *boundless* passion for her, a longing as fervent as my desire, independent yet almost simultaneous, to have all that actually stop happening to me. She knew that with the whiskey in the house my mind would fortify her image even more; she also knew I was going to spend the entire weekend mulling over images that would remind me of the fact that it was her favorite whiskey *as well*, the images of the two of us talking over that whiskey on myriad occasions. She knew," he said, "that I would be making countless circles around the telephone, wanting to dial her number, her number at home, to ask her 'Why?' again and again. Yes, I think in a certain sense Olga knew *a lot*, knew instinctively. But not only that: she was also capable of keeping secret those things that ordinarily surface during the first extensive conversation between two people, between a man and a woman, that is, who meet one evening for drinks and who go on drinking and talking until almost daybreak—I mean drinking, talking, and doing *everything* that can be done during two such wholesome pastimes as drinking and talking. Yes," he said, "at times I even thought she was mocking me. It took me a long time yet to realize that she didn't know how to mock anyone. The capacity to mock a person must have been atrophied in her. Yes, but despite that she did occasionally make fun of me, in some sense. One day, for example, she picked me up in her damned car, and I could see she had a book in the back seat. But it wasn't an ordinary book, I mean escapist and all that," said Hans, "no, it was a book by Freud. A thick book with his name printed in black letters: Freud. How dreadful," Hans said. "Yes, I think we'd been seeing each other for over three months, about an average of three or four times a week, and I was unaware of that fact about her. I suppose I told her something along these lines: 'What is this, are you playing psychologist with your unsuspecting office mates . . . ?' Olga replied with a dry, negative monosyllable, and I, amused at seeing her a bit tense, persisted: 'Or perhaps you're carrying that book about to impress your passengers?' You want to know what she replied, do you really want to know?" Hans asked, not even glancing at me. "Well, she observed me with a look that I could swear was full of tenderness, yes—but of *real* tenderness, almost sadness—and said: 'I study psychology.' That's what she said, yes: I was frozen, like an iceberg. At first I wondered whether or not to believe it, but I soon realized it was as true as the fact that my hands were beginning to tremble. To top it off, the only thing that occurred to me to say was, 'Why didn't you tell me before?' and ask whether she had deliberately intended to make me look ridiculous, to which she replied: 'Well, you never did ask me, "so what do you do?"' And she smiled, promptly changing the subject. But despite everything, I don't think there was any cruelty on her part when it came to such things. The fact is, that book of Freud's was there and it was I who asked about it, who kept on insisting until I found myself with a bullet between the eyes. Because at times, I think, Olga had a way of saying things that felt rather like bullets. Yes," he said, "*real* bullets: not blanks, but bullets that penetrated your flesh, causing a painful wound that she alone, sometimes in a matter of seconds, was able to heal with a particular word, with a particular gesture upon uttering it. Think about that. Psychology," Hans said in a mournful tone. "I hate, I abhor psychology, I think it's the one thing I hate most in the world. Olga hated politics, that's what she hated most. There I was, like an idiot, telling her how much I hated psychology, and she smiling, with a guileless expression on her face. Yes," he said, "but in spite of everything I believe that as a person Olga was extremely *political* in her behavior, I never told her this, first of all because I didn't believe it so positively at the time, and secondly because I know she would have been quite hurt by it. Yes, she was political, her attitudes were often very political. Olga's program for living was as meticulous as that of political parties at election time. Her strategy with people who sought something from her, or who she thought were seeking something, was a political strategy as well, I'd almost call it dialectical. Olga made it clear through her silence that it was impossible for her to do anything other than what she was actually doing, which was generally nothing but what she *wanted* to do. There's something, nevertheless," Hans said, "that's clear to me, or I suppose it's clear, and that is that Olga managed to play her role to perfection. And of course—just as with so many other things about her, I won't tire of repeating it to you, because I believe it's a basic element in understanding what is going on with me, if indeed something is going on—that was something I finally realized once I was here, while working on marble, in the *noisiest* moments with the drill, when it seems as if your eardrums are going to fly out in pieces. I suspect that if I had been aware of it then, of how well Olga played her role, I would have flung myself at her feet to worship her all the more. But then out of my love for drama. Yes," Hans said, "a typical example of what I'm talking about occurred as a result of the gifts and presents that I gave her all too often, even when various circumstances were manifestly against it, and I recall my difficulty in seeing that she got them at work without anyone noticing it, her discomfort in the presence of a gift she had inspired, the obligation to *somehow* reciprocate the gift that had suddenly materialized before her. I recall my own fear of overwhelming her with so many gifts, gradually causing them to lose all value for her, if at some point they'd had any. I've already mentioned that to you, yes. I think I did. And how, on one occasion in particular, after having bought her something I no longer recollect, but which did seem to disturb her more than it delighted her, she drove me to my neighborhood. I thanked her for being such an efficient driver. She then encircled the steering wheel with her long, long arms, yes," Hans said, "she embraced it as though it were a loved one and lowered her head over it, letting her hair partly cover it. Yes, I think there was a remote tone of nostalgia in her voice, and of weariness, as well. 'Thanks for your offerings,' she mumbled, her voice scarcely audible. But she said 'offerings,' not gifts or presents or anything else. No. *Offerings.* I was rather confused by that term at the time, but I'd soon forget about it. It was later, once I was here at Chemnitz, when that word laden with such special resonance revived in my memory: offerings. I think, or rather, when I remembered I thought, that what subjects generally present to their kings, what ambassadors give to their hosts, is offerings. Yes, the word acquired a fresh dimension in my mind. I understood right then and there that Olga knew herself to be the mistress, the empress of my whole being, of everything that sprang from or was connected to me. And thus anything I gave her, even if it were a worthless trifle, would assume for her the quality of an *offering*, never a mere *present*. Perhaps that was the reason for the nostalgia and weariness I believed I had detected in her voice. Nostalgia at knowing she was the mistress and lady at a time when I suppose

that's unusual. I don't know," said Hans, "weariness, perhaps, at not knowing what to do in the face of so many offerings, of such an absolute display of
faithfulness and submission. Yes, that was one of the keynotes of our relationship, if not the primary one," Hans said, "and I suppose that it lay at the
root of Olga's gradual loss of interest in me. Yes, I believe there are certain
platitudes which, however trite they may be, are true now and will always go
on being true. My great error lay in betraying my unconditional surrender
to her, I should never have done it, yet the truth is I lacked the strength to dis-
semble. But getting back to what I was telling you about the offerings, I was
nonetheless moved at the thought. I was deeply moved by the fact that Olga
should acknowledge with such candor her condition as queen in my life, as
a goddess whose image nothing and no one could sully. Yes, I suppose everything was like a medieval dream," Hans said, "or a nightmare, I don't know.
Which, translated into her own language, so prone to call things by their
name, would be, as she was bold enough to tell me once (after one whiskey
too many, of course): 'Listen, this thing you have for me cannot be, it simply
cannot be. It's rather like a Coca-Cola romance,' and then she burst into peals
of laughter. I looked at her, solemnly agreeing, but I didn't comprehend until quite a while later, mulling all that over and over in my mind, that in some
sense Olga, too, had *understood*. Yes, by acknowledging her condition as
queen, as goddess, she agreed with me to an extent, or rather she agreed with
my unconscious, because I had always pictured her precisely with a crown
on her head. Yes," Hans said, "the moment I saw Olga I think that was my
first image of her, my first impression: seeing her with a crown, like a Ni-
belung princess. Yes, that was undoubtedly the first sensation I had on seeing
Olga, that of knowing I was face to face with someone right out of a myth-
ical legend. Well, I suppose I was never able to stand before her without feeling like someone who has abruptly stumbled across a Wagnerian being. Yes,
an authentic Walkyrie, that's what she looked like, with her straight hair falling occasionally across her face, with her arched brows and her almond eyes,
blue as the sky in an oriental tale. The truth is, I think, that from that very
moment, a lot of things in my life changed radically. Well, quite a few things.
Yes. It's as if until that moment, until I met her, I had been naked, as if I had
gone through life *naked*. Suddenly I was fully aware not only of what my situation was, but above all (and this was undoubtedly the hardest part) of what

my *limitations* were. Yes, and I think it was then that I also came to understand that the magical equation of love isn't always fulfilled, that a feeling isn't always reciprocated in equal or like measure and is never, of course, in direct proportion to the breadth with which such a feeling radiates from us toward the other person. Yes, I think I had always gone through life naked," Hans said, "and suddenly, I suppose, I became aware that I was clothed, conscious I was wearing something that might please Olga to a greater or lesser extent, as for example a jacket she said she liked on several occasions. I don't know, it was strange, very strange. Yes, the fact of knowing she liked that jacket made me become aware of such an item, look at it repeatedly, attempting to find an explanation as to why Olga liked it. Yes, very strange. Time and again I saw myself clad in the jacket she liked, strolling before the mirror in my house, a very large wall mirror. Side view, front, and back. Yes," Hans said, "I think that from then on, clothing became one more obsession, another great obsession. *Selecting* an item of clothing could occupy me for several hours, and I was capable of starting out of bed in the early hours to iron the cuffs of a shirt I thought was wrinkled. Yes, I'm well aware that she never paid attention to those details, I know that, but it was a resolution I'd made for my own sake, I mean, a discovery that I could take somewhat greater care of my outward appearance, which until then, except on rare occasions, hadn't concerned me in the least. It was quite exciting. A challenge. As if in doing so I could conceal the inward: that which couldn't be seen, which couldn't be ironed. Naturally I at once became aware not only of my own clothing but of *hers* as well, of Olga's clothing, of the clothing everyone else wore, at work, on the street. Yes, I went about then, instinctively comparing. Women had never worn clothing as far as I was concerned, by which I'm not trying to say they didn't wear any," Hans said, framing a smile, "it's just that I paid no attention to that sort of thing. Mostly, I think I began to notice *women's* clothing with uncommon interest, as I mentioned. I kept up with the frequency of their recycling of certain garments, the special way they matched them, the color combinations improvised by all the women I knew or dealt with on a more or less daily basis. Yes, and there Olga always displayed a very definite tact, I mean in knowing how to get the most out of a wardrobe that I suppose must have been fairly limited, or at least certainly not as ample as she might have wished. I know there were some garments she preferred over others, and I also realized that she wore them—I mean, that she wore these garments rather than others—on special occasions, or ones she must for some reason or other have deemed special. Yes," Hans said, "I remember a blue summer shirt with short sleeves and a print in which you could make out a beach motif. I used to call it 'your Hawaiian shirt' and she, of course, would protest, saying it wasn't Hawaiian. But she couldn't conceal the pride she felt, not because of the shirt itself, but the effect that seeing her wear that shirt would have on others, in this case specifically on me. Although I should stress that the whole business about clothing—mine, hers, everyone else's—was only the outer layer of a heightened awareness of much greater scope, yes," Hans said, "an awareness whose roots went deep into the past, into my own past, I suppose, and once I stopped seeing her, I mean once circumstances were no longer favorable for us to go on seeing each other, I again fell into an acute apathy regarding this business of clothing. Negligence," said Hans, "yes. I suppose it was a way of punishing myself, of expiating, through the proof of my own slovenliness, my guilt at how ridiculous it had been to dress *only* for her. For the first few weeks I was here at Chemnitz I found it impossible to shave. In fact, I expect I relished the sight of my unshaven beard. And Olga hated beards, did you now that? Yes," he said, "and mustaches. She always noticed people's *mouths*, they were undoubtedly the part of the body that most attracted her. 'The mouth, the lips, never lie,' she said once. Yes, from that time on I would shave at least *twice* on the days we were to go out. But the truth is there were a lot of ridiculous things, or things I think Olga may have considered ridiculous and that she did in fact consider ridiculous when I mentioned them. As soon as I met her, for example, and as if there were a veritable conspiracy orchestrated against me, I began to see yellow cars all over the city, models like hers or others— which didn't matter, they were yellow just the same. I recall in particular a yellow Volkswagen like hers that used to be parked right in front of my house, right in front of the garden gate. Yes, well, I suppose it was a Volkswagen. I was afraid even to look at it. It was as though a flying saucer were parked there. No," said Hans, "worse yet: the voice of my conscience. Yes, sometimes I even thought it was actually a hallucination, that it couldn't be a car exactly like hers. And that was my first *glimpse* of the day, my first glimpse of the outer world. Yes, I was never able to figure out to whom that yellow car belonged, but the truth is I never really tried. I only know that on some mornings, or rather, many mornings, I felt like pouncing upon it the instant I saw it. Yes, I never told her that, but I know it would have struck her as absolutely ridiculous. Yes, I'd go out hugging the garden fence without so much as glancing over. And I know that if I had mentioned all this about the car parked in front of my house to Olga, she no doubt would have said something like, 'There's no reason why there should be only one yellow car in this city.' Yes, she would have made a remark of that sort. Something that would detract from the *actuality* of the yellow car parked at my door. It was never any different. Never. That was a very frequent habit of hers, I mean making light of everything. That situation, with Olga hastily and automatically dismissing something I said or did, recurred quite often, especially when, as usual, I immediately regretted having said one thing or done another. By now," Hans said, "you must have formed a rather robotlike picture of her, I suppose. Yes, imagine an unshaven fellow constantly making apologies for something. That's what she hated most. In any event, I think, dismissing certain things was very much a trait of hers. Yes. One evening, toward the beginning, I escorted her to her house, on a sort of knoll in the outskirts of the city. Sömmering wasn't there that evening, I don't know why, but it must have been one of the few days all year when Olga was *alone*. Yes, I think I was so drunk I could barely stay on my feet. I suspect that if I hadn't been so drunk I would never have dared go up there. There was hardly any light on the street and she was struggling to find the keys to the small gate that gave on to a little garden facing the house. Olga always carried a great bunch of keys. That was another of her mysteries, yes," Hans said, remaining pensive for a few seconds, the first time he had done so in a long while, which must no doubt have borne some relation to what he was recounting, "I was telling her that she reminded me of those gloomy *housekeepers* laden with keys, right out of some nineteenth-century novel, and she replied, yes, it must seem that way. In any case, she finally hit upon the right key for the gate and opened it. Yes, I remember I stood there facing her like an oaf, saying nothing, possibly wishing she'd ask me up for 'one last drink' or something of the sort, which I no doubt would have politely but promptly declined. Or perhaps not," Hans said, "I don't know, I really don't know what would have happened if I'd gone up with her that evening. But she was there, on the other side of the gate, and then I did something that must no doubt have surprised her enormously at that moment. Above all, I seem to remember, because it was the first time I had done it, or at least the first time I did it with a certain amount of *decisiveness*. She had rested her hand on one of the iron bars of the gate, and I moved my face forward a few inches until I was able to kiss it. I don't know how many times I did so. It was a long kiss, or kisses, and fervent. Yes, but Olga didn't withdraw her hand, she just gripped the door more firmly. It was instinctive, I suppose: first the neck, bending my neck, and then planting that long kiss on her hand. I noticed her long fingers, her perennially cold fingers, and I could have sworn that her whole body quivered. I don't know, I think that might have happened, but the truth is that her face betrayed nothing, absolutely nothing: she simply smiled with a faintly, but not terribly, confused persistence. Yes, it was a very special moment. I could hear my own voice saying: 'It's hard to go on living when you're not around.' That's when she resorted to minimizing the importance of a situation that, at least for me, was important indeed. She said, 'Come on, how can that be so hard?' I don't know, she realized, she had to realize that I was utterly beside myself, that I was really affected, yet she denied it nonetheless. She denied what was happening *within* me. Curious. Yes, she always did that. But that, I think, was the first time I kissed her hand—or one of the first, I'm not sure, later there would be others. I mean, on other days and especially other nights. Yes, I kissed Olga's hands the moment I had the slightest opportunity, although I must admit she was never very receptive in that regard. She always seemed somewhat on edge, not completely but just *a bit* on edge, as though restraining her agitation. It's also possible, I think, that if Olga had seemed too receptive at my obstinacy in kissing her hands, I would have ended up by devouring all of her, gobbling her up, hands, arms, body, everything. Yes, just as I felt the imperative need to besiege her whenever I saw her at the photocopy machine, the instant I kissed her hand, or both hands at the same time, what I really would have wanted to do was to gobble her up. Yes," Hans said, "every so often Olga would surprise me with mysterious things, with secrets, I mean with something I would never in the least have expected from her. For example, she once spoke to me about *her* secret, and on account of her tone, which she later used again when referring to her *great* secret, I asked her whether it was the one about the *wind*, something she had once started to tell me about but hadn't finished. Yes, as I told you, Olga seemed to lead a very intense internal life. When I asked her that, if she was referring 'to the one about the wind,' she smiled enigmatically and said: 'No, another one. *My* secret. The thing about the wind is no secret at all.' Taken aback, I then asked her whether it had anything to do with her nails, with the motive that drove her to bite them. Again the reply was negative, and I was left in the dark as to what secret she was referring to. At any rate," Hans said, "I understand that for a moment, even if only for a moment, she must have felt the need to share that secret with me. But she changed her mind soon enough, for what reasons I don't know. Yes, that's how it was. And as a matter of fact, on the evening I was telling you about, when I kissed her hand as it rested on the iron gate of the entrance, my relationship with her may also have changed. Who knows," Hans said, "I have no idea what Olga was thinking when she simply smiled and tried to make light of what I told her after kissing her hand. I've no idea what she was actually thinking. The truth is, I can't even imagine it. Nor can I remember what I myself thought just then. I do know, however, that she made a gesture I found terribly strange at the time. Yes, right at the very instant when she should have said, 'Why don't you come up for a nightcap?' or 'Good night, see you tomorrow,' at that very instant, I was saying, she turned toward the house and stared at it for a few seconds with an indefinable expression. I used to call Olga's house the 'Bunker,' and even Olga—though at first she seemed reluctant to refer to it as such—ended up in the habit of doing so. Olga herself used to call it the 'Dovecote,' which, in contrast to 'Bunker,' whose meaning I felt was perfectly clear, rather mystified me, as I didn't know what it might imply. Yes," Hans said, "she turned to face the 'Bunker' with a hint of resignation, and simply walked off without saying a word. Dozens, hundreds of times, I've imagined the phrase she should have uttered just then, yes. The phrase that, naturally, she didn't utter but which still resounds from time to time in my head. In that sense, I think, she exhibited all the *discretion* I lacked at those moments. Although her concept of 'discretion,' I think, was a direct threat to my own concept of discretion. I mean, from the instant it manifested, Olga's *discretion* was my *derangement*," Hans said, looking me squarely in the eye, as though weighing the effect his mention of the last word might have had on me. "Yes, because I remember it was precisely at

those moments when I strove to ensure that Olga not withdraw her hands
from mine, from my mouth, that she would remind me how much she liked
taking things one step at a time. And indeed, I also liked, and always have,
doing things without haste, but I think there must have been an abyss between my *without haste* and her *one step at a time*. Who knows, perhaps it
wasn't that way, perhaps it was the circumstances, I don't know, I really don't
know anything. What I do know is that every so often Olga made a disturbing gesture, as though wanting to postpone things until a later occasion, as if
she exercised genuine control over them, I mean, over the volume of things,
as though the things of the world and the earth passed before her without
affecting her in the slightest. Yes, but I also think that whenever I took Olga's
hand, when Olga, that is, would let me take her hand in mine, and the same
goes for any other sort of caress, it was always the *first time* I did it. I mean to
say I was always discovering everything about her, about Olga herself: her
gestures, her ideas, the things she spoke about were new for me each and
every time, even though I might previously have heard them. Yes," Hans
said, "quite strange, or at least that's how it strikes me. It was new to observe
how each and every time she ordered coffee, let's say, she politely refused the
packets of sugar the waiter presented her. She used to do everything with *extreme* politeness, and that was doubtless one of her great qualities. Yes, I recall being surprised, the first time, to realize someone could take coffee without a speck of sugar. But she, naturally, always refused any sugar, and thus I
was always surprised. And I think I wasn't so surprised by Olga rejecting the
possibility of having coffee without a trace of sugar, which I imagine must
be common among true coffee drinkers, as by the special way she did it. I felt
the same thing, I think, about her serene indignation over the little black ball
on the gear shift of her damned yellow car. Every single time she became upset, and every single time I was surprised as well. I don't know, in that sense,
I suppose, *my degree of absorption* with anything concerning her was directly
proportionate to the fondness she inspired in me," Hans said. "Yes, any number of times while witnessing such fits of anger, I would begin a mental enu-
meration of her flaws. Because when Olga's politeness changed to anger, it
could really be quite shocking. But perhaps it was a new, endless attempt to
put an end to her in my consciousness, to wipe her out. Doing that—thinking about a person's flaws—is, or tends to be, a tactic that never fails. It's hap-

hazard, but you always hit the mark, that simple. Thus with Olga. I think she, too, engaged in it without even realizing it. Yes," Hans said, "she even started doing it with me toward the end. But any resistance on my part was useless. Fictitious. Fake. Olga, I believe, exerted a negative effect on me, I mean, in my effort at trying to see her unpleasant aspects (to call them something), getting what little of her I could have, a date from time to time, politeness and charm galore, a fleeting or *not* so fleeting caress here and there, depending on the particular phase of our relationship and what I expected from those caresses, all of which kept reinforcing my image of her until it became solid as a rock. That's what Olga was for me," Hans said, "the gateway to marble: pure granite. I always managed to find convincing enough arguments to believe that such thoughts about her were biased and improper. Yes, each time Olga opened her mouth I adored her, as I might a sacred statue. That feeling of adoration would arise spontaneously. I don't know, strange as it was, I think it must have been the purest and noblest form of love I've ever experienced. And I can assure you I've experienced various others before, some much more *fruitful* than my spell with Olga. Earlier I mentioned the curious way she experienced certain noises, but there was more to it," Hans said, "yes, like her almost virulent obsession with crickets, for example. I had the chance to observe that a couple of times. I'll never forget the way she pointed toward the darkness and the shrubbery, saying, 'Listen, listen to them, do you hear them?' The chirping of crickets completely perturbed her, it was quite incomprehensible, or perhaps not, I suspect that in all that there may have been some relationship to the noise coming from the little black ball on the gear shift of her damned yellow car. Yes," Hans said, "maybe those sounds are similar. And she was also capable of cutting short a conversation, no matter how important, in order to *alert* me to a sudden warm gust of wind. Then she would remain sort of abstracted and murmur, 'Did you see?' Apparently I was expected to see what she had actually seen. As I said, at such times Olga would remain totally absorbed, with her gaze fixed on an indeterminate point in space. I can assure you it was impossible to remain aloof from the powerful influence of those gestures. To see them was to be swept away by them, and to see them up close was to succumb irremediably. Yes, it was especially unnerving to see the way Olga *dealt* with the wind, I mean it was one of the many unnerving things Olga would do. Her manner of disentangling her hair after the wind had mussed it, the special way she turned her head away or half-closed her eyes. Because Olga's eyes also changed color when it was very windy," said Hans, "yes, those eyes possessed the attraction of an extremely powerful magnet. I don't know if you've ever had the experience while talking to a person who has a pronounced defect in an eye—such as being cross-eyed or even having a glass eye—of not really knowing exactly where to look, so that your gaze shifts from one place to another in an obvious show of discomfort. Yes, I suppose that happens to a lot of people. The same thing happened with Olga, only in reverse. I'd feel observed, spied on from the depths of her pupils. And the discomfort of this observation was such that it really felt as though a whirlwind were dragging you *inside*, into its center. Yes, Olga's eyes would keep absorbing you, and within a few minutes of being in her presence—this would always happen to me—I'd feel totally immersed in that vertiginous spiral. Yes, I think I told you I'd explain this matter of the wind and Olga. Very well," Hans said, "I won't add or omit a thing, she herself was the one who told me this one night, or rather, one early morning, when autumn was still in full flurry. Yes. Have you ever heard about the *South Wind*?" Hans suddenly asked, and I was taken entirely by surprise, for I realized he had directed the question to me, rather than to himself, as he had done a couple of times before during the walk. Now he was expecting a specific response, but I could do no more than shake my head. "I see. It's unusual for people to know anything about it, even though it has quite a tradition, I mean in various places in the north it's firmly established in some folk traditions. Well, I don't know if you're aware that Olga was born in that part of the country, yes, very near Lübeck, in a little fishing village called Einsenau. It doesn't even appear on many maps, of course," Hans said, "one *couldn't* expect anything else of the place where she was born. In any event, according to her, in those coastal regions there occurs a rare meteorological phenomenon (to give it some sort of name) that *always* takes place during the autumn months, not *every* autumn, however, but rather every *few* autumns. She told me that it has to do with enormous masses of wind that apparently originate in Central Europe and arrive in those northern parts with a high index of insolation and nocturnal irradiation. Then," Hans continued, "when it arrives at Kiel Bay, that wind rapidly descends toward the sea, skirting the coastal areas, heading always toward Lübeck. It's during this descent, Olga told me, that it gains heat, at a rate of approximately one degree for every hundred meters. It seems that this type of hot, dry wind is also recorded in some regions of the Alps, where it is known as the 'föhn effect.' Yes, its principal characteristic," said Hans, "—and I'm repeating this story literally, just as she herself told it to me—its principal characteristic, I was saying, is that it hastens the ripening process of the fruits on the trees, especially chestnuts, which is why it's also known as the 'chestnut wind.' Yes, that's one part of the legend, I mean, of the reality the South Wind must apparently be in those regions, for among the peasants of the interior and the fishermen of the coast, it also has a reputation for causing an unmistakable sultriness in the atmosphere at a season when the temperature is very low. Yes, that night Olga talked in that relentless way I mentioned a while ago, I suppose you recall. According to her," Hans said, "the landscape takes on an astonishing translucency, almost crystalline, and if you fix your gaze on it, Olga said, it prolongs the horizon out to the infinite and what is *remote* seems *near*. It's at twilight, it seems, when the South Wind flaunts all its magic, something only the inhabitants of the region can recognize. I don't know if you follow me. That, as I was saying, is one part of the legend about the South Wind, but the *other* part," said Hans, "—the one gradually and sensually flowing from Olga's lips, from those two oval reefs of muted red coral on that night filled with alcohol and half-uttered phrases—the other part, I was saying, is no doubt the most appealing and the one that was more closely related to herself, to the air of mystery that seemed to enfold her. Since time immemorial, Olga said, in all those territories around Kiel Bay, all the way to Lübeck and Neumünster (encompassing, of course, the little seaside hamlet, to use her words, that was Einsenau), there have been widespread oral traditions that recount terrible things about the influence of the South Wind on people's nervous systems, especially those people who for one reason or another might be classified as more temperamental. Yes," said Hans, "according to Olga that odd phenomenon—though common as far as she's concerned—completely unhinges the most prudent minds. Yes, she said that when the South Wind blows, men are more prone to *violence* or rashness and women, in contrast, become more *affectionate* than usual, much more. A kind of collective sensual bewitchment, Olga said, yes, that's what she said: 'It's easier for us to be

tender and show affection,' she said, 'the body, the serene vibration of the atmosphere, that warm, sticky humidity all demand it, creating a sort of internal emptiness right here,' Olga said, pointing to the center of her chest,
'that makes you *crave* sensations.' Yes, I remember I laughed," said Hans,
"but now I realize it was nervous laughter. I've never been so nervous before
Olga as I was on that occasion, I think because that night she wasn't herself
but *someone else*, I don't know how to explain it. You should have seen her
while she was telling me, 'That wind sows a bit of madness in the head and
a lot of fire in the heart.' Yes, her head was resting on her hand and her hair
fell to one side, disheveled. With the palm of her hand pressed against her
temple, her eyes looked more slanted than usual. Yes, I believe I saw something dark and terrible in her. I laughed, as I said, but Olga insisted it was a
very serious matter. Yes, all at once she turned solemn. 'If we were in Einsenau you wouldn't laugh,' she said, and later she affirmed that at some point
in the past the legislators and judges of those parts deemed the blowing of
the South Wind an extenuating circumstance in certain kinds of crimes
committed during those periods. And it was clear, I think, just what she
meant by *certain kinds* of crimes, although she never actually told me. Perhaps she never knew herself, though she certainly must have imagined it, like
all the women in that place. Yes, and I felt that the earth was slowly beginning
to swallow me up," Hans said, "when Olga explained to me how apparently
in the woodlands of the interior it was said that there was a woman, a sort of
witch or nymph who during those autumn days entices men and, through
unimaginable wiles, makes them succumb. A kind of cruel harpy, I said, yes,
and I remember that Olga's expression became grave, almost melancholy,
and she replied: 'No, a lady, the most beautiful of all, the one before whom
all men kneel,' and then, while she tucked a lock of hair behind her ear, she
added, 'Some fishermen also claim they've seen her on evenings when the
South Wind blows strongly. Of course, all these are legends,' she said, tracing
a candid smile, 'but the truth is that the ancient history, and even the more
recent history of Einsenau and other nearby towns is full of dramatic inci-
dents connected with everything I'm telling you.' Yes, I remember that at
least half the whiskey was still left in her glass. And it was there and gone. She
took a swig and the whiskey vanished. Yes, she didn't make the least fuss
about it, and I didn't see her swallowing it, either, believe me, it's true: I didn't

see her swallow it, I mean I couldn't observe any movement of her throat that might indicate that a fair amount of liquid had passed down it. I was *nailed* to my chair," Hans said, "unable to shake off my amazement and she, seeing me like that, smiled again and added: 'Naturally, you're free to believe it or not.' As a matter of fact, that was the last time I saw her smile that night, the last. I don't know what happened afterward, but I imagine we must have gone to another place, I don't know. You may perhaps be interested in knowing what happened to me, I mean, getting some idea of the impression that conversation made on me. Some while after talking about all this, as I was about to say, we parted. Everything was as usual until, at nearly five o'clock in the morning, I got home. I know only that I felt as if I were floating, exhausted, deeply exhausted, but not sleepy. I went to bed and very soon *knew* I wouldn't sleep, that it would be impossible for me to sleep that night. And so it was," Hans said, "I remember I spent the rest of the night reading. The serious thing is that the same thing happened the following night. I didn't sleep even a single minute. They were two nights without a wink, but fortunately the next day was a Saturday and I had the entire weekend ahead of me to sleep, which I did almost without being aware of it. Yes, but the curious thing was not that—though on the other hand it had never happened before, I mean, spending two entire nights without sleeping, mulling over many issues, including Olga, of course—what was curious, as I was saying, was *what happened* when I awoke, I think at about six or seven on Sunday evening. Yes, before then I had gotten up half-asleep a couple of times, wandering about the house while eating something and then going back to bed. But when I really awoke," Hans said, "when I opened my eyes and sensed a slight headache, realizing at the same time that I wouldn't go back to sleep, the first thing I recall doing was searching among some papers in my nightstand. Yes, I pulled out an appointment book and began leafing through it. At last I found what I wanted: a pocket calendar. I don't quite know why I must have wanted to see the date on that calendar, possibly to see on what days the Christmas holidays would fall, I don't know, the truth is, I was merely obeying a very strong internal impulse. I looked at the current month, yes," Hans said, "I saw that it was November, the middle of November. Autumn, I thought to myself. And then, as if it were an apparition, I remembered that Olga, on the last night we'd seen each other—I mean, the evening of her curious revelation, a story I realize she had on several occasions put off telling me, for what reason I don't know—at the end of that evening, I was about to say, she remarked that her parents had written to her from Lübeck (as that's where they live), saying that everything was as usual in Einsenau, and also that the South Wind was the *strongest* the oldtimers could remember. 'You see, its wake must have reached this far,' she said. It was then, precisely then, I think, that I realized it was autumn. Yes, *autumn* and no other season. The impression this had on me, I recall, was such that I felt stunned for several minutes. Yes, I had a very peculiar sensation. Rather similar to coming close to having an accident, an accident that might befall you, that is, or some person you're watching. Yes, I'm talking about those first instants right after the *moment* when the accident might have taken place. And after that lapse," Hans said, "when I abruptly came out of that sort of stupor, I was gripped by a tremendous activity. What is certain," he said, "is that from that very moment I ceased to dwell on the coincidence between the current date, the weather in Einsenau, and what Olga had told me. Yes, I forgot all about it, giving it no further thought until a few weeks ago. I forgot everything *altogether*, as I said, but I think it's quite likely that this was due principally—besides being an obviously unconscious desire not to make room in my memory for what she told me—to the fact that Olga recounted many things of that *nature* and in that *tone*, yes, things that filled me with wonder and which I, of course, didn't entirely understand. Yes," said Hans, "I suppose it had to do with the manner in which Olga related specific things. The geometrical proportions of her arms, the sway of her neck, everything about her was the way it should be, just as it should be and no other way. Yes, Olga let long silences elapse while talking about those specific things. And within those dead *tempos*," Hans said, "one could construe a whole universe of suppositions. She would abruptly freeze as if paralyzed, only to suddenly drop a bombshell, a bombshell that could fall from her voice or from one of her gestures. Yes, her explanation about the South Wind was in that vein. And it was no different whenever she referred to her friend Rose Marie Zucksmeister, who died in the bloom of adolescence, although now that I think about it, that was actually a subject she tried to avoid as much as possible. At some point," Hans said, "I wanted to know more about that friendship, but Olga always closed up like a clam and refused to pursue it. I recall asking her

whether her friend's death had resulted from an accident, but she only answered with a flat 'No, from an illness.' I wasn't able to ascertain when, how,
where, or from what *illness*, but this very fact, I think, may give you an idea
of Olga's reserve when dealing with certain matters she must have deemed
of a personal nature. And I don't believe my interest in that girl, Rose Marie
Zucksmeister, arose out of a purely morbid instinct, no, not at all," he said, "I
hadn't a single reason for it. Although I expect the topic attracted me because
I realized it was Olga's only *experience* with death," said Hans, "yes, the only
time death had come near Olga, had grazed her. But as I was saying, Olga's
reticence on that occasion was considerable. Yes, she'd become really enigmatic when she peered into that neutral point of the void, which I've never
managed to locate anywhere, even only instants after she'd stared into it, for
it seemed to evaporate at once. Although the fact is, everything ever said or
done by Olga seemed to evaporate at once. Yes, whenever she mentioned the
word 'heart,' one had the feeling it wasn't she who had pronounced it. Or, if
she had, it was undoubtedly owing to a ventriloquy trick. Notwithstanding
that, as a closing to the few written messages she sent me, she would put 'with
all my heart.' Yes," Hans said, "I found the terms *heart* and *Olga*, if not antagonistic (which I really don't think they were), at least strange, somewhat
aleatory—I mean, aleatory with respect to each other. If I wanted to annoy
her—always in jest, of course—I'd call her 'heart of ice,' and she invariably
became annoyed. Yes. Just the same way she always got annoyed with the little black ball of the gear shift in her damned yellow Volkswagen or refused
sugar for her coffee with an angelic expression. *Heart of ice.* I don't know,"
Hans said, "perhaps at bottom it was aggression on my part. As far as she was
concerned, calling her that meant dubbing her insensitive, an idea that had
the power to depress her deeply, I would even say suspiciously. Because I
think anyone who didn't consider herself insensitive, I mean completely bereft of sensitivity, would attach no importance to it at all, no matter how
much she might be called that. Yes, that's what I think. But in spite of it all,"
said Hans, "I believe that was a happy period, yes, I suppose I must have experienced that phase as an enormously happy moment, although quite *agonizing* as well, I mean agonizing for me, because I doubt that she, that Olga
experienced it as anything beyond a somewhat conflictive moment. Yes,"
Hans said, "agony versus conflict. There lies the dilemma. The whole thing,

I suppose, was very disproportionate. I knew about her obsessions, which could have been a trump card up my sleeve, but wasn't. I'm talking about trying to get the scales of conflict and agony to tip more in my favor. Yes, Olga always feared I might become a true *conflict* in her life, which indeed I suppose I was, and I was obsessed with the idea of getting her to cease being an *agony*, which she undoubtedly was as well, from the beginning. I don't know why I didn't manage to channel or to benefit from her obsessions, but the fact remains that I didn't. And she was obsessed," said Hans, "by many things: the ones that secretly drove her to bite her nails, certain aspects of the life she shared with that Sömmering fellow. Yes, she was obsessed by many more things than she probably realized, and I suppose she demonstrated her intelligence by not dwelling on them too much. Yes," Hans said, "Olga lived surrounded by obsessions both humble and great, from the impossibility of finding a job that was even faintly creative, to the awareness of her own beauty, to crocodiles. Yes, crocodiles were part of her great mania in the realm of evil and misfortune. Crocodiles would quite often appear in her dreams, yes, crocodiles everywhere. And she was also obsessed by particular images from her past: a man in a raincoat whom she saw praying in a church when she was still very young; the relationship with her parents who, though they lived in Lübeck, as I mentioned before, had left a profound mark on her; or her scant, not to say nonexistent, ability to resist alcoholic beverages, although perhaps the latter *scared* rather than obsessed her. Yes, and at times I actually thought she was beginning to worry quite a bit, I mean, to be *obsessed* with the gradual turn our relationship was taking. In this sense I remember her reacting peevishly a couple of times, telling me a platonic friendship like ours struck her as ridiculous. Yes, that's how she categorized it. I asked her, I think, whether she meant the word 'platonic' in the ideal sense or in the sense commonly ascribed to the term, but by then, I remember, in an instant, her attitude had already changed and she was simply laughing. Yes, it was after knowing Olga well—I mean knowing her very well, or I suppose very well—that I began to realize *something* was going on when she laughed. Yes," said Hans, "and the more she laughed, the more consistently she laughed, the more there was something going on inside her. Because Olga used to laugh in *disparate* situations, I mean, at any gibberish I'd say or because she truly was nervous. But I don't know, all that belongs to the past, and the past, as somebody once said, is indivisible. Yes, to a past that seems remote to me now, though in fact it happened almost yesterday, or rather, this past autumn, last autumn. Yes, my *last* autumn," Hans said, and then I saw him taking several steps to the right and losing himself among some bushes. I stood with my hands in my pockets, indecisive, in the middle of the road we'd been following. Hans breathed deeply, letting his head fall back a few inches. At that moment I realized the light had noticeably waned. We were already in the small larch forest, and I occupied myself by taking in the surroundings. Through a clearing I could descry the walls of the sanatorium. "Well, it's about time we head back, or we'll soon have difficulty finding our way," Hans said, shrugging his shoulders in a gesture of resignation. "Yes, I usually come this far on my daily walks, whether it rains or it's hot, in a raincoat or in short sleeves. This is the place I head for. My *goal*, I suppose, though at times I've gone a bit farther in that direction," he said, indicating a vague spot through the branches, "yes, going for a walk is one of the healthiest pastimes there are. Since you're alone with yourself, there's no possibility of failure, I mean, as long as one isn't carrying failure within: the *concept of failure*. The truth is Olga and I didn't walk as much as I would have liked. No, far from it. But in spite of that," he said, "there are walks I'll never be able to forget. One in particular. We were coming down from a small deserted cabin located atop the Itsaspheim cliffs, by Oricksbald beach. That afternoon, numb with cold, we drank a toast with French champagne, and of course she never stopped laughing," Hans said. "Yes, I remember that at some point our hands grazed against each other in a fortuitous way—well, *almost* fortuitous. Olga started trembling, but soon after she took a deep breath and stopped. I never knew whether she had trembled because of the *cold* or because of *something else*, another sensation that had nothing to do with the cold. A sensation that, coming from anyone else, I would have understood and been able to define with no problem, but which in her I was unable to gauge, I mean, to understand what had made her tremble. It wasn't the caress itself, I'm positive of that. In any event, that happened at the beginning, I think, one of the first times we got together. It's curious, I realize I'm nearly always telling you about events that occurred at the *beginning* and not at the *end*. I don't know," Hans said, "it may be that I've always mentally refused to accept that end, or perhaps it might be that the phase after the beginning was too confusing to understand anything about. Yes, I've never understood the way situations come to an end, I've quite often been distressed by such denouements. I'm much more excited about *plots*, or even thinking about the *possibilities* for the denouement. It's always been so, with movies, with books, everything. And in that sense," Hans said, "every encounter, every situation involving Olga meant a new *denouement*. And the reason, I repeat, is that I was essentially unaware of the elements that were brought into play in Olga's thoughts and above all, her feelings. The truth is, I never knew a thing about her, about her feelings, not only toward me but toward everything. For example, I never quite grasped why she should be so thoroughly disgruntled by those horoscopes I dedicated to her in the local paper. As far as I was concerned, they were a joke like any other. Just one more. I think they could be regarded as important, on account of so many suggestive details about the absurdities I was willing to commit or was in fact already committing because of her—although of no real consequence. Who knows," Hans said, "that's why sometimes I say, I mean when I'm working I tell myself (though now I am telling you, as well) that Olga always disoriented me, yes, I suspect she was a few steps ahead of me. And that's why—if we're going to be dealing with specific things, and in saying *things* I'm referring, naturally, to deeds, such as my gifts would be—that is why, I was saying, I affirm that I'm incapable of knowing whether anything really happened between Olga and me, I mean in the sense that one could suppose something really does end up happening between a man and a woman when there are certain kinds of *contacts* between them. Yes," said Hans, "because indeed there were: *contacts* between Olga and me. At all levels and in every respect. But I don't know, the truth is I've thought about them so many times—not only in the sanatorium but also before coming here—that by now, I must be incapable of knowing whether I've imagined any of those contacts. Yes, that's why I say I'd rather not talk or even think about them, because I know that to think about them is to ponder them all the way to their *ultimate consequences*. And I don't know what such ultimate consequences might be," Hans said, "I suppose it must be something like an avalanche of fantasy—all the fantasy a mind aching and with obvious symptoms of disturbance is capable of—sliding like molten lava over reality," said Hans, and what he said made me shudder. I realized, on the one hand, that it had been a while since we had begun walking back, at in fact a much brisker pace than on the way out. On the other hand the words 'avalanche' and 'lava' were still resonating in my mind. I was stunned by how swiftly Hans had shifted from one image to the next, and also by his tone when defining his own condition as afflicted with "obvious symptoms of disturbance," something I would have flatly denied at that time. I let myself be led, both physically and mentally, like an automaton, for there was really nothing I could do to escape the personal magnetism he emanated, on the one hand, and the curiosity aroused in me by everything he was telling me on the other. "Reality, reality," Hans repeated as though he were chewing the words, "I suppose reality is the bride of death. And the truth is that our realities, I mean Olga's reality and mine, clashed spectacularly, I'd even say head-on. Yes," Hans said, "and I think my reality was *consumed* when I met her. Because Olga was incandescent magma emerging from the earth. She possessed a special power of attraction, and not until some time after we stopped seeing each other did I realize the destructive potential not only of that power of attraction (for after all it was nothing more than a psychological attribute like any other) but even of the memory of that power of attraction, or better yet," Hans said, "the presence of her characteristic power in my memory. And in this regard I think it would be better to forget forever her expression when I asked her, in a tone intended to be convincing: 'What woman could I look in the face after having known you?' But I only think about it, because in fact the more I think I should forget that face, the more its smiling image haunts me. And the same thing happens when I think about her telling me, in reference to our relationship and its presumed ending (to which I alluded from time to time, terrified that it might actually happen), 'It would be very sad, the end of something never begun.' Yes, that's what she said. Because for her, I suppose, our relationship never quite fully began. She didn't consider it begun because, for such a thing to have occurred, it would have needed to be she rather than I who took the *initiative*. Yes," Hans said, "my enchantment with Olga kept growing until finally it turned into a gigantic monster, a many-headed hydra that every day would feed on my entrails, on my mind. Yes, above all on my mind. On the bowels of my mind. I think it was just around that time when I dropped nearly ten kilos, yes, that's why I say that the creature Olga *transferred* into me devoured the best within me, the best in both a physical and a mental sense. And meanwhile I remained pretty much the same throughout, trying to put on an interested face and a suitable smile, always still as an idiot, absorbed in the dance of her immense eyelashes (like the wings of a condor soaring proudly through clear skies), and looking at her glistening lips as she told me how much she liked things left half-finished. 'Like those stories we overhear on the street, always half-finished, faces half-seen, half-finished phrases that leave us wondering,' that's what she'd say, yes. And I like an idiot, I repeat, as though in a coma, incapable of *reacting* as she might perhaps have wished I should. And the truth is that I was a passive being, a totally passive creature, waiting for her to finally carry out her threat of inviting me to dinner in Winschoten, on 'the other side' of the border. As though something mysterious were going to *happen* on that 'other side.' I'm still waiting for that dinner," Hans said, "yes, I'll wake up with a start some nights with one thought etched in my mind: to dine with her in Winschoten. 'I know a couple of places there, but I'll take you to a *different* one, which they tell me is better,' she said, yes. I believed her, just as I believed that some day I'd be able to glimpse one of those follies she threatened me with from time to time. 'I am not strict, Hans, I'm really quite *easy*.' I don't know, when I think about it, you see, an immense curtain of fog obscures everything else: reality, my own history, everything. It's as though nothing existed save those instants that time after time have delivered me from absolute nothingness. To meet Olga was to *yearn* instantly for her and thus to sink into the mire, into the bog of a relative void. It's only time, I mean, the passing of time exerting a great strain on my memory, that slowly ushers me into that other mire which is now the absolute void. I don't know," Hans said, "it's as though I were in a swamp and my legs had become entangled with algae, as though that algae were dragging me downward. Everything fits, everything seems to have been written since the beginning," he said. "I told you earlier about the South Wind and the tremendous impression that story made on me, didn't I? Well, when I was little, you know, when I was living with my parents, that is, I felt even then a special propensity for sleeping in a room that wasn't mine, located, moreover, on the other side of the house and which no one wanted because the wind could be heard perpetually blowing. In winter, as a matter of fact, its howling could be infernal. At any rate," Hans said, "whenever I had to sleep there for some reason, I spent the night huddled in a corner, with my eyes wide open, staring at the contour of the window, listening to the wind's continual soliloquy. Yes," he said, "I called it *the wind room*, and I can assure you that the presence of that room was always in my unconscious. Yes, I tried finding a place with similar characteristics in several houses I've lived in since. But I was telling you that the struggle against Olga was a struggle against myself and against oblivion, I mean against the awareness of oblivion I expected to fall into even then, and I'm talking about practically every time we saw each other. Yes," Hans said, "I constantly wanted to *forget* about things that pertained to her. Sometimes, dazed by the uproar from the marble, overtaken by weariness and fatigue, sleepy, I think I'm about to attain it, I mean, to begin to see those features fading away, the features of the experiences we shared together. But when it's about to happen," he said, "suddenly her face emerges again, that sort of triangle that rather resembles the figures Modigliani painted (as I once told her), that face of a virgin in a Byzantine icon. Nor am I able to forget, however much I try, one evening when I slipped my green raincoat over her shoulders. It was quite cold and she wasn't properly covered. Because Olga usually went about quite unprotected, and I don't know to what extent such an idiosyncrasy could be ascribed to carelessness or negligence, given that she was irremediably cold and came from a cold place like the northern part of the country. I'm rather inclined to think that on many occasions it had to do with a genuine need to *be* protected. Yes," Hans said, "the fact is, she liked that raincoat and it didn't look at all bad on her, just a bit large in the arms. I don't remember if it was when I was taking it off her that I told her that seeing her wrapped in that garment of mine gave me the feeling it was *I* who was embracing her. She simply replied: 'Yes.' I hadn't actually asked her if she'd had that feeling, but Olga replied, saying yes. And what matters is not what she said but *how* she said it. I expect it was moments like those that made me begin to see things in a really distorted manner, yes, totally *distorted*, to lose not only momentary control of situations but to lose track of reality. I'm not exaggerating, well, I suppose I'm not exaggerating," Hans said, "all that was a perpetual challenge before what ought to have happened next between Olga and me, which sometimes did happen and others not, something that, in any case, I suppose only *half-happened*, since I don't think there is anything that can happen between two individuals in a total manner,

there are always risks and doubts, transgressed limits and new goals to attain," Hans said, "something that for reasons unknown to me was always beyond my will, I mean, the scope of my will, but which at the same time made
me feel I was on a tightwire, the tightwire that was my only floor over the
void: the possibility of being able to penetrate her soul—and allow me to use
that expression, for I think it may give you some idea of what my *intentions*
were, something that she in fact asked me about continuously for months. I
didn't know then how to respond, while now, giving my thoughts free rein
like this, it's come out all by itself. Curious," Hans said, "this is an idea that
still needs to ripen. The tightwire, too, is an idea that comes quite close to that
whole situation. Yes, me, the great trapeze artist. I don't know, the truth is,
sometimes I came to believe that Olga was a really perverse being, truly ma-
lignant, who played with me just the way an angry child does with a toy he
has a special passion for," Hans said, "yes, sharp, precise blows to those parts
of the toy the child thinks might hurt it most. At some moments I felt jerked
about by Olga. And in that regard I think what happened with the key represented the height of the *perversity* I'm speaking about. I also suspect it
wasn't a conscious attitude on her part, but I'm sure she entered that realm
in response to some specific mechanism of her thoughts. Yes, as I said, Olga
studied psychology, that was a subject she must necessarily have mastered, I
don't know, I suppose she must have mastered it. In any event, one evening,
while we were having a drink, I remember her pulling from her bag the immense bunch of keys she always carried with her. I recognized that bunch
from having seen it on other occasions, yes, but this time Olga removed it
from her bag with special care, gently, almost in a show of prestidigitation.
She removed it so as to twist it about in her hands," Hans said, "yes, and I remember that on that evening her face and mine, her mouth and mine were
very near, especially *near*. As a matter of fact I don't recall ever having seen
her so tender. Yes, I suppose she felt comfortable with me that evening. It's as
though I could see it now," said Hans, still walking at a good pace and darting
brief, oblique glances at me so as to verify whether I was still abreast or had
lagged behind. "As I said, she took out her ring of keys and, without my having asked a thing about them, began to enumerate what each one was for.
Evidently," Hans said, "there were keys there that she hadn't used for years.
Yes, I think it was then that her fingers chose *one* among them all, and she

set it apart from the others as if it burned, poised at her fingertips. Then she said she hadn't any idea what that key might open. I remember wanting to possess that key at once. I assure you there was nothing in the world I desired more. Without that key, I think, I'd find it impossible to go on living, and I was almost on the verge of telling her so, but I held back. Yes, I aided her in her mental survey intended to ascertain the role of that mysterious key, with its intense metallic sheen yet lacking a past, about which Olga was uncertain even as to how and when it might have come into her handbag. She then began to make fantastic conjectures about the key, yes, with her lips ever closer to mine," Hans said. "The way she touched the key was ineffable, yes, I think she caressed it. I believe I told her that a key could be a very sensual, a definitely sensual, object, and that it therefore seemed dangerous to me that a decent girl like herself, I said, should carry a *definitely* sensual object in her handbag. She laughed at the joke, but half-heartedly, in a strange, syncopated manner, so much so that for a few seconds I was left wondering whether my remark might have displeased her. But no, Olga seemed distracted, I could have sworn even tense, as though expecting me to say something else. Yes, and I," Hans said, "mechanically as well, asked her to give me the key. I think normally I would never have asked her for anything like that, in such a direct, even abrupt fashion, but that time I did. 'I've always been fond of things that have no destiny,' I said. Yes, and it was absolutely true besides. In any event Olga, for her part, also did something I suppose she'd never have done under normal circumstances. She gave it to me at once, she almost *threw* it at me, I mean, she almost flung the key ring at me. Yes, it took us another several minutes to be able to slip it off the metal ring where it hung with the rest of the keys. Our hands fumbled together for quite a while. They were sweating. Yes. At that moment I was really thrilled about possessing that key of Olga's, a key (she herself said rather nervously) she had already noticed at some point, though without recollecting its function, yet she didn't actually *dare* to remove it, to separate it from the bunch. I expect that was one of the most special, indefinable instants I shared with Olga. Yes, in opposition to her special *moments* I had my special *instants*. I already mentioned there was something instantaneous about Olga. I was feeling and speaking in a special code, and for once, I think, perhaps just once, she spoke and thought in the same code. As to whether she could feel, I no longer dare surmise, but it's very likely she could; the fact is that in Olga as a rule all feeling ended up crushed by the weight of what she was thinking. By what she used to label 'my bloody realism.' Yes," Hans said, "I suppose that was one of the most *electric* moments in our relationship. There were others that were more *fiery* and, of course, richer in *nuances*," Hans said striving for accuracy in the words he chose to express himself, which he had done very rarely during the course of the walk. "With the key already in my hands I asked her, 'What does this key open, Olga?' She looked at me, saying nothing, and after a while I could hear a timid 'I don't know.' I insisted, not failing to notice I was seething inside. 'Surely it must *open* something of yours. Please tell me what it is.' And she replied, 'Possibly.' Then Olga averted her gaze. It was the first time since we had met that she'd made that gesture. For a long while her eyes watched the ice cubes floating in her whiskey. Yes, I remember simultaneously tightening my jaw and the fist holding the key. Never again," Hans said, "did we discuss that key. It wasn't necessary, I expect. I carry it with me always, it's my talisman. That same evening, upon arriving home, I thought about what to do with the key," he said, "yes, I spent hours attempting to find a place for it, a stable and *secure* place. Not even the most sophisticated armored safe in the world would have reassured me. I had the feeling they'd come to steal it from me, yes, that some burglars would break into the house and, instead of taking other valuables, they'd take that very key, the only thing of Olga's I had. Well, I had other things, yes, but that key was Olga herself, Olga in the shape of a key. Because if Olga had to be turned into an object, surely her fate was to be a key. Yes, or a crown," Hans said. "But more likely a key. The fact is that my fear of losing it was fairly justified, I mean, it was actually the *second* talisman or fetish I had gotten from her. Yes, before that, and not without insisting and harassing her for weeks on end, I'd persuaded her to give me a photograph of herself. Quite childish, I suppose, but as necessary as eating, I mean, necessary for me," Hans said, "absolutely necessary. One evening, I finally got her to bring me the photograph. It had been taken several years before, during a trip to Italy. A friend, so she said, had taken the photo in Naples. She had on a sort of ski cap that covered her hair. I don't know," Hans said, "some days before, she'd told me that was her *favorite* photograph, the one in which she looked best. The truth is that when I had it before me, I didn't entirely recognize that face looking with surprise into the eye of the camera. Olga in the flesh was much, undoubtedly much more beautiful, I think, than on that piece of paper. I suppose I confined myself to thanking her and showing little more than a reasonable enthusiasm. Well," Hans said, "inwardly I felt somewhat rebellious because it wasn't *the photo* of her I desired, the one I had imagined so often that I could swear it already possessed a certain substance in my mind. But I slipped it into a pocket and completely forgot about it. The point is, as soon as I arrived home a few hours later, I realized that the photograph was no longer in my pocket. It was lost. Lost *forever*," Hans said as he kept walking, giving those last words a pronounced emphasis. "I supppose I felt terribly chagrined, yes, I recall feeling that way. It was as if the possibility of holding on to Olga, to something of hers, had vanished forever, I don't know if you follow me. And I couldn't help feeling guilty about the fact that I had inwardly rebelled upon my first glimpse of that photo. Yes, a punishment, I realize it was a downright *punishment*. I think somehow or other I brought about the loss, I don't know how, but I must have done. That Olga, the one in the photograph, was not the one I knew. And it was also a lesson, yes," Hans said, "a lesson in humility, a remedy that curbed my egotism, at least partly and for a while. Yes, one of the great specters that hovered above us, or hovered over me (and I suspect this is something that no one who has a certain need to see another person can avoid), one of those specters, the one with the greatest reach, to my mind, was *possessiveness*. Yes, the tomb of passion, the chloroform that ruins, that corrodes all vestiges of normal strife in love," Hans said, remaining abstracted for a few moments, "accursed word, accursed concept that always ravages us insidiously. On top of my stupid, childish egotism in wanting to have a photo of her (something I realize was totally inappropriate, since at that time we were seeing each other often, quite often), on top of that absurd caprice of desiring her picture was added, I think, the even more stupid one that the picture should further be *exactly* like the ideal picture of Olga I had conjured up. Yes, I suspect it was a feeling of possessiveness that was almost homicidal, and I mean that in the emotional sense of the term. Possessiveness is rather like a beard. Or like, in the case of women, having prominent breasts. As adolescents we want more than anything in the world to have our beards grow, we regard our elders with admiration and envy because they have what we yearn for. Countless boys have rubbed their faces with pumice stone to make their beards appear sooner. We study our side-burns, upper lip, and chin with surgical attention. And later, when the beard accompanies us day after day, we no longer know what to do with it. That's how it is, I think, with possessiveness in love. Perhaps the same thing happens to a lot of people with fame, I mean, with the fact of being famous. Once they've attained it, they don't know in what corner of the world to hide. I don't know if you follow me," Hans said, "I was telling you that losing Olga's picture on the very evening she had given it to me made me think a lot about things, and represented a real antidote to my egotism. Which doesn't mean I didn't desire to have something of hers, and thus the possibility of possessing that key," Hans said, his eyes gleaming, "opened new doors for me, yes, doors that led to unsuspected *chambers*. That's why, the day after Olga gave it to me, I bought a metal chain made of very durable material and fastened it around my neck. Yes, look," Hans said, extracting his hands from the pockets of his sweat suit and showing me something that hung from his neck, "you can see it here, I always wear it. Furthermore, when I had it sealed shut, I made them adjust it in such a way as to make it impossible to slip it over my head. You see? It won't come off," Hans said, making an upward movement with the chain to illustrate what he meant, "it *stops* at the chin. I'm comfortable with it. When I shower, while sleeping, it's always with me. Yes, I'm aware of its cold contact and that spurs on my thinking. Yes, I reconstruct the scene about the key ten, a hundred, innumerable times. It's like a movie, though not always in color. There are times," Hans said, "when I see those images in black and white. Yes, as though it were an old movie, a very old one. After all, I think, that sensation of being with me, of being there, I mean, of Olga being there, in the key, is nothing but a transposition of what she was when she was wholly, physically present. Loving her came to be an instinctive act, or perhaps I should say an instinctive *sensation*. Yes, I wouldn't have known how to do anything else. But there are several levels of instinctive sensations, some of which arise, I think, from an instinctive act. In the case of experienced drivers, for example, it would be like stepping on the clutch every time they change gears. No one gives any thought to that gesture. You simply do it. But I don't believe it's a matter of *pure* instinct, because a stiff clutch, or stepping on it with an injured foot, or any other reason, may suddenly make us *aware* of that clutch pedal, I mean physically aware.

Pure instinct would be, in the ultimate instance, the ongoing but intermittent act of blinking. Yes, every blink is the will of life to go on being that essential," Hans said. "Each blink signifies a response in the face of total inertia, I mean, before the total and definitive inertia of death, yes," he said, "and
of sleep. But that's assuming we don't blink in the midst of sleep, even
slightly and every so often, and further assuming that sleep is something
more than the outer gates of death. Yes, *that which we are*, which we cannot
renounce, which we do because anything else lies at the fringes of thought.
Pure instinct," Hans said, "that's what Olga was for me, that's what it was to
love her. When she wasn't there, everything was left shrouded in darkness.
A desert in the midst of a sandstorm. Yes," he said, "and when she was there
I felt nimble and cheerful as a circus acrobat, I felt like doing somersaults in
the air. I don't know, I think that, although I concealed it, I really felt as over-
joyed in her presence as those shaggy little dogs that play with a pillow, chewing on it and shaking it furiously, knowing that in so doing they elicit the
gratification and enjoyment of their masters. She my mistress, always, without a doubt," Hans said, "and I sometimes the little dog and others not even
that, only the pillow. All that notwithstanding, I actually felt the utmost
pride at being and feeling I was a pillow, because I wasn't just any pillow, no,
I was *her pillow*, the fluffy pillow on which who knows whether she slept,
was sleeping, or could at some time have slept a placid spell. The fact is that
this key was my point of contact with everything, and I suppose anyone
wanting to snatch this key from me would have to saw through the chain,
and I assure you it's quite strong. Yes, I asked for the *strongest*. 'I want something that won't break,' I said, 'I don't care how heavy, only how sturdy it is.'
Yes, I vaguely recall the features of the young man in the hardware store I
went into in order to buy the chain and have it sealed. He was surprised that
I should want to hang a common, ordinary key from it. That's what he said,
but I explained to him that it was a whim like any other. Perhaps at bottom
Olga herself was a whim, though I think some whims may be very harmful,
yes, very hazardous. But I didn't tell the young man that, no, I remember
thinking it, I even considered saying it, though in the end I didn't. Yes," Hans
said, "it truly was a common, ordinary key, there was nothing special about
it, except that it looked brand-new and, therefore, as I mentioned, it shone
quite brightly if one held it up to the light, but that young man said 'com-

mon, ordinary' with an ingenuous tone that greatly disturbed me. Normally I would have taken that as an insult, I expect, but that young man had no way of knowing what I knew. Yes, I suppose at the time I could still analyze such situations more or less objectively. *Common, ordinary*, he said. *A whim*, I insisted, simply a whim, moreover a whim for which I'd be charged a tidy sum because, as I told you, I'd asked for the best chain, the sturdiest. 'Say, you want to be buried with it, right?' the young man asked jokingly. It was an untoward remark, in rather poor taste, yet made without malice. 'Yes,' I said. I meant it, I really *meant* it. And the truth is I've spent perhaps hundreds upon hundreds of hours wondering what Olga's key (this key I carry about like one more part of my body) might open. I've conjectured until I was dazed as to what secret of Olga's one might gain access to with this key. Yes," Hans said, "but I always wound up dazed, as I said, simply dazed. At first, perhaps two or three times, musing while half-asleep about the key that by then I carried with me everywhere, I even became excited, I mean *physically* excited, noticing an unmistakable stirring in my blood, in my entire body. It was an odd sensation. It vanished swiftly in a veritable avalanche of images. Yes, then a daze, an odd sort of stupor would come over me. Because thinking about her in those terms always left me totally *exhausted*. But I still keep Olga's key, yes, the key I know must unlock some mystery which has been obliterated even from her memory. I suspect Olga has never given another thought to that key, I'm certain of it, but I also know that some day, while talking about keys, or looking at keys, or making a copy of some key, or thinking about secrets and mysteries, she'll remember the key that for several years remained in her keeping. Yes, that's when she'll remember me, she'll remember my knees grazing hers, and my hands clasping it and my eyes looking at it when she gave it to me. I expect she'll never be able to see my mouth kissing it at the most unexpected moments, I mean, at those moments when I kiss this key. Yes, it's an automatic move, much like my *mental inclination* toward Olga, as though she and the memory of her marked my center of gravity. I slip my hand in through here, pull out the chain and give the key a quick kiss," Hans said, "as though this metallic object were my only link with nature, as I mentioned earlier. Yes, myself and nature: a minuscule bud amidst a phenomenal swarm, united by this minuscule metal object in the form of a key, which I've often thought was not really a key but *something else*. Yes, I think of this key as my treasure, the only thing I have. I suppose I must have more things, but in an etymological sense. I have or may have many other things, but I know that in reality this key is the only thing I have. If I were to be deprived of this key not only would I cease having it, which is obvious as long as one regards it as an object, but I'd *cease to be myself*. I don't know, I suppose it would be as though that part of Olga I still preserve here, within," Hans said, pointing to the chain with his index finger, "as though that part, I was saying, were to dissolve forever. And mind you, oftentimes I forget that I have the key with me, even a day or two may pass without my being aware the key is still here, just below my throat. You see, that tells me I'm very scattered, that *I, too*, am very scattered, something I discovered mostly after Olga admitted to me that she was *completely* scattered, which she must have repeated almost incessantly, so much so that I now suspect it was an excuse, I mean, that by reminding me how scattered she was, perhaps she meant to justify a certain *passivity* on her part in some situations. In any event, Olga helped me to realize that I'm one of those people who, when they're about to enter through a sliding glass door, always get confused and try to open the side of the door that *doesn't* move. I've never managed to open those doors in a single movement," Hans said. "But Olga, too, was scattered. Last winter, I remember, people were already going about all bundled up, and she hadn't yet noticed that the cold weather had arrived. Yes, as though she lived perpetually in a cloud. She once told me she *recognized* winter because of the pajamas, that's what she said. 'I'm suddenly aware of the presence of pajamas, of the feel of pajamas that have been in my bed for several days. That's when I tell myself: winter has arrived.' Yes, she was very scattered, but that, no doubt, enhanced her personal charm. From then on, I think, not only did I become aware of how scattered I was about so many things but, I suppose, I became even more scattered about many others of which, until that moment, I'd never taken any notice. I don't know, perhaps instead of saying 'scattered,' I should speak of it in terms of a gradual loss of my notion of reality," Hans said, "of a slow *dissolution* of my reality into the real, collective reality. Or, to make it thoroughly explicit, in terms of a non-existent insertion of the surrounding reality into my personal unreality, into the plane of my own unreality. Yes," Hans said, "I started to acquire habits I'd never had before, I'm talking about when I stopped seeing Olga or, more specifically, from the moment I realized I was going to stop seeing Olga because for her the situation had reached its *ceiling*, which she occasionally called its *limit*, challenging me to figure out what that limit was. The fact is that, in a general sense (and I certainly prefer not to dwell too much on this topic), I became aware of that deviation in Olga's course right at the moment when, after having agreed to have drinks, as on so many other occasions, she told me she was *abstaining*, yes, that for a certain period she preferred not to drink anything alcoholic. That was like severing the umbilical cord that joined us. Yes," Hans said, "but I was talking about the odd habits I acquired around that time. The ease with which I did those things was astounding, yes, as though I'd always done them. For example: I'd place my feet in a tub of hot water and salt, with very hot water, so hot it would burn me and then my feet would be livid for several hours afterward. 'That's a good way to relax,' someone had told me at some point. I think I did want to relax, somehow to *relax*, whatever the cost. And as I inserted or kept my feet in the water," Hans said, "I strove not to move a single muscle of my face, not one nerve, nothing, as though my face were not attached to my body. And at last I succeeded. Around that time, I think, I also realized I was incurring injuries and wounds, small injuries and little wounds, *voluntarily*. Yes, I realized that all those strange wounds—the tiny cuts I had from some weeks back, especially on my arms and legs, wounds I didn't exactly recall having inflicted anywhere—I myself had caused through something I instantly recognized as a suspicious negligence. And I realized it upon seeing myself trying to open a tin of food with a lame, rusty can opener that I'd already cut myself with while handling it on other occasions. I noticed how I grabbed the broken can opener and how bent I was on opening a tin. I saw how I cut the tip of my finger, felt the prick at the same time I saw a red drop emerge, and right then I recollected all or nearly all the past images of myself doing *inappropriate* things with objects that could cut me or cause wounds. Yes," Hans said, "I think it was one more way of punishing myself for something, an absurd way, I suppose, but one that little by little had ended up becoming a daily practice. And I say *practice* because I also realized then that I continually had red Mercurochrome stains on me, Band-Aids and gauze strips that I applied myself, very unskillfully in fact. Yes, it was a strange period, a period in which certain obsessions reached their peak. I don't know, I was often absorbed, too often I mean, much more often than during the period when I wasn't yet going out with her habitually, and also more often than when our encounters were more or less systematic. And that absorption, I think, was beginning to give rise to hallucinogenic effects and results. I'd look at the scrapings from a plateful of melon seeds, for example, and on it there *were* mice whose snouts and tails had been amputated, yes, horrible creatures with bulging eyes, their bodies transfixed. Yes," Hans said, "every seed was one of those creatures. I became obsessed by such things as observing the way in which the hinges of my garden gate would crush a snail, although in fact it wasn't being crushed at that moment. The sight of a snail being crushed by the gate, a sight I had witnessed some time before, would then be systematically *reproduced*. Everything was cause for disquiet, for suspicion: the strange grimaces a little girl made with her nose while eating a smoked ham sandwich in a delicatessen, the flashing of a traffic light in the street, the grayish smudge on a flower petal, everything," Hans said, "absolutely everything. Naturally I sought to relax, to calm down by every means at my disposal. I don't know, there have always been things that had the power to soothe me, yes," he said, "I think clocks, for example, have always had the effect of soothing me, the more clocks together the better. In that respect a watchmaker's shop, a watchmaker's workshop, would be *paradise* on earth. Another thing I find soothing is old people rummaging through garbage, I could spend hours on end watching them, yes, and also storms. A mighty storm usually leaves me exhausted but serene. The point, as I was saying, is that I avidly sought my own equilibrium. It was during that period, I suppose, when I stopped listening to the radio and the top forty hits, only to begin watching television with abandon. I want to make it clear, in case you haven't yet realized, that everything I did then was *at full throttle*, to employ an exaggerated expression they tend to use in sports jargon. Television, as I was saying, was also something of that sort. At first I'd wait until the end of programming, yet without including the farewell and sign-off segments in that distinctly masochistic activity. Later on I needed to watch, to feed myself with those images of farewell and sign-off too, even going so far as to sit for a while watching those bars that come up on the screen once the broadcast is over. In the end I became absorbed by the little white dot in the center of the screen that would appear when you pressed the Channel 3 button once the color bars came up. Yes, it was always early morning, I lived in an endless early morning full of fireworks, I mean, fireworks that arose spontaneously in my head," Hans said; "my days were reduced to meandering from one place to another without really knowing where I wanted to go. And at the office I was the embodiment of *internal* paroxysm. I would work with my gaze fixed on the papers, sensing Olga in each and every object, every obsessive minute of those hours when she was *there*. Yes, that's what I devoted myself to," Hans said, "to afternoons of wandering through the streets and through my house without knowing exactly what I was doing or thinking, evenings of impatiently awaiting the *redemptive* appearance of the little white dot in the center of the screen. Yes, sometimes I turned off the sound, and others I had the television at full volume. It was a very peculiar whine, not at all like the one from the black ball of the gear shift of Olga's car or the one produced by the drill against marble, no. The noise of the white dot was altogether different, it brought to mind a million flies buzzing around a pot full of honey. Yes," Hans said, "sometimes I would doze off amid the cloud of flies, wondering whether instead of honey it might not be excrement, because flies, in contrast to people or, to be more precise, just like certain kinds of people, are not very selective. Olga, as I said before, was selective, viscerally or irremediably *selective*. Her bloody realism obliged her to be, I think. Yes," Hans said, "I might wake up close to dawn with my head about to burst, always thinking that my head was going to burst at any moment. And that's if I had managed to sleep at all, which for a long time was nearly impossible. It's curious," Hans said, "but on the same evening that Olga told me about the South Wind, she also made reference to a custom of the inhabitants of Einsenau during their holiday celebrations. Yes, during these celebrations they evidently engage in something they call 'The night goes on,' which means nothing in particular save that it consists of spending all night in the bars of the town and the neighboring villages, drinking and carousing. As she described it, it has to do with spending the night, letting the night go by in a merry, festive way. During my horrible bouts of insomnia I often thought about that phrase: 'The night goes on.' And the night," Hans said, "went on right by me without my being able to hold it back, or failing that, to immerse myself in it so as to rest. Not too far from my house there's a cemetery, yes, and during that period I was able to hear the bells ringing throughout the night, for dozens of nights on end, especially after three or four in the morning. It was dreadful, really. First one bell, and then another, and another and another. In the middle of that solid waiting for dawn, for the redemptive ring of the alarm clock, I'd repeat every so often: *The night goes on.* And sometimes, when Olga saw my weary face, the circles under my eyes, she would ask me what was happening. Naturally, this was on the days following those hellish nights of shadows and bells in the distance. 'What's going on with you?' I'd hear her asking, worried and having not the faintest idea what was actually happening to me. And I would think: 'The night goes on.' Yes, my nights went by like a cavalcade, like an army of impressions that left me utterly spent. It was those long and terrifying spells of insomnia, I think, that brought about my ruin: I would brood relentlessly over the most insignificant words or gestures Olga might have said or made, I'd think about what I would say to her the next time we saw each other, I would imagine her possible responses and my reaction to those responses. She had already told me on various occasions that I thought too much. Yes, she was right, entirely right, for my feeling of impotence with her, in getting something *real* from her, would begin the moment I'd realize, after one of those nights I've talked about, that Olga arrived *spotless*, ready to talk or do anything. I, in contrast, would unconsciously sally forth with a whole preconceived strategy, a strategy I would then not implement because her mere presence, Olga's presence, so filled me that I was unable to think about anything else. But my tension must have been manifest somehow, I'm sure. Yes, and to some degree that extends even to the present. *The night goes on.* A difficult period," Hans said. "I also suffered bouts of temporary amnesia, yes, I'd forget what I might be doing, for example, with a plate in my hand, standing still in the middle of the dining room, when in fact I was neither hungry nor had any need at all to use that plate; nor, what's most curious, could I even faintly recall having removed it from one of the kitchen cupboards. It was a refined form of sleepwalking, which as a rule surprised me more than anyone. Under the circumstances, I thought, it was conceivable that I'd been roving about the house, plate in hand, for hours on end. Just conceivable, yes. And I also forgot commonsense matters, things people refer to as such, though that's something I've never quite understood, I mean, why something *logical* should be common or, what amounts to the same thing, *quotidian*. I don't know, it was like being on a treadmill of strange gestures, alien to one's own essence," Hans said. "All of a sudden, for example, I'd find it impossible to remember whether the central part of an egg was white or yellow. Somnambulism or dyslexia, I think. Incredible transpositions of color took place in my head, and the more I thought about it, the more confused I got. Yes, it was like tobogganing down the rainbow. And another symptomatic aspect of that period was one affecting my person. I would forget to groom myself and even tolerated a certain amount of *dirtiness*. But it must have been an internal dirtiness, I suppose, an awareness rather than a tangible dirtiness. Yes, I would think about myriad things, over and over, especially in connection with Olga, and that incessant thinking would end up making me feel brutish," Hans said, "that's how it struck me and that's why I would sometimes run to the bathroom and wash my face with soap, rubbing it vigorously, scrubbing my hair, my cheeks, my neck, everything. That sensation relieved me a bit, but in a few minutes I felt dirty again. I would ponder over and over, trying to define or to find an explanation for those things that affected me and affected Olga insofar as she, at those moments, was a *refraction* of me," Hans said. "I would think about love, yes, about love as a concept and as the feeling I had toward her, but even those thoughts were becoming sclerotic, yes," he said, "my capacity for abstraction was diminishing in giant leaps—I mean, my abstract capacity to reflect on events whose point of reference was something that had happened to me. On these sleepless nights I would think that love must be like a frying pan with traces of water placed over the fire, like those drops of simmering oil that spatter because of the water in the pan when you fry chicken. Yes, drops that, in striking the skin, leave little scars that, though painless, remain there for some time, like tiny spots. Painless, perhaps, but present. Olga the frying pan, the water, the simmering oil, the scar. And I, the fried chicken," Hans said. "But that sensation of boiling, of moving in an atmosphere that was always seething, of my life being spent in a perpetual simmer, never left me throughout the entire period I'm talking about. Yes, I would see myself, or rather, I was aware of myself looking at everything through the eyes of a fish sizzling in hot oil. That bloated, stupefied look must have been my own for quite some time, yes," he said, "that's why I would try not to lift my gaze from the papers at work, as though among the papers could be found that constant boiling point which, one might say, was my *natural element*. That mortifying point to which my gaze, if it wandered ever so slightly, was promptly returned. On the other hand I remember that Olga used to eat fish almost every day, yes, she detested meat, especially if it was still rare, and she was no devotee of vegetables, either. Being, as she was, from a fishing village, however, her predilection for fish was almost logical. But my period of insomnia was also totally nerve-wracking. Yes," Hans said, "a stupid comment from someone, an irritating noise coming from some machine or other, a slightly raised tone of voice, any gesture, anything at all, could make me come unhinged. Yes, to this day I suppose the whole thing strikes even me as odd," he said. "It's as if I myself were another person, as I mentioned to you already. There was one moment," Hans continued, "when I realized I was copying Olga's mannerisms—yes, you heard me. I would make gestures typical of her, without even being aware of it until nearly the end. It was a day when I had guests over to the house, I don't remember why. While saying yes, laughing at someone's joke, I realized I had *imitated* Olga in a gesture characteristic of her. Later, in a matter of hours, I discovered several others I had adopted as my own over the past few weeks. Yes, everything proved very confusing," Hans said, "because it was also around that time when I used to spend long spells in front of the mirror, looking at who knows what, as if the person reflected there before me might resolve my problems. It was also about then, I think, when I had the onset of anemia. I was refusing to eat. For four days straight I didn't touch a mouthful," he said, "well, I'd have one of those packets of soup every day, quite frightful. Yes, I remember that on the last day I wasn't even hungry. The mere sight of food made me gag. Some sort of blisters appeared on my fingers, and a doctor friend of mine assured me that it was in fact the onset or first sign of anemia, as I mentioned. Naturally I didn't fret over it, I simply *resumed* eating, out of inertia. Taking vitamins out of inertia, eating out of inertia, walking out of inertia, living out of inertia. To ingest no food whatsoever for so many days was an irrational, a totally infantile attitude, I know that, but one I was compelled to adopt in order to externalize my desperation. Yes," Hans said, "because it was with desperation that I observed that the sole thing in my life I didn't do out of inertia was to love Olga. Of that I'm certain," he said, "I never loved her out of inertia, which eventually, I think, disturbed my entire vision of many things, for example that what approximated my concept of the infi-

nite—I mean, my love and affection for her—didn't necessarily fall within
the bounds of inertia, Olga and inertia were, and are, incompatible terms.
Olga, Olga, Olga, Olga," Hans said compulsively, yet with his mouth almost
entirely shut, "Olga, always Olga. Olga everywhere. Olga the ocean and I the
oblivious coral swaying in her depths. Olga's frenetic presence in everyone,
in everything. Olga!" he suddenly exclaimed, now as if he were gnawing at
an invisible bubble of chewing gum, "*Olga*. Simply by pronouncing her
name I felt as though I were someone else, I mean, a different person. That
other person I told you about before, I suppose. The *other* man. Yes," he said,
"at times I think Olga would be amazed if she knew how many times I've
spoken her name aloud when she wasn't there. The point was to utter her
name. To myself, to the drink that was my only company in a bar, to the
branches of a tree someplace, to the curtains you part in order to glance into
a street you can't make out, to the steam rising from a pot, to the cloud dis-
appearing beyond the corner of a window, to the nibbled cap of a pen. Yes, I
remember that on those days when for some reason she didn't go to work,
I'd invent any excuse to go into her office and find a way to pronounce her
name. Naturally, I think, no one noticed it. No one. 'So *Olga* didn't come in
today,' I would say, smiling knowingly, puffed up with unaccountable pride.
And if for some reason I wasn't heard, I would persist: 'Is *Olga* sick today?'
In saying 'Olga' I'd raise my voice in a tone of contained joy, then say 'sick
today' very softly. I repeat, the point was to say her name, even if only to the
walls. Saying her name was addictive, as was looking at her things, anything
directly or indirectly connected with her," he said, "and of course I'm also
convinced that she would be utterly amazed if she knew the number of
times when, hidden in the shadows of my car, I've looked at her car until my
vision became blurry. Yes, at her damned yellow car parked next to Sömmering's damned green car, at the door of her house, of her damned house.
I know she'd never comprehend what it was like to remain staring, in the
middle of the night, shivering with cold inside the car, to watch almost without blinking the light burning in her house, the light of a room in which she
was at that moment in his company. And I down below, biting my fists or the
steering wheel, saying time after time, 'Olga, Olga, Olga.' Yes," he said, "I
suppose all that belongs to a part of the story she'll never know. And the curious thing is that those episodes occurred much too often, I mean, when we

had gone out together barely a few times as well as when we had *done* many things together. Yes," Hans said as he darted a quick glance at me, the real meaning of which I was unable to decipher, "I know you've probably been wondering all along to what degree Olga and I *did* things together. I know, it's only natural," he said, "but I'm not lying when I say that even I don't know with any certainty, I mean certainty as an element that allows one to evaluate an affective relationship. But yes, I suppose there was a moment when she and I *were one*, yes, a single reflection from two mirrors, one of those moments when heaven and earth kiss, when dawn and dusk softly touch, trembling to the very same rhythm to which bodies tremble when they *surrender* to one another. Because if I'm convinced of anything," Hans said, "it's that the adventure of Olga's body was nothing but the reverse of my endeavor to draw near to her soul. But I don't want to talk about that, no. Keep that in mind. It's hard for someone who's seen paradise for a few instants to return almost at once to the world of mortals. I prefer not to remember that whole symphony of tremors because, in contrast to a sonata or a concerto, which are much more direct and closer to the bone, every symphony has about it something of a mirage. Now, for example, I want to remember the moments when Olga was *chamber music*, more intimate and accessible. Yes," he said, "the memory of her eyes is quite enough for me. Symphonies or string quartets illuminate me equally. She, Olga, I don't yet understand. And despite everything, I still love her oddities, her caprices. Yes, I love the adolescent who, without knowing why, would draw seagulls in different angles of flight. I love the person who can't stand faces with extremely fine eyebrows, the one who bragged about not having a palate for gourmet food or for liquors of the highest quality. Yes, I suppose the Olga I fell for was the one whose nature was initiatory. But I say *initiatory* in the sense that it is initiatory to observe the bored purity of old women whiling away the afternoon hours in cafes and pubs. Simply *observing* them is or may be initiatory, and they themselves are as well. Yes," Hans said, "and in the same way that we might be able to unravel the secret—the acquiescence in human relations ever since the world began—in the particular way that a beautiful woman, without being seen, looks at another woman who is also unquestionably beautiful, in that same manner, I was saying, I would watch Olga on and on without ever tiring of it, as if through that perseverance in my contemplative attitude I might arrive at a major *revelation*. Quite probably, however, this was an anomalous phase in my life, I mean in my internal life. And that might perhaps be due to the initiatory quality of my relationship with Olga, of which she, on the other hand, I think, never became even faintly aware. I can't seem to find a way to explain it to you," he said, "it's like when, after years of turning over in one's head the concept of elegance, one suddenly happens upon Olga's timid gesture, a gesture of puzzlement before something that enchanted her, even though she couldn't explain *why* it enchanted her. I don't know, elegance is touching, it's true, but false elegance chills the soul, makes you feel pierced by an invisible rapier, while you smile with a grin of approval. And there you have a chasm that can only be resolved by continual reflection, in this case about elegance. And sometimes I think that despite everything I'm lucky, enviably lucky, since for me that dilemma was cleared up by Olga's smile, her modesty and innocence before everything and everyone, the faith she professed in her own beliefs (those four or five very *clear-cut* ideas of hers), and her hunger, her thirst for deriving the greatest possible benefit from existence. An anomalous phase of my life, as I said before, but at the same time a very rich one. There was a little of everything. Yes, around that time, I think, things that had always annoyed me became genuine enemies in my daily routine. Yes, routine," Hans said, "from that moment my life was routine. I remember having uttered that word just once in front of Olga, yes, and her whole countenance changed. I think her cheeks went pale, and I recall even getting scared, for of course that was a topic she didn't want to discuss under any circumstances. The truth is I was left with an urge to know why the mere mention of that word, *routine*, seemed to upset her so. Perhaps the key, her key, *this* key," Hans said, "could've unveiled that secret to me, yes, because in fact the negative way she would slip the word 'routine' into an ordinary conversation also wound up augmenting the ample list in which I was mentally accumulating Olga's enigmatic aspects. One after another, yes, until they formed a veritable mountain. Because Olga herself was like one of those abandoned mansions the mere sight of which overawes the senses. Yes," Hans said, "the sensation I experienced first on *approaching* her, and later on *being* with her, was precisely that: of slowly infiltrating an abandoned mansion, its splendor intact yet at the same time encircled by an invisible and enormous curtain of ice. A garden full of frost, I think. And I say *infiltrating* in the literal sense, yes. I suppose that was a mansion in which I ended up being the ivy, that ivy that climbs up walls and stone fences, up partitions and columns, seeking out the sky. Ivy indeed, parched ivy, ivy tortured by all kinds of insects, ivy that when it has no place to cling, to creep up, becomes entangled with itself in a long lament," Hans said, "grows desperate and dies; ivy whose mortal enemy is the air, the *air* that in my language came to mean the distance Olga put between us from week to week, month to month, that gave her strength to withstand a new attack I would aim directly at the foundations of her sensibility (and also perhaps at some of her needs, which she doubtless had, no matter how determined she was to make me believe the opposite), attacks, I would say, that weakened me more each time, wore down my imagination as I prepared to approach her in order to do or say things that might please her, to suggest alternatives that might tempt her even if only a little. Yes, but I think in some sense Olga was a sort of woman with *no* alternative, I mean, without alternatives, since we never have just one but rather several, I think, many alternatives. She carried within her an almost volcanic potential to violate all the rules—her own and those of others, of everyone around her. I suppose that's how it was, and one had only to see certain things she did or said—especially which she said, since only with difficulty did Olga decide to slip into *action*—one had only to see them, as I said, to know there was a volcano there, yes, a sleeping volcano that once in a while must have also been beset with gloomy nightmares. Yes," Hans said, "one had only to see her mouth when she said that more than anything she was obsessed by people's mouths, that she always observed the *lips* of those speaking to her so as to know 'who she was dealing with.' Yes, that's why she was so annoyed by men's beards and mustaches, as I told you. But I don't believe her judgment was of a voluptuous nature, no, Olga was incapable of that. Her sensuality, I think, was of a different cloth. It was exactly the kind of sensuality, to give you some idea, that the enormous abandoned mansion might inspire, a world brimming with stories that *must* be floating in some part of the atmosphere, with fog enveloping it in concentric and zigzagging circles. A place where the sounds, where any sound is legend even before it's born, a place where everything *could have been* and who knows whether at some point it was. Yes, I think I was always aware of slipping inside like ivy, I mean, inside that ancient deserted house which Olga sometimes seemed to be, and the fact is, I think, she promoted those obsessions, which I suppose must have always been with me, to their maximum point of effervescence. Yes, it's obvious that all our flaws are rooted in our childhood and we do no more than recycle and at times refine them because, after all, our *flaws* also give us character. I don't know," Hans said, "for example, I've always been annoyed by people who cough too much—and I'm not saying in a concert or in a cinema, no—by those people who are unable to suppress their coughing. I can't help it. Yes, I understand it's not their fault, but a cough irks me no end. Yes, just as I can't stand ladies who are called Ulrike (that name that sounds like onomatopoeia), nor caged birds, nor people who shout instead of talking, nor shoe stores. Yes," Hans said, "I'm unable to bear the sight of so many feet *unshod*. And now I can't stand yellow cars anymore. Yes, they strike me as moving abominations that should be banned by decree, by law, yes," he said, "perhaps if severe economic deterrents were imposed on people who drive them, the massive consumption of that sort of iron sunflower, so diabolically vexatious to the sight, would diminish a great deal. Yes, that's what would need to be done," Hans said in absolute seriousness, and I seemed to notice a slight hint of irony in his words, but his expression (which I saw in profile while his gaze was lost in the confines of the ground) was not that of someone speaking in jest. "Although ever since, I was saying, since that period when particular obsessions were at their zenith, which was more or less immediately following my incident with Old Handke, my life was reduced to a *sheer lost instant*, to a vain wait for something or someone I still can't name. It was as though the vital thread had disappeared, as though everything I might have learned since I ceased being a child had disappeared, yes. But in any case, I think strange things of this sort tend to happen in cities, that a city breeds them, I mean, at birth we're *already* urban dregs," Hans said, "and I assure you that a brief sojourn here at Chemnitz would convince you of everything I'm saying. We are warped, I mean the human race, and as a rule everyone does exactly *the opposite* of what they'd really like to do. Raise this problem to several hundred thousand or several million and you'll have the face of a city. Yes, that was something about Olga that attracted me," he said, "I mean, the city *wasn't there* in her face, it was not *yet* there when I met her—that is, just over a year ago. But not even Lübeck was there, no. In each and every one of her features was

Einsenau, the little fishing village of Einsenau, glimpsed by the seagulls soaring over Kiel Bay as a mere reddish and white dot. Yes," Hans said, "and I'm not implying the question of ecology and such, no, not by any means. I'm referring to *something else* you might perhaps be able to suppose. I don't know," he said, "happiness has completely withered, many decades ago now, from *all* the urban faces, and the same holds true of the lively, scintillating look in people's eyes. Yes, in that sense Olga was an exception, I'm sure. The three years spent in Düsseldorf weren't at all evident, not in the least, and I have no doubt that some day in the near future disgust, routine—the routine she so feared—and pollution will forever petrify on her face the grin of purity I saw there. The fact is that in the city, as I was saying, everything is more difficult, even existing, something any animal achieves almost by inertia, yes," Hans said, "in the city one sometimes has to fabricate excuses in order to go on taking the whole affair of existence seriously. It's a subterranean battle of all against all and of each against everything and everyone. I think there are people—or at least it's true for me, and in this respect I believe I represent a certain social behavior that's fairly widespread—there are people, I was saying, who are in the habit of always having breakfast at the same place. Yes," Hans said, "and one fine day it's closed for some reason. And at that point one feels *lost*, having no idea where to go, as though there were no other bars or cafeterias in the city. I suppose the same thing happens to people who are in the habit of always using the same pen or stamp pad or type of stationery. If they suddenly find themselves without it, they may actually feel they're unable to think when using something unfamiliar. And in a certain sense this is what happened to me with Olga, yes, I don't think one could say that I had Olga, that she occupied a central physical or visible niche in my life, yet the fact that days, weeks, months might pass without her being near me nonetheless intensified that feeling of absolute *destitution*. That's why I would approach her in desperation, as I said before, yes, just like a hawk so delirious with hunger that even his vision has begun to fail him and he winds up dashing himself against the rocks. As a child I would go every so often to visit an aunt of mine, in Dortmund, I mean once a year, for Christmas and such. Yes, my aunt used to have a gorgeous white cat. I don't recall her name," Hans said, "I don't know, my aunt was quite a unique character and it's very likely the cat didn't have a name, I mean, my aunt would sooner throw her out a window than call her 'Miez' or some such thing. The point is that on one occasion I was amazed to observe that this cat with no name had yellowish patches in its fur, right on the side, on its hind legs. The reason, as my aunt explained, was that with the arrival of the first snows and great drops in temperature, the cat, frozen stiff, would literally *charge* up to the stove, attempting to get into it even while knowing, I suppose, that if she went too close she'd be burned. That's how cold she was. Yes, and that's how much I needed Olga. For in just that way and no other I would approach her," Hans said, "knowing all along I'd get *burned*. I believe I've always been more or less conscious of that," he said, "and also from that time on—since the moment I realized, I sensed, that I couldn't keep *advancing* into Olga's terrain, into the morass, into the quicksand that was Olga—I did or I experienced more and more odd things. I dreamed about swords of fire and deformed creatures, I dreamed continuously," Hans said. "I drank and drank. The days were a painful wandering through the immense, rugged jungle into which my own house seemed suddenly to have been transformed. And I sought the most efficient remedies, I would hunch my back, clasping my shoulders, and sway for hours like a bulrush stirred by the wind. Yes, I'd come to a halt in some street or another, watching a sudden flurry of doves or listening to the conversation of a few women in some cafeteria. Something *commanded* within me, I know that, I'm not merely supposing it, I know it with absolute certainty. That was the moment, I think, when silence, which until then had been my best, virtually my sole ally, began to frighten me, that was the moment, I was saying, in which, besides being frightened by silence, I realized I had almost ceased to think, I scarcely thought: rather *I was thought* by the pounding current in my brain. I don't know how to explain it any better, Andreas," Hans said, and in speaking my name, quickly put me in mind of who I really was—something that, given the psychological siege I was being submitted to, and the effort I was making to follow his words, I had entirely forgotten—"the point is I realized I had to do something, and without delay, that was quite clear. But I'd no idea what," Hans said. "The truth, I suspect, is that I hadn't the strength to go back to Mozart and Webern, to my books, to that small or great heap of things that constituted my daily world, no. Olga's eyes could never be found in a book. At the very most, I suppose, in a good photograph, yet such an image would nonetheless lack the spark of her intensity, as I already mentioned regarding what happened when I saw that picture of her taken years before in Naples. Therefore I decided to *think*," Hans said, "to think continuously, even to the exclusion of sleep, because in my dreams I would succumb to her: as she wore my raincoat; as she gave me the key, and I accepted her gift; as she smiled ingenuously after I'd kissed her; as she asked time and again, 'But what have I done to make you feel that way?' while caressing my cheeks with both hands; as she smoothed back my hair; as she reminded me every five minutes in a kind of excuse to herself how terribly *indecisive* she was about everything, when we both knew that was absolutely false, that Olga never had any doubts about what she wanted; as she grew ever more nervous," Hans said, "while I stared at her, speechless, listening carefully to everything she said to me; as she laughed conspiratorially each time we toasted in our peculiar way—which we'd do whenever we drank, no matter what we drank—clinking glasses not just with the top but also with the *bottom*, with the base, which at first, because we tried to be nimble about it, entailed getting soaked a few times, but in the end it was almost a single stroke in which the liquid barely wavered—because you cannot imagine Olga's gesture, her gesture every single time, which consisted in biting the *tip* of her tongue with a characteristic flair at that very point of the toast when the lower part of the glasses would touch, yes; thus," Hans said, "I succumbed to Olga, especially, I think, as she'd say no, no, no, *denying* what was obvious—she who, while saying no, was surrendering, and I also think that what she was truly saying *no* to was the idea of surrendering further still, of taking another step and another and yet another. Because I imagine (though I merely imagine this, mind you) that Olga knew quite well what her limits were, at least with respect to the people who ordinarily surrounded her, but I also imagine she often lost sight of that with me, that I threw her off completely. I don't know, for the first time in her life a limit she had perhaps imposed on herself went against and directly threatened her will. But I insist that I always experienced that unconsciously, not wanting to see it, understanding it superficially but never assimilating it. And therefore," Hans said, "I acted *accordingly*. I have to assume I imposed it upon myself not to transgress Olga's limits even though I could have done so at some point merely by forcing a little the vacillating, invisible course of things, things still to come, I mean. I was aware that at some level she was fearful I might compel her to go beyond those limits, to exceed them even through force. I don't know," Hans said, "that's probably the reason I was shackled in her presence, yes, *shackled*. That's why, I suppose, she never got around to inviting me for dinner at that place she alone seemed to be familiar with, in Winschoten, that's why she never explained to me the motive behind biting her nails, that's why I never did hear from her lips what that key opened or might open, *this* key I mean," Hans said grasping the key with his fingers. "Because, as I think I've already mentioned, if at first I suspected that through the parable of the key Olga was perhaps hinting that it might open the secret of her body, I mean, that I might learn that secret, as time went by I realized that it really had to do with something else, or at least *included* something else, that this key might perhaps open the chest containing all the desires she had sublimated throughout her life, desires that I in some measure stirred up and revived in her memory by talking to her about committing *real* follies with her, by mentioning terms she found so abhorrent, such as 'routine' or 'alternatives,' you know. Olga recognized that her life was going to yield to routine and she couldn't stand that. Nevertheless," Hans said, "she knew she was drawn to a certain degree of routine, which she admitted, something prodigiously routine, like the sparkling, serene perfection of a Renaissance fresco. 'Yes, your life,' I once told her, 'is like a lovely canvas that nothing can ruffle,' I suppose I told you about it at some point. Yes," Hans said, "that's how she wanted it to be, a lovely, untouchable painting which one can only approach like those throngs of stupefied tourists of all nationalities who swarm just like bees around the hive. Thus with Olga, yes," he said, "even against her wishes there was about her an air of art, of honey, of nectar, of the queen bee. That's how she liked things to be, I think, but nevertheless I suppose that at some moment, I mean to say, I may have come to be or to represent the possibility, the *alternative* to her perfect picture, that which lay beyond the actual dimensions of the canvas, I don't know if you follow me, I'm saying the vessel that might have actualized one or another of those desires contained in the chest, I mean, the chest of desires that have never been desired rationally but have always been desired *intimately*. For example, not to be as one is, desiring to think, and especially to feel, otherwise, something I suppose happens to a great number of people who don't realize it, something I suspect at least half the world goes through, while the other half—though well aware of it—wants to ignore it. Yes, ever since then I haven't stopped mulling all that over in my head. Time after time, until I'd get dizzy from thinking about it so much, yet I suppose that *somewhere* there must be as much misery as there is here," Hans said, his index finger indicating his head as he traced a feeble smile, "and in just the same way that (so they say) ballpoint stains can only be removed from certain garments by rubbing them with milk, similarly, I think that my only possible means of removing Olga from me is by thinking her, thinking her and pondering her until I wind up bloated. I don't know, everything used to refer directly or indirectly to her, that still holds true for me, yes. If I say the word 'milk' I think of how looking at Olga would remind me in a way of something they always used to say back home: if you fix your eyes on milk while it simmers it will never overflow. It's when you get distracted for a few seconds that the milk rises and suddenly boils over. According to that curious theory," Hans said, "the milk *knows* it's being watched and restrains its boiling, awaiting your lapse; it's capable of bubbling for a long while, gnawing at your patience without deciding to boil all the way. Thus with Olga, I suppose. It always seemed she would boil from one second to the next, but no, I'd fix my eyes on her and the *definitive* bubbling would subside as if by magic. It was when I turned away, when I wasn't there, that the boiling apparently occurred. And if I say 'ballpoint,'" Hans went on almost without giving me enough breathing room to know what he was talking about, "I immediately think how I often saw myself in relation to her (before being with her and especially after having been with her), as being one of those pens whose tube is damaged and all the ink leaks out inside, yes, like a pen that bleeds. That's how I felt, I think, that was Olga, I mean, that's how *I* was for Olga. Yes, because that sense of suffering a hemorrhage of feelings was with me from the beginning. And now at the end, after having thought those feelings so much, I ended up doubting whether I really felt something or only *felt* the thoughts. Yes, my thoughts would feel by themselves, as if they had a life of their own. Everything, with Olga, inexorably ended in *hemorrhage*. Encounters, phone calls, gifts, caresses, conversations, everything. It was like those wounds from which blood just keeps gushing and we can do nothing to stop it. As you see, she *saturated* everything," Hans said, "that's why I chose to keep thinking about her until I overcame her, at least in my mind. Yes, because as my sister Angelica advised me not long ago, to do things in a frenetic way would only succeed in removing her to one corner of my mind, creating a focus there, a tumor that, I'm fully convinced, would one day resurface with greater vigor, if that's possible, than before. The problem nonetheless," Hans said, "lies in the fact that though I do consider myself capable of relegating Olga to the furthest corner of my brain for an indeterminate period of time, I mean, of exiling her, of banishing her to the attic of my memory, it is also true—and I'm becoming aware of this through purely physical perceptions—that Olga has utterly drenched my soul, that my whole being has become her *sponge*. Yes, I'm filled with her, and the sun could burn me or kill me, but not *dry me out*. Yes, that's what I think. Though being aware that everything was left half-finished, that everything would remain half-finished—since I couldn't free myself of that thought even when we saw each other habitually and there was actually evidence pointing to the contrary—that awareness, I was saying, won't cease hounding me wherever I go, it's like my shadow, an extension of my own skin, an ache I drag along like some sort of leprosy that makes me the first to try to flee from myself," Hans said, "I the first and only being to be horrified by what he is. Yes, the impact that might have on others never worried me too much, I mean, as long as it wasn't Olga. Because I'm well aware that my depressions, my constant depressions at the time were especially intense in their outward manifestations. Yes," he said, "I felt as if entangled in the cobweb of anguish, it was then I found what the taste and the feel of anguish were like. Anguish in my chest, in my eyelids, anguish in my mouth, yes, there above all, lodged deep in my throat. I often felt like crying. Yes, I thought about it coolly and found it ridiculous, but my need to cry didn't go away. And I don't know whether I actually did or not, I suppose I did. There was a moment, I think, in which the terms were reversed and I noticed I didn't feel like crying but I did *think* I felt like crying," Hans said, "rather strange, yes. But that's the way I would see myself, yes, I the fugitive from what I am, I the one cornered by my reality, I think, surrounded, frisked, tortured by my limitations and by the ever unfulfilled wish that the dam of my limits, contrary to what she wanted, might completely *rupture*, yes, and several times, I mean, countless times I've tried to erase everything from my memory, at times sedately, like a teacher who, alone in his classroom, erases from the blackboard a theorem written there; while at other times, gripped by great agitation, like the student who, for the amusement of himself and his peers, has written 'The teacher is an idiot' on the board and realizes the teacher is on the verge of entering the classroom. Yes, but the attempts to *erase* Olga from the blackboard of my memories have always been closer to the latter. I suppose I only went so far as to smear the chalk all over the board, clumsily and chaotically smearing rather than erasing anything. But I had made that attempt at erasing her, I suppose, before I devoted myself to doing just the opposite, to thinking and rethinking everything continuously, beginning with her and everything concerning her and then on to my attitude toward her and everything concerning that, I don't know if you follow me. At some moment I made a mental effort, as I told you, to exterminate Olga from my memory, yes," Hans said, "but I think for that to have been possible the operation would have to have been unconscious, as perhaps she herself had done with me from the instant she realized I was interested, deeply interested, I mean interested in an obsessive manner, in knowing what was unlocked by this key that in some way, I think, goes on being *hers*, even though it's the one thing truly hers that I have, that I possess. Yes, I think it's incongruous to preserve it without knowing its use, what the key opens. Yes, it's a punishment, I know it must be a punishment but I don't know the source of that punishment, from whom it comes. I also believe it's not a punishment in itself, of course, but rather one more punishment. Yes, sometimes I fear I'm losing my mind when I think that's the only part of her I have left, when I can't remember precisely what I felt on kissing her hands chapped by water and cold, her cold, elusive hands; when I don't recreate exactly the taste of her mouth and her tongue, when I only *approximate* the idea. I go mad thinking about what she meant, what she had in mind when she spoke of being fascinated by things left half-finished, yes, *raving* mad," Hans said, "and not even the sound of marble, the marble dust sprinkling my face, not even alcohol attenuates those whiplashes, which are sometimes terribly frequent. I go mad from thinking I must stop looking at the calendar, transfixed on seeing her birthdate, as though that day, by the mere fact of having an excuse to phone her and congratulate her, might change anything in all this, yes, and I especially go mad thinking about the way she'd say the word 'terrible,' half-closing her lips in a manner at once demonic and angelic, contracting them and then initiating a slight expansive movement to display her white smile in all its glory. Yes," Hans said, "I lose my mind, I think and I know that I go mad at the thought of Olga's smile, like a snow-covered landscape at dawn, but even then, when I had the opportunity to be with her from time to time, I think I began to feel I was losing my wits at not having learned what those *follies* she occasionally seemed to be proud of might have been, and at not having gotten her to commit them in my presence, for me, *with* me. But in reality, I suppose, Olga always expected me to take action, to quit thinking on and on about what I was going to do from one moment to the next, and to *truly* do something. Yes," he said, "perhaps that was the only possible form of *commitment* for her, but the fact is, though I was more or less conscious of it, I didn't realize to what extent I was losing battles on that ground every time that, instead of *doing*, I thought about what I ought to do, and either told her so or brought it to her attention. Yes, although that, too, proved comfortable for her, since not at any moment did I oblige her to make a decision with respect to me, I mean, a decision of *any kind*. She confined herself to simply being there, to not entirely losing her composure when we were together. And I was totally blinded by her radiance, because I don't know whether I've told you that Olga would glow, or at least I would see that glow. There were occasions when I asked her: 'But what are you doing here? Why are you really with me?' To which she would reply: 'I'm here, isn't that enough for you?' And perhaps the problem, the genuine problem," Hans said, "is that I wanted her to be there in a particular way. You know, the ghost of possession, well, I suppose so, or perhaps it was egotism. Although a passion without egotism, I think, wouldn't be a total one, yes, so it seems to me. Look, we're almost there," Hans said, signaling forward with his chin, and indeed there in the distance, to the left of some beech trees, I could glimpse the sanatorium, "we'll arrive before nightfall, yes, here, at Chemnitz, it always seems as if it's on the *verge* of nightfall. I'm not sure, though it's quite possible that impression may result from an internal image projected externally, I mean, here (and this is something obvious almost upon arrival), night falls *mentally* for many patients, day by day, month by month. It's a long twilight of which they're unaware. The fact is my relationship with Olga was rather like that, a gradual nightfall in search of a Milky Way that I'm afraid I alone glimpsed. Olga never looked at the clouds, no, she'd look down at her feet, she wanted to live with her feet planted firmly on the ground. But, despite everything, I suspect Olga, too, ended up feeling a certain passion toward me, toward what I might represent at a given point in her life, toward what I could offer. The truth is," Hans said, "I don't know what that could be, I truly don't know, I don't think I ever found out. I've wondered about it countless times, as you might well suppose, and I don't come up with any answer whatsoever. A particular sensibility, I expect, a different way of seeing life, at least in some respects, a different way of interpreting or engaging in follies that might perhaps complement her own, the ones carried out at some point, as well as those she'll *never* dare externalize even if she were to awaken each morning with a desire to do so. A detonator," he said, "yes, that's it, a *detonator* for her. Because that's indeed what she ended up becoming for me. The fact is, I think, when I faced Olga, on the one hand I stopped thinking, yes, I automatically stopped thinking and confined myself to talking, just talking, attempting to envelop her in the cobweb of my own insecurity, of my nervousness upon realizing that I was not making the impact on her that I'd desired, and I'm talking about the initial impact. Yes, and on the other, gaining *positions* day by day in the huge fortress that was her personality— resulted in an erosion from which even now, I suppose, I haven't fully recovered, I mean, from which I haven't recovered at all. Because if there's something I'm very clear about," Hans said, "it's that my life is being divided up not so much into before Chemnitz and after Chemnitz, but rather with Olga becoming the equator, yes, my life will be cloven as if by a machete into *before* meeting her and *after* meeting her. And that may not be justified, no, perhaps you might think it's not at all justified, and for my part I, too, might think that, but I really do think it's otherwise. Hence I say that my feelings *think* on their own and that thoughts *feel* in a symbiosis at once destructive, I think, and generative of fleeting sparks of joy, I feel. Yes, that's how it feels, I can't help it," Hans said, "no, I can't quit thinking, thinking about Olga, about me with respect to Olga, about Olga with respect to me, thinking over and over about everything with respect to both of us. Thinking the thoughts so as not to think anything other than what's *pure*, you know," Hans said, looking at me, I could have sworn, in search of some reply, whether of approval or understanding I don't know. "Yes, now I'm no longer with her, but if I keep thinking and thinking that I am, if I do that intensely, I end up truly *being* with her, being so in reality. Yes, I know it's a mirage, but I expect that mirage is enough for me, in other words, I think, I suppose it suffices. I should think she's not there, I know that, I ought to think that I couldn't or didn't know how to hold on to her, that I couldn't or didn't know how to hold on to myself in her company, was unable to do so. But neither was I able to make her understand that if many times I didn't resolve to stop thinking in order to act, as she wanted, I think, or might have wanted (for I'll never really know), it was quite simply because even then, at those moments, in being with her, I understood for the first time in my life that what delimits the exact magnitude of the love felt by one person for another is the degree of rejection he believes it possible to endure from the other person. And mark that I don't say he endures, but rather that he believes it *possible* to endure," Hans said, "which in other words would come to mean the importance that person— one of the lovers, the one who loves, never the beloved—confers upon the transgression of time, by wanting to know and to see beyond what is given him, I mean the present. Yes," he said, "that's why when Olga would tell me she was there, was with me, it wasn't enough. I could have shouted no, she wasn't, over and over, I could have wept," Hans said, "I could have thrown myself at her feet. Yes, and I think that magnitude I mentioned before was infinite in me, my concept of infinitude being Olga herself, I think, what she represented within me and for me—that magnitude, I'm saying—could never have been measured in mathematical terms, to speak of it somehow, it *transcended* the body, the air, the essence of the body and the essence of the air, everything, I think," Hans said, "yes, and therefore the fear of being rejected, even if indirectly, constituted in itself a reason for visceral panic, an indivisible state of panic, a state of atomic agitation, I don't know if you follow me. That sensation flattened and buried me," Hans said, "it rendered me useless to do anything other than talking and talking uninterruptedly while I was with her, just as I'm doing now, I think, awkwardly embellishing those conversations or those monologues, yes, always awkward and punctuated with a caress *here and there*, mostly out of place, out of line, caresses I sought to give her not so much because they really arose in me spontaneously or because I craved them at just those instants and not at others, but rather because I was convinced she expected them. That was the other side of the problem," he said, "the one she never actually saw, not to mention that if she had, it wouldn't have meant anything, I mean nothing that would have *substantially* modified her attitude toward me, the attitude of her feelings toward me and toward my thoughts, which of course she didn't know, but which she perhaps guessed, because, as you know, she was very intuitive. I was telling you," Hans said, "about those instants, about the caresses. For me the day's instants were merely an extension of Olga, of Olga's voice and Olga's gestures, I think, and when the instants *truly* arrived, when she was before me, I waged a silent, desperate battle against all the laws of time and space to arrest those instants, to freeze them. Yes," Hans said, "the truth is that at bottom a caress seemed a meager thing to me, and I say meager not because it lacked importance, which is far from the case, but on account of it being an ephemeral sensation, something that couldn't be preserved by any means. My whole being, I think, was a caress for Olga, a great prolonged caress over each and every part of her body, her soul, what she had touched, what she was going to touch. And," he said, "at the same time I know I was suffering the effects of uncertainty, knowing that wasn't how she understood it, and that even if she did manage to understand, it would be useless to her, as I was saying. Yes, because Olga was a practical person in general and a *very* practical woman in particular, tremendously practical. Whenever she had to study, however much I might suggest the possibility of going out for the evening, it was clear that she was going to spend that evening studying the question of the *ego*, the *superego*, and the *id* in Freud. Yes," Hans said, "and whenever she mentioned that frightful term, the *superego*, of which we can never free ourselves, I mean, of which the *ego* can never be free, she would make a characteristic gesture with her hands, she would shape a figure in the air and it always seemed to me she was sketching the outline of an invisible Bunker. But as a matter of fact Olga's practical spirit never surprised me one bit, no, I saw right from the start that *that's* what she was made of. Even the first time we went out, the very first, I remember she spent virtually the entire time telling me how she always observed, always saw, always watched everything and everyone carefully, and then *chose* whatever best suited her. I thought it was akin to selecting fruit in the market," Hans said, "yes, and I told her so, I think, but she ignored it. I understand she really had no reason to heed me, since that tactic had produced optimum results anytime she'd engaged in it and, as she admitted to me, had in recent years become an instinctive act—I'm talking about that peculiar method of selection. She was very definite about this selection process with people having yielded very good results, as I said. Yes, I suppose she even did it against her will—selecting, I mean," Hans said, "Olga always selected everything. I think it was or purported to be a way of being on *top* of things. She needed to do it because she, too, must have been conscious of her other *ego*, the subjected one, the one tyrannized by that other *superego* of her particular, comfortable lifestyle, the *ego* of the woman who at certain moments would start to tremble. And indeed," Hans said, "she tended to do that when we were on the street, the hour quite late and the night's full chill upon us. Olga was very susceptible to cold, as you know and I suppose I've already told you at some point, maybe even today, but the truth is, I think, I'm beginning to find it difficult to pinpoint exactly what I've mentioned to you and what I haven't, but what I do know is that the *majority* of things I know about Olga I have *not* mentioned to you, not to you nor to anyone. As I was saying, Olga was extremely susceptible to cold, yes, but the instants when she'd start to tremble—not the way she did it, which was indeed just a result of the cold—those instants, I was saying, marked the rhythm of the other Olga, with her *internal* cold, I think, with her never resolved contradiction between fire and ice. Yes," Hans said, "perhaps that other Olga was something evanescent, something that as far as she herself was concerned never existed, that she didn't admit to herself as such, something similar to the *other side* of the border, to the invitation to dinner on that other side at once so near and so remote," he said, "something that though she might not recognize it in herself, perhaps she *foresaw*, she heard within herself very often, or fairly often, often enough that she'd dare to say on occasion that she really wasn't strict but terribly *easy*. Yes, that must have been her mental way out of propriety: thinking and knowing about what she was simply *capable* of. Her follies, I suppose, were the topic she must have liked to think about most whenever she didn't allow herself to be swept along by the tide of the mundane activity or inactivity that, deep down, so disturbed her. Her follies," Hans said to himself mechanically as we drew closer and closer to the sanatorium, now skirting an oak grove and finding ourselves almost directly before the building's facade, "her follies. A string of things she never carried out, will probably never carry out, but which she's certainly thought about until she has *actually* done them in her mind. Yes, something similar to the act of reproducing Olga's image, her presence, in my head. Follies that for her have acquired an identity as a result of thinking that someday she will end up acting them out, as a result of familiarizing herself with the ultimate significance of those follies which have been floating around in her mind over the years. Yes," Hans said, "I suppose Olga was what one would call a normal person, which doesn't imply that she lacked flaws or attributes—I mean, she wasn't particularly problematic. And she herself confessed she would like to be odd. Yes, that's what she said, 'I'd like to be odd, *very* odd.' That was her fantasy. But she knew she wasn't odd and that vexed her a little, only a little, I think, because the truth is Olga was frightened by oddities, by oddness, myself for example," Hans said, "yet in spite of that, I did always think she was odd, at least *rather* odd. Yes, and I believed it for two fundamental reasons: first of all, because if Olga hadn't been odd or at least rather odd, as I said, she would never have interested me, never. I suppose in that sense I, too, have my unconscious selective criteria. Yes, I'm sure her physical beauty wouldn't have been enough to attract me, or at least not to such a degree. There are many beautiful women out there, I suppose. Yes, I know there are," Hans said. "The bonbons that remove the bad taste left in your mouth by another bonbon you've lost, as my sister Angelica put it, yes. The fact is that at times Olga herself could be a sour bonbon, totally acidic, at least that's what I think, or what I believe I think. Yes," he said, "because on many occasions I unquestionably detected that *acidity* in the things she said to me and the way she said them. Consequently, I think, what always attracted me was not Olga's face, I mean, *not that alone*. Yes," Hans said, "it's always been obvious to me that from an early age I moved in a very broad aesthetic orbit. As I've told you before, I'm a child of Mozart and Webern, I think. Not just of one, but of both," he said, "yes, and in that sense Olga could be the offspring of Mozart, of a certain drowsiness, of a certain Mozartian lethargy if you like—though I repeat, in herself she was a completely Wagnerian being. But undoubtedly, I think, she could never have had any relationship whatsoever with Webern, especially bearing in mind the profound contradiction that lies in Webern as well. I don't know, I suppose two contradictions of such magnitude, Olga and Webern's music taken to their ultimate implications, could culminate in a split greater than our capacity to think about those elements separately. But in the end, I think, it's a matter of my own perception of the issue, yes," Hans said, "and I want you to understand me completely—I mean, a person captivated by Mozart's music, to give you an example, might have felt captivated at once by Olga's face, by her way of *moving*, but that example couldn't be extended to Webern's music. Moreover," Hans said, "I'm thoroughly convinced that someone captivated by Webern's music—the contradiction, the destruction within beauty, or at least of one *particular* idea of beauty—could hardly feel captivated by Olga's face, which was, of course, beauty in a *total* state, I think. Yet nonetheless," he said, "it did happen to me. But I don't suppose it happened only because of Olga's face, as I've said, but because of having apprehended in her, including in her face, the contradiction that made her so odd, inasmuch as she permanently trod a strange, slippery terrain fraught with dangers that frequently drove her to adopt a tense outlook on life. Yes," Hans said, "tense in the sense of contradictory. I suppose the follies she never committed were included in the realm of the unforgivable, of what she would never forgive herself for, but which in spite of everything she justifies for the sake of indulgence, of a smooth, placid existence beside the person she'd chosen to share that existence, along with elements she had also chosen in order to make that shared existence as lucid as possible, I mean, the least *conflictive* possible. Yes, because one of Olga's obsessions, one of the presumed follies I managed to coax out of her on one of the last evenings we met, after much talk, many caresses, lots of whiskey, was getting her to admit that she had always dreamt about going away to another place, but not just to *the other side*, no, I think she meant something else. Yes, I remember that at first she said 'to another place,' and then she added 'far away,' and later '*very* far.' When I asked her where, she bit her lips. Yes," Hans said, "she didn't want to tell me where, but at last I heard the magic words. I think she even pronounced them with her mouth closed: New Zealand. Yes, Olga said she'd always wanted to go live in New Zealand, at least for a while. But a few seconds later," Hans said, "as though she regretted having made that confession, she assured me she wasn't prepared to renounce everything she had here, in other words, that complement of her existence who was her other self in routine, Sömmering—the 'Bunker,' family problems, that feeling of being *useless but necessary* everywhere, which she didn't know how or couldn't or didn't want to give up—that other *ego* or *superego*. And as far as that's concerned, I think, I was absolutely astounded when she said that what she really wanted was to go to that faraway place, yes, but accompanied, with the *superego* tagging along. 'In all likelihood I'd go there with *him*,' that's what she said. I felt a deep sadness, I don't know why I felt sad, but I did. Although my thought felt sadness, I suppose it remained ice-cold. Yes, but the first time she said she wanted to leave for New Zealand, that she had always wanted to go live there, her eyes gleamed in such a way that I immediately knew the second part of the explanation—her assuring me almost emphatically, and a bit aggressively, that she'd go to such a remote place accompanied, and furthermore accompanied by the person who has accompanied her every day for several years, by the person who will probably go on doing so forever—I immediately knew or sensed, as I said, that the second explanatory part was a patch, I think, just a patch, a mend that she herself never believed, but which she felt obliged to acknowledge aloud so as to avoid *frightening* herself, to go on preserving intact the old dream of going away, of escaping to New Zealand, which I think would be nothing but a flight from her superego, from herself. But Olga wasn't cowardly, as I've said, she was simply pragmatic, which I suppose was squarely and irremediably at odds with the prospect of feeling satisfied with herself, I mean, with her way of being. I don't know," Hans said, "that devastating gleam in her eyes meant, I think, that the genuine folly, what she really would have wanted, was to go to New Zealand *alone*, to try out the adventure of living alone, of feeling and knowing herself to be alone, without someone not so much to lean on but rather to be guided by. Because I'm sure, or at least this is what I think, that deep within, Olga always had a complex about having been guided, in other words, *led* as a woman in our society so often is, a woman who lives with a man, of course. Yes, as for myself, I can tell you that in spite of my unconscious sadness upon learning that Olga had always desired to go to New Zealand, I was seized with such enthusiasm that in a matter of days I obtained whatever books dealt with the place, yes," Hans said, "with Oceania in general and New Zealand in particular. Although it involved renewing my encounter with the printed word," he said, "because I don't know if I've told you at some point that ever since meeting Olga I had found it virtually impossible to read anything, be it novels, essays, anything. She alone was fantasy enough. Yes," Hans said, "I devoured everything concerning New Zea-

land, everything, *gobbled it all up*. A sumptuous, gratifying banquet. Yes,"
Hans said, "I read everything about the place, its cities, geography, flora and
fauna, industry, mining, agriculture, livestock, communications, territorial
divisions, its political system, yes, its commerce, the legends and religions of
the area, its ethnography, its history. Everything," Hans said, "I came to feel
like a New Zealander myself. Yes," he said, *"just another New Zealander*. I
was only at ease among New Zealand *things*, among New Zealand phenom-
ena and history. Yes, reading about New Zealand in libraries, in its consulate,
among books and dozens of notes about its people and their customs. I suppose I was a sort of New Zealander infiltrating everywhere, yes, a sort of
New Zealand *spy* who spent the evenings immediately following the discovery of Olga's desire to travel reading and reading stories about the indig-
enous Maoris, said to be one of the most beautiful races in the world, until
close to daybreak I would fall asleep, overcome with exhaustion, convinced
that I myself was a Maori who the next day, or rather three or four hours
later, would dress in ordinary clothing and go to work, as on every day, in an
office entrusted with the administration, advertising, and technical matters
of an explosives concern. Yes," Hans said, "ordinary clothing that, I came to
fear, might not perhaps entirely disguise my distinctly Maori *origins*, my in-
digenous features, of which no one, on the other hand, seemed to take notice.
Yes," Hans said, "as a matter of fact, the unpleasant incident with that hysterical old codger Handke occurred shortly after that period. I think I lost
control, I recognize that, I never intended to harm Handke, only to remove
him from my sight, I mean, to physically remove him from my sight, give
him a little lesson in return for all the years he's indiscriminately dumped his
sour temper on the people around him. I suppose my *Maori stage* was the one
immediately preceding my transfer here, to the sanatorium, which as you
know, Angelica arranged at my own request. But at any rate I suspect," Hans
said, "that incident, the 'attempted murder' as the old idiot must have called
it amidst great histrionics, signaled just one more link in the long chain of
events in which I found myself suddenly submerged, I think, after I stopped
seeing Olga, I mean after I stopped seeing her alone from time to time; from
that point on, seeing her at work became absolutely unbearable. Yes, that's
when the dizzying bustle of the treadmill must have begun. One turn, another, and then another. And at each turn, I think, more suppressed gagging.

Suppressed or *evacuated* inward, I don't know. My relationship with each and every object in my house started becoming tragic," Hans said, "yes, tragic in the *theatrical* sense. I expect I was perfectly aware it was happening, but there was nothing I could do. Yes, that's when I *recovered* my toothache," he said, "suddenly my toothache started to ail me again, so I *dashed* to the nearest supermarket to pick up a case of cognac. And that," Hans said, "getting soaked on cognac daily, soaking myself like a rag, right down to the bone, was also a serious contradiction. Yes, I don't know if I've ever told you that I abhor cognac, I don't like it at all, I'm *repelled* by it. As a matter of fact it's a taste I can't stand. Yes," he said, "drinking cognac by the liter is, or was, like being completely bereft of Olga's lips, those lips that, mysteriously and without my understanding why, she would open freely and avidly in the midst of a kiss, of a caress, swallowing me, making me feel that I was about to *flow into* her from one moment to the next. The fact, as I was saying, is that I would have relieved the toothache with whiskey, with that whiskey Olga and I always used to order, the one we liked best, which I no longer know whether I liked for the actual *contents* or because she once remarked how she loved the *design* of the bottle. Because the fact that Olga had studied design for several years meant that she tended to go around noticing the design of everything, I mean, I suppose she had a detailed vision of everything, she'd see the skeleton, the original mold. Yes," Hans said, "and I think that was true with things, with objects, but also with people and situations. I'm quite sure the glasses would have broken in my hand had I tried to drink that whiskey just once, I mean, just once more *without her*. Yes," Hans said, "I've never tasted it again, I don't dare, I'm unable to, I know I'd be torn up inside if I tried to drink it. Taking cognac as a remedy was torture, I assure you, or at least that's how it seemed to me then, but I didn't know what else to do. And I also think my *relationship* with particular household objects deteriorated substantially," Hans said, "for example, the electric razor, the toothbrush, and various items that reminded me inexorably of Olga. Yes," he said, "I bought the shaver shortly after meeting her, I think. Had I not met her or, more to the point, had I not actually gone out with her, I surely wouldn't have bought it. In fact, I'm positive. Yes, I would have gone on with my old shaver. And it was much the same, I think, with my toothbrush. I'd had one for quite a while, a yellow one, like Olga's damned car. It was falling apart,"

Hans said. "Then, when I started going out with Olga from time to time, I realized I would instinctively go to the store once every two weeks to buy a new toothbrush. Yes, I quickly—decisively, I suppose—threw out my old yellow toothbrush. Later those purchases started becoming more and more frequent. It reached the point," Hans said, "where each time we'd go out, even if it was a matter of two days in a row, I felt *compelled* to run to the store and buy a toothbrush. I remember that having sparkling teeth became an enormous obsession, yes, I'd spend the entire day probing them with the tip of my tongue. That was a ludicrous obsession that caused me to make queer grimaces everywhere," he said, "and I would realize it when, for example, I stepped into an elevator that had a mirror. Before me would appear a fellow moving his chops this way and that. 'But it's you,' I'd tell myself. Of course," Hans said, framing a smile as he lifted his gaze toward the sanatorium, which was now but a few dozen meters away, "one should also bear in mind, I suppose, that this was about the time when I could step into an elevator and spend quite a while waiting for the elevator to *guess* what floor I wanted to go to, because I would lose any awareness of what I was doing there or where I wanted to go. In a sense, I think, one might say that the time I spent cleaning my teeth increased in just the same way. In the end I would stand there absorbed in thought, my mouth full of foam and my gums sore from so much scrubbing. I suppose that was the *hygienic* manifestation of the process of constantly cutting and wounding myself with some object or other. Yes," Hans said, "and I also think my real obsession was my breath, I mean, it was one of those solid obsessions, which you start noticing as though they were a heavy chain. I've never been able to bear foul breath, which is true for most people, I suppose, and the fact is I genuinely feared something of the kind would happen to me with Olga; and that's why, in addition to my compulsive relationship to toothbrushes, I also got into the habit of chewing gum several minutes prior to our encounters. Yes, always mint-flavored. Around that time, I suspect, my mouth must have been a sort of fragrant icebox, almost a perfume *factory*. Yes," Hans said, "I consumed inordinate amounts of gum. I did so, I think, to exactly the same degree that my dentist from the other side, I mean *her* dentist from the other side, warned me that gum was harmful, *deadly* for my teeth. In any event, Olga must have wondered about not ever having seen me chew gum and all of a sudden never seeing me without it. Suspicious, she must have thought, or perhaps not, because as I've said, Olga was unpredictable. I'm not sure, for all I know she realized it, but she never said anything to me, not a word. But there came a time, quite near the end, when I could kiss Olga without fear of her refusing at any point, I mean, naturally it hadn't always been *so*. Yet such a moment came, without my even realizing it, I think, just as the first light of day arrives and catches us sound asleep, yes, I'm talking about that sort of daily ambush of light," he said. "At first she always *eluded* my caresses and later on, suddenly, she'd remain a little more *still*, and then a bit more, and more, until she finally became *rigid*, sometimes totally rigid, I mean rigid except for the whirlwind of her mouth. Yes, the whole thing was very odd," Hans said, "very odd. Then the business of chewing gum also began to escalate, I mean to a matter of hours, I even chewed gum in front of her, that's right, yes, *especially* in front of her. But the fact is I'd never had gum in the house, never, mainly because it destroys the teeth, which I already knew or could suppose long before her dentist from *the other side* told me. As a matter of fact, I recall, my entire house was gradually filling up with packets of gum, some still unopened, on hand in the event of an unexpected date. When we stopped seeing each other, or rather when Olga began to make serious and insurmountable objections to continuing our dates, I'd get to feeling really nauseated just by thinking about the flavor of gum. I remember throwing heaps of it into the garbage," Hans said. "I would have thrown myself away along with those packets, yes, like one more bit of chewing gum. Because when everything's said and done Olga, in her own way (which I don't by any means believe was malicious or intentional) squeezed me out, chewed me up, took away my best, or rather the best *of me*, because ever since I met her everything mine automatically became hers. I myself was not my own but simply *of me*, I don't know if you understand," he said, "I only had things that were *of me*. And yes, I think my capacity to love was chewed to its limits by Olga. I believe the word *limits* had a magic resonance to her ears, I know it, it was rather like *the other side* of words, of language," Hans said, "and as far as *perseverance in chewing*, I doubt that Olga had ever been so deeply occupied with anyone, I suppose. I gave her a free hand to do to me, or with me, whatever she desired. She was aware that the least of her gestures was welcomed by me, I think, with the boundless joy of that shaggy little dog I mentioned earlier, you know," he said, "the one with the pillow. I remember that as soon as she appeared before me, I became the image of supreme happiness, yes, and she had to notice it," he said, "because in the same way that a child with its face full of chocolate is the paramount symbol of happiness in someone, so too was my own happiness in her, I mean, *through* her. Gluttonous and irrational, I suppose, smeary. Yes, the truth is, even now I often look instinctively at my arms, my legs, my whole body, to see whether I'm still *smeared* with Olga. And she, I think, always knew that perfectly well. Yes, Olga, in a certain sense, must have become aware of that effect even momentarily, but I doubt she also realized that she had *chewed up* my future, my future capacity to love anyone. Yes, I think it would have been very hard for her. I don't know," Hans said, "it must be rather complicated to understand, I suppose. But I assure you I would have thrown myself into the garbage had I been certain that there I would have ceased feeling cornered. Yes, I think I've already told you before, but I think that's exactly what was happening to me then: I felt cornered everywhere. Yes, like the bad guy in an old gangster movie when all the lights are suddenly turned on him by the police, who've set up an ambush in a squalid blind alley. I think I never knew how and deep down didn't want to prevent the *dazzlement* entailed, first in meeting Olga, and later having her in front of me. Yes," Hans said, "I felt cornered out in the open and cornered in my own house, in my room. I had the sensation of being cornered even when I'd curl up, tremulous, in one corner of my bed, perspiring alcohol and letting myself be carried away by a tangled wave of thoughts. Because Olga, I think, was a *flood*, a water spout that demolished everything, a tidal wave in my veins," Hans said, "a hurricane in my lungs. To see her was to hear, to sense, to perceive a wave bursting within me, yes, one of those huge waves we went to see several times, breaking against the wharf at Emden harbor. I constantly asked myself where the zero point of the burst of my attraction to her could have originated, yes," he said, "but observing those waves, sometimes with her, but most often alone, observing the upswell of those huge waves, I realized that there's no answer to the question as to the exact place where the wave *bursts*. Yes," Hans said, "I still remember one evening when, looking up at the stars, I asked Olga if she could imagine where the night's blackest point could be. She, utterly confident, fixed her eyes on a point in the firmament and said without hesitation: 'There.' That's how Olga was. And I felt cornered, as I said, from the very instant I realized I had transgressed the bounds of *affection* and fully entered those of *idolatry*, when I realized she was morphine and opium for my pain and anxiety, when I realized that at the same time, I mean, at exactly the same time I was doing anything—working, walking, eating, whatever—I was seeing her jasper lips as if they were an immense maw, the entrance to a cave in whose recesses lies hidden the treasure we've yearned for, through each and every man of other ages and centuries gone by. I suppose I couldn't free myself from the prison of my body," Hans said. "Yes, perhaps my thought wasn't made of thick bars but was rather a sort of armored steel shutter that separated it from the outside. And I was on the *other side*, I think, on my other side, that is to say, inside that armored steel shutter, loving her in a bedazzled, total way, with no turning back, loving Olga vociferously. Yes, because I know I loved Olga to the point of hearing myself perpetually shouting to her how much I loved her," Hans said, "and ever since then, I think, my life was reduced to a sheer, contained shout. Yes, I'm sure it was impossible to love Olga any other way. That's how I loved her," he said, "shouting inwardly, even though she usually liked people who shouted outwardly, people who always externalize what they feel. That's why, I think, she detested talking on the telephone, because it was something internal, subterranean, something taking shape not in the open air but through all sorts of hidden channels that aroused her insecurity and timidity to the utmost. Whenever Olga chatted with me in the corner of a bar, even when she did so *quite at ease*, and of course I suppose when she wrote those few messages intended for me, or when we spoke over the telephone, whenever she'd do any of that, I think, a part of her brain was anesthetized. Olga was herself when she was trying to douse me with water she'd stored in her mouth, having collected it from the jet of a fountain; Olga was herself," he said, "giving free rein to whatever her body called for. She was a person overflowing with life," Hans said, "and I don't believe that's a cliché, no, I've seen it with my own eyes, I mean, with my own eyes I've seen *life overflowing* from Olga's eyes, her lips, each and every pore of her skin; I've seen her overflow with the serene inertia of lava from a volcano sliding down the slopes of a mountain. And I loved her, I think, in both modes, I mean, pirouetting in the middle of the street or chatting quietly in a bar. Both things," Hans said, "she would perform without *stridency*, yes, I think so, as if it were the prelude to a melancholy concerto. And before both I would have shouted that I wanted to penetrate into the womb of her silence," he said, remaining quiet then for a few moments, as though he had really been shocked by what he had just expressed, "yes, I suppose I would have shouted something that doesn't pertain to any language or vocabulary whatsoever, something that transgresses, as I was telling you, the boundaries of the spoken word. Because I can go on talking to you incessantly about Olga, but the physical sensation I'm left with once I've done so is that of finding myself very far from what I want to say. Yes," Hans said, "I suppose I always gave too much weight to what I said to Olga, as well as to what she said. The cycle would be inexorably fulfilled: I was so worried by what I needed to say to her and how I ought to say it that I, too, often found myself speechless all of a sudden, my mind would go blank, as though I were opening my eyes onto the very heart of the deepest crevasse of a glacier. But the fact is," Hans said, "that I also experienced that sensation of talking uselessly on and on with her, yes, the same way I feel to some degree with you is how I felt with her, as well. I really emphasized certain remarks I wanted her to notice, so as to create an immediate impact, but Olga didn't pay much heed to whatever polished phrases I might use. Yes, for example, I think I said goodbye *definitively* dozens of times. And at those instants I would do it in all truth," Hans said, "there was not one shred of fiction in it. 'I'm happy to have known you,' I would say, I suppose with a lovelorn look. And Olga, entirely unruffled and only mildly concerned, would reply: 'Well, if that doesn't sound like a genuine farewell.' I would look at her then with an expression full of anguish or nostalgia. And she'd go on: 'You're so extreme, you need to exaggerate in order to really believe what it is you see or feel.' I don't know," Hans said, "perhaps she was right. But in any case, I think Olga never believed what I told her, I mean about the sensation of irksome stinging, of lassitude, of pain toward the end, which I experienced when she was not around. I don't know," he said, "it was, I suppose, an ambiguous sensation. Just as I can say that the sanatorium is only a few meters away, that we're gradually approaching it, so, too, can I say that I loved her in every way imaginable and even *unimaginable*," he said as he lowered his eyes toward a handful of dry leaves that crunched under his feet, "I loved her through my gifts or offerings, through my horoscopes or lengthy letters explaining my feel-

ings, through each and every gesture of my life, from those mechanical gestures that proved effective, to others that were totally useless and to which I
became accustomed without worrying too much about them. Yes, that was
the worst thing once she was no longer there. I would take interminable, repeated sips from an empty glass, and I was loving Olga through that gesture,
I truly was, just as I was when I'd take a spool of thread, tear off a piece, and
proceed to cut it with a pair of scissors. Yes," Hans said, "into fragments pro-
gressively smaller, more diminutive. In the end I'd be left with nothing but
dust on my fingers. But even so I'd keep on cutting, cutting in a totally uncontrolled way and at the risk of piercing the tips of my fingers. Yes, I suppose at *some* point I must have done that," he said, "I've already explained to
you how around that time I would hurt myself, all too often causing sores
and cuts. I was aware that it had to do with an obviously destructive drive
involving all my surroundings, the wall that still protected me. But the center
remained, the part where wounds never suppurate: my thought. Yes, that
was the beginning, I think, of the siege of my mind by my own thoughts,
which of course knew perfectly well all the secret codes and passages that
had to be used, first to make it vulnerable, and later to take it by storm. Yes, I
think there came a moment of almost total paroxysm—when Olga and I
were still seeing each other but the frequency of our encounters had, at her
behest, conspicuously decreased—when my thoughts in particular, I mean
one by one or in perfect and synchronized operative groups, rebelled against
my thought in general. At that time," Hans said, "what I had deemed a guer-
rilla enclave of no importance, or of but relative importance, became a full-
fledged popular *insurrection* of thoughts, yes," he said, "the masses of
thoughts thronged the streets, the cities, the country of my mind, its memory, instinct, subconscious, everything, hoisting the flag bearing Olga's face,
her voice, her smile. I suppose the *collective wrath* of those thoughts was irrepressible. And I realized I lacked the only element or argument that might
have saved me," Hans said, making an effort to stress this last point. "Something of which she had plenty to spare: lucidity. Yes, something that proved
impossible for me to even consider because for that to have happened, I
think, I should have to have been very clear-headed about exactly what I expected from her, which as I already told you, I never knew. What I mean is
that I know I was slowly destroying myself on account of my blind obsession

with a person who, I suppose, could be no more than a detonator for a heap
of other reasons I don't recognize; I was perfectly aware of that even though
I myself denied it. Yet at the same time," he said, "I also knew that Olga was
the greatest thing that had ever happened to me. Yes," Hans said, "up until
then I had been a *vegetable*. And when the eruption of Olga's volcano took
place beside me, I felt overflowing with life, I felt that the life brimming over
from her had entered me, I don't know how or why, and to tell the truth, I
sometimes think I don't much care to know the reasons. They won't change
anything, I suppose. On the one hand I was fully aware that it was necessary
to destroy her image, Olga's image within me, yet on the other, I repeat, I
knew that in destroying her I would destroy the best part of my life," Hans
said, "the most vital, the only vital part. Because upon meeting Olga, I realized that Mozart and Webern and everything they might signify were dead,
I mean dead *in comparison* with her, with the crackling rivers of lava. Yes, I
was slowly destroying myself, as I said, with gestures that were often uncontrolled and that, once made, I knew were nothing but *tokens* to Olga, tokens
she never knew about and would naturally have considered ridiculous had
she known their true nature, but which, nonetheless, at the moments I made
them—the gestures, I mean—struck me as the only possible (and of course,
furtive) alternative to the prolonged scream that threatened to issue forth,
rending the clouds in the process. Even now I'm ashamed about many of
those *gestures*," Hans said, "deeply ashamed. Yes, I'm talking about such adolescent gestures or attitudes as something I did several times at work, I don't
know how many times but it was in fact several: I spied on her. I became a
spy, a common spy," he said as though swallowing the words, and with his
eyes steadfastly fixed on the white facade of the sanatorium, "and the reason
lay in my *asthma* for Olga, in not being able to breathe when she wasn't near.
It was horrible, I was really horrified about doing it," he said, "but had I not
spied on her at those moments I would have screamed, I think, I would have
said something that, by doing so in front of co-workers, would undoubtedly
have hurt her. It would have been worse, I suppose. I don't know if you understand, I *need* you to understand," Hans said. "Yes, well, you already know
that the bar on the corner is located some forty meters from the company's
back door. Well, though you may never have thought about the fact, I suppose you'll at least remember. Yes," he said, "the point is, one day I discovered

that from a particular washroom, the very one facing the central part of the
building, one could overlook that entire stretch, all the way from the back
door to the bar. Yes, Olga and some other women from Administration used
to go out for coffee once or twice every morning. I knew when those times
were," Hans said: "between ten thirty and a quarter to eleven, and (if the second break took place) between a quarter past twelve and twelve thirty. Yes, I
was well aware that by climbing up on the toilet and peering through the angle of a small metal window, I could observe that stretch without being seen.
Naturally, I mean of course, I didn't do that as many times as I *wanted* to,
which still doesn't erase, I think, the fact that when I did it I'd feel like a
wretched spy. Yes, it was only on particular days, when my chest seemed
about to be split open as though a herd of maddened buffalo were charging
through it," he said, "days when for some reason or another I would have
found it impossible to stand before Olga, I mean, to be physically *near* Olga,
which was at times the greatest torture of all. It was then that I'd spy on her
like that, when I loved her, I suppose, in such an infantile and peculiar fashion. I do know, however," Hans said, "that if by some fatal coincidence the
washroom—that washroom—had been occupied on one of those days, I
would have smashed in the door, yes, I would've broken it down and kicked
out whoever was there. And I think, for example, that my *exploits* in her office must have been innumerable. More than once, I would have kicked anyone out of there too. You can't even imagine the ruses I had to contrive, often
on the spot, in order to leave a message for Olga, yes, or some fetish," he said,
"some object that would bring me a bit closer to her and, consequently,
would also bring her a bit closer to me. In other words, I think it was an attempt on my part to bring us *mutually* closer through those objects and fetishes I'd leave for her. Because I'm not sure whether I've already told you
that I believe I filled Olga's life—or at least one phase of her life—with fetishes. Yes," he said, "my incessantly giving her fetishes, I expect, testified to
my internal *drought*, to the drought in my consciousness and my spirit during that long period. Emotional or sentimental drought, I suppose, who
knows. But I was telling you about my exploits in her office," Hans said suddenly, swaying his head, "yes, I imagine I myself brought on some rather
comical situations, of which I don't know whether anyone else was ever
aware. Whenever I wanted to leave something in her drawer (which inci-

dentally she never locked, something she could have done) and I'd bump into one of her co-workers milling about, always on *the verge* of leaving, always about to take flight, yet always parading their loathsome bodies about, I came very close to losing control. First of all I'd go directly to the cabinet to pick up an eraser, a pencil, a new typewriter ribbon, anything. Naturally, I'd have to leave without consigning my fetish or my message (or on innumerable occasions, both my fetish and my message) to her drawer, defeated and each time more hysterical. A couple of minutes later, I would burst into her office once again, always when she wasn't there, of course, thinking everyone had already left. But they hadn't. The excuse was an envelope, a writing pad, a file, an ashtray, whatever. I recall rather confusedly a loathsome body and loathsome face looking at me strangely. Yes, and I doing a juggling act, real prodigies with my imagination so as to linger there a few seconds more, but the fact is in the end, I don't even know how, I managed to leave the fetish, or the object, or both fetish and object tenderly and silently united in the bottom of her drawer. Thinking about the gleam in her eyes when she opened the drawer and discovered it the next morning would bring me a rare happiness, a joy I can't explain. The certainty of that happiness, and consequently, the certainty of the awareness and hence of the reality of that happiness, prompted me to *find* the moment to leave all that for her, although I repeat I don't know exactly how or when or by what means I achieved it. But the risk was always worth it," Hans said, "yes, well worth it. Because Olga didn't forget, she never forgot, and moreover I think she was quite appreciative. Several days could go by when suddenly, right out of the blue, she would say: 'I found that,' while she smiled, nodding, even though she might not say another word about it. Yes, I think her thought process was always incredibly complex, extremely complex, and her way of appreciating things or, on rare occasions, of showing her affection, was therefore just as complex. At times she even astounded me. I felt she was *reading* my mind. Those, I believe, were spectacular discoveries about portions of her character which, I suppose, very few people have known or will ever know. A couple of times we were discussing topics that had nothing to do with anything *sensual*, to designate it somehow, though I admit *that's* where my mind was drifting. Yes, a small but ardent flame was burning in a remote quarter of my mind while, at the *same time*, we were chatting about work or people from work, which after all was the excuse, distasteful yet convenient and ideal, to gaze for a long time into each other's eyes. Then Olga, shifting her gaze, said with utter candor: 'I, *too*, want it.' I got so nervous feeling I'd been found out that I said: 'Fräulein, I thought you and I had a Coca-Cola romance, not a telepathic one.' But she seemed to have already forgotten the whole thing. The fact is, it was only much later that I realized the extent of our interpenetration. Yes," Hans said, "I've already mentioned that in many things Olga was hardly subtle. In certain matters she would flaunt her brashness, would play it, employ it. If we were in one of those so-called *refined* places, for example, her first reaction was to order a hamburger. Yes, sometimes she'd *shout* her order. 'A big, thick one,' she'd insist. Perhaps she did it knowing full well I didn't particularly relish the sight of a hamburger. Then, when she noticed my expression, she would shrug her shoulders and assume a look of contrition. But I knew she liked to appear a little unpolished in my presence, perhaps as an immediate response to what Olga herself labeled my 'outdated manners,' manners which, on the other hand, I know delighted her, or at least aroused her curiosity, even in a morbid way, I fear. Not in vain did she sometimes call me 'my favorite gentleman.' But I also have to say that her subtlety in other areas compensated for those provocative fits that, I suspect, she had with very few other people besides myself. On one occasion I gave her a foulard of mine that I'd worn barely a couple of times. It was gorgeous, made of white silk, and she seemed quite thrilled by this token, which, I can assure you, was entirely spontaneous on my part. The days went by," Hans said, "and not once did I see her wearing the foulard. Not once. That's how Olga was. Weeks, and then months, went by. I had almost forgotten that scarf when one fine day Olga showed up with it wrapped around her neck. Yes, that was a *very* special day, I remember it was an unforgettable day. We both knew it would be unforgettable. At some moment I touched the scarf with my finger and told her it really became her, which was true. 'It's only for special days,' she replied, and then gave me a long kiss. I don't know, on that day I suppose I felt compensated for all the silence, the intense bombardment of silences to which she had subjected me for so long on account of that garment. Yes," Hans said, "and the same thing happened with those clothes of hers that I liked best. She wore them only on those special days which, as with Ravel's *Boléro* and her special moments, must have had a sacred value for her. Yes, I think Olga was extremely frail and vulnerable but at the same time, without even intending to, she realized that she, too, could inflict harm, assert herself *by force* in the most diverse situations. Very often, probably much less often than she would've liked, she'd ask me: 'Am I hard, you really believe I'm *so* hard?' Yes, she was tortured by that doubt because she considered herself far from hard. And in the same way she was concerned about her lack of what she labeled, with an insolent and essentially contemptuous idolization, 'ordinary problems, the mundane variety.' Not having any real, overwhelming problems, as did everyone else around her, lent her attitude toward me—one of those people overwhelmed by *inordinate* problems, whose roots were often as metaphysical as they were absurd—a more aggressive turn than normal. Yes, I remember that 'normal' was one of those words she really liked to use in referring to herself. 'Is it my fault that I'm normal, absolutely normal?' she once asked me in a half-mocking, half-anguished tone. 'People are consumed with such lofty problems: *I think I'm not who I am*, or *I fear I am someone I know I'm not*. Rubbish. I have girlfriends who show up at the door one fine afternoon looking dismal. You think something serious has happened to them, and suddenly they burst out that they think their sexuality has become atrophied, or they doubt their identity to such a degree that on hearing their own voices, they don't even recognize them. Such things don't happen to me. And perhaps that's what sets me apart from the rest. I don't need those sorts of problems, you understand? I don't need them. If someday they come up, we'll see, but right now I haven't got them. Is that my fault?' That's how Olga was. Oddly enough, I think her greatest problem lay precisely in not having any in a world where problems, tremendous, insoluble ones, are consubstantial with the substance of our being, naturally a being that even from the embryonic stage is totally problematic, I think, but is at the same time *distinguished* by just that quality from all other beings in creation. Yes, stress, that terrifying modern malady afflicting society today," Hans said, "is already within us at birth, yes, we're born out of a *coitus of stress*," he said, smiling, as though the idea had amused him, "hasty and presumably unsatisfying. We secrete adrenaline right from the cradle. We pump out adrenaline incessantly, and therefore only a death or a madness that is *total*," he said, emphasizing this last word first through a pause and then by modulating his voice, "can manage to put an end to the constant bombardment of adrenaline. Thus, I think, one way or another I wind up saying that, in my judgment, there are also *partial deaths*, though this is only a supposition," he added now with a triumphant smile, which rather disconcerted me. "Yes, I suppose the world is divided between those who cultivate that kind of partial death or madness, I mean, the slow pilgrimage toward the *total comprehension* of death and madness, of death and madness understood and experienced as a totality; it's divided, as I was saying, between that type of person on the one hand and, on the other, those who neither develop nor cultivate that perpetual mental exercise. Olga, I believe, falls into this second group of people, yes, I'm positive. She is forever marked by the fact that she lacks problems—I mean problems that at some particular point one deems *worthy* of a psychiatrist—or at least by being thoroughly convinced of having none. Personally, I think Olga adjusted to life quite intelligently, yes, she adopted a chameleon approach—though not for that matter cynical or base—to the environment, her environment. As you already know," he said, "she is the middle sister, not the eldest or the youngest, which, I think, involves both advantages and disadvantages. Well, once, without making any fuss about it, she told me something that, with time, I've learned to appreciate in what I consider its due measure. A *blow* changed her intellectual life, yes, it entirely changed the course, the evolution of her intellectual and, I'd even dare say, her emotional life as well, which is, after all, logical in a world where one learns by blows. It was very simple, yes, but I've concluded that life's feats are forged through simple details or acts. She would usually sit in a particular armchair in her house, when she was still really a child, perhaps twelve or thirteen years old, to watch television. Olga has never been at all drawn to television," Hans said, "and the process of settling down in that armchair and no other was rather a ritual for her, an affirmation of a territory wherein her identity, I suppose, was reaffirmed, whatever it might take. In any event, one fine day when her parents were out, she went to sit in her armchair, as she customarily did, and her little sister—considerably smaller to a twelve-year-old girl—this seven- or eight-year-old sister, I was saying, had her heart so set on that chair that she tussled with Olga. At some point the child dealt Olga such a blow, right in the face, that Olga was nearly left reeling. 'With a clenched fist,' I remember Olga telling me when she recounted the incident. There was no need for Olga to tell me how much her attitude toward her young sister had changed from that point on. Yes," Hans said, "I know her well enough to realize that on that very day, at precisely that intense moment, began Olga's actual mental, spiritual, and physical domination of her quarrelsome little sister. She gave me no more details, but I know that on that day, immediately after receiving the blow *with a clenched fist*, Olga didn't even feel like crying, no, I'm sure she felt only vaguely humiliated, since in addition to the assault itself there was the fact that it came from someone younger; but she at once lowered her sails, changed her attitude or strategy on the spot, swallowing her wounded pride, her trampled pride, mingled now with her pain. Never again did she use violence or force with anyone to attain her goals. From that day and that blow she learned, I think, that there are other, more *effective* methods to attain what one wishes from people. And," Hans said, deftly digging into the earth with the tip of his sports shoe, "I really fear that today her little sister, now a full-grown woman, might be one of those people who are in some sense subjugated and even *enslaved* by Olga. Yes, because Olga has something that fascinates you at the beginning, which is later withdrawn without your fully realizing it, and in the end you've pretty much got to make a superhuman effort to be able to glimpse it again. Or to overcome it. You think you know *enough* about Olga, and suddenly you learn something that tears down all your preconceptions. I've already told you she's very contradictory. About everything, yes. Even with animals. Not only is there her terror of dogs, which I, by the way, always found overly theatrical, no, there's also her obsession with cockroaches. As a child, when she was still with her family in Einsenau, there used to be cockroaches in the old kitchen of their house. One night she got up half-asleep and headed to the fridge for something to slake her thirst. When she realized she was *barefoot* in the kitchen, the scare almost gave her a heart attack. That sensation of coldness from the floor, pressing against the soles of her feet, has haunted her to this day. She told me so herself. A common nightmare for her is one where she's stepping on a cockroach. And note that it's an *auditory* nightmare, not a visual one, for she only hears the *crunch* of the cockroach bursting open under the weight of her bare foot. There's that on the one hand," Hans said, "and you may well think a lot of people would be revolted by the same thing. But on the other hand, there's her *boldness* in certain things. For example, I know that several years

174

ago she traveled to a country in the Near East. There were snake charmers about, along with the usual hurly-burly of the markets in such countries. I know for a fact that Olga became adamant about holding and touching one of those enormous serpents with which the locals try to tempt tourists into having their picture taken, thereby getting a little money out of them. In any event, to the horror of the people accompanying her, Olga was *bent* on picking up that serpent and coiling it around her neck. 'It had to be done,' she told me. I suppose that sort of voluntary struggle between Olga and the serpent doesn't fit into the system of values we might attribute to a person who, even today, dreams about *stepping* on cockroaches and who jumps back in sudden terror at the sight of a dog. I don't know," Hans said, "perhaps I'm mistaken, it's possible. But I imagine that in all this I'm simply trying to provide *data* so you yourself, to whatever degree possible (which I fear will be only vaguely approximate) can construct or try to construct a psychological picture of Olga that's true to reality. I *need* to share this with someone, I know you understand that. Yes," he said, "it's a treasure that is of no use to me alone. After all, they say one always ends up sharing what one loves most, isn't that so? But I insist that her capacity to surprise those who at some point presumed to really know her (and of course I count myself among them) was inexhaustible. There were—there are—*disquieting* aspects to her. Without going too far, I'm thinking about her tendency to constantly observe life, while, incidentally, being none too observant of people. Olga was capable of bumping into all the street lamps, into each and every tree in some park where we were taking a walk, you know. In theory, I think, that would indicate that observing her surroundings appealed little to her. Yes, but only in theory," Hans said, "because it would be very interesting, I think, if one day someone were to decide to speculate about, or more accurately, to elaborate *a theory of Olga's theories*. I'll give you an example: we had been seeing each other for many months when, one afternoon, while we were near some cliffs, she seemed to have become lost in thought. I attempted not to disturb that silence, which at those moments struck me as sacred, full of wisdom, yet *filled* with thoughts. From time to time I caught her looking at her watch. I finally resolved to ask her not *what she was thinking*, which would have been normal considering that nothing lay before us but the sea, but rather *what she was watching*, which as it turned out didn't seem to disturb her in the least.

'The Green Ray,' she said solemnly. At first I thought she was pulling my leg, that she was simply, purely, and plainly mocking my always insane curiosity. But she was not. She ended up explaining to me her *Theory of the Green Ray.* According to her," Hans said, "sometimes, on the horizon, just at that instant when the sun disappears beyond the last line drawn by the sea's silhouette, just at that instant—which normally lasts no more than a second or two—if the atmospheric conditions are favorable, a sort of greenish segment or ray appears, the intensity of its color increasing in direct proportion to the clarity of the sky. 'Like a short rainbow, but a green one,' she specified. The curious thing is that for Olga—who had in one respect already arrived at an utterly *empirical* approach to her Theory of the Green Ray—for her, I was saying, there was an obvious relationship between the appearance of that optical phenomenon and her particular mood. The intensity of the ray was, in her own words, like an accurate barometer of the stage she was going through. Yes," Hans said, "Olga's tendency—of which many people were un-aware—to observe carefully everything around her was curious, really curious. You see, as I was marveling at that practice of visually tracking the horizon, Olga surprised me even further by making a remark that, incidentally, I think defines her character quite well. According to her, if you lie face down and look at the horizon without blinking, the slight curve ev-ident when it's observed from a normal position becomes pronounced to a surprising degree. It becomes almost a semicircle. 'It's incredible,' she said, 'I've done it quite often.' 'Done what?' I asked almost out of habit, though I knew what she was referring to. 'Just that,' she replied, 'looked at the horizon lying face down and tried to see the fleeting appearance of the Green Ray. That way everything is *complete*.' Yes, even now I haven't fully gotten over imagining Olga doing such acrobatics. I think about it and it's like floating. And I have such a peculiar feeling because I realize this person has almost nothing to do with the other one, the one everybody or nearly everybody knows. I knew there were two Olgas: the one who feared even alluding to or talking about death in more or less straightforward terms, and the one who, while still an adolescent, liked to go to cemeteries alone and collect little white pebbles, arranging them in little pyramids on the graves. Alone or in company, it didn't matter. I think at heart Olga has always been alone. I don't know whether it was from the moment I saw her observing the horizon or some other moment, but the fact is I began to feel as if I were floating ceaselessly. Yes, I suppose it was during that period when I learned the secrets of simulated *levitation*. I simply began to fly. Only at some harsh noise would I land. Yes, or when Olga suddenly appeared *in person*. Then, inside me, an emergency landing strip would take shape, with foam spread over the runway, sirens, the whole thing. It's true. I'm serious. Seeing Olga, even from a distance, even *from behind*, alone or with someone else, meant an instant and irrepressible desire to shout out loud, I mean, to allow all those other long-repressed shouts to manifest externally, condensed into a single shout. That's why my innocent spying, I think, was nothing but one more shout directed inward. One of those shouts she didn't like, but that nevertheless, I suppose, created no conflicts for her. And Olga wanted no conflicts. I've already told you that, I think. Conflicts were a necessary yet dreaded revulsive that called into question her most ironclad modes of thought and moral preconceptions. Consequently, I think, Olga loved the possibility of flirting, I mean, of flirting in the good sense, naturally, of *getting close* to such conflicts, while at the same time knowing she must flee from them almost at once if she wanted to preserve a good measure of her mental well-being. Olga, as I have said, would grow *dizzy* whenever conflict, in the form of something or someone, loomed up in her life. Yes," Hans said, "that's why she eliminated me from her life. And she did so in a decent, polite manner, without excesses, I'd even say affectionately, yes," he said, "I suppose almost without my fully realizing she was doing it, and I believe, or rather, I'm thoroughly convinced, without her realizing what she was doing, what she *herself* was doing to me. Yes," Hans said, "I think Olga was always very affectionate, terribly affectionate, but there was something that paralyzed her at certain moments, something that made her go stiff as a bamboo reed in the middle of some sultry, asphyxiating summer evening in the jungle, impassive as a rag doll accepting with resignation the grotesque posture she has been and goes on being subjected to year after year in a dusty, forgotten attic," Hans said, now weighing his words more before uttering them, as if it proved more difficult to do so while attempting to express those images, "yes, inert as a statue, or rather as an *effigy*, I think, because at heart Olga was very much like that. She seemed to be made of marble, of a marble which from time to time gave off sparks, or rather, actual lightning flashes. Yes," Hans said, "I suspect that it was in one of those sparks or flashes of lightning, in one of those chains of lightning Olga left in her wake when she spoke, when she smiled, when she kissed, and especially at the moment when she would leave, I think, that I was completely charred. Or perhaps not," he said, "perhaps it was through each and every one of those thunderless lightning flashes, after all of them, that I was consumed by the searing marble that was Olga. And by contrast," Hans said, "I also think the opposite happened to her, precisely the opposite, I mean I don't think she became gradually disappointed after our brief nocturnal encounters—though at times they were diurnal as well—I don't believe she became disappointed through a long, internal process paralleling those encounters, but rather that something scared her, something very definite and specific that I said or did. I don't know, or perhaps it was something Olga not so much said or did but thought or desired. Yes, I suppose it was something that happened *within her*. But I repeat, I'll never know for certain what Olga and I *did*, and if at some point I do come to know, I doubt I'll manage to understand it," Hans said. "And vice versa: perhaps I may understand it intuitively some day, but I'll never know for sure what it was. My awareness of what we did, as opposed to what we said, what we used to say to each other, has almost entirely vanished. All that remains is a thick cloud of dust," he said. "Yet it's clear that *we did something*, the sensation still lingers on my skin, even though I've explained to you before that I often confused desire with reality. Yes," Hans said, "we must necessarily have done something when she got frightened. Or perhaps she got scared by something she was *on the verge* of doing, as I was saying. Yes, or even about something she thought I might do at any moment. I don't know, I really don't know. To think about all that now is to suppose it, merely to suppose it. And the fact is," Hans said, "when I think about it now the only thing that comes to mind is the sound of marble, the marble I polish from sunup to sundown, yes, and also marble itself, the curtain of marble that Olga had for skin, her lips of marble, her tongue of marble," he said, "yes, that tongue that could writhe with the fury of a frightened scorpion, but that nonetheless never ceased being marble, yes. I suspect something kept her chained within, something prevented her from unloosing herself, I'm positive. Yes, I suppose it was the fear of breaking away from her old life, her dull and at the same time programmed, pleasant, and absolutely uncomplicated life. Because Olga was and will always be an adventurer of the heart, not of Reason. The fear of the *new world*," Hans said. "Yes, it's very clear, after that half-finished relationship, as she preferred things to be, that New Zealand as well as myself were or could be the *new world* for Olga, I mean, the *new world* in a particular sense and at a given moment in time when both circumstances, that place and myself, might or could acquire a common resonance in her brain. Yes," he said, "and I surmise, given that character—I mean Olga's character, which I believe I know quite thoroughly, to a degree of depth that matches what she and I *did*—I surmise, I was saying, that Olga lived in hell, yes, as I've already mentioned to you, but in a placid hell," he said, "in the most placid of hells, which is not, I think, to suggest that it didn't have all the characteristics I imagine an infernal abode ought to possess. I suppose I'm referring to her 'Bunker,' which she fancied was similar to a dovecote. Though I imagine she was probably right, absolutely right, when she affirmed that there *was* happiness there. Knowing her, I believe such happiness must have been feigned, to what extent I don't know, but feigned nevertheless. Though not, for that matter, any less real than some other happiness that isn't feigned," Hans said. "She believed in it and that was sufficient. She was intelligent enough to find warmth in hell, yes, but she would never have dared to consider the possibility of *another* hell, symbolized in this particular case by me, I think, and regarding which—in contrast to the one she already knew, where she operated daily—she had no idea how dangerous its flames were, I mean, how hot it was. And I," Hans said, "would have made Olga *melt*. Yes, like clay in a forge. Exactly. But in any case I'll always be confined to suspecting what it was that scared Olga away and prevented her from going further, or at least *allowing me* to go further. I don't know, I suppose Olga and I both know at some unconscious level just what we did," Hans said. "But I often ask myself, plunged into this cataclysm of marble that surrounds me, into this perpetual oratorio of shrill tones in the shop, just what the meaning of *doing* is. I don't know if when I say *we did*, I think about what we did, or think about the act of thinking or attempting to think about what we did. At any rate," Hans said, "I suppose no matter how much I may try time and again to avoid or shy away from this *subject*, which you may perhaps be particularly interested in, it might still interest you nevertheless. If that's the case I'd be really sorry, you must believe me. Yes, but it's also imperative for you to believe me, for you to

have believed me every single time I told you that I don't know the true extent of what I actually did with her, aside from the fact that I don't think it
matters at all, at least not when severed from the other reality, the *reality* that
went beyond her body. Yes, bodies rot away, Andreas," he said pensively and
as though musing over his words, "but the same thing does not occur with
the other reality I'm talking about. And it doesn't happen for the simple reason that this other reality is invisible. And furthermore, I think it can be reflected only partially on paper, always only partially, and at best in the memory of someone who loves you. Not so the other, not with the body. Nothing,
I believe, is so delusive as the apotheosis of the body. By the same token, I
think, few things are as pathetic as a body that has obviously been defeated
and has surrendered. Yes," he said, "*body* and *doing* seem to be synonymous,
phases or stages that can by no means exclude each other. In terms of doing,
as you know, I don't quite know what I did. That, ultimately, concerns only
me, I think, and therefore I alone can know the range of that knowledge,
which in any case, I suppose, is a knowledge founded upon thoughts and
therefore latent, living. And as for the body, I can tell you that the mere mention of that word brings not only to my mind but also to my body the full
sensation of her body. *Every* body is *the* body: Olga's. But it's precisely Olga's body that I cannot, I *don't want* to talk about," Hans said in a suddenly
excited tone, "I haven't ever talked to anyone about Olga's body, never. Not
even to myself. Yes, I think that talking to myself about Olga's body, in the
silence of memory and through objects or by means of marble, is frustrating
and leaves me with a void I don't know how to fill. What's contradictory is
that I have only to mention, not to discuss but simply to mention or even
think about Olga's body to feel totally, immediately *replete*, filled with that
body. Olga's body . . . God, her body!" Hans exclaimed, seeming to contain
the rest of his thoughts by biting his lips, leaving me totally disconcerted at
such an unexpected change in attitude. "What could I say about her body!
Even now I feel my stomach contract when I think about it. Olga's body
smelled of blood, yes, all of it smelled of blood," he said, "and in turn I
smelled of blood along with it. Blood, blood, blood—blood everywhere!!"
Hans cried almost rabidly, making me gulp with discomfort in the face of
such behavior. He had let loose a kind of piercing, hysterical shriek that was
gathered into the vault of the trees and reproduced like an echo, taking sev-

eral seconds to fade away. "Yes, my apologies if I've shocked you," he said
shortly, "but everything, at the mere mention of Olga's body, becomes incredibly bloodied. I remember one evening, some evening or other in her
damned yellow car. I said: 'I want to know your body.' She said: 'All right.'
Then, as if someone were tickling her, she started to laugh compulsively. Yes,
she was drunk, I mean, I suppose she was drunk, otherwise she wouldn't
have said 'All right,' but something else. You know, she would have asked me
'What for?' or even worse (and typically she'd ask this with more conviction
and emphasis), 'Why?' When I asked her why she was laughing, she replied
that perhaps that night it wouldn't be possible because it was a very *particular* day. My expression must have been indescribable because in the end she
had to confess to me, laughing and slapping the steering wheel, that she was
having her period. 'How ridiculous, my period!' she just barely managed to
say as her forehead knocked against the glass of the door, making it impossible for me to see her face. All that was like falling into a sweet *abyss*, I think,
and the first clear thought I had was the image of my face, completely covered in blood, in front of a mirror, several hours later. Blood on my chin, on
my cheekbones, in my eyebrows, blood under my fingernails, between my
teeth, on the tip of my nose. Red stains on every single part of my body. Naturally, I remember going about staining everything the minute I touched it.
Yes," he said, "sheets, nightstand, walls, light switch, faucets, soap, towels,
everything, everything spotted with blood, but that wasn't just Olga's blood
anymore, no, it was also *my blood*, I think, besides the fact that in a certain
sense her blood belonged to me, because my blood was in there, too. That
I'm sure of, yes," Hans said, taking a deep breath as though he strove to con-
dense into his lungs all the air from the small forest clearing we were now
crossing, "that evening a *covenant of blood* took place between Olga and me,
which nothing and no one will ever change. The indescribable rapture provoked in me by that sensation, I mean by the awareness of being entirely *saturated* by Olga's body through her blood, even now causes me to shiver. Yes,"
he said, "because when I mention Olga's body I immediately think of Olga's
blood, and when I think I'm thinking about her blood, I also smell it, perceive its bittersweet taste, feel its warm moisture seeping into the creases of
my lips. Yes, and it's because of that whole series of thoughts and sensations
that I finally end up hearing, through that orgy of amorous blood, her laugh-

ter, yes, her laughter of a mad goddess, of a vestal virgin quivering with simultaneous pleasure and fear, pressing my face almost furiously, amidst
queer moans and tender words, against the fountain, against the *spring* of
her blood, the cave of her blood. That was not only the smell of Olga's blood,
the smell of our two bodies daubed with blood, I think, but was also the
smell of *life*, the only smell of life possible for me to conceive ever since. Yes,
a smell capable of enslaving the fragrance of a rose, a smell that could make
ambrosia blush and dye the flowers' nectar black. Ah, well," Hans said, "the
truth is there were other times, I mean other times *without* blood, or at least
I suppose there were other times, but those *other times*, those other partial ap-
proaches to Olga's body, since every form of contact with it was nothing but
an *approximation*, those other times, I was saying, were invalidated by the
phantom of blood. Yes, I would say that rather than a night of love all that
had been a sort of medieval pact, a sabbat of murmurs and entreaties inter-
mingled and thus also intertwined, as were our bodies, and in which the
words I most often heard from her lips were 'Say it again,' while from mine
I think what she must have heard most was perhaps 'eternity.' But I was telling you about Olga's body," Hans stammered after a brief silence, "Olga's
body, *that* body," he would repeat slowly, "*her body*. Yes," he said, half-
closing his eyes, "my porcelain vase, my liquor on troubled nights, her body,"
he said, "my uncut gem, my aurora borealis, and my destructive scintillation.
Her body, Olga's body—what can I say about it that you haven't already
imagined? It was my water in the desert, my sun amidst the ice, my favorite
aroma, the most exotic morsel. But no, I don't want to talk anymore about
Olga's body," Hans said, vigorously shaking his head from side to side, "in
all things, silence is the surest token of respect, and therefore I think I *must
keep quiet*. Yet nevertheless, I think, each time I reflect on that body I discover
new facets of myself. Yes, a veritable earthquake of memories and images
suddenly assails me. I shut my eyes, think about something related to that
body, about those approximations to the quicksand that was her body, and
what comes to my mind, powerfully, is the thought of myself, while still a
child, eating strawberries with cream. Yes," he said, "the *feast* it meant to dip
a strawberry into the cream and then swallow it, is always or nearly always
duplicated at the thought of Olga's body. I don't know, I suppose that if
everything that's gone through my head, I mean everything going through

my head since I met her, could somehow or other be rendered into a plastic image or some such thing," he said, "it would be the delight of more than one psychologist. Yes, even my own sister Angelica, were she not connected to me through family ties and a shared life experience, at least up to a certain age, would celebrate a geuine *banquet* at my expense. I'm quite sure. I know that what's seething in my head would constitute a lavish repast for psychologists, those fiends who revel in torturing the collective unconscious of history and mankind. Yes," Hans said, "I don't know whether you've noticed at any point that the human species is the only one in all creation that, since the beginning of time, miserably wastes time studying itself. Yes," he said, "mankind is studied from every angle. Philosophers study what you *intuit*, politicians what you *do*, those feeble-minded psychologists what you supposedly *ought to think* or not think, sociologists what you *are*, anthropologists *where you come from*, and as far as doctors are concerned, they simply *split you open*. The spectrum is broad and terrifying. I don't think there's any way out. They study you under cross fire, they deal your body dozens of blows if you don't obey the command 'Stop!'—a command they try to utter very softly, so you can't hear it. Yes, I expect they are interested in every sort of individual except the kind who *supposes*. One who merely supposes can prove to be dangerous, and one way or another they immediately and discreetly deal with him like a *spiritual fugitive*. The day will come, I fear, when an individual reading in the park will not be deemed odd, but rather suspicious. You see, that supreme instant when one portion or another of the spirit is cut out has already come to several countries throughout the course of history. And I don't believe that what annoys others is the fact per se that an individual should be reading, but rather his impertinent solitude. Yes, I suppose in the near future we'll arrive at the demented phase in which an individual's solitude will provoke the instantaneous *irritation* of the masses, united in their devouring inertia. I think the blows come from all sides, because even the disciplines that theoretically ought to decay to a lesser degree, in actual practice wind up being vile watchdogs for those I mentioned before. Yes," Hans said, "because whether dentists scare you or cause you misery isn't the least bit important, what is serious," he said, "is to have historians explain your past miseries, the disgraceful behavior of the civilizations that preceded us, forcing you to take them as *behavioral norms*. Now that's really cerebral decay. Yes, and it's also very serious to have poets bent on explaining what you *feel*, given that any worthwhile poetry is collective, everybody's. Yes, that's the root of the problem: our social nature, a nature that conceals the component of innate animality we carry within, which in order to avoid surfacing doesn't even surface in the majority of the masses throughout the long torment of yawns and jolts that constitutes existence. I don't know, I think nowadays anyone who constantly supposes is dealt with as a fugitive, as I was telling you before, but anyone who *imagines* is annihilated. I know I'm not revealing anything to you. What's astounding about all this is that everyone knows it but no one does anything concrete to prevent it. Yes," Hans said, "these days anyone who imagines is sent directly to the madhouse. Madhouses, I think, are filled with people who simply imagine. Society allows you to moralize fatuously or to produce relentlessly, but not to imagine. Then the place for you is the madhouse, and I'm talking about *authentic* madhouses, not places *like this*," he said, indicating Chemnitz with his glance, "which are harmless sanatoriums, health resorts. Yes, as you can see, here I can only *imagine* Olga's body. But deep down I don't suppose I desire anything else. It horrifies me to think of that body full of wrinkles, that body in a few years, plagued with problems, including mental ones, like some kind of smallpox. No, for me Olga's body will always be strawberries with cream," Hans said, "yes, and her body will be my sated vampire's face reflected in a mirror that I recall bore unmistakable traces of rust. I don't know if you understand why I don't want to talk about what we did or about Olga's body. Perhaps there dwells within me the horrible sensation of doubt," Hans said, "I suddenly hear the tumult of that cruel mental corrosion, *doubt*—and I begin to fear that what will illuminate my own consciousness for as long as I live will on the contrary tarnish hers. Yes, I think she always felt very guilty because of what she did with me, what she ended up discussing with me, and, above all, I suppose, what she thought about me and in regard to me. I feel a deep sorrow about that, so deep I prefer not to think about it," Hans said. "As deep a sorrow as when, still a very small boy, I recall, I would burst into tears on seeing that my mother's nails got dirty when she prepared artichokes in the kitchen. I don't know why that happened, but I suppose I associated that image with something frightful in a being I supposed was beyond good and evil. Yes," Hans said, "and beyond uncleanness, of course. On one occasion my mother, looking very distressed at the sight of me crying on account of her green nails—which I remember filled me with genuine dread—said something foolish like, 'But mama is a normal person, someday she'll die too.' That was *definitive*," Hans said, "ever since, the sight of an artichoke has made me feel dizzy. It's not merely an artichoke, I think, but my mother, death, I myself dead one day, you, everyone. The dizziness is *thought*, not felt, I mean, nothing whirls about me, nor am I debilitated. It's only my thought that gets dizzy, and hence for a few seconds it can't keep functioning, it stops thinking. And the sight of an artichoke also brings me sorrow, I think, an automatic, unmitigated sorrow. That particular tone of green condenses in some part of my brain the idea of mortality which, I suppose, has tormented the entire human race ever since the advent of History as such. That greenish rugosity on the nails acquires a supernatural dimension, I assure you, that green, you know, is all the loved ones who have passed away, my fate, everyone's," he said. "Being and ceasing to be without ever understanding in the least this orgy of dawns that usher in days laden with routine, this ephemeral yawn of life that must hold something, when no matter how many misfortunes it brings us, we always cling to it with the *murderous* desperation of a ship-wrecked soul who glimpses a plank just a few meters away from him in the middle of a tempest," Hans said with his gaze now lost in the horizon. "In just the same way I feel a profound sorrow at the thought of Olga, I mean, at the thought of her not only not thinking about me but gradually tending to forget me, in direct proportion, I suppose, to the deterioration of her neurons. Though, mind you, I occasionally feel seized by an odd happiness. I know it's spurious and that the blackness will soon return, but during those brief instants I feel I'm the happiest man in the universe. My love encompasses the infinite, I mean, the infinite in that sensation of *being* with her. I recognize it's a realistic way of understanding love, yes, rather like loving the *idea* of love, loving its mystery, I suppose, I don't know. Although that's usually fleeting; later the sorrow returns," Hans said. "I know that when I start thinking about Olga—about her phrases and her gestures, what we did and what we never *actually* went so far as to do, since one can always do more, I think—I descend into the pit of sorrow. I believe it's a kind of solidified sorrow, yes, and I think it's a similar sorrow as far as its physical effects, as far as its external manifestation, I mean, as an objectification of itself, a sorrow very similar, I'm saying, to the one I experienced when, as a child, I had a stuffed bear that lost one of its eyes and my parents replaced it with a thumbtack. I suppose I would have preferred for my little bear to be one-eyed rather than such an abomination, seeming to have a metal eye, I mean, *having* a metal eye, an execrable metal eye that lent him, I think, a truly frightening aspect, a sinister laugh conveyed not *in* his mouth but *through* that silver eye, chillingly bright. What's more," Hans said, "when I was almost an adolescent, I once again saw my old stuffed bear with the thumbtack stuck in his eye, and the feeling of sorrow hadn't entirely left me yet. Naturally, by then I could look at it *face to face*, which for a long time hadn't been possible," he said, "but the sorrow lingered. It's the same with Olga, I think, even though several months have elapsed now since the last time I saw her. Yes, several months, though the truth is that I often wonder whether or not there really was a *last time*. It's impossible for me to know," said Hans, "it really is. I do know there was one day, one specific afternoon, when I suddenly understood everything clearly, yes, I realized what she was trying to tell me. I suppose it was the almost immediate result of hearing her voice telling me that the *emotional gap* in her life was already filled. Yes, filled, *filled* is what she said. I believe Olga had in fact spoken to me often about wanting us, above all, to be *friends*. That was her obsession from the beginning, I think, and for me the word 'friendship' in reference to Olga transgressed outright not so much the issue of possessiveness, which concerned both of us so much, but my concept of what was or ought to be the loftiest, most superior phase of love. The difference between Olga and me is that she kept her capacity to generate and even to give love completely *curbed*, she gripped it through invisible reins, while for my part I didn't care one bit if that capacity were to be completely unbridled. Emotional gap, she said, yes, I suppose that was the instant when I felt a gush of cold water run down my spine. *Filled emotional gap*, she said. Just remembering that moment I feel a vibration pervading everything, accumulating in the atmosphere, making it dense. And that, as I said, in spite of the fact that a lot of time has gone by. So," Hans said, "at this point I'm not going to deceive you, it would strike me as rather dishonest, yes, *rather dishonest* is exactly what I mean to say. You should know it, you should know *everything*, yes, you've been here all this time listening to me without saying anything or, to be more precise, I've been here with you all this time not allowing you to say anything, which I don't think changes anything; the truth is I don't believe it's fair to conceal from you that I know *exactly* how much time has passed since Olga and I last saw each other. Yes, I know it *perfectly*," he said, "here time goes by very slowly, extremely slowly, as I've already told you, and there's always the possibility of thinking about it, I mean, how time passes. To think about the passing of time while time passes. Although the distinction I would make when referring to Olga is that, when I think about her, time does not pass but rather *advances*. Yes, the essence remains, the sensation of time, but there is something beyond that essence, I mean, beyond what the senses can somehow or other retain, there is something, I was saying, that slowly advances. I don't know if you follow me," Hans said, "but I'll explain it in another way. I know that a hundred and thirty-six days have passed since I last saw Olga's face, yes," he said, "exactly that long, over four months, almost four and a half months. Saying it is *easy*," Hans said, scanning the thicket with his gaze, "but it's very hard. Three thousand two hundred and sixty-four long hours without hearing Olga's voice, without hearing it *at all*, not once. Would you be able to hold your breath for one or two minutes? Something like that happens to me whenever I think about her. An interminable, painful succession of one or two minutes holding my breath. Yes, I can't avoid thinking about time passing without her, I mean, with her in the most perfect and cruel state I know: *without her*. Yes, by now it's been a hundred and ninety-five thousand eight hundred and forty minutes since I last felt the electricity of her hair on my face. And I can't help being surprised, at least up to a point," he said, "by your astonished expression on hearing this. I understand your astonishment only relatively. I don't know, I should be astonished by exactly the opposite, I think, in other words, at a lover who doesn't *count* the time that's elapsed without being with the person he loves. Yes," Hans said, "at all times I keep a more or less strict account of that sort of *crime* that destiny and time have committed against me by depriving me of her, of the remote possibility of her, of consummating that long series of things we left *half-finished*. But what grieves me most," he said, "much more than thinking about Olga, about everything concerning Olga and about everything that was refracted outward *from* Olga, is to think that when I think about her I do so in terms of the past. Yes, because you must have noticed I'm talking in the past tense and, consequently, even when I converse with myself mentally through and amidst the noise in the marble workshop I'm unable to do it in the present tense. Yet nevertheless Olga *exists*: I suppose on the one hand she does so objectively, I mean, at this very instant Olga is existing, though she may not think she exists, but the fact is she also exists *here*," Hans said, pointing with a furious, almost violent gesture to the key hanging from his neck, "she exists and I can sense how she moves. I sense her just as I sensed her during that last spell before leaving the firm. Yes, at the time I placed my desk so that I was facing away from the photocopy machine, thinking that way I wouldn't see her. But Herr Reinicke's office was right across from me, and every time she went out to make copies I would see her reflection in the glass of his office. I think I also *sensed* her in my skin then, even if I didn't look directly at her. I don't know how a mother senses her child when she is carrying him in her womb," Hans said, "but I do know that I sense Olga *moving* inside me. Yes," he said, "I even feel slight contractions every so often, especially if I recall something I had forgotten, but which at the time had a profound impact on me. I think Olga is in my head, yes, but the *sensation* of Olga comes directly from my stomach, though at other times it comes from my chest as well, or even from my palate. I've often tried to analyze that sensation of bearing Olga within me to its ultimate conclusions. Yes, and it usually depresses me. I told you before that she nearly always ate fish," Hans said. "Well, I suppose my situation is much like something Olga told me, remarking how it had made quite an impression on her, and which I quickly understood as a perfect metaphor for what was happening to me with respect to her. 'I was eating a turbot,' she said, 'when suddenly a little anchovy turned up inside it.' Thus my *pregnancy* with Olga, I think. Yes, I believe I managed to somatize Olga entirely, there came a time when she was in my cells. I don't know," Hans said, "I suppose *somatize* is a word she would have been surprised to hear from my lips. Yes, as I was saying, almost everything is felt in the stomach, I suppose: happiness, uncertainty or anguish, everything. Nothing *happens* in the head except thought," Hans said, "yes, and the incessant thinking about scenes involving Olga tends to affect the rest of the body, especially the stomach, I think, rather like a baby turning over from time to time. Sometimes I could even swear that the noise of marble bothers her, I mean, that it in turn provokes a reaction in that being, causing something akin to slight *spasms*. Yes, then I feel a sharp pang in my stomach. It's as though an internal voice were telling me: 'Quit.' And I do," Hans said, "yes, I do so at once. Then I sit calmly and think. I think and then think again about what I just thought, yes, I think about why I thought it, what the reason was and why at just that moment and not another. Last of all, I think about what I might have thought if I hadn't thought that. Yes," he said, "and believe me, that's a very debilitating process. But her *presence* gives me strength to keep going. I've already told you, I expect, that even though Olga belongs to the past, she goes on being here, inside my body. The past flows into my memory and thus into my mind. As though I ever had any mind at all!" Hans cried, trying to give his expression an air that proved unmistakably false. He then looked at me attentively, remaining silent for several seconds. "Well," he said apologetically, "I don't know why you're looking at me like that, but I suppose being in this place implies, if not being *totally* mindless, at least having a stomach that also *thinks*. Yes, and a mind that *eats*," he said, framing a smile that, in contrast to the glacial expression of his look, put me quite ill at ease. "Thus the nature of the being within, that's right, my memories devour everything happening in the outer world, I know that. By now, you see," he said, "it's been one hundred and ninety-five thousand eight hundred and forty-three minutes *without her and with her within me*. The entire sum of lacerating minutes, except for a few spells of sleep, when I expect I cease thinking about her entirely, or at least I don't remember doing so. Yes, because I still haven't fully managed to calculate the consequences of that relationship. For example," Hans said, "I always had the impression, as I may have told you at some point, that every time I was about to see Olga it was like undergoing an exam. Yes, it was terrible. I was convinced that *everything* was at stake on each date. And so it went month after month," he said, "but those exams in the dark of night began to extend not only to the eves of our dates but to many other nights as well. I would wake up with a start, thinking I had failed some course, that because of that failure I would lose my job or some such thing; it was as though out of the depths of night there loomed the *silhouette* of an examining panel to grill me about things I didn't feel responsible for, because to begin with, I think, I'd no knowledge of them. I don't know," Hans said, "I suppose that feeling of being constantly examined was nothing but the literal translation of the fact that I knew I was inferior to her. Because the problem was, I think, that I *fell in love* with Olga, while she simply ended up *getting used* to my devotion," he said, "to my devotion transformed into a veritable cataract of things done, things said, and things supposed. Things that at first surprised her, I think, even if for no other reason than the allure of novelty, which then flattered her, even flattered her quite a lot, and later on, I suppose, by dint of having felt *excessively* flattered, I think, caused her to become scared or to cease finding them amusing. I don't know. The truth is I barely struggle against the chronometer that went off inside me the day I saw her for the last time. It's futile and I know it, I mean, that *struggle* is futile. I understood some time ago that attempting to change anything of hers that she was not entirely certain about was virtually useless. And with regard to me, I think, she was never certain. At times she found me charming and at times glum. Yes, she always accused me of exaggerating, of being an extremist. That *immunized* her against me, I mean, she wielded that accusation in order to protect herself, to avoid giving a response in any sense of the word. The fact is," Hans said, "I learned to live with the awareness of futility concerning anything I did or said for her sake and in her presence. Yes, and thus I devoted myself to thinking about futility, I wound up accepting it, and now, I believe, I try to use it as I deem fit, I mean, however it might cause me the least harm. Yes, I know that up to a point it's useless to remember, but I also know that I can't *believe* I don't remember her. It's a lie," he said, "and that's the reason I always know which is the *last* minute without Olga, that is, the one hundred and ninety-five thousand eight hundred and forty-fourth, for example," Hans said nimbly, not pausing for even a moment to think about that number, which went through my head like a streak of lightning, "but I know too that I often think about the *first* minute I saw Olga, the first time I saw her and the impact that first vision had on me. It's one of the thoughts that most often hounds me. Yes," he said, "I remember having seen her on the street, in Emden, some weeks before she came to work with us at the firm, yes, I remember her perfectly well. I believe she was accompanied by someone I paid no attention to, whether by one person or several, I don't know. Next to her they seemed to be mere *shapes*, yes. At that moment, I recall, she was crossing a central street. Even that first impression was explosive, I think, totally, devastatingly *explosive*. At first I felt I couldn't breathe," he said, "and then that something threw me or thrust me back, in the opposite direction to the one in which she was walking. Yes, as though it were a blast. I once felt something similar during some tests carried out in some quarries near Essen. Yes, it was as if your ears were plugged and all at once that force hurls you backward, almost before you hear the explosion, I mean, right between the instant when the explosion has in fact already occurred and that other instant, within tenths of a second, when the ear registers it. Yes," Hans said, "a sort of *funnel* between the nose and the brain. That day, I think, something similar happened to me. I believe it was then, almost immediately after that first impression, that I felt something like a slap of searing hot air on my face, turning my cheeks red and making me break into a sweat like a man sentenced to death. Yes," Hans said, "but it was a sweet sensation, as though grief could be sugared. Rather strange, I admit. Because what I felt on seeing her, I think, was in fact a *painful plenitude* that I couldn't even begin to describe. Rhetoric and Olga are utterly antagonistic elements, I suppose, yes, and I imagine that to a great extent—assuming that at some moment I might have *had* her in one sense or another—I lost her thanks to my rhetoric. As I was saying, I suddenly saw the outline of those honeyed lips, yes, I remember it perfectly, I saw them for but a fraction of a second as they crossed in front of me, and I thought, 'There, there she is.' But she had already gone by and what for a fraction of a second had been, as I was saying, plenitude, swiftly turned to *pain*, yes," Hans said, "the pain that inevitably derives from being unable to grasp, to caress, to hold in our hands the plenitude that has flooded our being, leaving us at the mercy of the most absolute helplessness, the tremendous lack that henceforth every hour and minute will become, yes, these one hundred and ninety-five thousand eight hundred and forty-six minutes of remembering the plenitude of that moment, of those moments, because there were indeed many moments. Moments like a string of firecrackers with a kind of initial *Great Fugue*, because I've concealed something from you," Hans said pensively, "yes, I've concealed it as we went along because for a while I thought you, too, might think I am exaggerating, I mean, that I have a distorted perception of things. The fact is I didn't *simply* come across her, no, the whole thing was a lot more extraordinary, yes," he said, "I think there was something of an *apparition* about it, because Olga did not emerge from around a corner or out of a group of people, I mean, from the group of *shapes* with whom I believe she was walking that day. No," Hans said, "Olga *issued forth* from the light, from the innermost core of the light. As you know, in the city it's usually overcast, the days are gray and cheerless. It clears up only from time to time and always tentatively. Well, I remember it was a winter morning, yes, but the sun shone radiantly in the sky, which at that time of year is remarkable. Everything seemed crisper, more alive, you must believe me," Hans insisted somewhat vehemently, yet without looking at me, "yes, everything happened in an instant, in just *one instant*. There was an intersection of two streets where the sun was reflected in a most singular manner. It seemed as though all the rays had concentrated at that very corner. I think it was a coincidence," he said, "though I'll confess there were times when I wasn't so sure about that. The fact is, coincidence or not, there was such brightness in that patch of street that when I looked directly at it I was rather dazzled for a few moments. I recall thinking it was a pleasant and comforting sensation. That's when Olga emerged from it, from the medley of light, and came walking toward me. In all likelihood, I made the instinctive gesture of raising the palm of my hand to shield my eyes, yes, quite likely. She couldn't have had that sensation of dazzlement, I think, because she walked with her back to the sun. I also remember," Hans said, "that something I've often been intrigued by is the almost absolute certainty that I felt the same sensation, first of dazzlement, and then of warm air on my face, the sultriness that flooded everything, once again when she told me about the South Wind that blows during some autumns in those northern regions. Yes," he said, "when she explained the effect of that strange wind, the *memory* of the explosion, of the luminous tumult that seeing Olga for the first time had been, came to me again. Those were the same *symptoms*, I think. Yes," Hans said, "and I also recall that when I saw her show up at work something very similar occurred, though at that time I was stunned. A hallucination, I thought. But no, it wasn't, I had to make a great effort to keep from running toward her, taking her hand, raising it to my heart and saying: 'Listen.' At that very instant, I think, my heart went rampant and my head began to function in a peculiar way, I mean, with *another cadence*, yes, to a serenely feverish rhythm," Hans said, "a fever that perhaps reached its peak when, well into my subsequent relationship with her, she spoke to me about the South Wind and the psychic influence which, according to the legends of Einsenau, that odd atmospheric phenomenon exerts over certain people. And also at that moment when I saw her appear at work, my brain started to function like one of those jewels of fine watch-making that are in fact true *timing devices*, a challenge to the imagination. Olga herself, I think, with all her contradictions, was always a *challenge* to my imagination. Yes, and mind you, I believe I've always been quite an imaginative person, I mean very imaginative, yes. A challenge that my imagination couldn't overcome, I suppose. The fact is, I understand that in some way or other I'm still fully immersed in that challenge," Hans said, "yes, otherwise, I think, I would not be *here* at this moment, nor possibly would there have occurred many things that have indeed happened, I mean, that happened and continue to happen within me and which I suppose happened in the outer world as well. What I have not wanted to accept under any circumstances," he said, "is the possibility of believing that such a challenge really isn't one, that it doesn't exist. Several months passed from the time I first *saw* Olga until the time I managed to *break out* of her, almost half a year that our more or less intense relationship lasted, and then my time here. By this stage, I'd think it would be imperative to believe that I *understood* something about all this. No," Hans said, "I understood absolutely nothing, and I don't know why, but I imagine she must have experienced something similar. I know the obvious, what left traces," Hans said, "I know that during that time I dropped several pounds, got a few gray hairs, yes, quite a few, a lot of them, I know I became acquainted with the horror of insomnia, that malady which doesn't hurt but can annihilate whomever it chooses, I mean, annihilate them in the middle run, not in the long or the short run, in the middle run, as I suppose Olga chose to do with regard to me, even if at an unconscious level. It was also around that time," Hans said, "when I realized I had circles under my eyes, though mine were completely distinct from hers, yes—hers, I think, were almost imperceptible shadows that one only noticed when looking at her very *closely*. The bluish undertone contrasted with the blue of her eyes, forming a harmonious whole inseparable from its parts, I mean, Olga without those dark circles would not have been herself. Mine," Hans said, "suddenly cropping up in a matter of months, were two bags full of impatience, of frustration, of fear abruptly and mercilessly concentrated there. But as a matter of fact, I think, that stage passed, yes, I honestly believe that to at least some degree it passed, or perhaps what it did was to advance rather than to pass, as time has ever since I met Olga. It advanced over me, I mean, because the difference between time passing and time advancing, I think, is that the first does so, I believe, *through* everything that surrounds us, ourselves being an infinitesimal part of those surroundings, yes, it affects us directly insofar as it is indeed slowly killing us, yet indirectly in that we tend not to be fully aware of that subtle process of extermination. Yes, in contrast, the second, time advancing," he said, "does so directly *over* us, yes, it's as though the entire weight of time were concentrated *here*," Hans said, pointing to his forehead, "it's a time that is witnessed at nearly every moment by thought, which knows all the while that the battle, the war with time is lost, and is therefore crushed by it, pitilessly and continually crushed, allowing awareness to witness, as I was saying, that *self-immolation* it undergoes throughout each and every minute of the day. To face this with determination, I think, ends up being the least painful way out possible, which is, incidentally, what has happened in my case. That's what I've learned at Chemnitz," Hans said, "the course of destiny can never be diverted, but if you can ride on its back, in a certain sense you control its movements, or rather in my case, its *convulsions*. Being in contact with its infinite superiority, you become better acquainted with its workings, and in some way, however remote, you also become part of that infinitude. Yes," Hans said, "you're like a horseman of the Apocalypse. My hours are spent between the workshop and going for walks. If the weather is mild I stay to meditate until I feel the first signs of exhaustion. Yes, that happens almost always in the afternoon. Then I go back to the marble. I know trying to read is fruitless, for example, nor do I have any use for what the other patients call 'recreation rooms.' I drink vast amounts of tea. Yes, lots of tea. No cognac, no toothaches, that's over. No whiskey either. I don't think I could take another swig of whiskey. Yes, the very thought makes me gag. But in any case there's little else to do here besides think. I hate being bombarded by images from the television and noise from the radio that my mind is unable to follow. Yes, there are few things I hate as much as those. I have quite enough with *my own* bombardment, I suppose. Yes, phosphorus bombs hurled in my direction by myself. Napalm, perhaps, I don't know," Hans said, "it's all the same, I think, the effects must be nearly identical. I devote myself to thinking strictly from the perspective of the process of active thought, not from that of contemplative passivity. I prefer to think about everything I at once hate and love, in other words, Olga," Hans said, "because I think I still love the sacred memory of her smile, yes, and I hate her special way of saying or doing certain things, for example, when she acknowledged that she usually emerged *victorious* from certain situations. Yes, 'victorious,' she said. I don't know, the fact is that every victory implies an instant loser, I suppose. But what distresses me even now is not my own awareness of being the loser—which if I actually did have it, I also had the certainty of having gotten from her, from Olga, a lot more than most of the people who have surrounded her throughout her life—what distresses me, I think, is to remember, almost photographically, some moments directly connected with her when I felt a dejection similar to the one provoked by watching the *felling* of a gigantic tree. It's as if they were amputating a hundred, two hundred years or more of history. Yes," Hans said, "I once saw one of those centenarian trees hacked down, and I can assure you that what went through my being on quite a few occasions when I was with Olga—especially toward the end, of course, when I was aware that each date I managed to wrest out of her would be just that, a partial and momentary victory on my part, only the *mirage* of a desperate, pointless victory—I assure you, as I was saying, it was a very similar sensation. My whole being was stunned, left paralyzed and in utter silence, just as happens seconds before the sawed tree topples down. At those moments," he said, "all of nature seems to remain motionless, shocked that someone should dare to do *that* to one of her children. That's just how it was," Hans said, "an immense tree would topple down within me each time she left, each time she *had to leave*. Many times I asked myself how it was possible for her not to realize what she left in her wake, because I think it was very obvious, yes, or at least quite obvious. You can see the extent to which our survival instinct can actually befog us," Hans said, "and I'm speaking about her, about her reaction toward me, because I've no doubt she was perfectly aware what *condition* I was in. I know she was aware of it because I think she, too, experienced our relationship, right from the start, as a protracted *farewell*. And despite all that, she appeared not to notice it. 'See you tomorrow,' she would say, always in reference to work, of course. Yes, I think Olga used to say it with all the ingenuousness in the world, not realizing that right before her a tree was toppling down, slowly splitting," Hans said, "at first leaning only a little, then a bit

more, until it finally fell in a mute crash, raising a great cloud of dust, a confused dance of splinters, leaves, and earth. I also experienced that impact, I
think, with the images of a building being destroyed. Yes, I remember mentioning it earlier. A tree or a building, it makes no difference," Hans said, "but
you know, several months had to go by before I understood why I liked going
to the Sörolt, whether I was alone or had to choose some place to meet her. It
was a dirty bar, not particularly attractive in any sense," he said. "Yes, there
wasn't *a single element* to justify my instinctive preference for the Sörolt. I've
lost count of the number of hours I must have spent there thinking about
Olga, sensing her presence in that atmosphere. And one day, quite by chance,
I think, completely by chance, I looked up at one of the walls, noticing a small
picture that had never caught my eye before. Yes," Hans said, "it was a
framed photograph, a rather deteriorated photograph in which was preserved the instant when an old building was being dynamited. The central
tower was beginning its fall and a cloud shaped like a mushroom or ring encircled the structure of the building. Yes, the photographer who took it, I
think, chose the *exact moment* I've been trying to describe to you all along. I
don't know," Hans said, "I suppose, or might suppose, that I must have seen
that picture at some point, though I assure you that my mind didn't register
it at all," he said, "and nevertheless I had *always* gone to the Sörolt looking,
I think, for some trace of her, which I wouldn't even have been able to define.
Yes, imagine my astonishment at discovering that photograph. I think I set
foot in the Sörolt another three times, but always because I had agreed to see
her there, for it was Olga herself who ended up being partial to meeting at
that bar. I never again went back to that place, no," Hans said, "nor did I mention to her the matter of the photo. It would have taken too long to explain,
I think, much too long. Yes, I don't suppose Olga needed explanations to do
as she pleased. She needed to live, to live as intensely as possible. As though
her life were going to end the following morning. Yes," he said, "I think
knowing Olga implied a splendor no one was ever able to see, not even the
people who knew me best, not even you, with whom I'd shared all that during a certain period, not even Olga herself, being always more concerned
about continuing to be loved than about loving, because that, I think, would
have implied taking a decisive step in her life. I suppose that step would have
meant a *qualitative* leap between her ideal willingness to change everything

196

and her real capacity to withstand that change. Yes, because I repeat: she was aware of having been born to be loved. I don't know, perhaps because of her beauty, most likely," Hans said, "but, being the sensitive person she was, it was wearing her down from day to day, relationship to relationship, because I've no doubt that before me, and aside from her partner, she'd had relationships with other men. Yes, it had to be that way, I think. There will be others later on, that's the order of things, I think. Because Olga's ability to withstand a certain kind of *pursuit* is very limited. 'I'm human,' she used to say by way of an excuse. And I would think, 'No, you're a goddess.' But I wouldn't tell her that. It was fruitless, everything was fruitless with her. Yes, in that sense I think she was *also* predestined to succumb to the destiny she herself had chosen. When one of those pursuits, be it through perseverance or the effectiveness of its methods, seriously began to worry her—which I suppose happened in my case when our relationship reached a certain pitch, when it threatened the foundations of her sensibilities—at that point she would make a mental *break* with everything. She would then grapple with the matter, 'turning it over a bit' in her mind. Yes," Hans said, "and you can see the outcome. Olga always emerged victorious in everything, as she said herself, not without a certain mixture of pride and compunction. But I suppose the awareness of being born exclusively to be loved leaves its mark. It's like a tattoo we see without even looking at it. She had an intuition of what a great thing it is to love, I think, surely she must have needed to experience *that* some time, as well, but I imagine her capacity to really surrender herself was becoming more sclerotic by the moment. Yes . . . look, there's Dr. Littbarski waiting for us," Hans said, indicating the sanatorium with a nod. "He's a nice fellow who's never given me any trouble, I mean, trouble since I've been *here*, in the sanatorium. I suppose one of these days I'll find out when he intends to declare what he labels my 'phase of autonomous recovery' complete. Yes," Hans said, "at the beginning I explained to him in general terms what was happening to me, and also what it was I wanted: to work with marble, to lose myself in marble, yes; and *the other*, that is, to think my problem out, the Olga problem, the *quote-unquote* problem, as my sister Angelica used to call it. Ah well, but I think I've already told you about all that. The truth is I have an enormous jumble of thoughts in my brain. Yes, and I often lose the drift of what I want or don't want to say and, still worse, of what I've said and what I haven't managed to say even though I have thought it, I mean, thought about what I have to say. For example," Hans said, "the phrase *quote-unquote problem* reverberates frightfully in my head, believe me. I think during the long winter nights I've heard it myriad times, either mingled with the noise of marble or else unaccompanied, harmonious as a church melody. I still hear my sister saying it. I see her lips forming it. I see myself saying it to you who knows how many times, saying it here and now, during our stroll. Yet nonetheless," Hans said, "I am, I believe, only partly certain of having done so, I mean, of having mentioned it to you. My sister's damned invention, you know. Yes, I told you before, I suppose Angelica is one of the most intelligent people I've ever known. She always saw everything, knew everything, yes. But I think in my case she was blind, I mean, *totally* blind. Because there are *seeing* forms of blindness, I think, and hers was not of that mold. No, hers was an unseeing, total, anachronistic blindness, yes, I suppose it was the worst kind of blindness, the kind that tends to reinforce itself—I mean the idea of blindness—because she's at a loss about how to break out of the vicious cycle of absolute darkness. You *at least* listen," he said, "you remain silent and I don't know what you're thinking, though I imagine it, I mean, if I attempt to think about what you're thinking I end up doing so, or at least I think I do, but I assure you that, even while having a relatively valid basis for judgment, Angelica has seen nothing, has understood nothing," Hans said, "or maybe she *has* seen, *has* understood, but has chosen to *turn away*, not to see or understand for fear of broaching a problem, even a *quote-unquote* one, that doesn't fit into her scale of values. Yes," Hans said, "come to think of it, I suppose the greatest stroke of intelligence my sister has ever displayed, her greatest stroke of ingenuity, was to disregard and make light of what was happening to me. And in a certain sense I think Olga did something similar, though in her case I can understand it, since she was the motivating agent of a problem she had never even dreamed of creating. 'I know an ideal spot in Chemnitz where you can regain your former equilibrium, Hans,' Angelica said. A certain Vogt, a *qualified* colleague, in her words, was the one who had mentioned Hohenstein-Ernstthal Sanatorium. In other words," Hans said, "I'm here thanks to this fellow Vogt, yes, how curious. I think my sister's outlook *betrayed itself* on that occasion. 'It'll cost,' I remember she specified, as if that detail were going to set me at ease. It's just that for my sister, I think, as for all psychologists, it's quite likely that behind the problems of the mind—or rather the *peculiarities* of the mind, of each mind that theoretically refuses to function in unison with the rest of the minds that make up a given milieu—behind those problems, I was saying, ultimately there's money as well. Yes, I suppose that's the world we live in," Hans said, "a world divided into those who charge and those who don't. That's how it is. I don't know, I suppose I've learned there are only two things beyond the reach of money. Yes," he said, "I'm referring to love and death. You can't *buy* the one or *bribe* the other. Though in essence, I think, perhaps inasmuch as the destiny of all love is death, maybe it is precisely death which is the apex, the summit, the perfection of every great love. Yes," he said, "because in the last analysis love is a psychic quality that stems from a living and therefore finite being. Nevertheless, I think, the only positive part about having an awareness of *rejection*—which you no doubt must think is exactly the case with me, which I won't deny, though one could certainly be fastidious about it—having that awareness, I was saying, helped me to *grasp* finitude ahead of time. Yes," Hans said, "to lack hope is to *hold* the future in your fist. The spectrum of non-hope, or to make myself better understood, of utter hopelessness, I think, is pierced by a blinding ray of light. And light, I believe, cannot be explained. Either you see it or you don't. Yes," he said, "a whole erudite treatise on the theory of light is a mere trifle in comparison to the twinkle of a light bulb when our eyes, for whatever reason, *need* a bit of clarity. Yes, in speaking about light or clarity, my mind inevitably conjures up Olga's image. I think I've already said that Olga lies in my instinct. Because the sensation of being without Olga is much like that other sensation we sometimes experience of leaving *something* behind in a place we haven't yet left. That certainty that we're leaving something behind, that act of putting our hands to our pockets and musing pensively for several seconds is, I think, precisely what must take place in the cold chamber of my heart. Yes," he said, "the perfect void. But furthermore, I think—just as at some moment Olga evoked that splendor nobody noticed, which I mentioned before—furthermore, and almost simultaneously, she entailed a cerebral hecatomb, yes," Hans said, "a hecatomb *of thought*, rather than of the senses themselves, which no one ever perceived either. Yes," he said, "because whom can I speak to about Olga? I often wonder about that. Only the marble listens, its coldness retains whatever I'm able to impart to it, yes, but it also *expresses itself*, it responds to me somehow in a language I don't understand but do comprehend. Everything that I think, that I am and do, I think, am, and do *for* Olga, for her alone, of that I'm positive. Thus I believe I can say that I *go on being* for her, which doesn't mean I have any hope in regard to her, I mean hope in the sense, for example, that she used to say she wanted my friendship, that we should simply be friends, *great* friends. My only hope with her," Hans said, "might perhaps be a long-term one, excessively long term, yes, I'm talking about the fact (which at times I've come to doubt, while on other occasions I've been thoroughly convinced of it), the fact, I was saying, of slowly becoming *integrated* into her life, into the process of her life, into her memory, I suppose. Though that will depend, I think, on the course her life takes, on the importance Olga herself might ultimately confer on all those things that are connected in one way or another with me. She knows what they are, yes, she knows perfectly well. There are things that for Olga will always be me, I know that. Even if the weight of oblivion were to bury me, even if she totally changed the manner and place in which she lived, there are not one or two but many things that will always remind her of me. Yes, I think that's the only thing I can aspire to," Hans said, "being the *king* of her Invisible Kingdom, I mean, the Invisible Kingdom of her memory. Yes, in the same way that she fills the entire mental and physical space that's always with me, just so do I hope to fill at least a part of her mind's *domains*. Because Olga is the mover that animates me, that moves me *even now*, yes," he said, "she is the source, she's the energy, the nourishment, she's the shape of each instant, the sweating nape of time, she's every sound and every object, she is the air's blue eyes, and her voice the fiery chariot emerging from the horizon. She is *the voice*. I don't know," Hans said, "I think today, during our entire walk, I've discussed her with you, or rather I suppose I've confined it to *me* talking *to you* about Olga. At times rather poetically, you might think, and hence not without exaggeration. That's likely, I think, but I mentioned earlier that lately I find it very hard to control my thoughts when I attempt to verbalize them. But I suppose doing this, talking to you about her, has been comforting, yes, *comforting* is the word, I believe. And the truth is I don't know what will become of me in the near future, I mean, when I leave here. Yes," Hans said, "perhaps I'll ask the company director to transfer me to Oldenburg, who knows, I think in the long run it might do me some good to finally work on the technical end of things, in the lab. Yes, that's possible," he said, "quite so. Perfectly possible, I think. In any case I suppose that soon, perhaps within a few weeks, I'll return to work, yes, and I fear it will be difficult to face her once again. I don't know, I just heard myself say *difficult*, when the word that really came to mind was *impossible*. Note that though I wanted to say *impossible*, what came out was *difficult*. My thoughts, the instinct of my thoughts imposes itself on my will, as I've told you. Yes, I think it will be virtually impossible for everything to remain the same, yet I'll have to do something, I suppose, but I'm merely supposing, mind you. You already know that here one ends up supposing everything," Hans said. "That's the risk involved, I suppose, in thinking not so much what you think but how and why you think it. Then you end up, I expect, by supposing your thoughts and, in a parallel fashion, thinking your suppositions. Perhaps you've already realized it, I don't know. Yes," he said, "the final stage, I believe, is supposing your suppositions. That's the only way it can be, because otherwise one couldn't maintain anything, I mean, one could *no longer* maintain anything. But not for that matter do I stop supposing it will be rough on me when the time comes to return to work. I say *work* and once again I'm thinking about Olga. I don't know, perhaps if I didn't put up such resistance to thinking what I then say, everything would turn out to be more fluid, I mean, I would say what I'm really thinking. Although I suppose that's impossible, as well. I'm shocked myself at thinking what I think, not what I say, which is but a minimal part of the former, and consequently, I suppose everyone else would be shocked, too, if they knew it. There are things that cannot be known, that cannot even be thought, like what really *occurred* between Olga and me. The one favor I ask of you," Hans said, gripping my elbow in a reaction that completely disconcerted me, "is that you *never*, under any circumstances, speak to her about any of this, about anything I may have said here, about anything I may have thought without really knowing whether or not I said it to you. You must also suppose what I *haven't* wanted to say and yet have ended up saying. Yes, I think you mustn't ever tell her about this. No matter what," he said, removing his hand from my arm and smiling broadly, something I hadn't seen him do in such a way until then. "That *too* would be fruitless. Yes," he said, "like a pantomime performed before a mirror in utter darkness. I suppose you'd worry her needlessly," he said, "yes, but I also suppose that the things I've said to you, what I've told you about myself and about her, are so numerous and so confusing that conceivably within a few minutes, while driving back to the city in your car, you may recall absolutely nothing. Yet the memories linger, in spite of being unremembered they linger there, like the picture at the Sörolt, like that building slowly collapsing amidst a curtain of dust, like that slow collapse *seen* by the senses but not the eyes. Yes," Hans said, "I remember meeting her on a winter day, as I told you, she was dressed in black, I don't know whether I mentioned that detail before. Perhaps it was an insignificant detail, I expect so. In any event, I was wearing a blue overcoat that I have *never* worn again, naturally. I don't know," he said, "the fact is, the other day, while working in the shop, I thought that without her even knowing it, she was dressed *in mourning*. And one day, I mean, the very day I realized I had lost her, had lost her forever, on precisely that day, I was saying, Olga wore her black dress again. I glimpsed it under a sort of parka. Yes, I think I only saw her in it on those two occasions. And that day," Hans said, "I mean, on that cold and rainy afternoon I did something bizarre, yes, upon leaving the bar where we'd had a drink, I did something that must have surprised Olga quite a lot, especially because I did it right in the middle of a street bustling with people. Yes," Hans said, "as on so many prior occasions, I felt I was bidding her farewell, a definitive farewell, even though we might see each other at a later time. But it would no longer be the same. I think I had sensed it, I knew it at that very instant. And in some way or other Olga knew it, too. Yes, I believe she was a *match* for the occasion, beyond a shadow of a doubt. What I did was to come to a halt as we were walking in the rain, before we each went our separate ways. Yes, even I don't fully understand the reaction that rose up inside me, that I suppose someone else *carried out* through me," Hans said, "yes, I can see it as though it were happening right now. I brought my face close to hers and kissed her on the lips. Then I knelt down, yes," he said, "resting my left knee on the wet ground as I thrust my right arm forward, slightly bowing my head as a sign of respect, of submission. I don't know, I think it would have been normal on Olga's part to glance around her, I mean, around us, to notice what effect my pose was having on the passersby. But she didn't. I remember she smiled broadly as the raindrops slid down her forehead and cheeks. 'What are you doing?' she asked me, somewhat startled and amused. And I, thinking it unnecessary to explain that embodiment of a knightly oath, was even more surprised than she, I suppose. Yes, when I finally managed to respond I remember telling her: 'Take my sword.' Then Olga's smile changed entirely, yes, it's not that she *stopped* smiling, but rather that her smile ceased being conspicuous only to become intimate. I think it was then that, eccentric as it all seemed, she realized I was speaking in earnest, completely in earnest. So much in earnest, I think, that I was on the verge of crying, yes. Later, having gotten to my feet, I remember she said she would never forget that *gesture*, yes," Hans said, "I believe it was at that very moment that I thought: 'Requiem,' but I didn't say it, I suppose I didn't go so far as to say it, although I'm sure I thought about it. Yes. *Requiem*. What I do remember is my repeating that she mustn't forget that, even if only symbolically, my *sword* was hers forever and she could claim it whenever she pleased. 'I'll bear that in mind,' she replied. Then I watched as she disappeared through the rain. Yes, on that occasion, as I mentioned, Olga was dressed in black, just as she'd been the previous winter at about that time, when I saw her issue forth from the sunlight. And in between, I think, the autumn, the warm sensation that *enveloped* me from the final days of summer, then throughout autumn and a good part of winter. Yes," Hans said, "I *knelt down*. An extraordinary gesture, I think. Look, there's Dr. Littbarski now. Well, you've no idea how much I appreciate your having come, Andreas. We'll see each other at work soon, I expect—that is, I *hope* we'll see each other there soon," he said, "I suppose I think so, otherwise I wouldn't be saying it. Yes, I think so, I really do think so. Thanks, Andreas, so long."

Hans offered me his hand in farewell and immediately began taking long strides toward the metal banister on which Dr. Littbarski was leaning, having been joined by a nurse and another young man clad in a white smock. He'd given me no time to react, not even to say a few words in parting. And, in fact, as Hans himself had predicted just minutes before, my head was in such a muddle that I found it impossible to say or do anything at all. I do know, however, that I gestured with my hand to Littbarski, with whom I had talked a few seconds before seeing Hans, though without knowing his name. Dr. Littbarski at once returned my wave, and I walked mechanically toward the parking lot, located next to a pond. At that very moment I realized it was almost night. I got into the car, but fumbled about for some time before I managed to start it. I was deeply affected by what I had just heard, though I didn't actually know whether I should feel stupid for not having opened my mouth to say anything or whether, on the other hand, I should run back to Hans and simply remain with him. I realized he was in need of help, but also that I was unable to provide such help, and so was Dr. Littbar-ski who, judging from Hans' words, had virtually turned his back on his 'case.'

The truth is I didn't snap out of my bewilderment for quite a while. The more I thought about it, the more surprised I was at my need to keep listening to Hans, when in fact the jumble of phrases engraved in my mind was such that I was barely aware of what I was doing.

I made the entire return trip with my eyes glued to the road, trying to put in order everything Hans had told me. At least in some order, perhaps chro-nological. But I was only able to see his lips moving incessantly. From time to time, I recalled, he had stopped in the middle of his monologue as though all of a sudden he had completely forgotten who he was, to whom he was talking, and what he was doing in such a place. And I myself had just that sort of doubt at some moments. I was bothered by the sensation of having spent all that time in the presence of a person who, I was certain, didn't fully recognize me. Though he had called me Andreas two or three times, and had even made some specific references to our workplace, deep down I was quite convinced that Hans hadn't recognized me in the least. I had merely been the silent audience he'd required for reasons unbeknownst to me. Probably to unburden himself, as he had acknowledged toward the end of our peculiar and memorable walk.

But I was perhaps even more disturbed by another aspect of what had happened that afternoon in the environs of the Hohenstein-Ernstthal San-atorium. First of all, and what I found most odd after reflecting on it a bit more calmly, there was the fact that Hans was unaware, or pretended to be unaware, that I knew Olga Dittersdorf as well, that I had known her about the same length of time he had, though in a different way, of course. Even if I had never really come to know her well, we had in fact happened to meet while eating or having drinks at the corner restaurant-bar and, if memory serves me, at some spot elsewhere in the city. Hans knew this because I had mentioned it to him at some point after his relationship with her had begun, well before the unfortunate incident of his assault on old Handke took place, when I was in some sense his only confidant throughout a passion that had increased from moment to moment without, I admit, my fully realizing it. And in this regard I should say I never knew why he specifically chose me as the one to whom he trickled out those confidences, which began as simple remarks uttered almost in jest and at random, the magnitude of which I would manage to understand only later. Ruminating about it, I've come to the conclusion that perhaps it was because I was the colleague closest to his desk. That's likely. Or perhaps I inspired his trust for some reason I can't discern.

Secondly, I also found it totally incredible that Hans seemed likewise unaware that it was none other than his sister Angelica who had informed me of his whereabouts once he'd been taken to the sanatorium, and that it had been Hans himself who had asked her to reveal nothing to the people at work, 'except Andreas Dörpfeld, I'd enjoy seeing him later on.' Those, according to his sister, had been his words. And that's why she had given me the message, in light of which, before visiting him (bearing in mind that 'later on' meant Hans didn't want to see anyone in the near future) I had prudently chosen to wait nearly two months from the time Angelica Kruger, in a telephone call to the office, informed me about the circumstances and wishes of her brother.

The more I thought about it, I should say, the stranger I found it that Hans seemed to have forgotten that both his sister and Olga were people I knew, particularly the latter. But the fact is that not at any moment during the initial stage of veiled confidences over our breakfasts together had he asked my opinion while speaking of Olga's beauty, never at any moment did it seem to have entered his mind that I might differ with him in anything, be it only in some insignificant detail. Even then he was supposing everything. And to observe that the pedestal on which he had placed Olga not only remained intact but had acquired outlandish proportions, as it were, is what most disturbed me, once several days had passed after my visit to the Hohenstein-Ernstthal Sanatorium and I was able to take stock of the mental state in which I had found Hans. And, still more troubling, the state in which I'd left him.

I can say that for a period of several nights I had a hard time getting to sleep. The overwhelming monologue I'd had occasion to hear from Hans' lips in the woody environs of Chemnitz haunted me wherever I went. And the fact of seeing Olga at work almost daily doubtless contributed somewhat to my inability to forget everything Hans had confessed to me, or at least some of what he had confessed, for the more I tried, the more problematic it became to reconstruct, if only approximately and with some semblance of order, a discourse uttered no doubt for his own sake, yet which I wouldn't know whether to classify as a mere accumulation of chaotic ideas and feelings or as a marvel of perspicacity.

That was my general impression—of not having understood what had brought all that about, yet being unable to quit thinking that in everything I'd heard from him there was an unmistakable undercurrent of coherence. Because one thing I was fully convinced of as the days went by: there was, in what Hans Kruger had told me, no small degree of lucidity, I'd almost venture to say, an enormous lucidity. He certainly didn't try to convince me of anything, nor was he justifying a specific stance or attitude before me or even before Olga. He had done no more than explain to me, in the only way he knew how, the way he felt about a woman. He was merely obeying the orders, translated into images and in turn into words, that his brain had given him. A brain that, as I was able to observe, was still totally occupied with Olga. In this sense I was extremely surprised that the passing of time had made no dent in him.

In general terms, however, that was the greatest surprise I encountered upon arriving at the sanatorium: Hans' obsession with Olga. An obsession that not only hadn't diminished one speck, but which on the contrary was becoming inordinate; personally, I must confess I didn't feel the least alarmed by this, though I was concerned by the fact that he was continually aware of it and yet seemed quite unprepared to take the steps necessary to resolve it.

Until that time, of course, I'd thought that what had occurred between Hans and old Handke had been the culmination of a long depression on Kruger's part, but a depression probably rooted in several sources.

Little by little I began to realize I was mistaken, at least partially. Hans' life was methodical and even somewhat dull. He lived in a comfortable, spacious house, with a nice garden I had never seen but about which he often spoke with pride at work. His leisure time seemed to be taken up by what were in fact quite normal forms of escape, like reading, going to films, or listening to music. As he had told me himself: "My life, my evenings, were filled by the ample gamut of melodies ranging from Mozart to Webern." At first glance, then, there was no reason other than Olga to have lapsed into that great, mounting depression. His income was more than adequate, and I don't believe his solitude weighed too heavily on him. Furthermore, I remember that on some occasion he intimated, through rather vague allusions, that in the past he had tried sharing certain living arrangements with some young woman, but the results had been unsatisfactory, at least for him. As a matter of fact, he never struck me as one of those people who live alone because a variety of circumstances obliges them to do so. Quite the contrary. Hans Kruger was rather good-looking, enjoyed good health, and led a comfortable life, in which he could even permit himself a few luxuries. If he lived alone at thirty-six, it was because he wanted it that way.

I must admit, however, I always thought it impossible that in this day and age someone could become obsessed with a woman in such a manner. No matter how much I turned it over in my mind, it still struck me as something outdated, something wont to happen in movies or novels, of course, but not in real life. And in that regard, although I had experienced Hans' obsession directly and, I repeat, as probably the sole witness, my thoughts coincided with his sister's. Olga was very beautiful indeed, a young woman who attracted attention on account of her beauty, but there were also other remarkable women about. I would have understood his initial obsession, at any rate, but never the constancy and tenacity of such an obsession, especially considering that he seemed to have overcome the greatest obstacle to the permanence of this kind of passion: time. Time and distance, because Hans had already been separated from Olga for several months, many kilometers away from her, knowing nothing about her life. But even while knowing all that, I never really thought the existence of that young woman, the profound impression she had left on his life and his character, was the sole cause of the depression that had seized him. Never until my visit to the sanatorium at Chemnitz.

Several weeks elapsed, just how many I don't know, and I began to forget the whole affair. From time to time, when I saw Olga at work or noticed Hans' empty desk, or even when someone happened to sit there, I would recall my visit to Chemnitz, and several times I was on the verge of telephoning his sister to suggest the possibility of paying him another visit. But something held me back. I recognize that I truly dreaded the possibility of facing Hans again. Not knowing what his present condition might be restrained me all the more.

It's curious, but Hans' problem—which, insofar as it concerned me, I believe I should have resolved with practical solutions, for example by going to visit him again at Chemnitz or by deciding once and for all not to do so—started to become a mental problem for me as well. My thoughts revolved around him, and whenever I saw Olga laughing with the other women from Administration or with anyone else at work, I couldn't help feeling a certain remorse at the thought of him. Seeing her so happy and carefree, I would feel what might perhaps be termed remorse or discomfort at something I was not a party to. On several occasions I was even about to go talk to her and tell her everything, yet that would have been not only a betrayal of what Hans himself had requested of me in the matter, but a lack of tact on my part, an unjustifiable interference.

I remember one such occasion in particular, when I had to make a great effort to check myself. I felt extremely annoyed that she, being the indirect protagonist of the whole affair, should not be participating at all in that particular situation. Perhaps a rather ridiculous one, to be sure, but also unpleasant and, I would even venture to say, pathetic, at least where he was concerned, whether he admitted it or not. Because it was clear that the person directly involved was Hans, and then myself, for of course after that long walk I knew much more than his sister. But Olga went on as usual, charming with everyone, having, I came to believe, forgotten Kruger entirely. Although my feelings might be completely dismissed as selfish or even contradictory, seeing her like that became a great source of irritation to me.

The truth, on the other hand, is that Olga didn't seem to have been even faintly aware of what she had provoked in him. For instance, one detail I recalled after a while is that Olga wasn't present when the incident between Hans and old Handke took place, resulting in the latter's trip to the clinic amid threats of filing suit and great pandemonium at the firm. She had gone on vacation for a few days and consequently must have learned everything about the incident through the grapevine, because from the time the unpleasant altercation took place until Hans requested to be sent away from the city (and in fact asking his sister to arrange it was an appeal to be confined), they hadn't seen each other again at all. I also imagine that for several weeks prior to the scandal Hans hadn't seen Olga alone, owing to her express desire not to do so, which in all likelihood aggravated his irascible nature somewhat, as was only logical.

Because of all this, and even though I knew Olga was aware of only one aspect of the drama she herself had provoked (whether wittingly or not didn't matter), I tried to restrain myself and not fall into something that might perhaps be more than an indiscretion, by which I mean any discussion of the issue with her. The problem was that having witnessed the unfolding of events more or less from the inside, and almost from the moment they began, I felt I had the right to make decisions like that of talking to Olga, which in the end, as I said, I chose to curb.

I can't pinpoint how much more time elapsed, but it might have been approximately a month and a half before Katz, a colleague from Publicity, spoke of having heard in Management that Kruger would be rejoining us shortly. He went on to mention, though not without some suspicion, an ulcer requiring a lengthy and difficult treatment, which, officially, was Hans' ostensible illness. But the truth is no one seemed to make too much of the fact that he would be returning to work, which could hardly fail to surprise me at first, and later to distress me somewhat. I think that's when I realized what even less than half a year can do to people's relationships. As for me, I can say that from the instant Herr Reinecke, the personnel manager, verified that indeed as far as he knew, "Kruger would be back on the job next Monday," I felt an enormous impatience, as well as a great desire to go and tell Olga. After all, I thought, she'd be the person Hans was closest to.

It may have been owing to cowardice or to simple complacency, but the fact is that even on the occasion of Hans' return I didn't make any attempt to mention it to her. Whenever I firmly resolved to do so, I very soon had misgivings, thinking I didn't want to become the apex of a triangle consisting of Olga, Hans, and myself, were I to intervene in their private matters.

On the Friday prior to the week Hans was expected to return, I received a letter. It was from his sister, and in a few lines of nearly indecipherable handwriting, she apprised me of Hans' return and of the improvement she had remarked the last time she was at Chemnitz. She also informed me that he had been at home for several days already, getting everything in order. "Although we have plenty of room, he didn't want to stay with us." She also said he seemed quite excited about his return to "the civilized world." I can't explain why, but that last phrase had a strange effect on me, as of repulsion. It was as though Hans had suddenly been able to transmit to me what I knew to be his profound contempt for what Angelica Kruger labeled, in a tone at once solemn and trite, the "civilized world": psychology, a certain family order, and a long series of eternally unfulfilled desires. But in her brief message she also noted that he seemed excited and ready to "begin anew." I couldn't help heaving a sigh of relief, while at the same time thinking: Mozart and Webern.

On Monday, the day Hans was supposed and expected to return, I was somewhat nervous, and around noon, when I realized he wouldn't be coming in, I felt quite naive about having thought that I alone might be responsible for giving him a warm welcome. I'd even thought about the possibility of having a bottle of champagne ready, but I gave up the idea, fearing it would bother him by making him feel he was the focus of everyone's gaze and, of course, the center of attention all day long, which would no doubt happen with or without champagne and notwithstanding his vain hope to pass unnoticed. I finally decided that in order to celebrate, if it seemed a good idea to Hans, we could go have a meal in grand style at one of the city's fine restaurants.

But coupled with the initial disappointment of his not coming in until Wednesday was the coldness with which he made his entrance into the office. It was not exactly coldness, but rather an attitude between insouciant and evasive, which betrayed something I realized right from the start: that he was having a very rough time of it. Nevertheless, I guessed there was more to it than timidity, which on the other hand would have been perfectly natural. Not even with me did he seem very expansive. He made no reference whatsoever to his stay in the sanatorium, nor of course to my visit, nor for that matter to anything concerning the past. Now and then, after we had exchanged the customary greetings, he would joke about matters relating to work. It was as if he had been sitting at that very desk the preceding day, and the one before and the one before that, as if on that day he was simply in a better mood than on other occasions.

The fact is, I couldn't help feeling disappointed at Hans' behavior. He appeared polite to everyone who approached him to inquire after his health. He would dispose of them with a few phrases and a broad smile, and if anyone pressed him for details about his condition, he made some enlightened reference to the ulcer problem. But he would say it so earnestly that at some point even I started to believe that a problem ulcer was what had made him take so many months off. Curiously enough, on that first morning Hans appeared self-assured, I'd even say eager to regain people's confidence quickly. Yet, without being sure of the reason, I was on guard, tense and unable to stop wondering whether he had already seen Olga, whether he had come across her on his way in, whether or not they had spoken.

Several days went by and Hans' remarks began to taper off, until they disappeared almost entirely. On the surface there was nothing abnormal, since one couldn't claim he had ever been outgoing at work, but I realized that he had been back for nearly a week and the only times I heard his voice were when he spoke with someone on the phone, when he would ask me for a light, or when it was I who asked him a specific question. Nevertheless, no one observing him would have said there was anything bothering him. Everything about him seemed normal and, judging by his behavior, was indeed perfectly normal, save that he displayed a certain weariness. But that's just what prompted me to worry: Hans' normality. And perhaps it did so because I was expecting something else from him. I can't explain it, I only know that even without looking at him directly, I was aware of each and every move he made, as well as his words whenever he spoke. And my own worry exasperated me at times.

The result of that situation was that I, too, tried to avoid saying more than was strictly necessary. And I could swear that at some level he noticed the change on my part, beginning little by little to talk with greater frequency and ease. To my surprise, however, he still made not a single allusion to the past, and now spoke quite eagerly about what he called his "new destiny." I learned then that he had requested permission from Management to work in the labs—something he had mentioned in passing at the sanatorium, though I didn't exactly recall the specifics—and to that end was taking some sort of accelerated course. But the labs as well as the central warehouse were located in the outskirts of Oldenburg, prompting me to point out to him that to begin with, such a step would mean leaving town, his home, everything. Hans replied that it wasn't really so bad. After all, he said, he'd already moved several times in his life and was sure he could find "a nice place there for my books, my records, and even for me, if I'll fit."

He seemed excited about the change, and naturally I ended up sharing his enthusiasm. He even told me that for quite a while now he had been going all the way to Oldenburg in the evenings "to visit the area and make myself feel at home there." I knew, since he had mentioned it to me, that the company manager had at some point suggested he transfer there, with the promise of a substantial raise in salary, so he could take full advantage of his knowledge. But Hans spoke modestly about all that. What really seemed to excite him was the change of air, to which he constantly referred.

"The truth is, one ends up exhausting all the possibilities of a place, still more in a small city like this one," he had confided to me with the utmost calm. "Strange as it may seem, I've discovered that listening to old Martin's stories in the warehouse from time to time can have its share of charm. Besides, I've always been bothered by the climate, by turns cold and sultry, of seaport cities. It sticks to your skin. Yes, going inland appeals to me."

Under other circumstances, had I learned that Hans intended to move to another city to somehow free himself from Olga, I believe I would have found it a very sensible decision, especially after having witnessed the way he had been affected by that problem and having made a fair evaluation of just how far things had gone. But his seeming not even to remember her meant, as far as I could tell, that those were certainly not the reasons compelling him to distance himself from the city as soon as possible. I felt reassured, therefore, though somewhat baffled. And so I remained for a couple of weeks, until one morning when I saw the two of them talking in one of the office corridors. I greeted them briefly and then withdrew. Olga was smiling but seemed rather stiff. She had her arms crossed over her chest. The fact is I barely glanced at Hans. Yet I could have sworn that he was leaning with his elbow against the wall and that my presence abruptly cut short whatever he seemed to be telling her.

The truth is, all of that worried me, and my worry kept increasing as I observed that time was passing and Hans did not come back to his desk. I knew it wasn't possible for them to have gone on talking in the hall for such a long time. That would have exposed them to the gibes of more than one sardonic co-worker. But Hans finally returned, and I felt as if someone had poured cold water down my spine. He was pale and his eyes shone strangely. Not even at the sanatorium had I seen him in such a state. He tried to assume a suitable smile and organize the papers strewn over his desk. I knew at once that he'd been drinking. All the while he had been at the corner bar. Just then I could no longer restrain myself and blurted out all at once:

"Listen, Hans, I think it would be extremely stupid, and above all unfair to yourself, for you to become obsessed with that girl again," I said, striving to give my words a convincing yet not vehement tone.

Hans raised his eyes toward me. Never until that moment had I heard him make so cruel and ironic a remark as he did then, keeping his gaze squarely on my face:

"Are you talking about Olga, Olga Dittersdorf?"

I was offended by that, I'll admit, but I realized before it was too late that Hans was in no condition to withstand the anger aroused in me by his cynical question. I told him I was indeed referring to her, and that it was entirely unnecessary for him to mention her surname in order for me to know who he was talking about.

"Right, right, of course . . . she simply mentioned that she's going away for a few days," he stammered, suddenly averting his eyes. "Apparently she's accumulated four days' vacation and plans to go away somewhere till Monday. She has a cabin in Zizurkwald. Yes, next Monday she'll be back at work."

I realized he'd gone into his shell and that it would be useless to insist. I made note of the fact that it was Tuesday and there was a holiday that week. Then it occurred to me that I might suggest he join me for the evening. We could go out, I said, to a film or just anywhere. Hans didn't respond. I expect he hadn't even heard me. The pale tone of his cheeks flushed beneath his eyelids, leaving a sort of pinkish trace along his cheekbones.

"Tell me the truth, Hans. Is it possible you haven't yet rid yourself of her, is that possible?" I asked, availing myself of his silence. It took him several seconds to reply, but he finally did so in a tone of voice diminished almost to a whisper:

"I can't say, I don't know the answer to that question, Andreas. Olga understands only a particular kind of language. A cryptic language that derives from a very strict code of values." While saying this, he ran his hand through his hair and attempted another smile. "Well, never mind, I guess it's foolish, but I needed to talk with her one more time, at least one more time. I'll devote myself to doing something productive, active, I have an urge to do that," he said quickly and with a sudden exhilaration, which in turn made me calm down a bit. "Yes, maybe I'll devote myself to training hummingbirds, to raising chickens for wholesale, to cultivating orchids, to doing horoscopes here and there, who knows . . ."

I laughed, proposing again that we go out together, but over the weekend, since he couldn't do it that evening. Hans had placed a sheet of paper into his typewriter and was typing away vigorously. He told me it would be impossible for him over the weekend as well. "Another, perhaps," he added. When I asked him the reason his reply was terse:

"I have to go to Oldenburg."

The rest of the morning I was very busy with a string of pending matters, and Hans made several trips, at least three, to the Management office. The next day I saw him for only a few minutes. He came in and greeted me while he gathered a couple of things from his drawer. Then he asked me to please take messages if any calls came in. I recall that Friday was a holiday, and on Saturday morning Hans didn't come to work, even though it was his turn. I surmised, therefore, that he must be in Oldenburg, as he had indicated.

From that point on, everything happened as though in a dream. It happened with such precision in regard to time and place that I can remember the unfolding of events in a completely objective, impartial manner.

When I arrived at work on Monday morning, shortly after punching in, I saw Olga chatting with a friend from Administration. And I expect it was precisely the certainty of knowing that Hans had slowly and truly begun to rid himself of her which enabled me to perceive the extreme beauty of her features. I had seen them on countless occasions, it's true, but never until that moment did I fully grasp how attractive she was.

I must have been working for a couple of hours when the telephone rang and someone at the switchboard said there was a woman asking to speak to me. I assumed it was some work-related call and was rather taken aback when I recognized Angelica Kruger's voice. Yet the voice sounded odd, as if she were hoarse or had a handkerchief over her mouth. In few words, she explained what had happened, and I remember saying absolutely nothing. I would even swear that I felt nothing in particular. Nothing save that my legs were tingling and by no means would I have been able to rise from my chair. I also remember that she repeated everything again and said goodbye with a kind of guttural onomatopoeia, saying we would probably see each other.

The story was as follows: Hans had committed suicide that very morning around nine o'clock by detonating a powerful explosive charge attached to his body. He had done it in the garden of his house, apparently initiating the explosion by means of a battery. All the windows of the neighboring houses had shattered, as well as those of many cars parked in the vicinity. Of Hans there was nothing left. According to Angelica, he had literally disintegrated. The commotion in that remote part of the city must have been tremendous.

I don't know how much time elapsed before I was aware of getting up from my desk, prepared to go to the site where it had taken place. I knew his sister would be there, and I also knew she was the only person I wanted to see at that moment. Someone said something to me, but I don't recall who or what it was, and as I was starting my car to make for Hans' house I remembered that Overath, from Publicity, had asked me that very morning, just after punching in downstairs, whether I'd heard the noise, a muffled noise that seemed to come from a distance. At the time, of course, I'd paid no heed to his remark, because in a city one hears countless noises of all sorts every day. In all likelihood Overath was referring to a blowout.

I must have spent quite a while driving down streets that were still wet from the recent drizzle, and I suppose I must have taken a wrong turn at some point, because I didn't arrive there until nearly eleven thirty. The street was cordoned off and from a distance I could see three or four police cars, an enormous tow truck, two ambulances and a fire truck. There was a large crowd of onlookers periodically ebbing and flowing, through which I was allowed to make my way once I said I was related to the victim. Presently I glimpsed Angelica, in dark glasses and with a muffler concealing half her face, beside a tall, brooding man whom I supposed to be her husband. Someone who seemed to be with the police was speaking to the couple, and when I approached her the fellow turned to pick something up from the ground. Then he headed in the direction of two other men who were looking at something wrapped in plastic. They were discussing its contents.

Had it not been because in essence, as it were, the whole thing struck me as perfectly logical and natural, I would have believed I was at the gates of hell. The lawn was scorched. The wooden cornices of the house and the roof were still smoking. The walls had been seriously damaged by the expansive wave. Two trees at one end of the garden, some eight or ten meters from a deep pit in the ground, were completely charred, no doubt also as a result of the blast. Of Hans there was not the least trace, only something that might perhaps be the remnants of a shoe. Where the explosion had taken place there was a crater several feet deep in the earth. The fog hovered about the swollen lawn, turning everything into a Dantesque vision. Men in dark uniforms crossed back and forth, carrying bags in their hands. However much I looked at them, I was unable to make out their faces.

I don't even know where I found the strength to ask someone a question, but in any case I addressed one of those men carrying plastic bags, so as to find out exactly how it had happened. Seconds before, Angelica had made a remark about something that had to be taken care of at the firm, but I didn't understand her. What I do recall is the voice of one or perhaps two of those men explaining to me that, according to all the evidence they had gathered so far, and judging from the extremely powerful detonation, Hans had blown himself to bits with twelve kilos of ammonal distributed into thirty cartridges of four hundred grams apiece, which he must have tied to his body, probably around his shoulders and waist, with a cartridge belt.

I recall one of those men with vacant features remarking that such an amount and type of explosive, intelligently placed, could demolish a building. The other one kept repeating that he had never seen anything like it. The explosion, they said, must have occurred at one minute past nine, because they had a testimony to that effect from a woman in one of the nearby houses, who had been listening to the news on the radio at that very moment.

The commotion generated throughout the neighborhood defied description. The explosion had been brutal, and a young man who happened to be passing through the area even had to be treated for injuries to his eardrums as a consequence of the phenomenal blast. Had the explosion taken place inside the building, one of the other policemen said, the entire house, and even part of the surrounding area, including some adjacent dwellings, would have suffered severe damage. One could surmise, then, that Hans had taken this into account. For him to have chosen a spot as far as possible both from the fence separating the garden from an adjoining alley and from the nearest house indicated that he had worked out the technical fine points of his deed quite thoroughly.

In spite of my comprehensible horror, all this continued to strike me as the final, I might even say foreseeable, step in a process that was already clearly limned in Hans' eyes, not only while he spoke to me at the Chemnitz sanatorium, but also later, in their serene, intense gleam after he had returned to work. That was why I couldn't help feeling a certain skepticism when I heard "How dreadful! How dreadful!" incessantly repeated all around me.

Curiously enough, my reasoning at the time centered around the idea that physically Hans had suffered much less, in all likelihood, than those of us present would when our time came. I understand, however, that this was a rather vain way of consoling myself, not so much for the loss of Hans—since owing to the odd nature of our relationship we had scarcely had time to consolidate our friendship—as on account of the extraordinary (though not, I insist, illogical) manner in which I was faced with his definitive absence forever.

But all I could do during those moments was to wander about the garden mechanically. I walked among the rubble, and only the first time I came across a black, totally charred object did I feel a pang of nausea at the thought that it might be Hans, some fragment of him. But it was not: Hans had simply evaporated. He had finally fulfilled his wish to be hurled into the instantaneous in the shortest possible time, just as he had confided to me at the sanatorium.

And however much I looked around me, it didn't strike me as dreadful. I know that one part of my brain was making an unconscious effort to convince me that the whole thing was dreadful, but to no avail. It might have been the gates of hell, as I said, but it was not without a certain order. Time and again I came back to the thought that, aside from the spectacle presented by that smoldering scene, with its unmistakable smell of burning, any of the deaths that occur through illness every day, all around us and yet without our being aware of them, were infinitely worse. I suddenly recalled, as though someone had planted the images in my mind, how at Chemnitz Hans had remarked that there must be nothing so swift as the devastating effect of ammonium nitrate for making the instantaneous transition from being to nonbeing. I also recalled, and now at last understood, his reference to the previous autumn as his last.

His decision, then, must have been made some time before, and once he had again taken up his normal life, every movement he made had been aimed at tying up loose ends so as to consummate the deed that morning in his garden. First of all, seeing and talking to Olga, with completely negative results, as was only to be expected. Later, that series of trips to the Oldenburg labs and warehouse, from which he no doubt must have been extracting the explosive materials, an endeavor that must surely have benefited from his friendship with the night watchman. Although, in fact, everything indicated that his trips to Oldenburg had begun even before he spoke with Olga. Furthermore, I don't believe that his choice of the hour, substantiated by a neighbor's testimony, had been a coincidence. Hans had activated the battery of that fatal mechanism at exactly one minute past nine. Neither before nor after, but at one minute past nine. That, as he had mentioned during our walk through the woods at the sanatorium, was the time when Olga punched the clock at the Personnel office, always one minute late as a sign of open rebellion. It was also the day on which she would be returning from her brief vacation, having already talked with him for the last time, which led me to conclude that Hans had waited until that very Monday to blow himself up. It had been his way of giving her a welcome, as it were, at once macabre and epic—consummated, paradoxically, in the manner of a farewell.

Suddenly, I saw clearly what Hans had been referring to when he alluded to Olga's black dress, and I also understood his comments about the damp but sultry climate he seemed to feel everywhere since his recent return to the city. I couldn't help experiencing a slight shudder upon remembering his flashing smiles during our last conversation as he declined my invitation to go out over the weekend because he had to go to Oldenburg.

Then, while walking about the garden as though in a daze, I began to feel

218

somewhat queasy. My eyes were stinging a great deal. A few seconds before, I had looked up at a nearby three-story building. All the windows had shattered and the neighbors were now huddling within the frames, looking in my direction. And it was just seconds after observing the mute consternation of those people, who had perhaps watched him on countless afternoons as he devoted himself to the care of his spacious garden, that I felt my eyes smarting most intensely. But I soon realized that it wasn't owing to any shock or distress I might have suffered—which, I repeat, was not at all the case—but rather to a thought that gripped me as I walked among the crushed stems of flowers and petals blackened as though smeared with soot: Hans' key. All at once I wondered where the key Hans wore around his neck might be. It was metal, very hard—perhaps it hadn't entirely disintegrated. Perhaps it had only been scorched and, even though unrecognizable, could be lying about in some corner.

I thus spent quite some time crouched over, scouring the garden. At last I realized the absurdity of my search. It struck me when I saw the dark blotch visible on the front of the adjoining building, imagining for the umpteenth time the magnitude of the explosion. Either that key no longer existed or it had been flung a distance of so many meters that it was by now mixed up with some rubbish. At any rate, the moment of weakness passed and I went over to Angelica to let her know she needn't worry about any matters concerning her brother that I might be able to take care of at the firm. She responded that she would call me later, and we parted after an affectionate embrace.

The next morning at work, people naturally spoke of nothing else. Fortunately no one had found out that I had been at the scene, and thanks to that I was spared unpleasant questions, which in any event I would have been incapable of answering. I came in somewhat late, having spent a very fitful night, and the switchboard operator told me that a journalist had telephoned several times, asking to speak to me. After a while I received a call and learned that it was Hans' friend from the newspaper, whom he'd mentioned at Chemnitz. He said he knew about me from references Hans had made, and that he was terribly affected by what had happened, asking presently if I had seen the previous day's paper, that is, the one published the very morning of the event. I told him I hadn't, whereupon he explained that Hans had

shown up at the paper's editorial department the preceding Friday afternoon, looking well and in surprisingly good spirits, saying he had a favor to
ask. This consisted of publishing, the following Monday, a horoscope he had
written for the Taurus sign, in order, as he put it, to give someone a surprise.
"Up to your old tricks again," the journalist said he had commented ironi-
cally, to which Hans had simply replied, "Yes."

That was truly a blow. Before me, on my desk, lay a copy of the day's paper, as well as one from the previous day. I was tempted to throw away the
latter, but after I'd thought about it a while I carefully folded it, stuffing it into
my coat pocket. I couldn't bear to remain there any longer, so I left, roaming
aimlessly up and down the streets. At last I sat down on a bench, opened the
paper to the entertainment pages and quickly read the horoscope dedicated
to Taurus. It did indeed seem to be addressed to Olga, to her absence over
those days, and undoubtedly to something that must have had some bearing
on what they had discussed during their brief conversation in the halls only
a few days before.

Just then I felt a renewed desire to rush to Hans' house and look for the
key in his garden once more. But I didn't. I merely kept reading the Taurus
horoscope, over and over. For the next several days I didn't see Olga either,
though it is possible that she had come to work and we simply hadn't run into
each other. When she finally turned up, there was nothing about her that
might indicate she had been particularly affected by what happened to
Hans, which she had surely learned about on the same Monday the tragedy
occurred. An event that in one way or another, even though her behavior at
work was apparently normal, must inevitably have made an impact on her.
Her enormous blue eyes gazed with assurance and her lips still traced the
same candid, infectious smile.

I spoke no more with Olga Dittersdorf, nothing but routine greetings
when our paths would cross. After a few months she left the firm. But I
know that if at some point I had come face to face with her, I would have
asked her several questions, many, which perhaps she might not have been
too eager to answer. I would have asked her about her nails, and why she gave
Hans that key. And also, of course, what that key unlocked. I'm sure that,
even while attempting to evade the magnetic influence of her pupils, I would

have asked her to talk to me at length, endlessly, about that mysterious South Wind and the effects it had on some people.

In all honesty I should say that I don't know to what extent it might be of interest for me to cite certain facts pertaining to the conclusion of this affair, which Hans' sister conveyed to me some weeks later. It is my belief that, as I stated in reference to my own name at the beginning of this narrative, these facts have very little bearing on its content. Yet they are there, nonetheless, and it is not for me to deny their significance. So I shall state them concisely.

Inside Hans' house, on the morning of his suicide, the police found a freshly opened bottle of whiskey beside a brief note written in his own hand, which read: "Tell her I await her there." Apparently there had also been a record playing on the turntable at the moment the explosion took place. That's what the first people to arrive found, the grooves of the record spinning away idly, waiting to be stopped by some hand. It was Mozart's Kyrie in D minor.

When I learned of this I understood that in some sense, Hans had found redemption. And only then did my eyes fill with tears.

Design by David Bullen
Typeset in Mergenthaler Granjon
by Wilsted & Taylor
Printed by Maple-Vail
on acid-free paper